DUPLICITY

Books by Jane Haseldine

THE LAST TIME SHE SAW HIM

DUPLICITY

Published by Kensington Publishing Corporation

DUPLICITY

JANE HASELDINE

KENSINGTON BOOKS
www.kensingtonbooks.com

KENSINGTON BOOKS are published by

Kensington Publishing Corp.
119 West 40th Street
New York, NY 10018

All Kensington titles, imprints, and distributed lines are available at special quantity discounts for bulk purchases for sales promotion, premiums, fund-raising, educational, or institutional use. Special book excerpts or customized printings can also be created to fit specific needs. For details, write or phone the office of the Kensington Special Sales Manager: Attn. Special Sales Department. Kensington Publishing Corp., 119 West 40th Street, New York, NY 10018. Phone: 1-800-221-2647.

Kensington and the K logo Reg. U.S. Pat. & TM Off.

Library of Congress Card Catalogue Number: 2016955148

ISBN-13: 978-1-4967-0407-8
ISBN-10: 1-4967-0407-X
First Kensington Hardcover Edition: April 2017

eISBN-13: 978-1-4967-0408-5
eISBN-10: 1-4967-0408-8
First Kensington Electronic Edition: April 2017

10 9 8 7 6 5 4 3 2 1

Printed in the United States of America

To my husband, Darrel, for always giving me the time to write and never thinking it was time wasted.

Acknowledgments

This book would have never seen the light of day without the help and guidance of some pretty tremendous individuals. A big thanks goes to the following people: my literary agent, Priya Doraswamy, for being my constant advocate and wickedly cool pitch-woman extraordinaire; my editor, John Scognamiglio, for his always spot-on editorial insight and for taking a chance on me; my husband, Darrel Cole, and brother, Michael Haseldine, for the reads, re-reads, and brutally honest critiques; retired police detectives Steve Baty and Ray Hansell for all the fact checking and for being two of my all-time favorite sources on my former crime beat. And finally, to my lovely mother, Marjorie Haseldine, for always taking me to the public library every Saturday while I was growing up and for helping me follow suit in her lifelong love of books, especially kick-ass mysteries.

CHAPTER 1

Glenlivet, light on the rocks. A cocktail waitress with bright fuchsia lipstick delivers the drink and motions her head to two tables down, in the direction of a group of aged fifty-something women. The recipient of the cocktail turns his head toward the hoots and low whistles from the likely recent divorcées who are ogling him like participants in a lusty spectator sport.

"Want to join us, hon?" the ringleader asks, and adjusts her leopard print halter top to reveal an extra inch of orange, tanned cleavage. In case her intent wasn't clear enough, the woman scoops a sugar cube from her champagne cocktail, places it between her teeth, and starts sucking.

"No, thank you," the businessman answers coolly, and places the unwanted drink back on the cocktail waitress's tray.

He turns his back on the spurned women and locks in on a tall, willowy blonde in a white dress that clings to her slender curves as she moves fluidly in his direction across the casino floor.

She pauses at his table, slides into the empty seat across from him, and carefully tucks a leather briefcase between her legs.

The rowdy commotion from the neighboring table of women abruptly stops as they wordlessly concede that they've been bested by a thoroughbred.

The businessman slips an Italian charcoal gray suit coat over his tall and tightly muscled frame. He tips back the last few sips of the drink he ordered for himself ten minutes earlier and heads toward the lobby, not bothering to look back. He knows the blonde will follow.

In the elevator, the mouth of a camera lens captures its occupants' activities. The pair stand close, but just far enough apart so it doesn't look obvious they are together—just two attractive strangers heading up to their respective rooms. The blond stunner holds the briefcase in her left hand and takes a risk. She lifts her pinky finger up and brushes the back of the businessman's hand for less than a second.

The elevator arrives on the VIP floor, the best the MGM Grand has to offer.

The blonde bends down, slides a keycard out of the front pocket of the briefcase, and opens the hotel room door. Inside, the man stands in front of the floor-to-ceiling windows. He takes a quick pan of downtown Detroit and then snaps the curtains shut. When it is safe, when they are alone, the blonde, now anxious and wanting, drops the briefcase and goes directly for his zipper.

"Wait." He takes the briefcase over to the bed, opens it, and fans the stack of bills across the mattress like a seasoned blackjack dealer some thirty stories below.

"Two million. You don't trust me now?" the woman asks with a contrived pout.

He ignores the question until the cash has been fully accounted for.

"Come here," he commands.

He starts to remove his coat, but she is already there.

"I've missed you," she whispers, and cups her long, delicate fingers around his crotch.

He reciprocates by running his hand across the thin silk of her dress directly over her breast, and then squeezes until the blonde lets out a gasp.

The blonde easily submits when the man pushes her down hard on the bed, letting him believe he still has the upper hand, that he is the aggressor. She stares up at his beautiful face, his breath coming faster now as his body starts to move in a rapid, steady rhythm above her. She doesn't mind when he closes his eyes. He wants her again, reestablishing her position of control, at least for now. That's all that matters.

When they are finished, the businessman turns toward the wall in disgust.

"I knew you weren't through with me yet," she says. "You take all your hostility out on me in bed. You're a rough boy, but I like it."

He ignores her, gets up from the bed, still naked, and heads to the bathroom. The blonde is useless to him now. She knows it but still holds on.

"The birthmark on your ass is so sweet. It looks like a crescent with a shooting star underneath," she remarks. "Come back to bed and let me take a closer look."

The man spins around, anger flashing in his eyes as if the blonde's comment violated something personal.

"Shut up," he says.

"No need to talk dirty to me. You know I'll give you what you want, as long as you give me my share of the money."

"When it's over, you'll get it. That's the agreement."

"How do I know you won't screw me?"

"Because I'm not that guy. The money will be in a safe place."

"I want access to it."

"I don't think so."

The door to the bathroom slams shut and she is dismissed. Inside the shower, he scrubs every trace of the woman off his body, hoping she will be gone when he comes out. But the blonde is still in bed. At least she is sleeping.

The businessman climbs back into his suit, grabs the brief-case, and closes the hotel room door quietly behind him. The second elevator in the hallway opens, and he disappears in-side just as elevator one chimes its arrival to the VIP floor. Its single occupant emerges—a man, squat and thick but moving swiftly like a gymnast. He wears all black—a bulky Wind-breaker, sweatpants, and a baseball cap as if he's just come from the hotel gym. He lets himself into a room with a key-card he extracts from a bulky fanny pack that flanks his waist. Inside, he quickly assesses the scene, pulls a tiny cam-era out from its hiding place inside a fake antique clock on the dresser, and tucks it into his coat pocket.

He then retrieves a razor blade and scarf from the pack and heads toward the bed where the blonde is still sleeping.

The man moves silently as he eases his body onto the bed. He inches forward across the mattress and then straddles the blonde, locking her in place until she is prone and pinned to the bed. Without opening her eyes, she smiles, thinking her lover has returned. She flicks her tongue across her lips and then opens her mouth expectantly.

"Shhh," he whispers. "You pay now. We know what you did."

The woman's eyes fly open, and she tries to scream out her assailant's name, but he seals one stubby hand across her mouth before she can utter a word. He lifts the razor from his pocket and gently glides the unsharpened side of the blade down her stomach until it reaches the top of her pubic bone.

"Please!" she begs. "I'll give you what you want."

The razor stops short before it makes its final descent.

His breath is warm and steady against her ear. "How do you know what I want?"

"Money. I'll give it to you."

He pauses as though considering the request and flicks the dull side of the blade back and forth across her skin.

"God, please. You don't want money then. Okay. Just tell me what you want and I'll give it to you."

He shakes his head and teases the sharp edge of the razor blade against her leg.

"Who is it?" he whispers as the razor makes a tiny, precise knick on the inside of her thigh, drawing a single drop of blood that trickles down her ivory skin like a crimson teardrop.

"The name. I'll give you the name!" she pleads. "Sammy Biggs, the Butcher. He's the one. I just found out, I swear. I didn't betray you. He did. Now, please! Let me go."

The hired hand sighs deeply, as if savoring an indulgent pleasure, now finally satisfied. But not quite. Lessons must be learned and never forgotten. The man stuffs the scarf down the woman's mouth to muffle the pain of her penance. It is ingrained in his soul that those who sin must atone. He clasps the razor blade between his thumb and middle finger and cuts off the blonde's left earlobe in one clean slice.

"Hail Mary, full of grace," he prays as he pulls out a locket from underneath his black T-shirt. He kisses a likeness of the face of the blessed Virgin Mary etched into the front of the gold necklace charm and stuffs his newly won keepsake from the blonde into his pocket.

CHAPTER 2

Concrete—gray, cold, and quickly passing—is the only thing Julia sees. The running started the previous summer when she was at the lake house, the place she mistakenly thought would be a sanctuary for her boys after the separation from her husband, David.

The runs started as just one lap around the rocky coastal loop along Lake Huron. But when Julia migrated back to the Detroit suburbs for a second shot at her marriage, her runs progressed; three times a week turned into seven, and the start times became earlier and earlier.

Five a.m. Julia conquers the stretch of her comfortable, suburban Rochester Hills neighborhood within five minutes. She expands her perimeter to downtown and then all the way to the Auburn Hills border. Ten miles today. No negotiation.

Julia races through the darkness just starting to break and ignores everything she passes—the funky downtown stores, the tidy homes with daily papers waiting on the icy driveway blacktops, and the Assembly of God church with its message board warning: "Sin: It Seemed Like A Good Idea At The Time."

None of the scenery matters. The steady rhythm of her sneakers pounding against the concrete pushes Julia forward, getting her closer to some invisible finish line as she races her one constant opponent: herself.

Spring officially arrived in Michigan a week prior, but the depressing mounds of frozen gray snow from another cruel midwestern winter obviously didn't get the memo. Julia pushes herself harder and starts to sprint as she passes the elementary school that her oldest son, Logan, attends—her half-mile mark to home. She breathes in deeply. The cold air stings as it goes down, but it's worth it. Julia is certain she can smell the ground starting its impatient thaw and the bulbs, in a deep slumber since October, beginning to stir. Change is coming, and she is ready for it.

A car drives by slowly, reaches the corner, and then turns back around in her direction. Julia instinctively moves away from the curb and reaches down toward her waist pack. Instead of a water bottle, Julia packs protection: pepper spray, and a folding knife with a three-inch blade. Paranoia always ran hard and deep after what happened to her brother when Julia was a little girl, compounded by twelve years covering the crime beat, not to mention a deranged religious fanatic who kidnapped her youngest son. For Julia, it all adds up to one thing: Trust no one.

The car slows to a crawl as it approaches a second time. A dark sedan, nondescript, probably a Ford model about five years old with tinted windows, Julia calculates, as her hand sweeps inside her pack. She runs her fingers across the flat side of the knife's blade as the car's driver-side window opens.

"Hey, Gooden, I thought that was you. If you're going to jog in the dark, you better wear brighter colors or you're going to get mowed down out here," Detroit Police Detective Leroy Russell says. Julia recalls that Russell lives somewhere in the Rochester Hills community, where his ex-wife is an assistant professor of journalism at Oakland University.

Julia finally exhales, her breath turning into a puff of white that disappears into the frigid March morning. Now knowing she won't have to engage in hand-to-hand combat, Julia fixes her gaze back on Russell, whose trademark Mr. Clean buzz cut looks freshly shaved. She feels the sting of adrenaline coursing through her body as the fear leaves her.

She begins to respond to Russell when the smell hits from the open car window. Julia makes out the distinct aroma of almost metabolized late-night, heavy drinking and Old Spice, the latter applied so liberally, it makes her eyes sting.

"How are you doing, Russell?" Julia asks. "Are you on the early shift?"

Russell reaches toward his glove compartment and extracts a green bottle of Excedrin, which he pops open, and then he crushes four white tablets under his tongue.

"Retirement party last night for Sergeant Walter Shaw," Russell explains. "I'm meeting Navarro for breakfast, so hopefully an order of scrambled eggs and home fries will soak it all up before a hangover hits."

"You and Navarro are meeting up to discuss the Rossi trial," Julia states, no question necessary. "I caught both your names on the prosecution's witness list."

"That's right."

Julia jogs in place without realizing it and strategizes how she can pump Russell for information for her story. The court part of the crime beat is her least favorite, despite the fact Julia is married to a lawyer. To her, courtrooms feel like tight little boxes where various versions of the truth run fast and loose amidst the big show, and the winner is often selected not by the culmination of the presented facts but by which side puts on a better performance.

"I heard there's going to be a surprise witness the prosecution is going to pull out at the last minute. Do you know anything about that? We can go off the record. You know I won't burn you. I just need a name," Julia pushes.

Russell reaches up and massages his right temple with his index finger.

"I don't know," he says. "Even if there is some last-minute witness, Judge Palmer probably won't allow it if they aren't on the list. Why are you asking anyway? You've got a much better source at home. You and David are back together, right?"

"We're working on it. I can't ask David, though. It would be a conflict of interest. The D.A.'s office doesn't want to get sued for leaking information to the press. Plus, David and I are pros. Neither of us would cross that line."

"Come on. You can't tell me you don't pull some favors in the bedroom to get your husband to talk. Sex is a woman's secret weapon. It always has been since the dawn of time. A sweet, firm ass has toppled many a mighty man. I'm more of a leg man myself, though," Russell says as he gives Julia's well-toned runner's legs a nod of silent approval.

At thirty-seven, Julia has long mastered the fine art of the dodge and weave around unwanted advances. Unless the guy is completely out of line, Julia ignores the come-on as if it never happened. The talent serves her well covering the cop beat, where egos and virility are often intertwined, enormous, and surprisingly fragile.

"Where are you and Navarro having breakfast?" she asks.

"Chanel's in Greektown. You want to join us?"

Julia gives just a hint of a smile. Dodge and weave successful.

"Thanks for the invite. I'll try."

"All right, Gooden. Tell the assistant D.A. we'll see him later. And be careful out here in the dark," Russell answers, and raps a red-chafed hand outside his driver-side window before he disappears behind the tinted glass.

Julia watches Russell's car pull away, and a small shiver runs down her back.

(Don't ever take a ride from a stranger, Julia, or, I swear, I'll kick your butt.)

The sudden childhood memory jolts her, and Julia starts to sprint as if she could race fast enough to outrun the passage of time and warn her younger self to lock the door the night her older brother, Ben, was taken.

Julia finally reaches home, nowhere left to run. She drops onto the front step, looks up at the first soft lights of dawn finally penetrating through night's heavy cloak of darkness, and chokes back a sob. She knows how to get through the pain. She always has. Julia pushes her emotions down deep and focuses on what she can control.

Her mind clicks off the pieces of the Rossi story she will have to assemble and file into some kind of compelling piece to run in the paper's online edition before opening arguments. The facts will be the bones of her story: Nick Rossi's illegal Detroit empire is believed to encompass hijacking and shipping stolen goods, mainly computers and electronics, illegal gambling, and drug trafficking. Both the feds and the Detroit PD had been trying to nail him for years. Rossi finally got busted in a city police sting courtesy of hidden cameras placed in the VIP suites of the MGM Grand Hotel. Images on the tapes showed payoffs to the former Detroit mayor and a city councilman, in addition to drug trafficking and cash exchanges for high-stakes gambling bets.

Julia kicks at the frozen ground with the toe of her sneaker and assembles the color elements she will add as sidebars to the main article, the ones that will make the story real to the readers and ultimately make them care: the seventeen-year-old West Bloomfield high school track star who overdosed and died at a party after he graduated that night from ecstasy to heroin for the first and final time, courtesy of Rossi's stash. Then there is the story of Rossi himself, only nine years old when he witnessed the rape and murder of his mother during a home invasion while the young Rossi bore silent witness as he hid inside a closet and watched the horror unfold through a crack in the door. Since Rossi's dad had taken off before his son was born, the young Rossi moved in with his uncle, Salvatore Gallo, who ran a moderately successful dry cleaning business with a small bookie operation on the side. Julia and Salvatore Gallo have history, and Julia makes a mental note to call Gallo before she gets to the courthouse to see if he'll talk.

Julia's cell phone buzzes inside her waist pack. She looks suspiciously at the phone. 6:15 a.m. Even as a reporter, no one calls that early unless it's an emergency, and she knows David is still at the house with their boys, Logan and Will, who are sound asleep. She is about to hit the ignore button but stops at the last second when she recognizes the number. Gavin Boyles, the acting mayor's chief of staff. The other piece of color she needs for the story.

"Gooden here. You're lucky I'm up."

"You told me you ran at dawn, so I figured I'd catch you before you got into the newsroom," Boyles answers. "I checked online a few minutes ago, and I didn't see your story posted yet."

"It'll be up later today. Do you have something for me?"

Boyles, a former TV news anchor before he became a flack, still has the oozing, ultrasmooth voice of a game show host. Julia met him ten years earlier at the scene of a major fire that obliterated a Detroit high-rise and eighteen of its residents who were trapped inside. Boyles showed up late and asked Julia if he could take a look at her notes and she could debrief him on the situation.

"Always working the story, that's why you're so good," Boyles says.

"You're too kind," Julia answers, and plays the pleasantry game while she waits for Boyles to cut through the bullshit.

"Are you including Mayor Anderson in the story?

"Acting Mayor Anderson?" Julia asks.

"Semantics. We'd prefer not to have Mayor Anderson's name mentioned unless it pertains to how he is working tirelessly to turn the city around since former mayor Slidell's indictment for his involvement in the Rossi case. If you write another story about how Slidell took bribes from Rossi to shut him up, you're doing a disservice to the people of the city. Detroit has suffered enough, don't you think? You could turn this into a positive story."

"And how has Anderson turned the city around exactly?"

"Public perception. I want to share something with you. This is off the record for now, all right?"

"Of course," Julia answers, and wonders whether the call might not be a complete waste of her time after all.

"Mayor Anderson will be holding a press conference today announcing a strategic task force dedicated solely to promoting all things positive in Detroit, including a volunteer-driven beautification project to help improve blight. It was my idea. Detroit is trying to make its way back. The residents don't need a rehashing of another corrupt city official story."

"Politics isn't my beat."

"Neither is business, but your articles are hurting the casinos. Detroit got gutted after the auto industry crashed, and God knows we can't afford to take any more hits. There's a responsibility, a fine line, we journalists need to ethically tow."

"I'm still a journalist. Last I checked, you weren't."

On the other end of the phone, Boyles blasts an obnoxious guffaw.

"Always blunt, aren't you? The press conference is scheduled for twelve-thirty on the steps of City Hall. I assume you'll be available since the trial will break for lunch. Mayor Anderson specifically asked for you to be there."

"Thank you for the invitation. I'll run this by my managing editor and let her decide who to send. You know how this works. It's not my call."

"Got it. I'll call Margie myself and put in the request. I'm surprised the paper is letting you cover the story when your husband is prosecuting it. Good for you, though. You won't have to work as hard this time."

Julia grits her teeth and forces herself to still play nice. She may need Boyles in the future.

"I always work hard."

"I just meant . . ."

Julia cuts off Boyles before he can finish. "Thanks for the call and the heads up on the press conference."

Julia gives her phone the finger, the sentiment she'd really like to give Boyles directly. Instead, she shuts her phone off and heads into the warmth of her house, which hits her like a blowtorch. She strips off her North Face jacket and then peels off her running pants and nylon shirt, which are sticking to her clammy skin. She frees her curly, dark brown hair from its ponytail and pads softly down the hall so as not to wake the boys. Inside the office, she leans over the desk and begins to search for her competitor's coverage of the Rossi trial. She pulls up the *Detroit News* website and feels a tug in her stomach. In addition to a big picture preview story on the case, Julia knows the *Detroit News* reporter is writing a sidebar profile on David as first chair for the prosecution and his likely run for D.A. next year, a promise David made to himself after he gave up a lucrative private practice partnership six months earlier to become a public servant. Still standing, Julia bends down closer to the desk and begins to search whether the *Detroit News* found out about the surprise witness or, worse, if they got the name before she did.

"Nice view."

Julia spins around to see David inside the office doorway. He is half-dressed for trial in a pair of blue slacks and an unbuttoned white shirt that hangs below his waist. Julia stares at his close-cropped blond hair he recently cut short for the case, finally losing his California laid-back surfer look and longer hair he had worn since Julia first met him ten years earlier.

"Do I know you, sir?" Julia asks.

"It's the hair, isn't it?"

"You look like a lawyer now."

"You say that like it's a bad thing."

"You used to have a Matthew McConaughey look going," she says.

"Not *The Lincoln Lawyer*, I'm guessing?"

"No, more *Magic Mike* or *Surfer, Dude*."

"Never seen either of them," David answers.

"You need to get going before the kids wake up and find you here. But it's still early."

Julia pulls away from the desk, still in just her running bra and panties, and tries to slide inside David's open shirt.

"I like your new look. It's like I'm cheating on my husband with a preppy stockbroker or something. Despite the hair, I bet you still have moves that would make Magic Mike blush."

"Sorry, babe. I have to get to the courthouse early. I don't have time for a second shower either. It's probably not a good idea for me to show up on the first day of the Rossi trial smelling like sex and my wife's sweat."

Julia, feeling suddenly exposed, spots one of David's University of Michigan sweatshirts hanging on the back of the door and pulls it over her head.

"Thanks for making me feel like a leper. Did I do something wrong?"

"I need to stay focused on the case and my A game this morning without a hot reporter distracting me. It would probably help if I could sleep in my own bed without having to run out in the morning before the kids see me. When do you think I can move back in? I know all the employees at the Marriott Residence Inn so well at this point, the front desk manager invited me to her daughter's wedding."

"I just need to be sure. I don't want the kids to get hurt if anything goes wrong again. Moving back to Rochester Hills to be near you is a good first step."

"A typical Julia Gooden safe step, you mean. The kids are going to be happiest if we make it permanent and become a family again. I need to be back here with all of you. I'm not myself otherwise."

"Let's talk about it after the trial is over. I know it would mean a lot to the boys."

"Is that the only reason? You are so damn romantic, Gooden," David says. He pulls Julia close and then turns her around so her back is facing him.

"Are we about to play pin the tail on the donkey or is something kinky about to happen?"

"Neither. I bought you a present. Don't turn around until I tell you."

Julia waits impatiently as David digs inside his briefcase.

"Okay, you can turn around now," David says, and hands Julia a small red box.

She feels a strum go off inside of her as she opens it and discovers a long silver necklace with a blue topaz in the center that glints against a shaft of morning light shining through the office window.

"It's beautiful," Julia says.

"I planned for the light to hit the necklace like that when you opened it, you know."

"Sure, you did. Can you put it on?"

Julia pulls her dark, wavy hair away from her face, and David brushes his lips against the nape of her neck as he clasps the necklace in place. Julia looks at their loving reflection in the mirror, a seeming portrait of domestic bliss but with some deep, hidden fissures that she knows still lie beneath. Julia fights an urge to turn around and tell David that she wants him back for good, but she knows what broke their marriage the first time. After ten years of trying to help Julia get over the loss of her brother and his growing concerns for Julia's hyper-overprotectiveness of their own children, David had walked. He packed up his suitcase one night after getting back from his practice and announced he was sick of trying to fix her. And following David's brief and clandestine fling with another lawyer during their separation, trust needed to be re-earned.

Julia feels stiff under David's embrace and stays firm in her resolve that she has to be certain about David moving back, not just for herself but mainly for Logan and Will. She won't let them suffer the consequences if things don't work this time, leaving them casualties of a failed marriage like those children who are reminded of their doomed status each weekend as their parents bicker bitterly during the ceremonial exchange of kids to ensure the court's visitation rights are met.

"The necklace is beautiful," Julia says.

"But it won't buy me a key back into the house yet. I can deal with baby steps if that's what you need."

"I started to see Dr. Bruegger again. I actually think it's helping."

"The shrink? Aren't you the one who called psychiatrists

useless quacks who take advantage of people's emotions and manipulate their thoughts by asking over and over, 'How do you feel?' "

"Dr. Bruegger says if I let go of some of the pain and guilt over what happened to Ben, it doesn't mean that I'm abandoning his memory. He says I can still love Ben without feeling the hurt that goes along with it."

"That's some serious progress. I'm proud of you, Julia."

David pulls Julia into his arms and is about to kiss her when his cell phone sounds on the table. David groans as he looks at the incoming number.

"Sorry. I have to take this. It's Don Brewbaker from the D.A.'s office."

"Get your A game back. It's okay," Julia answers as David retreats to the hallway and away from her curious reporter's earshot.

Julia thinks about her own A game on the Rossi coverage and returns to the computer to see what the *Detroit News* has on the story. A trickle of dread moves through her as she worries she'll get beat, the cardinal sin and biggest downfall any reporter can face.

Julia feels a temporary reprieve as she finishes a quick scan of the headlines and doesn't see a new story filed by her competitor. She plugs in a flash drive that contains all the information she's gathered so far on the Rossi case and the bones of the story that she will fill in and file later, after opening arguments.

The dark star of the article is Rossi, the once poor, young boy who witnessed his mother's rape and murder and was later adopted by Gallo. Julia pauses over an article about the mother's funeral, including a photo that shows a grieving and very young Rossi, his shoulders stooped in front of his mother's grave as Gallo's arm is draped protectively around the boy.

Julia clicks through the rest of the material about Rossi. He returned to Detroit four years ago from California to take over the family business after Gallo suffered a series of heart attacks. The police and Feds believe Rossi expanded his uncle's legitimate dry-cleaning business to a vast and powerful illegal empire.

Julia reviews her bulleted list that will run along with her main story.

Ten million: as in dollars, the annual estimated revenue Rossi reaps from his illegal and legitimate businesses each year.

Forty-two: Rossi's age.

Zero: the number of times Rossi had been arrested until now.

Julia quickly scans another folder that contains pictures of Rossi, the handsome criminal caught smiling in thousand-dollar suits.

"I've got to head out and meet Brewbaker before seven," David says as he reenters the office and leans over Julia's shoulder. "Is that your story?"

"So far, but it's got some holes. What's the name? The witness who is going to flip on Rossi?" Julia asks without turning around.

"How do you know about that? Did Navarro tell you?"

"If Navarro told me, I'd know the name as well."

David, still as strong as when he played lacrosse at Harvard, picks up Julia's chair and turns her around to face him. He drops to his knees so their faces are level. His green eyes shine with anger and intensity as he looks into hers.

"Listen to me, Julia. I mean it," David says in a sharp tone he's rarely used with her before. "If the identity of this witness comes out before the trial, he'll be killed. No question. I'm skating a razor-thin line here, and if I have to beg, I will. I've spent weeks trying to gather enough evidence to convict Rossi, and what I've got is circumstantial at best. Rossi is smart and didn't leave a trail that could connect back to him. I gave the witness my word I'd protect him and his family in exchange for his testimony. That includes not leaking anything to the press."

"The *Detroit News* can't get this story before I do."

"This isn't about getting beat on a story. It's about doing the right thing."

"That's the second time I heard that this morning," Julia says. "The witness should be in protective custody, if he's not already. The Feds should be handling this."

"This is my case. The FBI had its chance to nail Rossi on hijacking and selling stolen goods, but they couldn't. Now, stop digging around about my witness, understood?"

"It's not my responsibility to protect your guy. I have a duty as a journalist to write the truth."

"Bullshit. There's no public good achieved in reporting the name of this witness ahead of his testimony. Whatever mighty responsibility you think you have, take a step back and really think about it."

David puts his hand under Julia's chin and lifts her face toward his so she can't look away this time. "I know you. You're a good person. You would never hurt someone on purpose. Please think about what you're doing here."

"Okay. I understand where you're coming from, and I promise I'll think about it," Julia concedes.

"Maybe when this is all over, we can get away, just you and me. We can ask Helen if she'll watch the boys overnight and we can escape to Mackinac Island. No cars, no kids. No distractions. Just us."

"I'd like that."

"I promise I'll pull out my best Magic Mike moves."

"So you've seen the movie?"

"On a flight once. It's not a good thing for a guy to admit. I looked at it as merely research for my woman."

"So do we need a code of conduct in the courtroom?" Julia asks as she swings back to reporter mode.

"What do you mean?"

"I'm going to approach you in the hallway to ask questions, just as I would if you were any other lawyer."

David takes a moment to consider this as he buttons up his shirt and then begins to fasten a bright blue tie around his neck. "Good luck with that. The only comments anyone will get from me are written statements I'll send to every member of the press and whatever is said if we hold a press conference after the trial. That's it."

"You know how to use the press. You may need to plant something, and I know you've done it before. Just don't discount me. All I'm asking for is a fair playing field. And that blue tie is too monochromatic with your blue suit. You need some color," Julia answers, and hands him a light gold tie with blue stars.

"Lucky I still have all my clothes here. Not too obnoxious?"

"Much better."

"Tell the kids I'll see them tonight."

"Logan has a field trip at the courthouse, remember? You might see him there. I'm going to meet his bus at the courthouse when it arrives."

"How are you going to do that?"

"It's during the lunch hour. I'm the queen of multitasking, baby," Julia says. "I'm not sure if you'll have time this morning, but if you get a few minutes, I think I'll stop at Chanel's over in Greektown before I go into the newsroom. Navarro and Russell are meeting up there."

David shoots Julia a sideways glance and is about to respond when his cell phone vibrates on the desk. He snatches it up, looks at the number, and then shoves the phone into his pants pocket.

"You can take that."

"Not around you. This one can wait. It's nothing urgent. I'll call them back. How's Navarro doing? Still coveting my wife?"

"Now who's insecure?" Julia asks. "You have nothing to worry about. Never have. Navarro is dating some big restaurateur from New York anyway. She opened Chanel's and a couple of other restaurants in the Art Center and Eastern Market."

David stretches into his blue suit jacket and drapes his long wool coat over his arm.

"Wish me luck," he says. "Don't worry so much about what the *Detroit News* puts out. And stop your hunt for my new witness. Understood?"

Julia crosses her arms in a natural defense move. A light tapping on the front door tables any chance of a rekindled argument as David hurries down the hallway with a heavy briefcase in either hand. Julia follows his path and watches as David greets their housekeeper, Helen Jankowski, a painfully thin, older woman with a thick Polish accent and the best pierogi recipe in all of Greater Detroit. She nods at David and gives Julia's bare legs a disapproving glare.

Julia ignores the judgment and gives David a thumbs-up sign. "You're going to be great."

He leans in and whispers in her ear, "We'll take some time after this is over. I promise. Just you and me."

"We'll talk about your moving back in after you get a guilty conviction for Rossi."

"I like the way you think," David says. He walks out the door toward his car and then hesitates, turning back one last time as he takes a long look at Julia, who for a second thinks her husband is going to cry.

"Are you okay?"

"I just missed you guys and I'm glad you all came home. I wasn't myself without you."

The hot water of the shower runs over Julia's still cold body, which begins to thaw underneath the heat. Julia does her usual ritual, turning the water temperature to the coldest setting, and stands underneath the icy spray until her shivers become uncontrollable and she grants herself a reprieve.

Julia stands soaking and naked in front of the bathroom mirror, and a striking reflection stares back at her—her eyes, the same shade as her con man father's, a bright, startling light blue, contrasting against her olive skin and dark hair. But like most women, all Julia sees are her flaws. Journalism was the lifeline that first pulled her out of her often-crippling insecurity and gave her strength beyond the reserve she had stowed from her brother Ben's love and protection from the ugly life they shared as children. But then David and her boys became her salvation. Julia catches herself smiling in the mirror over her realization that maybe this time, she and David could really make it work.

The sound of little boys' feet tearing down the hallway breaks Julia out of her dark trance, and she hurriedly gets dressed, pulling on a fitted yet tasteful black skirt and a loose cream-colored top. She hustles barefoot toward the kitchen, carefully balancing her heels in one hand and her laptop in the other. She sticks her flash drive with the Rossi file in her purse and turns the corner to see the back of her two sons' heads pressed together over the kitchen counter.

Logan, her eight-year-old, sits on a barstool and is engrossed in his Minecraft game on the family iPad. Will, her two-year-old, teeters on the other stool as close as he can to his brother so he can watch the action on the screen.

Julia rushes over and rights the stool before Will takes a spill.

"Good morning, beautiful boys," Julia says, then kisses Will on the top of his golden-blond hair.

"Play with Lo Lo," Will says, and keeps his eyes riveted on the action on the screen. Julia smiles over the mundane domestic bliss and realizes she's already become second fiddle to Logan in Will's eyes, but takes comfort in the fact that the two boys will always likely have a close bond.

"Sorry to spoil the fun for both of you this morning," Julia says. She places an ABC picture book in front of Will and snags the iPad out of Logan's hands. Julia then gets on her tiptoes so temporarily she can tuck it away from his grasp on the pantry's highest shelf.

"Hey, Mom, why'd you do that?" Logan asks.

"You don't need to play video games first thing in the morning. Let's practice for your spelling test instead," Julia answers, and gives Logan a playful swat on his bottom with his homework folder.

Helen brushes into the kitchen and begins to stir brown sugar and raisins into a pot of steaming steal-cut oatmeal simmering on the back burner of the stove.

"That smells delicious, Helen," Julia says while handing Logan a notebook and pencil. "The first word is 'between.' "

"Between," Logan recites, the tip of his tongue poking out of his mouth as he carefully writes each letter. "Are you going to be there for my field trip today?"

"Absolutely. Next word is 'system.' There's a tricky letter in the word. One that is sometimes a vowel. I'm meeting your bus outside the courthouse at twelve-thirty."

"Don't be late again. The tricky letter is *y*."

"I'm sorry about that. I got stuck at work just one time, and I swear it will never happen again. I should be at the courthouse all day, so I'll already be there before your bus arrives."

"You don't have to volunteer for everything," Logan answers. "There's like four teachers and a bunch of other parents always at these things."

"Cities are dangerous places. You need to be very careful whether I'm there or not. Besides, I like participating in your school activities. I'm proud of you, you know."

"My friend Sarah wishes Daddy would go instead. She thinks he's hot."

"Good lord. Third graders shouldn't think anyone is hot," Julia says.

"I think you're beautiful, Mom."

Julia smiles and looks back at Logan, with his jet-black hair, dark eyes that turn up on the end, and a sprinkling of freckles that scatter along his high cheekbones. She is always amazed how much her son looks just like her brother, Ben. And Will is a dead ringer for David.

"That was a very kind thing to say. Thank you."

"Things are still good with you and Dad, right?" Logan asks.

"Everything is fine. Why would you ask that?"

"I thought I heard his voice this morning. Were you guys fighting?" Logan asks.

Julia curses herself silently for not being more discreet and for opening the door of possibility for Logan to hope that his parents may be reuniting.

"Daddy came by to pick up some work papers. That's all. Things are fine between your dad and me."

Logan nibbles on the inside of his cheek, a lingering nervous habit he picked up after the incident at the lake house last summer.

"Swear?" Logan asks.

Julia draws an X across her heart with her finger.

"Cross my heart. I'd never lie to you. You know that."

Logan gives Julia a small smile, seemingly satisfied with her promise.

Julia scoots Will's stool up closer to the counter as Helen places a bowl of oatmeal in front of each boy.

"I'll be home by five-thirty tonight. Six tops. Helen, please leave Will's door ajar when he takes a nap. You'll stay with Logan at the curb and not leave until he gets on the bus?"

"Of course," Helen answers. "I always do. I've raised four children of my own and all survived to adulthood."

"It's not that I don't trust you," Julia says, and pats Helen's hand.

"It's just the rest of the world she doesn't trust," Logan answers. "Don't worry, Helen. She does that to everyone. She just wants to keep us all safe."

"Please call me if anything comes up. I'll keep my cell phone on vibrate even in the courtroom," Julia says to Helen. "Something tells me you won't need to call me, though. I get the feeling it's going to be a great day."

CHAPTER 3

Seven-fifteen AM. The black Mercedes creeps along I-94, the Edsel Ford Freeway, and cruises off the exit ramp that hugs the forty-acre site that was once home to a Detroit legend, the Packard Plant. The name still resonates and stubbornly remains, even though the last Packard automobile rolled off the assembly line in the 1950s. Once a bustling empire that employed thousands in the east side neighborhood, it has long since become a gaping eyesore, mirroring the crumbling and decay of Detroit, a city with problems so big, many of its residents feel it was left to rot. The buildings that make up the abandoned Packard Plant are empty shells, except for trash, squatters, scavengers, and a matrix of graffiti strewn across the crumbling concrete remains, as crews of taggers tattoo what's left into a hopeless urban masterpiece.

The Mercedes pulls behind the south side of the blighted manufacturing plant. The car's driver is not worried anyone will notice their entrance, including the police. Bankrupt Detroit can't afford to pay to replace streetlights, let alone bankroll extra patrols for the high-crime areas of the city.

Inside the car, rules are being reset, in case they weren't understood the first time.

"It has to be small and compact but powerful. I'll pay up to one hundred thousand, but lowball at fifty thousand first. If you run into any trouble, you pull the trigger first. Got it?"

The two men—boys really, both barely older than nineteen—nod in agreement. This isn't their first job.

The two exit the car—Carlo, tall and thin, and Pete, muscular and short, both dressed in dark leather jackets and jeans, their hair black and shiny, the only thing beautiful against the backdrop of debris, unforgiving grey sky and cinderblock rubble.

They make their way up the side stairwell, carefully stepping over broken concrete as if dodging land mines, until they reach the sixth floor, the location where the salesman is supposed to await them.

"What are you going to do with the money when we get paid?" Carlo asks. "Man, when I get my five thousand, I'm going to Miami. Michigan can kiss my white ass good-bye, piece of shit. I hear they got sexy girls all over Miami who are just begging you to give them some."

Pete pauses at the sixth-floor stairwell and stares through a hole in the concrete at the cold sky. He closes his eyes and mumbles something.

"You praying, man? You're scaring me. What the hell you praying for? You think something bad is going to happen?"

Pete turns slowly toward him, centered and calm. "No. God is in control. If we die, it's His will."

"What are you talking about? If you aren't in this anymore, tell me now, and I'm out of here."

Something seems to pass across his friend's eyes as Pete turns back with fascination to the hole in the wall. Carlo pulls his Glock out of his pocket and points it at the back of his childhood friend's head. His finger hesitates on the trigger as he recalls them as two little boys, shy and holding their mothers' hands on the way to Communion.

"Take care of us, Blessed Mother," Pete says, and then crosses himself. "Put the gun away for now. We have a job to finish."

A small shiver runs through Carlo, who wonders if Pete has eyes in back of his head like the devil. He keeps a strong hold on the gun until he decides whether his friend can be trusted. He finally tucks the gun against the small of his back, praying that he is making the right decision.

Pete turns around finally and embraces his friend, giving him a kiss on each cheek.

"You're creeping me out, man," Carlo says. "You all right?"

"Of course. Let's go."

As they reach the landing of the sixth floor, Pete recovers the role as leader, pushes ahead, and scans the expansive, yawning cavity of the sixth floor before them.

In the far corner is a pile of metal, looking like a tall scrapyard of twisted steel and the picked-over carcasses of long-abandoned, rusted cars. Pete moves stealthily, almost catlike, toward the agreed-upon meeting spot until a voice rings out from inside a far room.

"The Madonna waits for no one," a voice calls from behind a door.

"Until pure innocence is found again," Pete answers.

A man surfaces from the hidden confines of the room. He's wiry and haggard, like a homeless man whose skin is now weathered and shriveled under the daily effects of the sun and frigid temperatures.

"How can I help you, boys?"

"We need a device that's compact and can do the most damage," Carlo says.

The bomb dealer lifts the handle to a sliding metal door that creeps up until his wares are in full view.

"I got the regular pressure cookers that would cost you fifty thousand or so, but for something that high-tech, I'd need one twenty-five, and that's a steal," he says, and wheels out an expensive-looking leather suitcase with something that looks like a miniature fat beer keg inside. "These are top-of-the-line designs just coming out of Russia. Maximum damage guaranteed. It's compact, and as you can see it fits easily into a midsize rolling suitcase. Dress someone up in a suit and have the guy leave it where you want the initial point of impact. After the Boston Marathon bombings, you have to be smarter. Anyone sees a nice leather suitcase sitting around, they're going to think some distracted businessman left it behind by accident. Then he walks away about three blocks and calls a number that belongs to the cell phone that's attached to the bomb. The cell phone is the activator, the call comes in, and *bam*, there you go. It's Fourth of July. This thing is guaranteed to cause major destruction. I'm talking a city block, half a building, or a jetliner, if you can get it past airline security these days. Like I said, a hundred twenty-five thousand. I'll even throw in the suitcase."

Pete reaches his hand inside his jacket pocket for his gun when Carlo speaks up.

"Seventy-five thousand. That's our top offer. You make this sale, there'll be plenty more opportunities coming your way."

The salesman digs at his greasy hair with long, yellowed fingernails and makes a decision.

"Eighty-five thousand and you've got a deal."

"Done," Carlo decides.

Pete stands beside him as still as a stone.

The bomb salesman rolls the newly purchased weapon of mass destruction in their direction and smiles at the young men like a car salesman who is about to give them the keys to a brand-new Bentley.

Carlo takes a long moment to study the case in front of him, trying like hell to pretend he knows what he's doing.

"Fine," Carlo says with authority. "This thing isn't going to blow up on us, right?"

"No, it has to be activated. It won't spontaneously combust, if that's what you're asking."

"Okay. Give him the money, Pete."

Pete stares back at the bomb seller with pure, unbridled hatred.

"Careful, boy," the bomb salesman says.

Money is exchanged, and Pete carefully holds the suitcase in his arms, cuddling it close to his chest like a newborn.

"Guy was a prick," Carlo says as they make their way back to the parking lot. "What do you think? All sales are final?"

The passenger-side window of the Mercedes lowers, and the driver motions the two men forward.

"Do you have it?" the driver asks.

"Yes," Carlo answers, badly wanting credit. "We had a little trouble inside, but I handled it."

"Then why is your partner carrying the goods?" the driver asks. "Come here, Pete."

"No," Pete says, staring back at the Mercedes without moving. "You come out."

"Hold on. Don't screw this up, man," Carlo says, and begins to walk toward his friend.

A single shot fires from the Mercedes and makes a perfect hole through Carlo's chest, just to the left of the breastbone. Before he takes his last breath, he thinks about banging the wild, sexy girls of Miami. The driver turns to Pete, considering more carefully how to deal with him without damaging or setting off the bomb. But the problem is already solved.

Pete tries to disappear behind the Packard Plant, leaving the small rolling suitcase on the ground in his escape. The driver fires, and the bullet penetrates the back of Pete's skull. Pete falls before he can turn the corner. The driver exits the vehicle, carefully scoops up the bomb, and returns to the Mercedes.

Directly across from the action, a junkie huddles behind a large cardboard box, praying to God the driver of the Mercedes didn't see him. He pulls the syringe of heroin, still halfway full, out of his arm and reaches inside a dirty plastic bag filled with all his earthly belongings. He finds what he's looking for, a card that he holds between two mud-stained fingers, and reads the name: Detective Raymond Navarro.

CHAPTER 4

Julia backs her SUV into a tight parking space across from the restaurant, fondly remembering her first junker of a used car she bought with her own money while a senior in college. On a full four-year scholarship to Syracuse University, she worked three jobs and was the only student in her dorm who had a vehicle their daddy didn't pay for. Her motto even back then was, if you came from nothing, you have to fight like hell to get something.

Julia slides four quarters into the meter and looks up at the flashing CHANEL'S sign, like a silver and gold strobe light illuminating the gritty Greektown block. The sign looks ostentatious and out of place in her city. To Julia, Detroit is a kindred spirit, an unaffected, scrappy survivor. And Julia believes Detroit is going to make it through the troubled times, just like she did.

Julia glances at her watch. 8:05 AM. She knows she'll have to make the meetup with Navarro and Russell quick in order to get to the courthouse in time. She waits for a second at the crowded podium and peers inside the restaurant, searching for Navarro amidst the gold leather booths and black lacquer tables with gold and silver stars hand-painted in the centers. Chanel's is Detroit's current "it" spot. Not the type of place Julia would normally frequent.

She spots Navarro and Russell parked in the best seat in the house: a booth in front of the open kitchen positioned in the center of the restaurant, where everyone can see them. Not Navarro's usual style, Julia thinks, as she elbows her way through the crowd.

A French press coffeemaker sits in the center of the table between the two detectives, who are studying some kind of handwritten diagram Navarro has drawn up.

"Mind if I join you?" Julia asks as the two men look up from their diagram. "Russell gave me the invitation earlier, and I thought I'd take you guys up on it if it's still okay."

"Didn't think you'd make it," Russell says. His eyes move down the curves of Julia's skirt, and he pats the seat next to him.

Julia slides into the booth and places her purse between herself and Russell to give a wide berth as Navarro picks up the piece of paper and stuffs it in his pocket.

"Official police business, huh?" Julia asks.

"How are you doing, Gooden?" Navarro asks.

Navarro runs his fingers through his dark shock of hair, and Julia spots his familiar barbed wire tattoo on his forearm, the one he got after they broke up about twelve years earlier.

At the time, she was just twenty-five years old and felt too young to accept Navarro's marriage proposal, no matter how much she loved him. Navarro took the rejection hard and the two separated romantically, but their friendship somehow remained intact.

"What's the picture you're hiding?" Julia asks.

"It's okay, Ray," Russell says. "Everyone's known for years you're her leak."

"I don't know what you're talking about," Navarro answers.

"Sure. I'll leave you two kids alone to talk about the weather," Russell says, and heads toward the neon restroom sign.

Julia clasps her hands together and leans down toward the table, as if she's whispering the next play to a quarterback in a huddle. "I'm not going to write about this, but I need to know. I hear the prosecution is pulling out a last-minute witness. I understand if he's identified ahead of time, he could get killed. That's not my intention. I'm going to have to file a story in a couple of hours, and I need as much background as I can get. That's all this is. Just background for a future story. No one gets hurt."

"David didn't give you anything?" Navarro asks.

"No. He says it's a conflict, and I have to respect that. I had to fight like hell with my editor to stay on the story because of David's involvement in the case. You know me. I swear to God if you tell me who the witness is, I won't write about it until it's public. I just need a jump-start. What do you say?"

Navarro's deep-set hazel eyes lock in on Julia and stay there until she looks away first.

"I won't give you a name, but I can give you something. The guy used to work for Rossi as a pretty high-up," Navarro says in a gravelly whisper. "He used to be Nick Rossi's henchman, I mean in the worst way imaginable. Remember Dwayne Brown?"

"Sure, the big hustler guy who was killed down by the Ambassador Bridge."

"It's rumored Rossi ordered the witness to off Brown because Rossi wanted Brown's territory. The guy David got to testify supposedly cut Brown's throat so deep, it almost decapitated him."

"How did David get the witness to testify?"

"Reduced sentence if he flipped. When the heat came down on Rossi after the mayor got busted, the guy fled to the West Coast. He just arrived at Detroit International."

"Thanks for this. But I need the name."

"No can do, Julia. I shouldn't have told you what I did. We have a deal, right?" Navarro asks and, to make his point, grabs Julia by the wrist. "This didn't come from me, especially if your husband finds out you got background on this. The guy doesn't like me as it is."

"That isn't true."

"You never were a good liar."

"I don't think David dislikes you."

"I don't blame him if he does. I wouldn't want my wife hanging around a guy she used to sleep with either."

"I didn't think you cared what anyone thought about you," Julia says.

"I care what you think."

Vintage Patsy Cline crooning "Walkin' After Midnight" softly pipes in overhead as a striking woman with dark red hair and a carefully made-up face steps out of the kitchen in a black sleeveless jumpsuit and cuts her way through the crowd toward their table.

The redhead assesses Julia as if she is a curious and possibly dangerous specimen, in a way only one woman can do to another. She leans over and gives Navarro a quick, territorial kiss on the mouth.

"Bianca, this is my friend Julia. Bianca owns the place," Navarro says.

"It's nice to finally meet you, Julia. Ray talks about you quite a bit," she answers with just a hint of a New York accent. "He tells me you're the best reporter in Detroit. I can't imagine how you can cover all the grizzly crime in the city and then go home to your husband and children and not take your work with you. But my skin isn't that thick, even though I'm a New Yorker."

"I've never had a problem," Julia answers.

"Of course not. Women like us, we're chameleons. Makes us dangerous and appealing. Please, let me get you a menu."

"Thank you, but I'm not staying long."

"Did you hear about how Ray and I met?" Bianca asks, preparing for her wind-up.

"No, he never told me."

"I was leaving here late one night. It must have been around one in the morning. I'm heading to my car when a mugger comes up behind me, grabs my butt and then my purse. The guy obviously had been stalking my place and knew when I'd be leaving with the bank deposit from the day's receipts. I'm about to scream when this big guy, all muscles and swagger, comes tearing across the street, tackles the robber, and cuffs him. That was about the sexiest thing I've ever seen in my life."

"Ray Navarro, the sexiest man alive," Russell chimes in. "We were leaving O'Sheas across the street after a couple of beers. I could have been the hero if Ray hadn't left me behind to pay the bill."

"Yeah, anyone would have done the same if they were there," Navarro answers, staring down at the table, obviously uncomfortable with the unwanted attention.

The food is delivered, and Bianca studies each plate to be sure it is perfect.

"Goat cheese omelet with kale, quinoa, and sun-dried tomatoes, a specialty of the house. It's the best seller at my Greenwich Village location," Bianca says, pointing to Navarro's plate.

"Isn't kale a weed?" Russell asks as he tucks into a plate of scrambled eggs and sausage.

"We need to get you and your husband in here for din-ner," Bianca says, ignoring Russell's comment. "Maybe we could make it a double date."

"Sure, that sounds good," Julia lies.

A pretty young woman wearing a black uniform with gold and silver stars hustles over to Bianca, looking as if she's close to breaking down into a fit of tears.

"Mayor Anderson is here early, and his table isn't ready yet. I offered him another window table in the back of the restaurant, but some guy who works for him said the mayor needs to sit closer to the door so everyone can see him."

"Another fire to put out," Bianca says calmly. "Very nice meeting you, Julia."

Russell carefully watches Bianca's retreat until Navarro clears his throat to redirect his partner's attention elsewhere.

"Keep your eyes to yourself, partner," Navarro says.

"Just admiring the view. Glad you found a good woman finally, Ray," Russell says. "No offense, Julia. I figure you and Ray have passed the statute of limitations by now."

"No offense taken, Russell," Julia says.

She fumbles through her purse to retrieve her cell phone, and a *Detroit News* alert flashes across the screen. A nervous shiver goes down Julia's arms as she clicks on the story, an-ticipating the worst.

David's headshot pops up first, and Julia quickly scans the color story about David's run for D.A. and anecdotes from his impressive, yet tragic, upbringing: David's mother dying of cancer when he was just eight; his affluent childhood with his father, a heart surgeon, in the affluent community of Grosse Pointe; David's success at Harvard Law School, where he was named editor at the *Harvard Law Review*, followed by his surprise move after graduation to work in Detroit's Public Defender's Office and then into private practice be-fore his move to assistant D.A. Julia's eyes flick across a family picture of David and the boys and then feels her pulse quicken as she scrolls down to the main article about the trial:

> *Prosecution in Rossi Case Pulls Out Last-Minute Witness*
> *By Tandy Sanchez*
> *(DETROIT) As the trial of Nick Rossi, widely believed to be one of the city's most violent criminals, starts today, the district attorney's office is poised to introduce a last-minute witness, who sources confirm is the former right-hand man of Rossi's local criminal empire and believed to be his hit man. The witness is expected to testify against his ex-boss in what is anticipated to be an explosive confessional in this ongoing story that has rocked city hall.*
> *A source close to the case said the witness will likely get a reduced sentence for his cooperation in the case.*
> *Whether Judge William Palmer allows the last-minute addition to the prosecution's witness list remains to be seen.*

"Son of a bitch," Julia says, and quickly scrolls through the rest of the article.

"What's going on?" Navarro asks.

"*Detroit News* story. I've got to go."

Julia hustles out of the restaurant and waits until she gets to her SUV to let out her anger. She pounds her fist against the driver-side door and accidentally drops her keys into a pool of slush underneath her car.

"Gooden, wait."

Navarro has followed her out, somehow not shivering in the cold in just a long-sleeved black T-shirt, jeans, and black motorcycle boots. He reaches under Julia's car and retrieves her keys.

"The *Detroit News* got the witness. They didn't name him, but they might as well have. Did you leak it?" Julia asks.

"It wasn't me. Probably the defense. They've got the most to gain. Before he comes out of the gate, it taints the witness as a snitch. Smart move. If Judge Palmer knows about your husband's witness, Palmer's going to be pissed it got out ahead of trial. If he doesn't know, he's going to go apeshit and probably won't give David a pass card to add a last-minute witness, since he wasn't on the list during discovery."

Julia assesses the collateral damage. Getting beat on a story is the worst sin a journalist can commit. It's a matter of personal pride and hell to pay from the entire pecking order of editors. But for David, the stakes are much higher: potentially the life of his witness and the outcome of the trial.

"We're screwed. David and me, we're both screwed."

"No one's screwed yet. It's day one. You're trembling," Navarro says, and begins to drape Julia's jacket around her shoulders.

"Give me the name."

Julia can feel Navarro's warm breath against her neck as he weighs her request.

"I'll do this for you. Just don't leave a trail back to me."

"You know I wouldn't."

"The witness's name is Sammy Biggs. His nickname is the Butcher."

CHAPTER 5

Julia dumps her laptop, purse, and jewelry onto the conveyer belt and hurries through the courthouse lobby security checkpoint, setting off the alarm in her haste. A red buzzer blares above her head like an angry hornet as a hundred pairs of curious and suspecting eyes turn their focus on the offender.

"Hold on, Julia," the security guard says as he waves a hand wand around her body. All is clear until it reaches Julia's chest.

"Someone told me underwire bras can do that," the woman behind her says.

Julia doesn't respond to the unsolicited comment, and her fingers latch around the one thing she forgot. "My new necklace," Julia says, unhooking her gift from David and setting it down in the basket. "Sorry, Gus."

"If there weren't two dozen people behind you this morning, I would have let you go on through," the older man says discreetly.

Julia takes the marble steps to the second floor two at a

time and searches for any sign of David, a long shot she realizes, since he and the defense attorney are most likely getting a smackdown in Judge Palmer's chambers to rival a WWE wrestling death match.

8:50 AM. Ten minutes to go. Julia carefully hunts back and forth in the hall to see whom she can hustle for information before she and the rest of the press get corralled into the media gallery of courtroom eight.

Julia catches a glimpse of David just outside of the Nick Rossi trial courtroom. David's expression is tight and intense as he talks closely with a tall, long-legged brunette in a tailored beige skirt and jacket. Conservative look, probably another lawyer from the D.A.'s office, Julia thinks to herself. She forces herself to stay put and not approach her husband for comment, and begins to scan the corridor for another source when the woman turns around. Julia's instant recognition of Brooke Stevenson makes her stomach twist. Julia was correct in her assumption that the woman was a lawyer from the D.A.'s office, and a point of contention in her recently revived marriage. David dated Brooke briefly at the beginning of their separation, a nasty little pill for Julia to swallow at the time, as Julia thought she and David were still trying to work toward reconciling sans any other third parties.

Brooke catches Julia's cold stare and reciprocates with a cool nod as she passes, like two adversaries sizing each other up for a rumble at sundown. Julia starts to move toward David, this time more for reassurance and to make sure he had told her the truth that Brooke wasn't working the case with him than for information gathering, but David disappears inside the courtroom to prepare for the morning's opening statements.

Julia brushes past her insecurity as her radar picks up the defense team's second chair, Ralph Charboneau, leaning up against the back wall, clad in a cheap-looking polyester suit. Charboneau is busy chatting up Tandy Sanchez, a bottled platinum blonde and the *Detroit News* reporter who scooped Julia. Julia's pulse quickens like a bull catching sight of crimson. Tandy's trademark braless cleavage is front and center in a tight-fitting emerald dress that appears to be at least one size too small for her. Julia's city editor, a former business writer back when he was one of her kindred crew, started calling Tandy "tits on toast," which through the years got shortened to Tot and the nickname stuck, at least behind her back.

"Nice suit," Julia says to Charboneau, not bothering to disguise her disdain. "I figured you were the leak, but I imagined you'd be more discreet. Nothing says 'I planted the story because I couldn't win the case any other way' more than having a private one-on-one with the *Detroit News* reporter you told about the prosecution's witness right here in the hallway for everyone to see."

Charboneau, a stubby man with a gut that protrudes over his belt by a good two inches, gives Julia a mean little smile, showing off his small, square teeth slightly yellowed by taking as many smoke breaks as he can fit into a day. Julia has had little use for Charboneau since his early public defender days, before he joined a lucrative private practice that specializes in representing Detroit's well-paying criminals.

"Ms. Gooden, I don't know what you're referring to, but I'd suggest you not insult me so early in the trial," Charboneau says. "I'm not inclined to speak to a rude and obnoxious reporter, even if her husband is a colleague. Now, if you'll excuse me, I have a case to try."

Charboneau waddles down the hallway, leaving Julia alone with Tandy Sanchez.

"Ralph is a walking oxymoron. A lawyer who hates confrontation, on a personal level that is," Tandy says. "So you read my story, I gather. I'm surprised you didn't beat me to it with your inside source and all."

"That story was reckless. Nick Rossi is a killer, and outing the witness puts him in jeopardy."

"The witness is also a killer. And don't tell me you wouldn't have written the story if you got the tip first," Tandy says, her pert chest shining with some kind of shimmering powder, as if it needed any more attention.

Julia snaps to respond but stops when she realizes she doesn't know the true answer to the question herself.

A heavy-set bailiff walks out of courtroom eight, and the scattered crowd of media, relatives, cops, and lucky residents who won lottery seats to the trial quickly jockey for positions so they can get a prime seat inside.

Julia weaves her way to the front of the pack and snags an empty seat in the center of the media gallery and next to a friendly face, Twyla Jones, the online editor for the *Lansing State News*. Twyla tosses her pink, blue, and brown dreadlocks that look like spools of multicolored cotton candy out of her knit cap and gives Julia a nudge.

"I'd ask you what was up with the *Detroit News* story, but from the look on your face, I think you'd strangle me right here in front of dozens of people and wouldn't care that there are plenty of witnesses to confirm the attack," Twyla says.

"Yes, don't ask," Julia answers, and pulls out her tape recorder and her old-school reporter's notebook and pen.

"How's Tot?" Jones asks. "Did she tell you who leaked the story?"

"No need. A friend helped me figure it out."

"All rise for the Honorable Judge William Palmer," the stocky bailiff announces.

Judge Palmer enters his courtroom looking like a wise monk with a long white beard and hair that is cut close to his scalp. Julia knows from experience that Palmer gravitates toward brevity, conservatism, and Jesus. She also knows he is a good and fair judge.

Judge Palmer, measuring in at an inch or so shorter than Julia's five-foot-seven stature, sits on his bench with almost regal authority. A tiny giant on this throne.

"Bailiff, please bring in the defendant," Judge Palmer instructs in his rich baritone.

The bailiff disappears behind a side door to escort Nick Rossi out. Julia tries to will David to turn around so she can at least give him a smile before the circus starts and to get a read on what happened in the judge's chambers earlier, but David stares firmly ahead, waiting for the defendant to enter the courtroom.

"I had no idea Jose Canseco was Detroit's biggest criminal," Twyla whispers in Julia's ear.

Nick Rossi walks into the room fluidly, like a panther. His resemblance to the former Major League Baseball player is almost uncanny. Rossi is tall and muscle bound, with impossibly broad shoulders, a square jaw, close-set dark eyes, and olive skin. He strides confidently over to the defendant's table and turns around, taking a slow pan of the crowd. Julia feels his eyes lock on hers for a second, and she holds his stare before he moves on. Julia scribbles down two words in her reporter's notebook: "intimidation" and "power."

"Now, before I let the jury in, let me remind counsel about the rules of my courtroom," Judge Palmer begins. "I do not like games. This trial is not reality TV or a game show that is going to be played outside of this room. I don't want any revelations going on anywhere but inside these four walls, and certainly not announced in the press first. Do we have an understanding here?"

Although not going into specifics, Judge Palmer obviously wants to give David and the lead defense attorney, William

Tarburton, a bit of a public slap for bad behavior, Julia notes to herself.

"Yes, your honor," David and Tarburton agree in polite unison.

"Unfortunately, an article in this morning's paper brought to my attention a matter that should have come directly to me first. Let it be known, I do not like surprises, not on my birthday, not on Christmas, and definitely not in my courtroom."

"Your honor," David interjects.

"Nor do I like to be interrupted after an issue has already been resolved. Assistant District Attorney David Tanner this morning made a motion to add a party after the discovery period passed. I have granted this motion in the interest of justice."

Round one: David, Julia thinks, and suppresses an urge to give a victory fist pump in the air. She then checks Nick Rossi's reaction. He is smiling, a look of amusement dancing up the corners of his lips.

"Now, bailiff, please bring in the jury."

Julia quickly draws the shape of a box with twelve circles inside. Once she gets a read on the jury, she will fill a "P" or "D" inside each circle, indicating whether she thinks that particular jury member will vote on the side of the prosecution or defense.

The jury shuffles in, day one always the hardest, as they face nerves, excitement, and pressure. At least one of them is probably fantasizing if they can land a book deal or at least an interview on CNN when the high-profile trial wraps. Julia does a quick analysis of the jury that consists of seven women and five men. The female jurors, who look to be between the ages of thirty and sixty, could go either way, Julia thinks. The defense could play up Rossi as a victim who witnessed his mother's brutal rape and murder when he was just a child. But David could win their sympathy by delving into the impact that Rossi's drug-trafficking arm of his business had on a wealthy West Bloomfield teen who OD'd. Based on the color of their skin, Julia deduces the ethnicity makeup of the jury is five whites, four Hispanics, and three blacks.

"Good morning, ladies and gentlemen of the jury," Judge Palmer booms. "In the coming days, you will be tasked with a great responsibility. I will remind you of your duties while you are serving as a juror in this case. You are not to read, listen to, or watch any media reports of any kind pertaining to this trial, nor are you to discuss the case in any way, shape, or form outside of this courtroom. Not with your husband, not with your child, not on your Facebook page, and not even with your dog."

A collective nervous hum of laughter fills the courtroom. The ice has officially been broken as Judge Palmer coaxes the jury to be more at ease.

"Now, before the counsel for the prosecution and defense choose whether to provide their opening statements, I'll reiterate, brevity is golden. This case promises to be a long one, so I will ask counsel to make their points and move on. Mr. Tanner, do you wish to give an opening statement to the jury on behalf of the state?"

David, looking to Julia like a white angel with his light blond hair standing out like a beacon among the dark suits and drab brown interior of the courtroom, stands up, an imposing figure to be reckoned with at a lean height of six feet. While some attorneys prefer to hold props such as pens or legal pads for utility or comfort, David does not. Julia knows he just wants to appear like a regular guy who stopped by for a little visit and a friendly chat with the jury.

"Yes, and thank you, your honor," David replies.

Judge Palmer does not exclude counsel from approaching the witness stand or jury box. David moves past the lectern and gets a few feet away from the twelve jurors, close but not too close that they invade their space and potentially make them uncomfortable.

"Good morning, ladies and gentlemen of the jury," David says warmly. "My name is David Tanner, and I will be representing the state during this trial."

David pauses for a moment and then emits a deep sigh. "I've been a prosecutor now for going on fifteen years. Never once have I gone off script and offered a jury even a hint about my personal life. But the stakes in this case and the ramifications should the defendant, Nick Rossi, go free are far too high this time. So here goes. I have two boys. One of my biggest fears as a father is for anything to happen to my children, including their exposure to drugs. Granted, my boys are young, but we've seen in our city that sometimes age doesn't matter. In the coming days, I will present evidence clearly showing that Nick Rossi masterminded a ruthless plan driven by greed and violence to bring heroin, crack cocaine, and methamphetamines into our city, intimidating anyone who got in his way, and hooking our most vulnerable and precious assets, our children."

David's approach is somewhat unorthodox but smart, Julia thinks, as she silently urges her husband to keep putting a face on the case to get the jury's attention.

"The defense will probably try to convince you that Nick Rossi is a good man, a law-abiding citizen, the only spot on his record a juvenile misdemeanor charge from his youth," David continues. "But as a key witness in this case is expected to tell you later this afternoon, this is because Nick Rossi has either paid off those he needed to turn the other way, including Detroit's own former mayor Willis Slidell, or intimidated innocents with threats of death to themselves or their loved ones. If drug trafficking in our city of Detroit and shamelessly paying off the people we voted in to look out for our best interests weren't enough, I will share evidence with you that Rossi operated an illegal gambling operation through our casinos, manipulating and luring employees through bribes and threats to ensure his business would continue. All the charges Mr. Rossi faces are astounding, but as a father, his drug business cuts the deepest. Two notorious drug dealers were arrested selling Rossi's crack cocaine during the lunch hour right across from a middle school near Mack Avenue and Helen Street."

David lets the sentence hang and pauses in front of an older black woman whose eyes shine with understanding.

"Many young lives have been lost, and our children have been taken during their prime because of the drugs Rossi has brought into our city," David continues. "Bryce Sullivan, or Sully, as the other members of his West Bloomfield track team fondly called him, overdosed at an end of season party, courtesy of Mr. Rossi. Now, the defense will try to tell you that Mr. Rossi is not facing murder charges, only drug trafficking, illegal gambling, and bribery charges. I will prove to you beyond a reasonable doubt that these charges are indeed true. But we all know the ramifications of Mr. Rossi's criminal operation did not stop there. Five million dollars worth of heroin, crack, and methamphetamines distributed and sold in Detroit means many of our kids will become addicts, and others, like Bryce Sullivan, won't live to see their high school graduation."

Julia pans the jury. They seem to be wrapped around David's every word.

"The witness who will be introduced to you later today is a former employee of Mr. Rossi, and he worked for Mr. Rossi for the past five years. This witness will take you through Mr. Rossi's carefully calculated operation, from its early front as a laundry and dry-cleaning operation that was actually Rossi's first portal to distribute drugs here in Detroit. But that was just the beginning. The witness will then detail how Mr. Rossi's appetite for the Detroit market grew to bribing and threatening employees at the MGM Grand, Greektown Casino-Hotel, and the MotorCity Casino Hotel. You will hear firsthand how Mr. Rossi bribed and intimidated the security in these hotels to ensure his gambling racket could take place on the VIP floors of these high-end establishments. But Mr. Rossi's corrupt influence did not end there. You will see recordings of the defendant in a luxury suite of the MGM Grand handing a city councilman and the former mayor hush money to ensure his illegal operation would continue."

David paces back and forth in front of the jury box as if deep in thought, and then hits them with an uppercut. "Don't let the defense convince you that their client is a helpless victim, forced to witness his mother's rape and murder at a young age. No doubt, what happened to Mr. Rossi's mother was a hateful and unforgivable act. I myself can't imagine what seeing something so evil could do to a child, or how it would affect their psyche, their later actions, and their very soul."

David lets the loaded statement settle in for a second and then continues.

"But no matter Mr. Rossi's past, it doesn't give him a pass card to become a criminal."

David skillfully ticks off a few more barbed points and then concludes. "I know each of you will use your good sense going forward, and you will clearly see from the evidence, Mr. Rossi is indeed guilty of the crimes he is accused of."

As David returns to the prosecution table, Julia notices a man with wide shoulders, a pinstripe black suit coat, and salt-and-pepper hair sitting on the bench directly behind Nick Rossi. The man turns around, and Julia recognizes that he's Rossi's uncle, Salvatore Gallo. The older man's eyes settle on Julia for a moment, and Gallo gives her an almost undetectable nod of recognition before he turns back around in his seat.

"Mr. Tarburton, do you wish to reserve your opening statement until you present the defense's case?" Judge Palmer asks.

"No, your honor. The defense will give an opening statement."

"Very well," Judge Palmer answers, not sounding surprised.

Tarburton rises, carrying a yellow legal pad and what looks like an expensive Montblanc pen to the lectern. As short and squat as Charboneau is, Tarburton is tall and reed thin, all bones and sharp edges underneath a classic black suit. Tarburton's strawberry-blond hair and heavily freckled face give him an almost boyish appearance, which he has often used to his advantage, as more than one witness has made the mistake of underestimating him during cross-examination.

"Good morning. My name is William Tarburton, and I'm representing the defendant, Mr. Nicholas Rossi, who has wrongly been accused of the crimes he now faces," Tarburton says in a calm, methodic rhythm.

Tarburton edges away from the lectern to hammer home what will likely be his mantra for the rest of the trial. "Ladies and gentlemen of the jury, let me put this to you simply: They got the wrong guy."

Tarburton lets sixty long seconds of silence elapse to punctuate his statement before he continues.

"I will prove that my client, Mr. Rossi, was in Traverse City with his uncle and ailing grandmother at the time these alleged and poorly made recordings were taken—the ones the prosecution alluded to, where city officials are supposedly caught taking hush money."

Tarburton turns around and gives a nod to an elderly woman in the second row sitting next to Salvatore Gallo. She looks to be about ninety and obviously the defendant's grandmother and Salvatore Gallo's mother. Nice touch, Julia concedes.

"Just like the grainy surveillance recordings you will see, all the evidence the prosecution will present is circumstantial, like trying to build a strong house that won't topple in the wind with just tissue paper and spit."

Juror number eight, the one who has been scribbling notes in a white notebook since David's opening statements, looks up for the first time and gives Tarburton a smirk. Julia fills a D with a question mark in the juror number eight circle of her diagram.

Tarburton moves to the witness stand and gives it a solid thump. "Mr. Tanner will parade a cast of witnesses in and out of this seat. What you must ask yourself is not only are they speaking the truth, but do they have something to gain by their testimony. You've probably heard the term 'jailhouse snitch.' The prosecution has indicated they will bring forward a witness—in some respects their hoped-for star witness, someone who allegedly worked for Mr. Rossi for years. This witness is a known and documented criminal who served time for aggravated assault and trafficking stolen goods. All illegal acts he did on his own. Now, the prosecution will try to slip in accusations of my client's involvement in other crimes. Keep this in mind. Mr. Rossi was never involved in these fabricated claims that Mr. Tanner will undoubtedly create, nor is Mr. Rossi on trial for them. This trial is simply about whether my client was involved in bribery, illegal gambling, and drug trafficking. As you will clearly see, the prosecution has no solid evidence to convict my client on any of the charges. As I said in the beginning, they got the wrong guy."

Tarburton hammers away for another ten minutes. He portrays Rossi as a victim who was traumatized after being forced to watch his mother's rape and murder, an unfortunate experience of convenience Tarburton uses to draw out sympathy from the jury.

Tarburton concludes, and Julia reluctantly admits that if she had to write a scorecard on opening statements, it would be a dead tie.

"Ladies and gentleman, as this is the first day of trial, let's break early for lunch. Please be back in the courtroom by one PM," Judge Palmer announces.

Julia turns her phone back on. 11:10 AM. She's already missed four texts and a phone message from her metro editor, Margie Kruchek, who demands an explanation on how the *Detroit News* got the bit about the Butcher before she did. Julia would prefer to file the story from the courthouse but knows she needs to try to diffuse Margie, so she makes the decision to go back to the newsroom and face the music. She realizes she'll need to make it quick since Logan is scheduled to arrive at the courthouse for his field trip at twelve-thirty.

Despite her time crunch, Julia decides to wait for the crowd to thin out so she can try to get a moment with David alone, but he is already up and heading down the aisle ahead of the pack. As he passes Rossi, the two men engage in a momentary stare-down, until David breaks and moves toward the door. Julia wants to give him a thumbs-up but realizes that wouldn't look fair and balanced, something she vowed to her editor she would remain when her boss threatened to take her off the story because of David's involvement in the case. Instead, Julia and David both give each other a polite nod. Julia watches her husband disappear out the door and feels a tug at her heart. She realizes she was wrong. Covering the case is not going to be as easy as she thought.

Six stories above Julia, Jim Bartello, the former head of security for the MGM Grand, ducks into an empty office on the eighth floor of the courthouse and places a call as he looks over his shoulder to be sure he isn't being followed.

"Yeah, they're taking an early break for lunch. Good news. Sammy Biggs declined special protection, so get in place and stay there. The cops will be escorting Biggs directly through the lobby of the courthouse at exactly twelve-thirty."

CHAPTER 6

Julia does the walk of shame across the newsroom, looking at no one, but she knows almost everyone is looking at her. She's worked in the business long enough to realize that news people are a fickle bunch, oftentimes fiercely loyal when one of their own takes a hit, but also rabid guard dogs when it comes to their beat. For most reporters, the story is the one thing, the only thing, that matters, and if it gets stolen, shame on you.

Julia sinks in her cubicle, hoping to be left alone so she can knock out a summary of the morning's opening arguments to be posted on the paper's website. She takes the flash drive of the Rossi case out of her pocket and stares at her blank computer screen, willing a snappy lead to come to her, but is distracted by the interruption of her ringing desk phone. The caller's name comes across the screen: Margie Kruchek. Julia bites the bullet and picks up.

"Newsroom, this is Julia Gooden."

"Come into my office right now."

Julia plans her strategy as she walks across the newsroom,

sparser now than ever after another recent round of layoffs last month. Julia decides her best defense is to simply throw herself on the sword and tell Margie she made a mistake and it won't happen again.

Margie, a round, middle-aged woman with a brown bob and square-shaped black glasses, sits behind her desk with her hands neatly folded in front of her. Margie has never pretended to be friendly since day one, when she got the job after being downsized at the *Philadelphia Inquirer* six months earlier. Julia was relieved when Margie replaced her former boss, Bob Primo, whom she detested, viewing him as a soulless viper. Julia ultimately decided to stay at the paper instead of returning to her former job at a smaller daily because of Primo's departure. The environment in the newsroom had improved, and Julia didn't even mind Margie's brutally honest approach. But this time, Julia wouldn't mind a few fake pleasantries from her new boss to soften the blow.

"I don't know what happened with the *Detroit News* story this morning, but I take full responsibility for not getting it first," Julia says.

"I made a mistake," Margie answers in an emotionless monotone. "I let you convince me bias wouldn't be an issue with this story."

"But I haven't been biased."

"I wasn't finished," Margie answers, her tone now cutting. "Everyone is biased, whether they want to admit it or not. If you and your husband weren't so worried about keeping up appearances, your ass wouldn't have been handed to you this morning."

"I don't understand."

"Your husband should be biased toward you. He should have given you the witness's name. Don't pretend to be naive. Journalists are supposed to work their sources so they will be biased. You want your sources to confide in you, not your competition. You don't write the story with bias, but you use whatever you've got to get the story, relationships included."

"David would never give up the name. He's too ethical to potentially risk his client's life."

"No one's life is at risk." Margie snorts in disgust. "I'm taking you off the story. Feed Patrick Conrad what you got from this morning, and he'll take it from here."

A flash of heat spikes up Julia's neck, and she forces herself to stay calm.

"This is my story. I failed. I admit it. But it won't happen again. It's a mistake to take me off it at this point. No one in the newsroom has the connections that I do, not even close."

Margie offers up one slow, hard blink. "Then use your connections. I'll keep you on the story, but if anything like this happens again, you're off."

"Thank you, Margie. I won't let you down."

"I've been thinking more about the coverage. It would be ideal to get an exclusive interview with Rossi. I bet Tarburton would bite. What better way to say 'my client is innocent' than having the wife of the prosecution tell the defendant's story about how he is wrongly accused."

"I've never known a defense attorney to allow a client to speak to the press during the course of a criminal trial. After the trial is over, maybe."

"Try anyway. See if we can get something, say, midweek. I'd love to turn the story into a big Sunday centerpiece, but we can't afford to wait that long."

A pit of dread begins to open in Julia's stomach. If that's the only way Margie is going to keep her on the Rossi case, then her chances of landing the interview are a long shot, at best.

"I'll try."

"You do that," Margie says, and turns back to her computer to check for any newly filed articles.

Julia hurries out of Margie's office and catches a glimpse of the clock above the copy desk. 12:00 PM. She calculates that it will take her about twenty minutes to get to the courthouse during the busy lunch hour.

She quickly grabs her laptop and bag and hurries out of the newsroom. Inside the parking garage, Julia checks for a phone signal. Not strong, but she wants to catch David before he gets buried in the trial again.

Julia expects to leave a voice mail message when he picks up.

"David Tanner here," he says, sounding hurried and impatient.

"It's Julia. I'll make this quick. You killed it during opening statements."

Five seconds of dead air on the other end, and Julia figures she lost the call.

"I can't talk right now, Julia. Let's catch up later," David says.

"I understand. I just wanted to tell you . . ."

The phone beeps in Julia's ear as she loses the call.

"Good luck," she whispers to the parking garage elevator.

Julia presses the down button and the weight of her conversation with Margie starts to hit. Although she didn't say it directly, Julia knows she is expected to work her husband for information, like some sort of sleazy con, just like her dad, who left town with Julia's mother, a drunk, when Julia was seven, right after Ben was abducted.

Julia looks at her distorted reflection in the silvery-gray elevator doors and feels cheap and dirty over actually considering Margie's directive to hustle her husband. She wonders if she'll inevitably wind up like her father if she stays in journalism. Self-doubt and insecurity start to rear up inside her, and she thinks back to the first person who saw something shining and beautiful in her, something she felt died when Ben never came home.

(*"I'll be here to take care of you now,"* Ben promised Julia *as the two children held hands and watched their father being escorted in handcuffs out of their broken-down doublewide trailer and into a waiting police car. "We were born into a bad life, but you're a fighter and you're going to fight your way out of it. You're good enough. You're more than good enough."*)

As the elevator makes its slow cruise down to parking level two, Julia feels the sting of tears start as she recalls her brother's words. She pulls out her parking pass and grazes her finger across the picture she's kept since childhood, the one thing that always stayed with her, even during a stint with an aunt who didn't want her and then as she struggled her way into adulthood. The photo is Ben's fourth-grade picture, the same one the police used in his missing person's flyer—a thirty-year-old case that has never been solved.

The elevator door opens and Julia tucks the memory away. She rushes over to her SUV, knowing she can't be late to meet Logan's bus at the courthouse. Julia pauses at her car when she notices a blackbird, sleek and shiny with tiny intense eyes that seem to be staring right at her, sitting on her driver-side rearview mirror—an unusual site, Julia thinks, as even the birds know not to return to Michigan's frigid temperatures until the ground begins to thaw.

"Come on, buddy. Please find another spot to hang out," Julia tells the bird. It stares at her for a beat longer, and then flies up and perches atop a cement beam above her car.

Julia jams the key into the ignition, and her car's engine makes a sharp churning noise that sounds like a fork getting stuck in a garbage disposal. After six tries of the engine fighting to turn over, Julia pounds her fist against the steering wheel.

"Of all the damn days," Julia mutters. Out on the street, she spends five minutes trying to catch a cab, but the only ones that pass are already occupied with fares.

David is out as an option for a ride so Julia calls the only other person who has always been there for her.

"Yeah, it's Navarro."

"Hey, it's Julia. My car broke down and I can't catch a cab to save my life. Logan's school bus arrives at the courthouse at twelve-thirty and I promised him I'd be there. Any chance you're headed that way?"

"I'm already at the courthouse. I'm meeting Russell in the lobby. Tell you what. I can leave him hanging for a few minutes. Tell me where you are, and I'll come pick you up."

"I owe you. I'm a couple blocks away from the Penobscot Building."

"I'll pick you up out front."

Julia weaves through the crowded sidewalks of West Congress Street until she hooks onto Griswold. Just as she reaches the forty-seven-story skyscraper, Navarro's unmarked Crown Victoria pulls up in front.

"You're a lifesaver," Julia says as she slides into the passenger seat.

Julia finally breathes out. 12:15. Plenty of time to get to the courthouse.

The sniper is patient. He has been in position on the fifth floor of the empty office building across from the courthouse for over an hour. The temperature in the room hovers just above forty degrees, but the sniper doesn't feel it. He wears gloves cut off at the fingers, so his hands stay warm and his fingers remain agile. His trained eyes scan for the target just in case, but he knows he will be called five minutes prior to the Butcher's arrival. He's an American-made killer who listens to Kid Rock and used to work at the GM plant in Pontiac. He first learned patience on the assembly line where he installed front and rear bumpers, the same damn thing eight hours a day, five days a week. But in ten years he never once had a safety incident. And he is still proud of that. He doesn't like pretty-boy criminals much, but money is money, and after being laid off, he needs it. So he brushed off the cobwebs of his early army training to find a new position. He considers himself a freelancer. And he wants to ensure that his tidy Dearborn rancher with the little garden in the back where he grows his tomatoes in the summer doesn't slide into foreclosure after the job is done.

12:25. The sniper's phone vibrates. He recognizes the caller—Jim Bartello, the former security guy from the MGM Grand, who hired him for Rossi. The sniper feels an electric hum going through his entire body. He knows there's nothing like the hard-on of a good kill.

"Can't you put your siren on? What's happening up there? I can't be late. Logan's bus is going to be at the courthouse in five minutes."

"The siren wouldn't matter, Julia. The whole block is stopped. There's nowhere to go around."

Navarro radios into the dispatch unit for an update.

"There's been a major water main break. Patrol is rerouting half of downtown to get around it," he relays to Julia.

"I'm going to make a run for it," Julia says, snagging just her ID, notebook, pen, and press pass from her purse and stuffing them in her coat pocket.

"In heels?" Navarro asks.

"I have no choice. See you there."

Before Navarro can respond, Julia the runner is out of the car and buzzing down the broken sidewalks like a bullet shooting out of a chamber. She gets just two blocks away and can spot the outline of the courthouse in the near distance. A school bus pulls away from the curb, and a heavyset man in a long black coat, and what looks to Julia to be a couple of undercover police officers trailing him, ascend the courthouse steps. Julia bets the heavyset man is the prosecution's last-minute witness, Sammy Biggs, although she doesn't see any sign of David and figures he might already be in the lobby.

"Hold on, Gooden," Navarro calls from behind.

Julia keeps running. As she nears the coffee shop on the corner, she is nearly rocked backward by a thunderous explosion. She feels something solid and powerful hit her in the back, and she goes down. On the sidewalk, the sounds of shattering glass, and a high-pitched keening of metal twisting against itself, play on like a macabre symphony around her.

In the abandoned building across the street from the courthouse, the sniper pulls himself off the floor and asks himself, "What the hell just happened?"

CHAPTER 7

A searing pain shoots up the side of Julia's skull from hitting the ground jaw-first after the massive blast. She opens her eyes to a sliver of gray sky and a barbed wire tattoo. She tries to get up and move the 220 pounds off her when she brushes against something warm and sticky. She quickly seizes back her arm when she realizes she is touching the remains of a man's severed hand. The thumb and index finger have been blown away, and the base of the hand is now just a stump of exposed tendon, raw flesh, and jutting bone. A gold band speckled with blood remains on the hand's ring finger.

The shrill peal of police sirens in the distance slices through the immediate eerie quiet after the blast. A second later, the yells and screams begin, as pandemonium ensues for the living and the dying beg for help.

"Julia, are you all right?" Navarro asks.

"Get off me!" Julia screams. "I'm not hurt. I have to find David and Logan."

"That had to be a bomb. Hurry and stand up before we get trampled."

Navarro jumps to his feet and pulls Julia with him as an oncoming wall of terrified people begin to flee from the scene of confusion, some pushing and shoving down the narrow sidewalk in their direction as pure survival mode kicks in. Navarro grabs Julia's arm and thrusts her into the entryway of a coffee shop away from the wave of people trying to escape.

"Stay here until the scene is secure," Navarro shouts, and sprints in the direction of the blast.

Julia feels as if she is outside her body, her world normal just one minute ago before the sonic boom. The ice-cold hand of fear begins to squeeze the life out of Julia as she follows Navarro, forcing her way against the tide, the air thick with an overpowering odor of acrid smoke, burned plastic, and something that smells like the spent remains of fireworks. As Julia moves forward, she takes in the devastation amidst the ruins. A plume of gray and white smoke rises in front of the courthouse entryway, and the exterior of the first three stories of the building has been completely shorn away. About two dozen bodies lie scattered on the ground, a few Good Samaritans hover over them as they wait for the first responders to arrive. Above them, a swirl of papers dances in a circle, then falls like confetti on top of the victims.

Julia begins to run, the courthouse just across the street from her now. She is so close, fueled by nothing but the primal instinct to protect her own. But what she sees in front of her path forces her to stop. A child, a boy, maybe Logan's age, is spilled on the ground with half of his left leg blown off. A foot away from the boy is a man, probably his father. Shards of misshapen metal and what look like ball bearings are embedded in the man's chest and torso. The lifeless body looks up at the sky almost peacefully without blinking. Julia knows the man is probably already dead and rushes to the side of the little boy. She feels for a pulse, which is thready at best.

"Hold on," Julia pleads. "Help! We have a child over here, and he needs immediate medical attention."

Julia's voice is drowned out in the melee. Not knowing what else to do, Julia strips off the belt from her white trench coat and wraps it around the boy's leg as a makeshift tourniquet.

The boy's pale blue eyes flutter open. They look glazed at first but then focus in on the strange woman standing above him.

"Where's my dad?" he whispers.

Julia shudders and grabs the child's hand.

"I'm not sure," she lies. "The police are going to be here soon to help you find him. Can you tell me your name?"

"Michael Cole."

The little boy trembles against the frigid pavement. Julia closes the boy's thin vinyl Detroit Tigers coat around his chest, as if that would somehow help him.

"I'm Julia. I need you to hold on until help gets here. Can you do that for me?"

"My leg hurts really bad. Can you please find my daddy for me?" the boy begs softly.

A choice has to be made. Julia's eyes dart back to the courthouse, where she searches for any sign of Logan or David. The lobby, now obvious to Julia as the place where the bomb was detonated, has been reduced to a dark, gaping hole. A man in a blue business suit emerges from it, running full tilt as he carries what looks like a small body in his arms.

Julia's choice is made for her. A caravan of first responders rush to the scene, including an ambulance that screeches up to the curb across the street. Julia yells louder than she ever has in her life as a paramedic exits the vehicle.

"Over here! Please," Julia cries. "A little boy is badly hurt."

Julia feels a tiny sense of relief as the paramedic hustles in their direction.

"Listen, Michael. You're going to be all right. Someone is here to help you."

Michael holds on to Julia's hand, his weak grip tightening.

"Can you stay with me?" he asks.

The request stabs Julia through her heart.

"I'm sorry. I can't. I promise I'll come back and check on you later, though."

Julia keeps hold of the boy's small hand until the paramedic takes over.

"His name is Michael Cole. Please take care of him."

Fire trucks, police cars, and ambulances line the front of the courthouse, the first responders assembling rapidly to the crisis. Julia searches the sea of quickly moving faces and the immobile victims who are being moved onto stretchers and wheelchairs while others still lie prone on the ground. Julia recognizes the battalion chief of the third district emergency crew team and latches her hand around his wrist.

"Brian, please help me! My husband and son are somewhere here and I have to find them. David is six feet tall with light blond hair. He may have been in the lobby waiting for a witness at the time of the explosion. My son Logan is eight. He has black hair and brown eyes. He's here with his class field trip. He is such a good boy," Julia cries.

The battalion chief, Brian Callahan, looks at Julia for a hard second and then back at the scene unfolding around him. "We just got here, Julia. You stay put and I'll have one of my guys tell you if we find them."

"No. You need to look for them right now. David is the assistant district attorney. I think whoever did this was trying to take out his witness."

Callahan listens to Julia with half an ear, most of his attention drawn to trying to lead and assemble the madness in front of him.

"I promise, we'll look for them."

Callahan pushes inside the courthouse. The scene is still fresh and mobile, and no yellow police tape has cordoned off the area yet. Julia weaves through the exploded cement bits of sidewalk and edges toward the entrance.

On the other side of the now-shattered glass doors, Julia looks in the distance and sees Detective Russell, unconscious and bleeding badly from a deep, open gash to his head. A paramedic and Navarro load him carefully onto a stretcher.

"Oh God, Russell," Julia cries.

Navarro looks up at Julia, rage and worry etched across his face over his downed partner.

"I told you to stay back," Navarro yells. "Get out of here. The building isn't safe."

Julia ignores him and quickly scans the victims and the dead. A foot away from the courthouse entrance, a large man with slicked-back dark hair and a long wool coat is crumpled in a heap next to the two undercover police officers Julia thinks she saw earlier. The big man, whom Julia suspects is the prosecution's surprise witness, Sammy Biggs, and the cop closest to him lie motionless on the granite floor. The other undercover cop is twitching uncontrollably, his body either undergoing shock or in the last throes of dying. Julia feels almost perverse in her relief that David is not among the group as she watches the man writhe beneath her.

"There's a cop over here! He's injured. Somebody needs to help him," Julia says in a raspy voice that no longer sounds like her own.

Navarro looks up in her direction. Julia knows he will find someone to aid the officer, so she continues on.

An older, petite woman covered in dust from the explosion looks like a walking zombie leaving an apocalypse as she limps past the security gate. Julia knows the woman, Beth Watson, a court scheduler who manages all the activities of the courthouse, including arranging tours.

"Beth, please! There was a group of students who just got off the school bus when the bomb went off. Did you see them?"

Beth's eyes snap back into focus, the task of her day-to-day job tipping her back into reality. "We had two school groups scheduled today. Carelton Elementary and University Hills Elementary."

"University Hills. That's Logan's class. Are the students in the building?"

"No. I gave a tour to the Carelton Elementary school kids. I escorted them back out to their bus and then got a call from the University Hills principal. He said his class was going to be late because they were stuck in traffic."

Julia feels her body ache with relief.

"What about my husband? David. David Tanner?"

Beth starts to pull away, her eyes narrow in fear. Julia realizes she is clutching the scheduler's elbow with all her might.

"I don't know. I just want to get out of here," Beth says, sounding like a petrified child.

Julia lets go of the woman and begins to sprint, dodging the rubble and almost falling on the slick floor, wet from the overhead sprinklers that automatically came on immediately following the blast. She puts her hand over her nose and mouth to make breathing easier in the thick dust and debris that fill the air. She stops suddenly to regain her footing when the lights go out. She realizes the power to the building has most likely just been cut to ensure there are no further explosions or fires set off by broken gas lines or electrical shorts. Julia clutches her cell phone and uses its light to help her navigate inside the now-dim structure. Once she checks the entire lobby, Julia then heads toward the stairs to the upper stories, where she will search for her husband room by room.

She reaches the top of the second story and feels the floor underneath her list slightly, the building's infrastructure weakened by the blast. Julia walks carefully down the corridor, sweeping past each of the courtrooms, but they are empty thanks to the lunch hour. Julia completes her check of the floor except for the last room on the right, courtroom number eight, where the Nick Rossi trial is being held.

Julia scans the aisle and shines the light of her phone across each row of the seats in the media gallery and the floor beneath them. She moves her tiny light to the prosecution table, hoping the impossible hope that somehow David will be there, having made it back to the safety of the courtroom before the bomb went off. The table has a legal pad on top of it. The light flicks across the yellow paper and Julia sees the initials I.R. with a question mark after it written in David's script. She shines the light under the desk. David's briefcase is underneath it.

"David. Are you in here?" Julia says, feeling the first flicker of hope since the blast.

A weak voice calls out from inside Judge Palmer's chambers.

"Julia. I'm in here with Judge Palmer. We're trapped. The judge is hurt. Go get help," David pleads.

Julia pushes against the door to the interior chamber. It gives about three inches and then bangs against something solid wedged up against it on the other side. She flashes her light inside the narrow crevice. The ceiling above the judge's chamber has completely caved in. Judge Palmer is unconscious on the floor, and a shattered wooden desk covers half his body. Julia darts the light to the other side of the chamber until she locates her husband, who is pinned on the ground underneath what looks like a metal beam.

"Oh, my God, David! Are you hurt?"

"Something fell on top of me after the blast. I can't move. Where's Logan?"

"He never made it to the courthouse. His bus got stuck in traffic. I'm going to try to push the door open."

The ground underneath Julia undulates violently, and she grabs the wall to steady herself.

"Did you feel that?" Julia asks.

"This section of the building isn't stable. You need to get out of here."

"I'm not leaving you."

The floor underneath them lets out a deep groan followed by a sharp snapping sound like thick metal cables beginning to sever. Julia throws her body against the door to the chamber, but it doesn't budge against her slender frame.

"Go now!" David commands.

"I'm going to grab a chair and try to ram the door open with it."

"No, you're not. You're going to get out of here. If you won't do it for yourself, then do it for Logan and Will. They need at least one of us around."

"Don't you say that. Not ever. Everything is going to be fine," Julia says, the words sounding hollow and untrue as soon as she hears them. "Help! Please, someone! We have two men trapped in here."

The floor begins to vibrate underneath Julia again, and she struggles to keep her balance.

"I love you, Julia. I always have," David says, his voice thick with emotion. "I'm sorry. Please remember that. You and the boys were always the best part of my life. Now go."

"I love you too. But this isn't over. I'm going to get help."

Julia runs faster now than she ever has, through the courtroom and down the hallway to the stairs. As she descends to the lobby, a massive crash rings out above her. Julia drops to the floor and covers her head as the weakened section of the second story severs and its remains free-fall down to the street below.

CHAPTER 8

Julia clutches her head between her hands and stares with fixed intensity at the sterilized floor of the surgery waiting area at Henry Ford Hospital. She drowns out the scenes of relief and devastation that continue to play out around her as families of the courthouse bombing victims receive news about their loved ones.

Julia prays for the first time since she was a child. She gave up praying when her brother, Ben, never came home. She gives God one more chance, considering the circumstances, and vows she will love and care for David no matter what condition he is in as long as his life is spared. She then says a silent prayer to herself that whoever did this gets what's coming to them. And if God won't bring the attacker to justice, she will.

Navarro sidles through the crowd and nabs the empty seat next to Julia.

"Are you okay?" he asks.

"No. I'm a bloody wreck," Julia says. "The surgery is taking longer than what the doctor originally told me. Maybe there were complications. Someone should come out and tell me what's going on."

"Hold on. If there was an issue, I'm sure you would have heard by now. I got you some tea. It's from the cafeteria, not the vending machine, so it should be okay. Are the boys coming to the hospital?"

"No. I don't want them here right now. It would just confuse and frighten them."

Julia picks up the Styrofoam cup filled with hot tea from the hospital's cheap Formica table and holds it between her hands, the warmth feeling somewhat soothing.

"Sammy Biggs, the Butcher, is dead," Navarro says. "Right now, we think the bomb was in a suitcase when it went off."

"How did it get through security?"

"It didn't. We think the bomb was planted outside the doors of the courthouse. From the video surveillance inside the lobby, it looks like the bomb was detonated just as Biggs got into position."

"I knew it. That's what this whole goddamn thing is about," Julia says. "Nick Rossi kills his snitch before he can testify. How many people did he kill?"

"Right now eighteen. Most were getting back from lunch when the bomb went off in the lobby. Thirty more were injured."

"Rossi better get the death penalty. If he doesn't, I swear to God, I'll take him down myself."

"Easy there. A few of the victims have been treated and released. Russell should go home by tomorrow. He was lucky."

"That's good news," Julia says. The overarching ache of jealousy slithers around her as she wishes David had the same luck as her friend.

"You know, I keep thinking, I would have been at the

courthouse with Russell if you hadn't called me. I might not have been so lucky. I owe you, Gooden."

"My car broke down and you were doing me a favor. Don't act like I saved your life. I didn't save anyone's life."

"From what you told me, there's no way you could have gotten into the judge's chambers in time to get anyone out of there. The building was collapsing, and chances are that was probably a steel beam blocking the door. I don't know if I could have moved it out of the way in time. Survivor's guilt isn't going to do you any good."

"I keep replaying everything, when David was trapped inside the judge's chambers," Julia says, her tears coming again. "David told me he was sorry, as if he did something wrong for getting hurt, like he was letting me and the boys down. He forced me to leave. I would have stayed otherwise to try to get him out, but he risked his own life to protect me and the boys."

"As he should have," Navarro says. "Did David tell you why he was in there with Judge Palmer by himself?"

"What do you mean?"

"Maybe he got wind of a threat and was in there telling the judge at the last minute before the jury filed back in. It seems odd to me that a prosecutor would be alone in a judge's chambers during a criminal trial without opposing counsel there, unless David approached him directly or the judge called him in about something."

"No. David didn't mention anything like that. Everything was happening so fast. I remember he told me the judge was badly injured. There wasn't much time to talk about anything else."

"Judge Palmer is still in a coma," Navarro says.

"Nick Rossi better be nailed to the cross for this," Julia says, a bud of fury blooming inside her chest. "What new charges are going to be filed against him? The feds should sweep in from here and charge him with use of weapons of mass destruction like they did with the Boston Marathon bomber. They should pile on as much as they can."

Navarro rakes his fingers through his dark hair, his usual subliminal habit when he is about to say something he'd prefer not to.

"There aren't any new charges. We've got zero proof right now tying Rossi to the bombing. The guy was in a holding cell at the time the thing went off. Tarburton is pitching a fit in the media right now, saying his client had nothing to do with the bombing and was put in harm's way since he wasn't offered proper protection after being falsely accused. Tarburton is threatening to file a civil suit against the state after the legal bullshit around the criminal trial is decided."

"Nick Rossi is no victim. He obviously had one of his minions pull this off at his direction," Julia says. "What about the criminal trial on the drug, gambling, and bribery charges against Rossi?"

"It's an unprecedented situation. The judge in the case hasn't regained consciousness, and the head prosecutor sustained major injuries, not to mention the prosecution's key witness was killed."

"Can't they find a substitute judge to hear the case? And the second chair from the D.A.'s office could handle the prosecution. I know David would want the trial to proceed without a delay."

"Come on, Julia. You and I both know that's probably not going to happen."

"Extraordinary circumstances. They're going to call a mistrial," Julia realizes. "They can't do that. Rossi doesn't get to just walk away from the charges, even if you don't have enough evidence right now to charge him with the bombing."

"You know how this works. It's not what's right or wrong. The law decides. If a mistrial is declared, Tarburton could claim double jeopardy and Rossi can't be tried twice for the same offense."

"But Judge Palmer isn't in any condition to declare a mistrial even if he wanted to, not now anyway."

"Last I heard, the Michigan Supreme Court Chief Justice is going to announce a decision. Unless we can find something that connects Rossi to the bombing, he could walk."

"You can't let that happen."

"The bomb squad is trying to get a print, but they've got nothing. The type of bomb, they think, is new, nothing like they've ever seen before."

"Everyone needs to work harder," Julia says.

"Believe me, everyone is working as hard as they can," Navarro answers, a hint of annoyance entering his voice. "We lost two cops, not to mention a couple of kids who died in the blast."

"There was a badly injured boy I tried to help, and I'm pretty sure his dad was killed. I talked to him while I was trying to get to the courthouse. He wanted me to stay with him," Julia says, knotting her hands into fists over the memory. "The boy's name is Michael Cole. If you find out he's here, can you let me know?"

"I've got to interview a witness, a guy who was leaving the lobby right before the bomb went off. He's in a room up the hall. He got pretty beat up in the explosion. Let me talk to him and then if I can, I'll ask around about the boy."

Navarro leaves to interview his witness and Julia is left alone to face her uncertain future. She tries to ignore her worst fear that David won't make it through the surgery and instead concentrates on trying to assemble the dangling pieces of the case. She pulls out her reporter's notebook and pen and starts scribbling down theories. If the bomber, working under Rossi's direction, made the explosive, it would be difficult to trace. But if the person bought it, there would be a paper trail, she figures.

Working the crime beat on the streets of Detroit for the past decade, Julia knows there's always a way to find someone to talk, you just have to know who to ask. Someone always knows something. Julia writes down the words *uncashed favor* and a question mark and recalls the promise given to her by an unlikely prospect, Salvatore Gallo, Rossi's uncle. Three years ago, Gallo had been arrested for the murder of Vincent Bombardi, a young hothead who was rumored to be rising up in the ranks of his nephew's operation. Bombardi had been found stabbed to death in his car parked across the street from Gallo's home. Julia investigated the story and uncovered a small-time hood had killed Bombardi on a territory dispute and had left the body in front of Salvatore Gallo's home so the cops would link the murder to Rossi. But the cops didn't see it that way and liked Gallo for the murder. After Gallo was released from prison, he asked Julia for a personal meeting, where he told her if she ever needed anything, he would help her. Julia taps the end of her pencil against the paper and decides if she reached out to Gallo to help her get information about the bombing, he'd obviously pick the side of his nephew, despite his promise.

The doors to the surgery wing open and David's neurosurgeon, Dr. Steven Whitcomb, emerges. Julia jumps to her feet and tries to read the doctor's expression to give her a clue on how the surgery went.

Dr. Whitcomb motions Julia over, away from the busy room, so they can talk in private.

Dr. Whitcomb is young for a surgeon, just a few years older than Julia, but she comforts herself with the reminder that he is considered one of the best neurosurgeons in the Detroit area.

"The surgery overall went well," Dr. Whitcomb says.

"David pulled through and we were able to relieve the pressure on his brain caused by the bleeding. It's too early yet to determine how much mental function, if any, he lost because of the hemorrhaging. The positive news is that he is strong and was in excellent physical health before this happened. But he sustained extensive trauma from the fall."

"What exactly are you telling me?" Julia asks.

"That we don't know yet how he's going to come out of this. Some patients suffer seizures, strokes, or permanent brain damage. With the type of injury David sustained, it could affect his vision for the long term. I've also had patients with injuries in similar areas of the brain who had minimal or no side effects. As I said, it's too early to tell."

"David is going to be fine. I know it," Julia says. "I want to see him."

"David is stable, but you need to keep this first visit short. Are your children here?"

"No, it's just me."

"David still had his wallet and cell phone in his jacket pocket when he was brought in here. His personal effects are in his room. Feel free to take them home with you if you like."

Dr. Whitcomb leads Julia to the room where David is recovering following the surgery. Julia tried to prepare herself ahead of time, but she is shocked over David's appearance. His perfect face is almost unrecognizable, marred with deep purple bruises and swelling. His recently closed-cropped hair has been shaved, and the thin six-inch scar from his recent incision stands out like an angry red line on his scalp.

Julia waits until she is alone with her husband, when it is just them again. She wills herself not to break down, pulls up a stool, and gently takes his hand. Julia closes her eyes and savors happy memories with David early on in their relationship.

("You can't be scared of lightning," David said as he ran his finger down the length of Julia's face, wiping off the single raindrop that had fallen on her as a harbinger of the coming storm in the distance.

Julia looked back at David, the two of them naked, covered only by a light blanket as they lay on a rug covering the outside patio of David's downtown Detroit penthouse.

"I'm not afraid. I just try to steer clear of anything that can kill me. Most sane people feel the same way."

"How do you feel about family?" David asked. "You never talk about your own."

"It's a long story, and not a very good one."

"If you want to remain a woman of mystery, I'll let you play that role, at least for a while longer. But my dad would like to meet you. He's finally talking to me again after his so-called painful recovery over my disappointing choice to work for the public defender's office instead of joining his Sunday golf partner's private practice. The guy makes huge bucks by representing the mob. I told my dad I'd rather be poor than a sellout."

"That's good you've reunited with your dad."

"Well, under one condition. I have to pay him back for all my education, considering he footed the bill and I chose to be a lowly public defender."

"That doesn't seem fair. And you accepted that? He should be proud of you."

"Life doesn't work that way, especially if you come from money. So you'll go to dinner? My dad has a new wife. I haven't met her yet and I could use some support from the cavalry, and what a very attractive cavalry it is."

"There's something I need to tell you first. It might make you rethink your invitation."

"What's the matter? Why won't you look at me?"

"I'm pregnant. I thought we were being careful. I'm sorry.

I realize we've only been together for six months, but I can't give the baby up. I understand if you want to walk away."

David pulled Julia as close as he could and kissed her as a boom of thunder rang out in the near distance.

"Hot damn. Julia Gooden, you're full of surprises.")

A profound hollowness settles in her chest, and the strong and comforting speech Julia had recited over and over in her head vanishes as she speaks from the heart.

"It's me, babe. I'm sorry I left you in the courthouse. You told me to go, and I did it for the boys," Julia says, and steadies her voice. "You did really well getting through the surgery. You don't give up, understand? Despite what's happened between us, the separation, the fighting, we put it behind us and I need you. Logan and Will need you too. Now listen, this is really important. You concentrate on getting better. That's your job. I promise I'll take care of the boys. But I know you, and you'd want me to take care of something else. Nick Rossi bombed the courthouse to take out your witness. I need to make sure justice happens for you and everyone else who got hurt. I'm going after Rossi. I know that's what you were trying to do. You'd tell me to be careful, and I will, but you wouldn't tell me no. I won't let Rossi get away with this."

Julia reaches into her purse; pulls out a framed picture of David, the boys, and herself, all tanned and happy at the lakeshore the summer before; and places it on her husband's bedside stand.

She notices a cardboard box containing David's belongings on a stand next to the bed, including his clothing he had carefully selected for big day one of the trial. Julia inspects the items in the box: David's cell phone, wallet, blue suit coat and dress pants, white button-down shirt and gold tie with the gold stripes she picked for him just hours earlier. Each item of clothing has been sliced down the center in an uneven crease, except for the tie, as the emergency room team obviously cut David out of his clothes when he arrived at the ER. Julia tucks the box under her arm as Dr. Whitcomb pokes his head inside the door.

"Ms. Gooden, I'm afraid it's time to leave."

Julia leans in close to David and whispers in his ear, "I love you. Fight with all you've got."

Julia pulls away and convinces herself she can see David's index finger raise just slightly, as if he were saying, "Damn right, Gooden."

Jim Bartello sweats before he makes the phone call, sweats even more than he did when the cops were sniffing around when he was still head of security at the MGM Grand. The cops never found enough evidence to directly link him to Nick Rossi, but it was enough to get him fired from his $75,000-a-year job by the general manager of the hotel.

Bartello spent his entire adult life around people who made bets, and he beat his own odds on not getting taken down in the Rossi bust. Bartello thought he'd won the cherry prize when Rossi's big dog, Enzo Costas, promised that he and Rossi would take care of Bartello for his loyal services. But his new services became much more than he expected and seemed to have no expiration date.

Bartello wipes the sweat from his palms across his gray vinyl tracksuit and reaches for his cell phone.

He can hear his heart thumping loudly in his ears as the phone begins to ring.

"Mister Jim," Enzo answers, his voice as deep and throaty as a Sunday morning evangelist preacher's.

"Mr. Costas, I don't know what happened. I did exactly what you told me. I hired the guy. He's the best sniper in the Midwest. I wouldn't steer you wrong."

"But he never fired a shot, is that right? Someone beat him to it."

"Yeah, that's what I'm trying to figure out," Bartello says as perspiration begins to drip down the back of his fat neck.

"That's what we pay you for. To figure things out so nothing like this happens. This bombing had many casualties. Nick's lawyer will try to get him out of this, but if he can't, our boss may be tied to this bombing. The charges will be much worse than what he is currently facing."

"I know. Christ, I know."

"What have you been able to find out about the bomber?"

"The bomb was purchased at the Packard Plant. I know that much. The bodies of two young dudes were found outside the building around the time of the sale. That's what my source said."

"You know who they were working for?"

"I don't know. I'm tracking them."

Bartello endures a minute of silence on the other end of the phone.

"Tracking them. That is not acceptable."

"I know. I'm close. I won't let you down. Right now, I think they were just contract kids for hire."

Bartello's body is completely wet with sweat as if he just ran ten miles in his tracksuit.

"And who hired them?"

"I don't know yet. But as I said, I'm real close."

"Tomorrow. You give me answers by tomorrow. Understand?"

Twenty-four hours. Bartello figures he can get to his hiding place by then.

CHAPTER 9

The sun begins its slow and glorious rise in Julia's rearview mirror as she pulls into her driveway. She stares out at the house she and David bought eight years ago, just before Logan was born. She can picture David walking around the backyard assessing the property on the day they first saw the house and how wonderfully foolish he looked in his suit coat and tie as he took a spin on the tire swing underneath the stately maple tree that still stands guard out back.

Julia rests her head against the steering wheel and tries to come up with strong and soothing words to say to the boys when they wake up. She wishes she could consult with David, always the calm one while she was the overreactor, about the right thing to tell them, but she accepts the fact she's alone on this one.

Julia looks up at her front porch. Perched on the ledge right outside the kitchen window is a blackbird. It stares back at her for a long minute and then soars high into the early morning air until it disappears into the thick nest of trees in the back of her property. She recalls the blackbird that waited by her broken-down car in the parking garage right before the bombing, and Julia realizes her stroke of extreme luck, because she would have most likely been at ground zero of the courthouse waiting for Logan if her car had started.

Inside, her house still smells warm and welcoming from a fire that Helen must have made for the boys the night before. She slips off her white trench coat, now tattered and filthy from the previous day, and tries to move silently through her quiet house. Helen lies ramrod straight on the living room couch, asleep with her shoes still on.

Julia gets halfway across the living room when Helen shoots up into a sitting position.

"I'm so sorry to wake you," Julia whispers.

"It's okay. The boys slept through the night. How is your David?" Helen says, and pats the empty seat next to her on the couch.

"He made it through surgery, but we're just waiting to see how and if he comes out of it."

Helen touches Julia's hand with her own weathered one, deeply creased and speckled with prominent brown sunspots.

"I prayed for David and your family all night. Such a good man to have a tragedy like this bestowed upon him. Do the police know who did this bombing?"

"No. Not yet. But I know the man whom David was prosecuting is responsible. The police don't have any evidence to convict him of the bombing, though, and he may go free. I have to find a way to prove he did it."

"Bez potrzeby wymówka, gotowe oskar enie," Helen says in her native Polish tongue.

"What does that mean?" Julia asks.

"A guilty conscience needs no accuser. People who know they have done wrong will reveal their guilt in what they say or how they act."

"It's not that easy."

"You go get a shower now. It will make you feel better. Maybe a little rest, too."

"Thank you, Helen, for all you've done. You should go home. I'm sure Mr. Jankowski would like you back."

"No. I will stay with you as long as you need, until David comes home. Alek brought me a suitcase from home last night, so I am fine. You go now."

"I'm not going to sleep, but a shower sounds really nice."

Julia creeps quietly down the hallway and peeks in on Will, his blond hair, just like David's, shining like brilliant gold against his red Mr. Incredible pajama top. She lingers for a minute, watching his chest move up and down slowly, and then heads to Logan's room. She peers inside and feels a stab of worry when she discovers his bed empty.

Julia hurries to her own room and finds Logan asleep on David's side of the bed. Next to his head is David's Harvard Law T-shirt, thin after much wear through the years, but David refuses to part with it.

Julia stands over her oldest son and resists an urge to hug him against her chest and tell him everything is going to be all right. She turns toward her bathroom when a voice calls her back.

"Mom. Where were you?"

Julia sits down on the edge of the bed next to Logan and wraps her arms tightly around her little boy. Logan's eyes are bloodshot and look swollen as if he has been crying.

"I'm sorry, sweetheart. I was at the hospital all night. I told you when I called that Helen would be looking after you and Will until I got home, remember?"

"But you didn't tell me you'd be gone all night."

"Understood. It won't happen again."

"You didn't tell me the truth. You said Dad got just a little hurt in an accident but that he was going to be all right,"

Logan says, looking wounded and small, tucked inside the king-size down comforter.

"Why do you think that's not the truth?"

"Because Sarah told me."

"Sarah from your class? Did she come over here?" Julia asks, her voice beginning to elevate several notches.

"No, she called when we were eating dinner and Helen gave me the phone. Sarah said there was a big bomb that went off at the courthouse and it killed a whole bunch of people and that Dad was hurt really bad. Sarah said her parents were watching the news and she saw Dad's picture on the TV."

She fights back an urge to call Sarah's parents, realizing the conversation would only upset Logan more.

"I wasn't lying to you. I just didn't want you to worry until your dad got to be treated by a doctor. Yes, there was a bomb that went off in the courthouse. Someone very bad did it, and it hurt a lot of people. Your dad was at the courthouse doing his job when the bomb went off, and yes, he did get injured. He had surgery, and his doctor told me it went really well. So right now we just have to be positive and give him lots of love so he'll continue to get better. Can you do that?"

"Yes. When do I get to see him?"

"I'd like you to wait until he's feeling better."

"I want to see him now."

Julia exhales and tries to figure out how she is going to handle this without making Logan any more anxious or upset than he already is.

"Okay. You can go with me later this morning. But your dad may still be sleeping. And he may look different than what you're used to. He got some bruises and his face is swollen, sort of like when you fall down and hurt yourself, and it takes a few days to heal. Just remember, he may look a little different right now, but he's still the same person inside who loves you very much."

"I don't care what he looks like. He's still my dad."

Julia smiles for the first time in the past twenty-four hours.

"You're my good boy," Julia says. "Do you want me to lie down with you for a little while?"

"No. I'm going to go back to my room and make Dad a card."

"I have to go to my job for a few minutes to pick something up, but I'll be right back. Fifteen minutes in and out. I swear."

"Sure, Mom," Logan answers, his tone betraying the reassurance of the words.

Logan retreats down the hall to his room, and Julia makes an internal vow that she will make it up to Logan later. She quickly showers and changes her clothes from the morning before, settling without thought on a pair of black jeans, a long-sleeved white shirt, and boots.

She grabs her laptop case and heads to the kitchen, where Helen is poised over the stove with a spatula.

"I've got to go to the paper for a minute," Julia explains. "I left a flash drive there with information on the Rossi case I need to pick up."

"You go to work at a time like this when your husband is in the hospital?"

"There's information David would want me to get that I left on my desk. It's important to the case," Julia says. "Forty-five minutes is all I need, if that. Keep Logan and Will away from the TV and computer today. I don't want Logan to find out anything more about the courthouse attack."

Julia can sense the buzz of adrenaline as she walks through the newsroom, the same electric jolt she has felt so many times before when she was covering a huge, breaking story that was going to go national. Julia knows her editors will be pulling all hands on deck to cover the bombing, even bringing in the sports desk for support. Not that any of the reporters would care. Everyone in the newsroom will want a piece of it. And right now, most likely a piece of her.

Despite the frenetic activity around her, there's a collective pause as Julia makes her way to her desk. She doesn't have to work too hard to realize what her colleagues are thinking: first, shock that she's actually in the newsroom, followed by a quick flash of pity and compassion, and then finally the dominant high of unexpected opportunity that supersedes everything else. Julia is no longer covering the story. She is the story, and every reporter is going to vie to land an exclusive interview with her before Margie makes her pick.

Julia pulls the flash drive she came for out of her desk drawer and stares at it, knowing she should just put it in her pocket and leave. But she can't help herself. She plugs the drive into her computer and clicks on the Nick Rossi file. Julia goes to a folder that contains images believed to be of his cruel handiwork against those who crossed him in business deals. The first photo is of hustler Dwayne Brown, whose body was found dumped on a bench near the Ambassador Bridge. Brown's neck had been severed down to expose the bone, a picture the paper's photographer took but was too graphic to run. Julia clicks on the final image, a family portrait of Rossi. Next to him is a stunningly beautiful woman with raven hair. A little girl, maybe two, wearing a white silk petticoat dress, sits on the woman's lap. The child is a dead ringer for Rossi. Julia reads the image's caption, *Nicholas Rossi with wife, Isabella, and daughter Christina,* and then the accompanying story.

Daughter of Suspected Detroit Criminal Killed
in Mall Shooting
By Conan Knox (Associated Press)

(DETROIT)—The two-year-old daughter of suspected Detroit criminal Nicholas Rossi was killed, along with her nanny, Beth Young, during a holiday shopping excursion to a retail center in Rochester Hills. The child, Christina Rossi, and Young, were both shot point blank as they exited their vehicle in a parking garage. While the shooters remain at large, police believe the victims were killed as a direct hit by rivals of Rossi's criminal operation.

Julia's hatred for Rossi ebbs ever so slightly as she knows nothing like that should ever happen to a child. Julia closes out of the file and ignores the sixteen new e-mail messages from fellow reporters that have popped across her screen since she sat down. E-mails work sometimes when trying to elicit a response from a potential source, but the old-school reporters know they have to work harder.

"Hey, Julia. Geez, are you okay? I was going to call you to see how you and David were doing, but I didn't want to seem intrusive," Joe Phillips, the city of Detroit beat reporter, says, as he leans just slightly over Julia's computer. Phillips is stocky, balding, and over fifty. As one of the veterans and, more important, one of the highest-paid reporters left in the newsroom, Phillips knows he has to hustle to make sure it's known he's still an asset when the next round of layoffs inevitably occurs.

"I'm all right. I'm just in here for a second before I go back to the hospital."

"I can't imagine what you're going through. I heard David was still in critical condition. What's the prognosis? We're all praying he's going to come out of this okay," Phillips says.

Julia is about to answer her colleague, but then stops herself. Whether Phillips actually cares or he's fishing for information, she knows the microphone is always on.

"Gooden, come with me." Julia turns behind her toward the voice and sees Margie, her managing editor. Margie's eyes are locked on the photo of Dwayne Brown's nearly severed head, still open on Julia's computer. Margie turns without another word and moves toward her office.

Julia clicks out of the file. She pops the flash drive out of her computer, puts it in her pocket, and follows Margie's fast-moving trail.

Once the two women are inside, Margie closes her office door and shuts the blinds. Margie then removes her glasses, presses her fingers against her temples, and lets out a deep sigh of frustration.

"What the hell are you doing here?" Margie asks.

"I needed to pick something up."

"There's nothing on your desk you needed so badly you would leave the hospital to come here. I saw the pictures you were looking at. What exactly is it that you think you're doing?"

Julia starts to stammer, something she hasn't done since she was seven. "I, just, um, I wanted to look through my Rossi file."

"You're not writing the story, if that's what you think is going to happen here. You're way too close. Actually, you *are* the story. A big part. If you're insistent, I can have Phillips interview you, but I'd just as soon tell him you gave me a 'No comment' for now."

"I have to say I'm surprised. I thought . . ."

"That I'd be a piranha and corner you the second you walked in here and force you to tell me what you saw at the courthouse, right? Sometimes other things are more important. Rarely, but it happens. I'm not the heartless witch that everyone around here thinks I am. If I was, I probably wouldn't have gotten axed in Philadelphia."

Julia stares back at her boss, momentarily speechless at her unexpected reaction.

"How's David? Not for attribution, okay?"

"Thank you for asking," Julia answers. "He's out of surgery. I called the hospital a few minutes ago. There's been no change."

"Keep me posted, and if you need anything, please let me know."

"Thank you," Julia answers, feeling awkward over the sudden generosity. "I think the Michigan Superior Court Justice is going to declare a mistrial. If that happens, then Tarburton could claim double jeopardy and Rossi would walk."

Margie leans back in her chair, considering how she will play out this latest story twist.

"We can't let that happen. Rossi is obviously behind the courthouse bombing," Julia insists.

"Phillips talked directly with the police chief. Linderman told him that at this time there's no evidence linking the bombing to Rossi. He was locked up in a holding cell when the bomb went off. There's no way he planted it."

"Oh, come on, Margie. He ordered the hit. The prosecution's star witness against Rossi was killed. I was told police believe the bomb was left in a suitcase on the courthouse stairs and was detonated just as Sammy Biggs went into the lobby. Obviously it's linked."

"Phillips thought of that already. We sent a Freedom of Information Act request to the prison commissioner to view the tapes of all Rossi's jailhouse visits. For the first time, government didn't move at a standstill. Phillips got the tapes this morning and went through them. The only visitors Rossi had were his wife and his lawyer. There's nothing on any of the tapes indicating Nick Rossi ordered a hit."

"Then there's something else. You're just not seeing it.

Chief Justice Waters is up for reelection. If public opinion is that Rossi did it, Waters might think twice about declaring a mistrial. Little kids were killed and maimed, Margie, not to mention my husband is hanging on to life by a whisper-thin thread. The paper has a responsibility."

"To report the facts. Phillips will definitely cover the angle that Rossi may be at the center of the attack. It's a logical possibility. But the criminal court hears dozens of cases every day. Phillips was told off the record there were threats of retaliation around the Laird Palmer White Supremacist trial that is going on at the same time as the Rossi case."

"I heard that a while back, but they were threatening to picket the courthouse, not bomb it," Julia says, and steam-rolls ahead with her point. "Phillips should get comments from people who believe Rossi ordered the hit—city officials, clergy members, regular citizens. You need to put the pressure on. And Berry should write an editorial making it clear this was a calculated and heartless act of violence that took innocent lives and Rossi is obviously responsible."

"What the paper does or writes, or what angle we cover going forward, is not your concern right now. I understand . . ."

"No, you don't," Julia interrupts.

"Let me finish. I understand you have a very personal and deep-seated interest in this story. But you need to walk away from it. I'm putting you on a mandatory thirty-day leave of absence from the paper, which can be extended at my discretion. During this period, I don't want to see your face in this newsroom once. Do I make myself clear?"

"Hold on. You need my help," Julia says.

"What I need, what you need, is for you to concentrate on your husband's recovery."

"David would want me to do this. He would want justice, not just for himself but for all the people who were hurt and killed at Rossi's hands."

"I don't know your husband like you do, but when something tragic happens, what we thought was important before usually slips away. The only thing that matters is that you focus on David and your family. Nothing else. Your obsession with Nick Rossi isn't healthy for you right now."

"It's not an obsession. He needs to pay for what he's done."

"As I said, if there is anything I can do to help you—meals delivered, dogs walked—I'm there," Margie says, and writes her home phone number on the back of her business card. "Anything else that has to deal with the day-to-day news coverage on this case, I'm not. Now go. I'll see you back here in thirty days and we'll see how you're doing."

"If you're not going to investigate this any further, then I will."

"I can't tell you what to do on your own time. But be careful, Julia."

Julia realizes the conversation is over. Her cheeks feel hot as she hurries back to her desk to collect her belongings before anyone else tries to engage her.

She reaches for an old notebook buried deep inside her bottom desk drawer. She knows she'll find what she needs in there. On the cover of the notebook is a business card attached with a paper clip: SALVATORE GALLO, GALLO FAMILY CLEANERS and a personal cell phone number written on the back.

Nick Rossi cuts a wide swath through the Marquette Maximum Security Prison dining hall as even the most hardcore White Supremacists scurry out of his way. Rossi emits a deadly aura of absolute power even in his blue prison jumpsuit, which clings to his hard-muscled frame. Rossi knows it's just a matter of hours now and he'll be a free man, but he didn't rise from a poor orphan boy to head one of Detroit's most successful criminal operations by just waiting around. He approaches a man sitting in the middle of a crowded table and leans into him. The man is short and thick with a cruel scar that looks as if someone sliced carefully on either side of his mouth to make an oversized, perpetual grin.

"The lawyer's still alive. He's in the hospital," the man with the scar tells his boss in a hushed tone. "The floor he's on is heavily guarded. The police are all over the hospital trying to find out who planted the bomb. It's just a matter of time before they pin it on you."

Rossi flexes his large hands into fists and shoots his employee an unforgiving ultimatum.

"Screw the police officers. I want the lawyer killed. Take him out in the hospital."

CHAPTER 10

Logan slips his hand inside Julia's and together they stare at the elevator numbers continuing to climb as they ascend to the twelfth-floor trauma surgery unit at Henry Ford Hospital. Logan's tender act catches Julia off guard, since he had just recently let Julia hold his hand again after the incident at the lake house the past summer. Julia fights back the bittersweet emotion and squeezes Logan's hand tightly in hers.

The elevator is about to announce its arrival to David's floor when Julia sweeps a sideways glance at another passenger in the crowded elevator—a woman, statuesque, with a few wisps of blond hair slipping out from a loosely wrapped, navy blue silk scarf. The woman is elegant in a pair of Jackie O giant sunglasses, her jawline strong and sleek. Julia would think the woman was nearly perfect except for an angry, red stump of flesh where her left earlobe should be. The stranger immediately caught Julia's reporter radar when she and Logan first entered the elevator, the woman's mouth receding into a thin line at their arrival before she turned away. Julia gives the woman a hard stare, feeling as if she has seen her before. Julia quickly changes her mind and realizes she would have remembered the woman, a contrast of beauty marred by such an unusual and nasty disfigurement.

Mother and son exit the elevator on the twelfth floor, and Julia pulls Logan to the side, squatting down so she is looking directly at him.

"Remember what we talked about?"

"Daddy may look different."

"That's right. And he's probably still asleep."

"I'll just hold Daddy's hand then and stay with him for a while. You think he'll know I'm there even if he isn't awake?"

"I have no doubt," Julia answers.

The waiting room has thinned out since the night before, as patients who were in surgery either didn't make it or were moved to recovery rooms. Julia and Logan find a seat while they wait for Dr. Whitcomb to brief Julia before the visit. Logan fidgets nervously in the chair, half watching a reality show where undercover restaurant employees capture the appalling behavior of real waitresses and cooks.

"Doesn't that lady work with Daddy?" Logan asks as he points toward the hospital corridor that leads to David's room. "Daddy took her with us to a concert on the river last summer."

Julia feels a wave of anger pound through her like a powerful tsunami as she sees the woman in question, Brooke Stevenson, arriving on the scene when her family is most vulnerable.

"Hold on a second, honey," Julia tells Logan. She gets up quickly from her seat and beats a fast path toward Brooke's solemn retreat to the elevator. Julia catches up and taps the woman hard against her shoulder blade to get her attention.

"Julia," Brooke says, clearly startled. "I was just . . ."

"Visiting my husband. I know. You were working the Nick Rossi case with him?"

"Yes. I thought you knew."

"No, I didn't. Lots of late nights. When did you two start seeing each other again? Or did you ever stop?"

Brooke inches away from Julia until her back is sealed against the closed elevator doors.

"It's over between us. It has been for a while now. He probably didn't tell you I was working the Rossi case because he didn't want you to be upset."

"Don't give yourself so much credit. My son saw you here. He knows who you are."

"I met Logan last summer with your other little boy."

"Big lapse in David's judgment. Let me explain how things are going to go from here on out. Do not come back to this hospital. Do not try to contact my husband while he is here. And my children are off limits. I don't want my son seeing you here again. Do we have an understanding?"

Brooke shifts nervously from side to side and stares at the elevator numbers ticking by, willing her safe passage to arrive on her floor.

"I'm sorry for what happened to David. I truly am."

The elevator doors slip open and Brooke hurries inside, nudging her way to safety until she finds a spot in the back of the pack.

Julia tries to brush the sting of jealousy and hurt that David lied to her off her shoulders and puts on a good face for Logan.

"Everything okay, Mom?" Logan asks.

"Just fine." She wraps her arm around Logan's thin waist as her cell phone buzzes in her purse. She is keenly aware of the hospital's no-cell-phone policy but sees Navarro's name appear across the screen and tries to be discreet as she answers her phone.

"Hey, Navarro. What do you got?" Julia says, her voice just above a whisper.

Despite her efforts to be inconspicuous, an older woman clutching a pair of rosary beads one row of chairs over hits Julia with a dirty look. Julia smiles at the woman apologetically and then turns her back to continue the call.

"How's David?" Navarro asks.

"I'm waiting to talk to his doctor before Logan and I see him. We're at the hospital."

"Keep me posted. That kid you were asking about, Michael Cole. He's alive but in critical condition. He's at Henry Ford, where you are, in room 313B. Apparently, he lost a lot of blood."

Julia flashes back to the makeshift tourniquet she wrapped around the boy's injured leg, her meager efforts obviously not enough.

"You were right. The boy's dad died at the scene. The nurse I spoke to said the kid's mom hasn't left the hospital since her son was admitted."

"Thanks for that. I'd like to stop by and see him later. I promised him I would. Is there anything new on the Rossi case? What's the status with the mistrial?"

"I've been told Judge Waters is supposed to issue her decision in half an hour."

Julia stares at the clock hanging on the visitor lounge wall. She feels a strange yearning, like a junkie who's late for a fix. She reminds herself she's no longer on the story and justice will have to march along without her chronicling it.

"Call me please the second you hear anything," Julia asks.

"Will do. Russell's about to be discharged. He's refused to go on medical leave and is heading back to the station later this afternoon once he gets out."

"He's a tough old bird," Julia says fondly.

Dr. Whitcomb, wearing a fresh pair of light blue scrubs, walks in Julia's direction. She quickly ends her call with Navarro and tries to tuck her banned cell phone back in her purse before she's caught.

"Julia, nice to see you again, and you must be Logan," Dr. Whitcomb says.

Logan stands up and extends his hand to the doctor.

"Very good manners. That's nice of you to come to the hospital today to see your father. I'd like to speak to your mother alone for a moment if that's all right."

Logan looks to Julia for direction, and she offers a smile of reassurance.

"I brought this just in case," Julia answers, and pulls out her iPad from her purse. "Do me a favor, just don't put the sound on, please."

"You know you aren't supposed to use a cell phone in the surgery waiting area," Dr. Whitcomb lectures as he escorts Julia to a quiet corner. "This is a very stressful place for most people, and we try to keep disruptions at a minimum for them."

Julia nods, knowing she will probably break the rules again.

"So we've had some good news this afternoon," Dr. Whitcomb says.

"I'll definitely take that."

"I thought you would. David's condition has improved somewhat. He is what we call comatose but responsive."

"Comatose. So he can't talk?"

"Correct. But his body is now reacting and responding to stimuli."

"That's good, right?"

"As I said, it's an improvement. A really good step. David

is also now breathing on his own, and I started him on an antiseizure medication."

"I could hug you right now, but I don't think you'd like that."

"You're a good judge of character," Dr. Whitcomb responds, and offers Julia a slight smile.

"Do you have any idea when he should wake up?"

"I can't say definitively. David has made some good strides today, though, so we will remain cautiously optimistic."

"Logan is chomping at the bit to see his dad. I prepared him the best I could."

"If a parent has a life-threatening event, it's usually devastating to a child. We have a child-and-family counselor on staff for Logan and for you, too. If you'll excuse me, I have another surgery in a few minutes."

Julia watches Dr. Whitcomb retreat through a door with a sign that reads MEDICAL PERSONNEL ONLY" and heads back to the sitting area, where Logan stares vacantly at the floor, the iPad's darkened screen lying faceup on the seat next to him.

"Are you sure you want to do this? Your dad wouldn't be upset if you changed your mind."

"He's going to get better, right?"

"Your dad is a fighter. And he loves you more than anything. So I have no doubt he'll fight his hardest to come back to you and your brother."

Logan reaches up for his mother's hand and Julia leads her little boy down the length of the corridor of the trauma wing to David's room.

"What are all the machines and tubes connected to Daddy?" Logan whispers as he hesitates outside the door.

"Nothing scary. They're monitoring how Daddy is feeling, checking his heart rate, blood pressure, and other important things."

Without a prompt, Logan pulls up a chair and slides it by David's bedside.

"Hi, Daddy. It's me, Logan. I drew you a picture. That's us, shooting hoops in front of the house. You told me playing basketball with me was one of your favorite things to do, so I thought you'd like it."

Logan waits for a response from his father, but none comes.

"Can I hold Daddy's hand?" Logan asks.

"He's got IVs in there, baby. So yes, but be very careful."

Logan gently puts his small hand on top of his father's and leaves it there, as father and son switch roles.

"When you get out of here, I was thinking maybe you, Mom, and Will and me could spend some time at the lake house until you feel all better. Mom and I will take care of you, and we can just hang out on the porch until you're ready to do other stuff. Just don't worry about anything, okay?"

Julia lets Logan continue his bedside vigil as the steady beeps and clicks of machines monitoring David's vitals play on in the background in a steady rhythm. After fifteen minutes, Logan stands up and pushes the chair back in the corner.

"I really thought he'd wake up when he heard my voice."

"He knew you were here. I believe that. Do you want to take a break for a few minutes? There's a gift shop down the hall, and you could get a candy bar if you like."

"You'll let me go alone?" Logan asks incredulously.

"This time is okay. The hospital is swarming with cops. Just don't talk to anyone you don't know."

Logan doesn't hesitate and hurries out of the room, leaving as fast as he can before Julia changes her mind.

"I guess now's not the time to be the jealous wife here,"

Julia says, and brushes her fingers against David's newly shorn short stubble. "But if I could play twenty questions with you, I would."

A heavyset, dark complected man in a pair of hospital scrubs pokes his head inside the doorway.

"Sorry, wrong room," the man says, and disappears into the hallway.

An instinctual worry tugs at Julia's gut. She follows the orderly and catches a glimpse of his wrist, heavily inked with tattoos, poking out from beneath a long white T-shirt. The man slips around the corner in a hurry and toward the stairwell door. Before it closes behind him, Julia spots another tattoo on the back of the orderly's neck, this one a single teardrop cascading from a densely inked half-closed eye.

"Hey!" Julia yells from the top of the twelfth-floor landing, but her voice echoes down the now-empty stairwell.

The orderly's out-of-place appearance sticks with Julia, and she hurries to the lobby to find Logan.

In the waiting area, a small entourage has gathered around a single man, Acting Mayor Lester Anderson, who is busy giving a big hug to the woman with the rosary beads. Julia looks past the crowd and feels relieved when she spots Logan by the gift shop. He clutches a candy bar and seems engrossed in a conversation with a police officer she knows from her beat.

Julia tries to walk in Logan's direction, but Gavin Boyles, Anderson's chief of staff, corrals her before she can escape. Boyles, a good-looking man in his early thirties, is tall and wiry with blond hair and wears an expensive-looking designer suit. His one distinct feature is a flat, red birthmark that trails up the side of his forehead, which he often rubs when the pressure is on. Boyles laces his fingers around Julia's arm and steers her toward his boss.

"The mayor is just devastated to hear about what happened to David," Boyles says. "What a tragedy this is. We just got word another victim died a few minutes ago. A child. Detroit is going to need to do a lot of healing to recover from this."

"It's going to be worse for the city if the person responsible for the bombing gets off. That's going to happen if Judge Waters declares a mistrial."

Boyles ignores Julia as his phone's ringtone, Fleetwood Mac's "Don't Stop," goes off and he reaches into his breast pocket to monitor the call.

He lets it go to voice mail and turns his attention back to Julia.

"Bill Clinton's theme song when he ran for president in '92." Gavin explains his choice of ringtone. "Imitation is the sincerest form of flattery. The Clinton years, now that was a winning team."

"I need to get my son," Julia says.

"Logan is in good hands. He's with a police officer. Hold on a second, Julia. Let me get the mayor."

Boyles nabs Mayor Anderson, who is a big bear of a man with a thick, barrel chest. And, he's a hugger. The mayor catches a glimpse of Julia and nearly lifts her off the ground in an embrace. Before he lets her go, Julia catches a small flash in the corner of her eye and realizes Boyles has just taken a picture.

"What the hell are you doing? This isn't a goddamn photo op," Julia says.

Mayor Anderson's sympathetic expression stays intact. "Enough with the photos, Gavin. Let me just say, Julia, I have been praying for David and the rest of the victims nonstop since the bombing. Your husband is a good man, and he's a tremendous asset to our city. You know, I think I almost had David convinced to delay his D.A. run for another year to come work for me as my lead counsel."

"I wasn't aware you two had that discussion."

"Over coffee in my office just the other day when he briefed me on the Nick Rossi trial. David told me he'd consider the offer and get back to me after the case was over. I want you to know, I'm here for you, Julia. I met with the governor this morning after the press conference, and he has given me his full commitment to help the city of Detroit get through this. We may be able to get some federal funding as a result. We also have a strong congressional delegation here in the state of Michigan that cares about what happened here to the people of Detroit, and they will push Washington for assistance as well. Gavin will give you the details, as I'm sure your paper will want to write a story on all the efforts behind the scenes. But of course, this isn't about money. I've organized an interfaith prayer dinner tonight at the Sweetest Heart of Mary Roman Catholic Church over on Russell Street. I hope you can be there. It's going to be big. I've got Congregation Beth Shalom, Second Baptist Church, Fort Street Presbyterian, and Historic Trinity Lutheran committed to being there."

A good cross-section of voters, Julia thinks to herself.

"I'm not very religious," Julia answers instead.

"That's okay. There'll be plenty of people there praying for you. So be sure to come down. I know Gavin would like a picture of David we can show during the PowerPoint presentation that will be playing continuously in the background. We're going to be showing pictures of all the bombing victims, so a photo of David with you and your boys would work real well. I obviously have great respect for your husband, and I know if he were able, he would be at the prayer breakfast. So please think about giving Gavin that photo."

Julia gives the mayor a flat smile, knowing there is no way in hell she'll offer up anything like that. She pulls away from the mayor's tight circle and notices Logan, no longer with the police officer but now in deep conversation with Tandy Sanchez, the *Detroit News* reporter. Julia plants herself between her son and Tandy, ready for her second battle of the morning.

"How did you get in here? There's not supposed to be any press up here bothering the victims or their families."

"I'm a guest of the mayor," Tandy answers. "Gavin Boyles invited me to join the mayor to cover his trip to the hospital this afternoon. I'm so sorry to hear about David. How's he doing?"

"You've got balls," Julia sneers as she feels Logan pulling on the back of her shirt to get her attention. "You sweep in here and corner a kid who's all alone to try to get some touching comment you hope he makes about his dad."

Julia spins around to confront Logan.

"Did you talk to her?"

"She's a reporter like you. I thought it would be fine."

"It's okay, Logan. You didn't know better. But she's not a reporter like me," Julia says, and turns her attention back on Tandy. "I swear to God, if one comment from my son shows up in your story, I'll sue you, your paper, and I'll go to every single media outlet in the state telling them what a sleazebag you are, cornering a helpless child to try to get a sound bite. You want to go to a bigger market, that stain won't go away. The only place that will have you after I'm through with you is the *National Enquirer* or TMZ."

Tandy takes a defensive step back as Detective Russell heads in their direction.

"Russell, members of the press are restricted from this floor. Tandy Sanchez just interviewed my son without my permis-

sion. She should be removed from the hospital grounds immediately," Julia says.

"Detective Russell, I was so sorry to hear you got hurt in
the bombing, but I'm glad you're okay. I'm not doing anything wrong. I'm here with the mayor," Tandy insists.

Russell, freshly injured but still unable to help himself,
takes a quick pan of Tandy's ever-present cleavage. "Sorry,
Tandy. Mayor or no mayor, hospital rules."

Russell escorts Tandy to the elevator. She calls out to catch
Mayor Anderson's attention, but Boyles whispers in the
mayor's ear and the mayor reacts with a friendly wave to
Russell, not wanting to catch any blame. Boyles hurries into
the elevator to do damage control.

"You should have followed her to be sure she actually left
the building," Julia tells Russell. "You don't want her roam-
ing around this place."

"Looks like she already had a date."

"Sorry to ask you to jump in like that. Listen, maybe I'm
being paranoid, but there was a hospital orderly I saw outside
of David's room a little while ago. He was a big guy, heavily
tattooed. Something about him didn't sit right with me."

"I'll take a look around," Russell answers. "We weren't
instructed to guard anyone's room. The theory around the
station is the intended target, the Butcher snitch, was taken
out, so no one should be at risk."

"Thanks. We just can't be too sure. Why are you here anyway, Russell?"

"I just got discharged and Navarro asked me to tell you
something personally. The Cole boy didn't make it. He died
a few minutes ago."

"Christ. I wonder if his mother is still here. She lost her
kid and her husband."

"I can stay with Logan if you want to check. Navarro said
the boy was in room 313B."

Julia leaves Logan in the care of Russell and takes the stairs up one floor, wondering what she will say to the child's mother. She searches for commonalities, something she always does to try to bond with sources on her beat. Both she and the boy's mother had loved ones injured in the attack. And while Julia never lost a child, she lost a brother, who was only nine when he disappeared, probably about the same age as Michael Cole.

Julia reaches the thirteenth floor and is ready to turn around, wondering why in God's name she is doing this, when she sees a young woman, probably mid- to late twenties, with strawberry blond hair and pale blue eyes, the same eyes that looked up at her with longing and fear on the sidewalk. The woman wears a beige polyester Dunkin' Donuts uniform with the name *Brenda* stitched on the lapel and clutches a Walmart bag that contains a child's Detroit Tigers jacket. The woman, Brenda, stares straight ahead as if in a daze.

"Excuse me, are you Michael Cole's mother?" Julia asks as she carefully approaches Brenda, whose eyes slowly snap into focus as she looks on with distrust at the approaching stranger.

"Yes."

"My name is Julia Gooden. My husband was injured in the blast. I wanted to tell you how sorry I am. I was there with Michael right after the bomb went off."

"You're that lady he told me about."

"I don't mean to bother you. I heard the news from a police officer who is a friend of mine."

"Michael told me you left him."

"I didn't want to. I tried to help him. But my husband was in the courthouse and I thought my son was in there too."

"Was your son there? Did he get hurt like my kid?"

"No. His bus got stuck in traffic. He never made it to the courthouse."

"I guess one of us got lucky then, huh?" she says, her accusatory tone ugly and cold.

"My son is fine, but my husband is still in critical condition."

"Mine died in the blast. I got two other kids at home, a two-year-old and six-month-old. You tell me how I'm going to be able to take care of them now," she says.

"I shouldn't have bothered you. I had told Michael I'd check on him. I made him that promise, but I guess I was too late."

"You got that right."

Julia, feeling foolish and guilty, turns to leave.

"Michael was a good kid," Brenda calls out to her. "He told me what you did, wrapping that belt around his leg to try to help him. I know you stayed with him until the doctors came."

Julia finally exhales. "Is there anyone I can call for you?"

"There's no one to call. You want to do something for me and my family, you find out who did this to them."

"I can do that. I promise."

"Make sure you kill that bastard when you find him."

Julia makes it to the staircase, hears the door close behind her, and then sits heavily on the first step. She puts her head in her hands and starts to weep.

Julia gives herself exactly one minute and then forces herself to get it together. As she rises, she feels her phone vibrating in her pocket.

"This is Julia Gooden," she says in a somewhat clear voice.

"It's Navarro. Judge Waters declared a mistrial. Tarburton is trying to get Rossi out by the end of the day. He's going to be a free man. Tarburton just called a press conference, and I hear he's supposed to claim his client can't be tried again because of double jeopardy, just like you thought."

"Son of a bitch. I've got to go."

"Hey, Julia . . ." Navarro continues, but Julia hangs up before he can finish and dials the number she committed to memory.

"Gallo Family Cleaners, this is Salvatore," the voice on the other end of the phone answers.

CHAPTER 11

Julia pulls into a space along Riopelle, directly across the street from Roma Cafe in the Eastern Market region of Detroit, and ignores a call from Gavin Boyles. She takes in the unassuming brick building with the red-and-white awning and does an internal check one more time to be sure she is certain of her decision. She's not confident Gallo will be true to his word to help her—in this case, give her information that could link Rossi to the bombing. But she's desperate enough to take the chance.

Four in the afternoon, the late lunch crowd is gone, and just a few older Italian men and tourists, anxious to visit a Detroit staple before they return home, sit at the counter or in one of the black vinyl booths.

"Can I help you?" asks a middle-aged hostess with dyed platinum blond hair.

"Yes, I'm here to meet Salvatore Gallo, please."

The hostess assesses Julia in one quick stroke of her eyes and then motions Julia to follow, leading her to a private room in the back. Julia takes a seat facing the door, and the hostess lays down a menu on the deep red tablecloth in front of her.

"I'm good for now, thanks," Julia says.

Julia battles her nerves as she waits for Gallo, reassuring herself that he isn't connected to the mob and gossip on the street led her to believe Sal wasn't involved in the darker side of his nephew's business. Gallo's only known brushes with the law were limited to his bookie operation. Just nickel-and-dime stuff. That's why it never made sense to Julia that Gallo would have been involved in a murder, and her instincts helped to exonerate him of the bogus charge that most people believed was Sal being framed to get to his nephew.

The hostess escorts Gallo into the room, and Julia quickly stands. Gallo is in his early seventies, with a thick mane of black hair with gray at his temples. He is of average height for a man, only a few inches taller than Julia, but he's big, with thick muscles and a wide neck. He approaches with a masked expression, leading Julia to wonder what he really thinks about their meeting.

"I heard about your husband, David. You have two sons as I recall. I hope they're doing all right, considering the circumstances," Gallo says.

"My boys are okay. My older son is taking it hard," Julia says, trying to downplay the defensiveness she feels creeping into her voice from Gallo mentioning her children.

"I'm sure your older boy is more aware of the gravity of the situation. Please, let's sit," he says, and motions to the hostess. "Dorothy, bring me an espresso, and for you, Julia?"

"Just water, please."

"Bring my visitor a pastry. She probably hasn't eaten in a few days," Gallo says, and then waits a beat for the hostess to leave. "Now, how is your husband?"

"There's been a slight improvement since his surgery. We're hopeful."

"I was surprised to get your call. I owe you a favor. That's why I agreed to this meeting. I keep my word. But what is it exactly that you think I'm going to tell you about my nephew?"

"He's responsible for the courthouse bombing."

Julia prepares for Sal to get up and leave, or worse, but he looks back at Julia with eyes that look like flinty steel.

"And you believe this because of what?"

"The target of the attack was his former employee who was going to testify against him."

"The snitch."

"Call him what you want. Sammy Biggs is dead, along with about eighteen other people. In addition to my husband, there was a little boy I tried to help. His leg was blown off. He died a few hours ago."

"For that, I'm sorry. But you're wrong to think Nicky had anything to do with the attack."

The hostess returns with an espresso in a simple white china cup for Gallo and a piece of rum cake for Julia. She then places an assortment of biscotti between them.

"That's very nice, Dorothy," Gallo says, and twists the slice of lemon rind between his fingers before dropping it neatly into the demitasse cup.

"So, what is it that I can do for you?"

"Did Rossi tell you he planted the bomb?"

"Of course not. Like I said, Nicky wasn't involved."

"But you have your doubts."

"Listen, I granted you this meeting out of respect for a promise I made you. But you're either foolish or you grossly underestimated me. Nicky has been under my roof since he was nine. I took him in as my own son after my sister was killed. Nicky was spirited, and rightfully angry after what happened to his mother. Nicky may be a hothead, but he's a good kid. He came back to Detroit to take care of my business after my heart attacks a few years ago. He did that because with family, there's loyalty and a bond that goes beyond anything else. You know this too, I imagine."

"Blind trust and loyalty to family is foolish, Mr. Gallo. Whatever I know about family loyalty was learned later on."

"I don't understand," Gallo says.

"When I was a kid, my brother was abducted. He was my whole world. My dad was a hustler and my mom was a drunk. My parents took off and left my older sister and me alone to fend for ourselves. I was seven at the time. My sister grew up to be a hustler herself and tried to exploit my children and me at one of our most vulnerable times. So if you're a bad person, you don't get a pass just because you're blood."

"You have a hard view on life."

"In all due respect, I believe you're a decent man, taking in your nephew like you did. And I bet you're pretty disappointed Rossi took over your business and turned it into something you're ashamed of. But I think you're covering for him now. If the police find out you're withholding information about Rossi's involvement with the bombing, you could face charges yourself."

Gallo leans back in his chair and lets out a humorless laugh.

"You've been hanging around too many cops. You're starting to talk like one."

"Will Rossi try to leave the country when he gets out of jail?" Julia asks.

"My nephew is a grown man with a successful business. He doesn't call me up every time he takes a trip. Now, is there anything else you want, Ms. Gooden? If not, this meeting is over."

Julia stands up, feeling foolish she thought for even an instant that she'd get anything out of Gallo. She turns toward the exit, but Gallo grabs her arm and gently pulls her back.

"What you told me about your family growing up, you have a chance for redemption with the family you have now. But if you pursue things you shouldn't, all that you've worked so hard to create for yourself could get taken away."

"Is that a threat?" Julia asks.

"No. Not from me. But it's a warning of things that could come. I owed you a favor, and by telling you of what could transpire should you pursue my nephew, the debt has now been paid in full."

Gallo holds the door open for her, and Julia feels a cold shiver run up her back as she hurries out of the restaurant.

She ignores Gallo's warning as she grabs her cell phone. If Gallo won't help her, she turns to another longtime source, her only other ace in the hole.

CHAPTER 12

Julia heads over to Corktown and parks her SUV on Bagley Street in front of Hello Records. She can hear the dull thump of an overamplified bass coming from a squat brick building across the street from the humble vinyl record store's location.

Julia hustles to the rear of the building and hits the buzzer three times, just as she was told. A giant of a man with skin as smooth and lustrous as pure ebony opens the door. The man wears a long, loose shirt made up of patches of brightly colored, mismatched fabrics and a knit Rasta tam hat. His other accessory is a gun holster and what looks like a Smith & Wesson tucked inside.

"What you want?" the man asks.

"I'm Julia Gooden. I have an appointment with Tyce," Julia says. "He's expecting me."

"So you say."

The thick back door slams shut, and Julia stomps her feet against the frozen mud to try to get the feeling back in her toes.

The door opens and the giant Rasta beckons her in. Before Julia can walk through the door, the man puts a hand the size of an NFL football on her shoulder.

"You carrying?" he asks.

"No. I don't even own a gun."

"So you say," the Rasta repeats, and begins to pat down Julia. She holds her breath, not out of worry Tyce's guard will find anything but more out of how uncomfortable she feels having a stranger's hands move across her body.

"You're good," the man says, and leads Julia inside. The walls of the first floor are covered in distressed brick, and the floors are a shiny cherry wood. Autographed pictures of rappers and R&B artists line the walls, and Julia is startled to see a picture of Tyce Jones shaking Acting Mayor Anderson's hand.

Julia follows her armed guide up to the second floor to a music studio. Tyce Jones's torso sways back and forth as he hovers next to a skinny, bearded white guy wearing a Beastie Boys T-shirt who is busy working the mixing console. In the sound booth, an ample female with a mane of red curls belts out what sounds to Julia like an aria from an Italian opera, and a black twenty-something young man wearing a bow tie, small square glasses, and a fur hat that looks like it came from Siberia lays down a rapid-fire rap to juxtapose the mood.

The mammoth Rasta taps Tyce on the shoulder to get his attention, and Tyce glances over at Julia.

"Okay. Let's take five," Tyce tells his crew. "Bromo, good delivery, man, but I want more feeling from you. Otherwise, you sound like you're doing karaoke at a piss bar in the projects. Cynthia, girl, you're killing it with the high notes."

Tyce Jones spins his wheelchair around in Julia's direction and reaches out his hand.

"Damn, Gooden. You don't come see me no more. You

just use me for my body and my connections when you need 'em," he says, and flashes Julia a naughty smile. "What you got? I'm hoping it's what I think it is."

Julia hands her source a plain brown paper bag that she retrieved after a pit stop at home following her meeting with Gallo.

"Mmm, mmm. Nothin' else smells like that. Helen made these?" Tyce says.

"Her very own. She still won't give you her pierogi recipe, though."

Tyce places the brown paper bag in his lap and wheels up a ramp that leads to the building's third floor. Julia follows Tyce into an office filled with white leather sofas and a gaudy red desk in the center of the room. Tyce wheels behind the desk and starts going to town on the Polish dumplings.

"You want some? I skipped lunch, so don't mind me," Tyce answers.

"No, I'm good. I need information on Nick Rossi again. This isn't for a story."

"Everything's about a story with you. What you want it for?"

"I need to know where Rossi is."

"And you think I know somehow? I'm a legitimate businessman these days. I don't run in the same circles as Rossi anymore," Tyce says.

"I think you keep track of your enemies, especially ones who put you in that chair," Julia answers.

Tyce's eyes narrow into angry slits, and Julia starts to second-guess her blunt approach.

"That's why I like you. You never bullshit. You'd be a tough adversary on the streets. Why you want to know where Rossi is at? He's probably hanging out in his penthouse apartment drinking Cristal and smoking Cubans now that he's out of jail."

"You watch the news?"

"Not if I can help it. It's too depressing. My life is filled with positivity. But I know what happens on the street. That's my business. You here about the courthouse attack?"

"Yes. My husband was the assistant D.A. who was trying the case against Rossi, and my husband was hurt in the bombing. He's got a long road to recovery, and we're still not sure if he's going to be the same as he was before. I know Rossi planted the bomb to take out his former employee who was going to testify against him."

"So you want revenge because the cops can't get it for you. I know a little something about that."

Julia tries to keep a poker face as she wonders if Tyce was the one who ordered the hit on Rossi's three-year-old daughter and her nanny.

"This is all off the record, right? Because if it's not, I like you, Julia. I really do. You were real nice to me and my momma when I was in the hospital after I got shot, and I knew it was genuine, not just you trying to hustle for a story. But I used to think I liked Nick Rossi as well and look how that turned out."

"I've never burned you."

"That's true. Okay. Here's what I can tell you about Nick Rossi. He never belonged back here in Detroit, and he knew it too. He was Hollywood, man. But he had loyalty to his uncle."

"Salvatore Gallo."

"Salvatore is a good guy, but small-time. He's your weak link in all this. He doesn't like the way his nephew has mud-died up his business, going into drugs and killing people. Sal is old school, and in his eyes Nick has brought shame to the family. Gallo might turn if you work him hard enough, make him feel badly about the bombing and what it did to his city."

"I tried," Julia says. "Gallo owes me a favor, but he wouldn't help me."

"So he's loyal. Blood, even if it's bad, that's more important to him than his word."

"I think my husband had something on Rossi that was going to come out in the trial."

Tyce leans back in his wheelchair and thumps one hand across his chest as he weighs giving Julia what she wants.

"First of all, you're thinking about this all wrong. Nick Rossi wouldn't plant the bomb. He was cooling off in a holding cell in the courthouse when the thing exploded, right? Mr. Pretty Boy ain't going to be putting himself in harm's way. If Nick wanted to take out the witness, he would've done it clean with a sniper."

"Where would he go to hire a sniper?" Julia asks.

"This is the U.S. of A., baby. Anything can be purchased for the right price."

"Then who planted the bomb?"

"Dunno. But I'm guessing it would be someone in his tight posse, someone real close trying to cover their boss's ass. But whoever it is, they aren't close enough to Nick that he'd confide in them about the sniper."

"Who replaced Sammy Biggs, the Butcher, when he turned on Rossi?"

"Enzo Costas. Nicky hooked up with him in California. Now he's the second big dog in the pack."

"How would I find Enzo Costas?" Julia asks.

"You don't. He's a freak. Word is, he's some kind of religious nut. And a badass killer. You got kids. Do me a favor. Don't go near Enzo Costas or Rossi."

"Would Rossi stay in Detroit, or would he leave Michigan to stay under the radar?"

"Nick? He wouldn't hang around here. He only came back

to Detroit to help out his uncle. After all the trouble he's had recently, it'd give him an excuse to go back to Cali."

"Where in California? I need an address."

Tyce shakes his head. "Damn, girl. You're stubborn. I'll give this to you, but like I said, don't get any ideas about trying to hunt this guy down yourself once he gets out."

"Of course," Julia lies, knowing nothing is off the table right now. "So he'd go back to L.A.?"

"Nah. He's got some sweet real estate in L.A. and Malibu. But he'd be hiding out at his compound a couple of hours north of there in the Santa Ynez Mountains. It's like his own personal panic room, but Big Nicky Hollywood style. He'd be hiding out there until stuff cools off about the bombing. He wouldn't want to make himself available, if you know what I mean."

"You've been there?" Julia asks.

"Once. I got business in L.A. too."

"If Rossi goes out on the West Coast, who'd handle his local operation? Salvatore Gallo?"

"Nah. Gallo is clean. Jim Bartello is your man. He's the former head of security for Detroit's MGM Grand. You want something? I'll give it to you. Bartello reached out to a colleague of mine to help him hire a contract worker, you could say."

"A contract worker? You mean someone to take out Biggs? If Rossi can't be retried on the drug or bribery charges, he could get nailed for attempted murder."

"There you go," Tyce says. "Now, are we good? I got business waiting for me. This opera-and-rap shit is going to be huge. Look for me at the Grammys, Gooden."

"I need the address of Rossi's West Coast place."

"You ain't afraid to ask big, are you? I'll tell you, as long as you got no ideas about going there."

"The address, Tyce. Come on."

"Yeah, well, that I can't deliver on because there's no address. Nick's compound is secluded on purpose. Way up in the mountains. But two roads can get you there, one back road up the northern side of the mountain that was closed a while back. There's another road on the southern end of the mountain. That bitch is accessible. But Nick will have the road guarded."

"So there's no way into Rossi's compound without being seen."

"Not true. Nick, he's a hard guy, but he's all into history and stuff, like that cowboys and Indians shit. When I was up there a couple of years ago, he showed me this map that totally got him off. It looked like something from a scavenger hunt or something to me, just a rough sketch of some old path that Nick said was used by Indians and farmers to get up and down the mountain like a hundred years ago or something. So Nick tells me, this path, it runs parallel to the road. A person can make it to the top by foot, or in an off-terrain vehicle. There's no signs or nothin', just markers."

"Do you remember what they are?"

"I didn't become the success that I am today by being stupid. Sure, I did a picture in my mind to remember the thing, like a lickety-split mental snap of a camera, you know? In case I ever needed to come back and pop the guy. In my former line of business, mind you, alliances can turn pretty quick. Case in point," Tyce says, and looks down at his withered legs. "Yeah, so the map. I remember the first marker is some joint named the Santa Maria Temple. It's at the southern base of the mountain, where the path starts. The second marker is a convent that Nick said closed about fifty years ago or something. The third marker is an old-ass rickety barn. From there, the compound is about another three miles up past a grove of avocado trees. Or it might have been citrus trees. Anyway, there're some trees up there."

"I owe you one," Julia says, and stands up to leave.

"You were always straight up with me. The cops didn't bust Nick for trying to take me out. They figured my injuries would get me off pushing on their streets. But the stories you wrote, you connected the dots to Rossi."

"He never got arrested."

"Yeah, he had one of his grunts take the fall. Dude's doing twenty years up at Wayne County," Tyce says.

He wheels around the front of his desk and gives Julia a knowing nod.

"You're smart and you've always had big-ass balls, Gooden. I'll give you that. But your problem, you're blind with emotion on this one. You try and bring Rossi down by yourself, it don't matter how smart or ballsy you are. Dead is dead."

"I'll take that into consideration."

Julia follows Tyce down the wheelchair ramp to the first story of the building.

"One more question," Julia says. "How'd you get that picture of you and Acting Mayor Anderson shaking hands?"

Tyce gives Julia a beaming smile, showing off his two gold front teeth.

"He came to the grand opening of my recording studio. I even got an incentive from the city to refurbish this building. Detroit is revitalizing, baby, and I'm gonna be a part of it."

Tyce reaches into his pocket and pulls out a business card on which he scribbles a number on the back.

"So here's the deal. I don't give this number out to just no one. This goes directly to me. We got an agreement, right?"

"This conversation never happened."

"There you go. You nail Rossi, I won't be crying."

"Thanks, Tyce. I appreciate your help."

Julia shakes Tyce's hand, stuffs his number in her purse, and realizes she has to find this Bartello person fast.

* * *

Jim Bartello shoots up one last time before he flees to his deer-hunting camp tucked far away in the woods in an unincorporated area of Michigan's Upper Peninsula. He lies back on his fake leather couch, finally relaxed after enduring the constant onslaught of fear and paranoia over the past twenty-four hours. The junk, just a little bit this time, starts to flow through his body now, making his head feel as if it is dancing above him, soft and buoyant like a giant helium balloon. Visions of his younger self nailing a three-point shot to win his Wyandotte Roosevelt High School's basketball tournament melt across his memory. Bartello's glory days slip toward the unconscious, and Bartello shakes himself hard before he starts nodding. He needs to be alert for the seven-plus-hour drive to Michigan's hinterlands of the U.P.

Bartello moves to his bedroom, which is cluttered with the belongings he will take with him—two suitcases, one with clothes, and the other with the hidden compartment where he can stash his balloons of heroin, the ones he was supposed to give to Rossi's guy in Flint. Next to the suitcases is his gun, a Sig Sauer. Bartello pushes inside his closet, his girth barely clearing its entryway, and gets on his hands and knees. At the very end of the narrow galley, Bartello taps until he finds his hidey-hole. He pulls away the frayed shag carpet and pries the loose section from the floor. Bartello plunges his fat little hands inside and retrieves a dozen neatly bound packets containing $25,000 in cash and what Enzo Costas slipped to him as he exited the MGM Grand, the flash drive with the surveillance footage that caught the uppity snitch banging the shit out of the blonde.

CHAPTER 13

Julia leaves the hospital, where she vowed to an unresponsive David that she is one step closer to bringing Rossi to justice, and waits impatiently at yet another private room in a restaurant—this time Chanel's—for Navarro.

"You need to eat something, honey," Bianca, Navarro's girlfriend, says, and places a warm piece of chocolate bread pudding in front of her. "You look like you'd blow away if a gust of wind came along. I've never had that problem. I've got more curves than straight lines, but we've all got to work what God's given us."

Julia looks with disinterest at the dessert and wonders why everyone keeps trying to feed her.

"Why aren't you at the hospital?" Bianca asks.

"I was just there. I need to talk to Navarro."

"He's been running around like a madman looking for that bomber. I've hardly seen him. Makes a woman nervous when her calls go straight to voice mail."

"Navarro's a cop. That's part of the job. He can't answer the phone sometimes," Julia says.

"He always seems to take your calls."

Julia ignores the comment and pretends to check a text message on her cell phone.

"Listen to me going on like that," Bianca says, and takes a seat across the table from Julia. "You've got enough to deal with right now, with your husband still in the hospital."

"Don't worry about it."

"You and Ray dated, though, right? He downplays it every time I ask, but a friend of his told me you two weren't just a couple. You lived together and Ray asked you to marry him. He neglected to tell me that bit of information."

Of all the things that happened in the past thirty-six hours, being interrogated by a jealous girlfriend takes the bloody cake, Julia thinks, and cups her hands into aggravated fists under the table.

"That was a long time ago. You've got nothing to worry about. Did Navarro tell you he was going to be late?" Julia asks.

"Ray talks about you a lot," Bianca continues, oblivious to Julia's question. "I brought food to his house while he was at work and found a box in his bedroom closet. It was filled with pictures of the two of you when you were still a couple. I tried to convince myself he was just hanging on to memories, you know, but then I found a photo underneath some clothes in Ray's dresser of you sitting on his lap at a police Christmas party."

"The picture was taken over ten years ago. You went through Navarro's things?"

"No. It wasn't like that," Bianca answers, realizing she's been caught. "Look, this is just a conversation between us girls. I figured you'd understand."

"In all due respect, I don't have time for this right now."

"I'm sorry. I realize my timing is terrible, but I need to know. Is there something going on between the two of you?

I'm not going to invest myself anymore in this relationship if there is."

"What? No. He's my friend and has been for a long time. I'm married. David and I have been together for ten years."

"You know, I hate to ask this, but if something should happen to your husband, I mean, from what Ray was telling me, there's no guarantee . . ."

"You've got to be kidding me."

Julia grabs her bag and heads to the exit. She shoves the front door of the restaurant open as hard as she can, nearly knocking Navarro over in the door's wake.

"Hey, slow down. I thought we were meeting inside. Did something happen?" Navarro asks.

"Ask your girlfriend."

"Just relax a minute. Let's go back inside."

"There's no way in hell I'm going back in there."

Navarro lifts his hand up as if telling someone to wait. Julia looks through the restaurant window and sees Bianca, anxious and looking somewhat sheepish, standing on the other side.

"Okay. Let's take a ride," Navarro says, and tips his hand to his ear, indicating to Bianca that he will call her later, and she reciprocates with an icy stare.

Julia slips into the passenger seat of Navarro's Chevy Tahoe and tries to exorcise the surreal encounter from her memory.

"What happened in there?" Navarro asks.

"Bianca seems to be under the false impression that you and I are more than friends. Apparently she found some old pictures of us at your house and thought we were either still an item or soon going to be if my husband doesn't make it."

"She said that to you?" Navarro asks, his face flushing with anger.

"Something to that effect. But let's just move on, okay?"

"I'm sorry, Julia. This thing has turned into *Fatal Attrac-*

tion. This morning, I came out of my bedroom and caught Bianca on my computer. She was going through my e-mails, digging around for who knows what. I'm going to call it off with her. I've got no time for this petty crap right now."

"Like I said, neither do I. What's the latest on the bomb investigation?"

"Just between us," Navarro checks.

"Per Margie Kruchek, I'm off the story. So right now, it's just two friends talking."

"As I said, between us, we found what was left of a small suitcase just outside the courthouse entrance where the bomb detonated. It was a sophisticated system, so we aren't dealing with a couple of amateurs cooking up crude explosives in their basement. We're trying to identify the type of explosive that was used. That way, we can narrow down if and where it was purchased."

"What was the trigger?"

"A cell phone. We're working to track all the calls made at the time the bomb went off. The cell phone is like a remote control and detonates the device. From the profile the feds came up with, the bomber was smart, and probably purchased one of those cheap, disposable cell phones for one time use at a convenience store and then tossed the phone when he was done. The FBI doesn't think a terrorist group is responsible, and none of the obvious players have come forward claiming they did it."

"The courthouse is in a central location downtown. There had to be plenty of businesses around with video surveillance."

"We're combing through all the tapes from local businesses now."

"You need to be sure Rossi doesn't leave Detroit," Julia says.

"As of one-thirty today, he was a free man. The judge didn't impose any restrictions on his domestic whereabouts. He just can't leave the country."

"I have information I need to share with you, but on one condition."

"I'm not guaranteeing anything until you tell me what you know. I've played this game with you before, and you know how it works," Navarro says.

"This is different. I'm not writing a story. I'll give you inside information on Nick Rossi, but you have to give me access to the investigation. I want to be there when you nail him."

"I can't do that. This is a very sensitive case, and everybody is involved—the Detroit PD, the state, and the FBI. Even if I wanted to let you in, it's not up to me," Navarro says.

"I'll ask Chief Linderman myself, then. He'll understand. You told me Rossi isn't considered a suspect in the bombing."

"Not at this time, no, he's not."

"You need to reopen an investigation against him for attempted murder."

Navarro lets out a low whistle and shakes his head.

"All right. Here we go again. I'll talk to Linderman, depending on what you've got."

"Nick Rossi hired a hit man, a sniper, to take out the Butcher. I spoke with someone an hour ago who confirmed a local guy, Jim Bartello, the former head of security for the MGM Grand, runs Rossi's local operation. Bartello reached out to my source, on behalf of Rossi, to recommend a hit man to take out the Butcher as he was entering the courthouse."

"If a sniper was in place, somebody else beat him to it. We interviewed Bartello during the Rossi bust. Bartello was vetted. He's a slimy little turd, but we couldn't find any direct evidence linking him to Nick Rossi's criminal activities."

"Then he got off when he shouldn't have. My source believes whoever did the bombing is at the center of Rossi's circle, working alone to protect the boss. I still believe Rossi did it. Whether he's in jail or not, the people who work for him would be too scared to try and undermine his authority, whether they thought they were doing this for his benefit or not."

"Who told you about Bartello?"

"I can't tell you that."

"You just told me you're not writing a story, which means you're not protected as a journalist under the shield law. That leaves you in a position as a citizen who is potentially obstructing justice by refusing to tell me who gave you information in a criminal investigation."

"So, there will be an investigation?"

"It's going to be hard to get a warrant to search Bartello's property based on hearsay, but let me see what I can do. The fact that Rossi was looking to take out the prosecution's key witness with a sniper makes it a lot more plausible to connect the dots to him and the bomb."

Bartello's Wyandotte end-unit townhome has remained dark for the entirety of the twenty minutes since the stakeout began, which means Rossi's local guy is either hiding inside or more likely out. Russell walks fast down the sidewalk in the direction of Navarro's unmarked police car parked on the corner. He blows into his hands for warmth as he leans forward in the driver-side window to debrief Julia and Navarro.

"Nobody's home. No lights, and someone left the side door to the garage wide open. There's no car in there either."

Navarro gives Russell a suspicious glare.

"The side door to the garage was wide open, huh?" Navarro asks.

"I just call it like I see it," Russell responds.

"Okay, let's see what we can find," Navarro says, and then

turns around toward the backseat to address his ride-along. "You know the drill, Julia. If I tell you to move or stay behind, you listen. Am I clear?"

"Crystal clear," Julia says as she pulls a black knit hat on her head.

The three walk briskly to the older townhome complex, its faded rust exterior looking shabby against the dull yellow glow of the streetlights.

"If Bartello was working for Rossi, he should have been able to afford a better dump than this," Russell whispers.

Navarro ignores Russell, moves toward the front door, and gives it three hard knocks. The only response is a curious neighbor who turns on their front porch light. After a minute, Navarro motions his partner and Julia toward the garage and the side of the home that faces a small wooded area.

"Like I told you, the side door to the garage was like this. Wide open," Russell says, somewhat unconvincingly.

The garage is dark. Navarro pulls out a flashlight and quickly pans the small one-car space, careful not to reflect the light in the narrow garage door windows. The sides of the cramped space are crowded with boxes, what looks like a never-used Stairmaster, and a framed and dusty picture of the Detroit Red Wings' 1998 Stanley Cup win. Russell begins to lift the lids off a few boxes in the corner.

"What do you got over there?" Navarro asks.

"A stack of old *Playboys* from the 1980s and some faded newspaper clippings from when Bartello used to play high school sports."

"Don't touch anything, Julia," Navarro says, but it's too late. Julia sifts through a black trash can next to the door that leads into Bartello's house.

"This guy used to be the head of security for one of the

biggest hotels in Detroit. He's not going to be stupid and leave something behind in the trash," Russell comments.

During her first year as a rookie newspaper reporter, Julia learned from a veteran journalist that people's trash cans are usually a hidden treasure trove of information. Julia's experienced fingers carefully pick through Bartello's garbage, including mostly fast-food and frozen dinner containers. She pulls out the plastic interior case from an Oreo cookie box and motions for Navarro.

"I don't think that's a condom," Julia says.

Navarro flashes his light inside the plastic container, which holds two spent balloons with the remnants of a sticky black substance inside.

"Looks like Bartello was using," Julia says.

"Heroin," Russell comments. "I think I may have heard someone in distress inside."

"Come on," Navarro tells his partner. "We didn't get the warrant yet."

"You didn't almost die in the blast. If you're not going in, I am," Russell says.

Navarro makes a split-second decision and turns to Julia. "Go back to the car. You and Russell. If you see Bartello or anyone else get anywhere near this place, you call me on my cell phone. I'll have it on buzzer."

Navarro kneels down and uses his lock picks with precision until the door creaks open.

"You didn't see this, Julia. Now get out of here."

"Five minutes. Don't be in there any longer than that," Russell tells his partner. He then grabs Julia's arm and leads her out of Bartello's place and to the car.

Julia returns to the backseat and sweeps her eyes back and forth down the street searching for approaching cars as the two sit in silence.

"It's been longer than five minutes. What's he doing in there?" Julia asks, her voice raw with nerves and adrenaline.

A black SUV turns the corner, passes them, and then makes a slow crawl past Bartello's townhome.

"Ah, shit," Russell says as he pulls out his cell phone and speed dials his partner's number.

"The car's turning around. They're coming back. We've got to go help Navarro," Julia says.

"Stay put. That's the worst thing you could do. You don't want to attract attention. Ray knows what he's doing."

Julia digs her fingernails into her palms until she can feel them begin to cut through her skin.

The black SUV snakes down the road, its headlights cutting a trail in their direction until the car parks on the street directly across from Bartello's place. Two men, short and wide and wearing all black, exit the vehicle and head directly to the front door. One of the men reaches his arm around to his rear waistband, and Julia can make out the shape of the butt of a gun. One of the men pulls a key from his pocket, and the two go inside Bartello's place.

"I'm going in. You stay here. You hear shots fired, you call for backup on the radio," Russell directs.

"Hold on, there's someone coming around the other side of the complex," Julia says.

Navarro appears under a street lamp walking casually in their direction, as if he's a neighborhood guy just out for a pleasant late-evening stroll.

Navarro gets to the car and calmly opens the driver-side door.

"Two guys inside who let themselves into Bartello's place with a key, and one guy still in the car," Russell says. "Talk about a close call."

The front door of Bartello's house opens, and the two

men exit and get back into the SUV, which then shoots down the street like a cannon.

"They didn't find what they were looking for, which I assume is Bartello. Did you get the plate?" Navarro asks as he slides his key into the ignition.

"Classic Michigan plate. Blue and white. I couldn't see the number from here, though," Julia says. "They have to be Nick Rossi's guys."

"How the hell did you get out of there?" Russell asks.

"I went out the bedroom window when you called. Thanks for having my back. The place was overall pretty clean. Looks like he hightailed it out of there pretty fast. Bartello took his clothes and wiped out a safe in the bedroom. But the guy is a junkie, so he got careless. His bathroom was clear, but I found his hiding place. He had a hole in his closet floor. He left a cell phone in there and a couple of grainy photographs that look like a man and woman having sex in a hotel room. From the quality of the pictures, it looks like they were copied from some kind of surveillance tape. There was also a piece of paper with the name and number of a woman written on it. I couldn't take the phone and the photos because we don't have a warrant."

"Shit," Russell says. "Those guys probably beat us to it. Did you get the name and number that was on the paper?"

"Yeah, I wrote it down. It's a local area code and the name of the woman is Isabella Rossi."

"Nick Rossi's wife," Julia says.

CHAPTER 14

In the penthouse suite bedroom, Isabella Rossi waits for her husband to finish on top of her. She closes her eyes and remembers the smell of Christina's head when she was a baby, as she rocked her daughter back to sleep against her chest, the cool night air misted with the smell of Lake Huron lazily wafting through the white organza curtains of the nursery.

Her husband, Nick, licks her neck and whispers in a husky voice that she is his whore, while Isabella drifts off to the days when she and her sister, Ava, danced on the sand while they waited for their father to get off his shift at the concession booth in the summer resort town of New Buffalo, nestled along Lake Michigan's southern coast on the western part of the state. Isabella closes her eyes tightly as she drifts off to the image of the younger version of herself and Ava holding hands as they executed sweet pirouettes and swore one day they would be ballerinas in New York City.

Nick Rossi finally arrives, the whole sexual episode clocking in under five minutes thanks to his recent lockup in jail.

As he climaxes, her husband lets out a loud groan that Isabella knows his two bodyguards can hear loud and clear in the next room.

She lies still until he rolls off of her, and then she covers her naked body with a sheet.

Rossi gets up, no modesty in his nakedness, as he sprawls with his legs casually wide open on a beige chaise lounge and pulls a cigarette from a pack, taking a long drag after he lights it.

"You changed your hair. It's like how you had it when I first met you out in L.A.," Rossi comments. "I liked it better before. You look like shit."

Isabella doesn't bother to fight the insult.

"I'm leaving tonight. The boys will drive me to Chicago and I'll take a flight back to San Francisco. LAX is closer, but I don't want the cops getting a lead on me if they're tracking the passenger lists," Rossi says.

"When do we leave?" Isabella asks.

"Change of plans. You'll stay behind. After all this crap, I'm going to have to scale back the Detroit operation. The future is out in L.A. anyway. I need you here to tie up any loose ends for me. That idiot Bartello took off. My men just left his house and he was gone, running away like a scared little girl. When I find him, I'm going to cut off his balls and make his mother eat them."

"Jesus, Nick. I don't want to hear that."

Rossi moves toward the bed and grabs his wife's delicate chin, forcing her to look directly at him. "What do you want to hear, Isabella? Do you want me to give it to you again? Three months without a man, I bet you're begging for it, right?" Rossi says, then laughs.

Isabella tries to look away, but Rossi squeezes her jaw until she fears it will snap.

"I'll stay behind and do as I am told," she answers.

"Good girl," Rossi says. He releases his grip and then smacks the side of his wife's ass.

"The bombing that I've been reading about, that was you?" Isabella asks.

Rossi stubs out his first cigarette, only halfway smoked, and pulls out another from his pack. "The five years we've been together, what have I taught you?"

"Not to ask about your business and to do what I'm told."

Rossi walks to the penthouse window and looks down at the city of Detroit, giving an entire and unabashed full monty to the Motor City skyline.

"I hate this shithole. Detroit's been nothing but bad luck for me since I was nine years old. It's cold and rundown, and I couldn't ever find a decent contractor who could distinguish his ass from his cock. The only good thing that happened here was that Biggs got what was coming to him."

"So you did kill the Butcher?"

Rossi takes a moment, still taking in the city view, and then slowly turns around to face his wife. He moves toward his wife and she cowers against the headboard, knowing what awaits.

Rossi gives her a hard open-hand smack across her face. Isabella doesn't cry over the assault. Not anymore. She thinks back to the one person she knows truly loved her once and feels brave for a moment.

"If my father were alive, he'd come after you."

Rossi opens his mouth wide, showing off his perfect white teeth, and offers Isabella a hard, mean laugh.

"Your father? He didn't care about you when he was alive. He let you run out to L.A. just to get rid of you. How did the Hollywood thing turn out for you, Isabella, huh? You're lucky I met you when I did. Otherwise, you'd have wound up doing soft porn flicks just to pay the bills like your sister did."

Rossi pulls on a pair of tight red bikini briefs and admires his muscular reflection in the room's full-length mirror.

"You leave tonight?" Isabella asks, and stares hopelessly out at the cold Michigan night.

"Yes, I have to start moving the Detroit operation, and I need freedom from the scrutiny. Tarburton should get me off so I won't be tried again on the drug and bribery and illegal gambling charges, but I need to lay low until this bombing investigation cools down."

"What if the police question me?"

Rossi slips on a pair of Italian custom-tailored black slacks and a light pink button-down dress shirt.

"Have I not taught you anything? You tell them nothing. You don't know about any of my business dealings. Play the stupid bitch that you are."

"And why am I here instead of with you?"

"Because my nana is sick, and you're here to tend to her until she gets out of the hospital. Tarburton was smart to bring her here for the trial, but she's ninety-two. The pneumonia will probably kill her."

"You don't care?"

Rossi dons a black suit coat and fixes his already perfect hair in the mirror. "She's old. People die. You spend too much time worrying or caring about what happens to people, you become weak."

Rossi leans down and gives Isabella a rough kiss on the forehead. "Now, remember what I said about the cops. I should get you back to California in a week or so. Once the lawyer is killed and I move the majority of my Midwest operation back out West, I'll send for you."

"You shouldn't take out the lawyer. Not now anyway. Give it some time, Nick. You don't want to make it too obvious that you hired the hit. If he winds up dead, all suspicions will turn to you. And you just got out of jail."

Rossi's dark eyes dart back and forth across his wife's face as if he's actually considering something she said.

"Maybe. You stay put, though, and don't mess up again."

"I won't," Isabella says, rolling away from her husband so she can face the wall. "There are some things I would still like to do here in Detroit."

"Yeah, spend more of my money. Prada this and Prada that," Rossi says. "Keep your legs closed unless I tell you otherwise."

"You made me a whore," Isabella whispers. But it's too late. Rossi is gone, and Isabella already knows she sealed her fate with him a long time ago anyway.

Salvatore Gallo declines the offer of a scotch or espresso by his nephew's thugs and feels the cool steel of his revolver in the pocket of his wool coat. Gallo has no plans on using it against his nephew, but he doesn't entirely trust the current crew around Nick or the recent business associates he added to Gallo's once fairly clean operation. Back in Gallo's day, the unspoken threat of retaliation against a wrongful act was as powerful as a bullet, like a known nuclear capability possessed by a dueling world superpower. In other words, you screw with me, I'll rain down an apocalypse on your entire village.

Nick Rossi comes out of the bedroom of his penthouse suite looking to Gallo more like a prissy *GQ* cover wannabe than the head of his family business.

"It's Easter already? Why you wearing a pink shirt?" Gallo asks.

"This shirt cost five hundred dollars. If you'd let me take you shopping, I'd show you how to dress, Uncle."

Gallo brushes the fingers of one hand in the air as if dismissing his nephew's suggestion.

"Come. Let's sit," Gallo says, and beckons his nephew to take a seat on the couch next to him.

Nick offers his uncle a strained smile but keeps standing.

"You never were one to obey orders," Salvatore says, and cocks his head in the direction of the bedroom. "You got one of your whores in there?"

"No. It's Isabella."

Salvatore shakes his head, looking suddenly weary and every inch his seventy-two years.

"You need to let that girl go," Salvatore says. "It's the right thing to do."

"You hated her friggin' guts when I brought her back from L.A. You said she was a gold digger. Now, what, you're her savior?"

"Whether I like her or not doesn't matter anymore. You married her and had a child."

"Our marriage died when our daughter did," Nick says. "If Isabella hadn't made the nanny run errands for her because she was too lazy to do them herself, Christina would still be here. Isabella's lucky I didn't kill her for what she did."

"A loss like that, it's easy to point blame. I could do the same for you, Nicky."

"What are you saying?"

"You think your little girl's murder was random?"

"Watch what you say next, old man."

Salvatore's jaw sets tight as the patriarch tries to regain control, a position he realizes deep down he lost years ago.

"You talk to me with respect, you understand? I spent years taking care of you, treating you like my own son, and you take my business and turn it into something ugly. My father, my grandfather, we never entered the drug trade. It was dirty. We never stole. And we only fought back when we had to. You kill people like it's sport."

"All rumors," Nick says, looking amused. "You should be grateful. I took your little business and turned it into an empire."

"Not an empire I ever wanted."

"Your choice not to take money from the other parts of my business. And don't worry about Isabella. I keep her on the payroll. She's still got some use for me."

"Then do what you want in your personal life. Look, I didn't come here to lecture you on your marriage. We need to talk."

"So talk," Nick says, and pours a shot of tequila.

"We talk alone."

Nick holds Gallo's gaze and then dismisses his help.

"You did all right in prison?" Gallo asks.

"I do all right wherever I go."

"Tarburton got you off. You were lucky. But all eyes are going to be on you now, even more than before. You need to lay low for a while. Think about selling off the parts of your business that got you in trouble. The Feds get you for hijacking and selling stolen goods, that'll be the end for you. And the drug business, you've got to give that up. Willie Robinson, he'd buy off that portion of your operation."

"I'm not giving up anything, especially to a nigger."

"Hey, watch your mouth. I need you to take some time to think about it. Go to my place in Traverse City for a while. Please, Nicky."

"You worry too much about other people, Uncle. You spend all your time thinking about how someone else feels, that's less time you're worrying about yourself. I'm getting out of Detroit. This place's been nothing but bad luck for me for a while now. I'm heading back to L.A. I'll be at my place in the Santa Ynez Mountains outside of Santa Barbara first until things cool down. I've got a local guy who'll take care of you if you need anything."

A look of disappointment creases the etched downturned lines along the corners of Gallo's mouth. "Who's that? Jim Bartello?"

"No, Jimmy's been screwing up. He's turned into a junkie, and I can't trust him anymore. I'm going to replace him with my guy from Flint."

"I won't see you anymore then if you go back to California."

Nick puts down his drink and places his hand on his uncle's shoulder.

"You're going to miss me? I figured you'd prefer it, me getting out of your town. Tell you what. I'll fly you out at Christmas."

"You do what you need to do, then. But Detroit will always be your home."

Nick sits down on the couch and pats his uncle's hand.

"Thank you," Nick says.

"For what?"

"For never making me feel like an obligation."

Nick gets up from the couch, his swagger fully back after his momentary slip of tenderness, and makes his way to the front door of the penthouse, the meeting now over.

"I see there's nothing I can do to change your mind. But please, be careful," Gallo says.

He begins to leave, but then turns around to face his nephew.

"I met with that reporter."

"The one who's married to that assistant D.A. guy who was trying my case?" Rossi asks. "What were you thinking?"

"I owed that girl a favor. Her stories got the police off my back. I could've faced some serious jail time if it wasn't for her."

"Bullshit. I'd have never let it get to that point. Julia Gooden is no real friend to our family. I heard she was sniffing around, trying to peg me for the Tyce Jones shooting. And her husband wanted to get me locked up for good. Your loyalty is with our family, not with some stupid journalist. What did she want?"

"She wanted to know if you were responsible for the bombing. I told her there's no way you'd be involved. That was it."

"Jesus Christ. Don't talk to her again. Whether you think she helped you out or not, if she tries to screw me over, I'll take care of her."

"No, Nicky. You can't do that. I won't let you."

"You take everything so seriously," Rossi says, and slaps his uncle on the back. "There are ways to take care of people without killing them."

"I've covered for you plenty in the past, Nicky. I didn't like it, but I did it to protect you. You need to be straight with me about one thing, though. Did you order the courthouse attack? If you're responsible, that's one thing I couldn't forgive, not for you and not even for my sister."

"You've always looked out for me, ever since I was a little kid. The bombing? I thought that was you."

CHAPTER 15

Julia clutches the topaz necklace David gave her just two mornings before and rubs it between her fingers as though it could somehow bring her luck.

Russell and Navarro flank Julia on either side as they ride the elevator up to Isabella Rossi's penthouse floor in the new luxury residence building that Quicken Loans founder Dan Gilbert purchased and renovated. The building sits directly across the street from his headquarters as part of his continued effort to revitalize the core of downtown Detroit.

"I wonder what the occupancy rate is in this place," Navarro says as the elevator pauses to let a pair of young professionals off on the concierge level.

"I don't know, but it gives me a reason to think about getting out of Rochester Hills," Russell answers. "I keep hearing about how the population is plummeting and the economy is sucking ass in Detroit, but tell that to the commuters on I-75. That drive is as bad into the city as it's ever been. I was stuck in gridlock traffic this morning for forty-five minutes."

"Did you get any sleep last night, Julia?" Navarro asks, and unconsciously moves his hand to the small of her back, a long-ago familiar gesture of his when he was worried about her.

"I slept for a few hours in the hospital chair. Thanks for asking."

"How's David?" Navarro asks.

"Improving. His doctor thinks he's going to be fully alert within a few days. Granted, he still may have issues with his vision and speech, but so far he's made a tremendous recovery considering the extent of his injuries."

"Yeah, I had a jumper, a guy trying to take his life by leaping off the roof of his building," Russell says. "The guy was an autoworker who got laid off from Ford and just wanted to end it. Ray and I were trying to talk him down, but the guy jumps anyway and does this belly flop off the building, but his body twists midfall and he lands headfirst on the sidewalk. It sounded like someone took a baseball bat to one of those giant seedless watermelons. Turns out the guy lives, but he had major brain damage from the fall and now he's a vegetable, just lies around staring at the wall in a diaper, and his poor wife has to take care of him twenty-four seven."

"Really, Russell?" Navarro says, and tilts his head in Julia's direction.

"Yeah, nice visual," Julia adds.

"Sorry. Just trying to lighten the mood."

Russell pulls out his phone and starts scrolling the local news stories.

"Mayor Anderson's poll numbers are way up. Take a look at that picture," Russell says, and shows Navarro and Julia an image of the mayor attending a funeral for one of the bombing victims. Anderson's arm is around the grieving widow as he faces the camera, his expression somber yet resolute. "Did you read the Tandy Sanchez story? It made Anderson out like he's so damn perfect he never took a shit in his entire life."

"I saw an ad this morning on Channel 9 with Anderson hugging people at the hospital," Navarro says. "I noticed you weren't in it, Julia."

"Thank God. I saw the same ad. 'Mayor Anderson. Compassionate Leader. Detroit Strong,'" Julia comments. "Boyles left me a message asking me to be part of his ad, but I refused."

"Probably smart on many levels. Mayor Anderson's campaign finance director was just fired. The chief told me," Navarro says. "Campaign funds went missing and apparently Anderson's money guy was dipping into the well. We're looking into it to see if we can pin the guy, and then he'll face charges. Gavin Boyles and Anderson met with Chief Linderman this morning to try and make sure it doesn't hit the press."

"Good luck with that," Julia says. "Don't look at me, though. I'm off the job right now."

The ride ends finally as they arrive on the penthouse floor, and Navarro takes the lead.

"How should I identify myself?" Julia asks.

"Just be honest. Chief Linderman agreed you could have limited access to the investigation as long as you continue to feed us any information you receive from your source," Navarro says. "I'm surprised Linderman went for it, but he knows you, and after the bombing no options are off the table."

Navarro gives three hard raps on the penthouse door instead of using the bell, subliminally already setting the stage for who is in charge.

A good thirty seconds elapse and Navarro raises his hand to knock again when the door opens. Isabella Rossi stands in the doorway, looking like some kind of exotic goddess in a loose, white flowing skirt and a turquoise off-the-shoulder fitted top, the early-morning sun casting a warm glow against her golden skin. Isabella is model tall, standing at about five-foot-ten, Julia estimates. She has straight, black hair that tightly frames her face and large, almond-shaped dark eyes. Although this is the first time Julia has met her, Isabella's face looks strongly familiar, and Julia remembers back to the newspaper photo she saw, picturing Isabella with her husband and the daughter who wouldn't live to see her third birthday.

"You're the police officer who called me?" Isabella asks. Her voice is fluid and smooth, without a hint of trepidation.

"Yes, we wanted to talk to you about an associate of your husband's," Navarro says.

"I don't think I can be of much help, but please come in."

Isabella leads them inside, through an entryway lined with black-and-white pictures of Lake Michigan.

Isabella catches Russell noticing the pictures and seems pleased.

"I grew up in New Buffalo. I took the photos you're admiring. I always felt if you were passionate about the objects you were trying to take pictures of, you could somehow capture their soul."

Isabella stops in the living room, which is banked by a wall of windows that overlook downtown Detroit. She takes a seat and gestures for her newly arrived guests to do the same.

Julia watches Isabella appraise Navarro favorably as he sits down, and then she turns to Julia and looks her up and down as well, but this time her face settles into an expression of distaste and irritation.

"Who's this woman?" Isabella asks Navarro. "I was told only two officers would be here."

"My name is Julia Gooden."

"I asked the policeman."

Navarro gives Julia a quick, sideways glance, and Julia forces herself not to respond, keeping with her promise to

Navarro that she will be there in the background only and will not ask or answer any questions.

"Julia is a journalist," Navarro says.

Isabella crosses her arms defensively, causing the six thin silver bracelets around her slender wrist to make a pleasant chiming sound.

"I wouldn't have agreed to this meeting if I knew a reporter would be here. My husband has had enough negative coverage," Isabella says, and turns to Julia. "I recognize your name. You wrote those stories about my husband, so many lies. Your articles damaged Nick's reputation and hurt my family. What you did, we'll never forget."

"I'm not writing an article," Julia answers. "But whatever you tell the police in my presence, I will not publish it now or at any future date. This is the agreement I've made with the detectives."

Isabella stares at Julia for an uncomfortable ten seconds and then turns her body in the direction of Navarro and Russell.

"I assume this man is your partner?" she asks Navarro.

"I guess I look like a cop," Russell answers. "I'll take it as a compliment."

"My husband would normally require me to have a lawyer here, but since his attorney is still embroiled in legal red tape, I'll agree to talk to you alone. As you'll see, Nick and I have nothing to hide."

"Where's your husband, Mrs. Rossi?" Navarro asks.

"Call me Isabella, please," she says, and gives Navarro a smile that is pure sexuality, a skill that has obviously worked well in her favor, Julia thinks. "Are you married, Mr. Navarro?"

"No."

"A man of your looks, I'm very surprised."

Isabella's play fails to disarm Navarro. "You didn't answer my question. Where is Mr. Rossi? Is he still in Detroit?"

"No, he's on a trip. My husband travels a great deal. He's an international businessman. I'm not aware of every move my husband makes. It's not common knowledge, but Nick and I are estranged and have been for over a year. My daughter was murdered two years ago. After that, our marriage was never the same. My husband has his life, and I have mine."

"I'm sorry to hear about your daughter. But you and Mr. Rossi stay married?" Russell asks.

"For now."

"Does your husband see other people?" Russell asks.

Isabella shrugs casually as if the question holds no great importance to her.

"It's possible. Nick is a powerful man. I'm sure Ms. Gooden can attest to the way men operate. Your husband works for the district attorney's office, I believe."

"Your husband told you this?" Julia asks.

Isabella points a long finger toward a computer on the sleek stainless steel kitchen countertop. "I keep up with the news. I read about your husband's injuries from the bombing. Such a shame. He looked like a very handsome man in the photos before the attack."

Julia forces herself to not throw herself across the table and wrap her fingers around Isabella's throat.

"Do you know Jim Bartello?" Navarro asks, steering the interview back on course.

"I've never heard of him."

"He's a business associate of your husband's, the former head of security for the MGM Grand," Russell says.

"I'd think I'd recognize the man's name if he worked for my husband. Let me get you something to drink."

Isabella slips into the kitchen and returns with a tray holding a glass pitcher of water with fresh-cut lemon slices floating on top. She pours a glass and hands it to Navarro, and then does the same for Russell, and then Julia.

"Please forgive my earlier reception. This trial and the media coverage have caused Nick and our family great pain. And then this terrible bombing. We were worried the police would blame Nick, so we were very nervous until he was rightfully acquitted. I swear to you, Nick had nothing to do with the courthouse attack. We've had our problems, but Nick is a good man. He loves the city of Detroit."

"Your husband was acquitted because the judge and the prosecutor, who happens to be my husband, and the key witness were either gravely injured or killed. If this case had gone to trial, your husband would not be a free man," Julia says.

Navarro holds up his hand for Julia to stop, but Isabella sweeps in.

"We are more alike than you may think, Ms. Gooden. Our husbands are both powerful men. When they are accused wrongly or hurt, we jump to their sides to protect them. As women, we would do anything to defend our family," Isabella says.

"Including setting off a bomb in the courthouse to take out a witness, a snitch who you and your husband once trusted?" Navarro asks. "You and Mr. Rossi may lead separate lives as you say, but if he went to prison, his assets would be frozen and you wouldn't be able to afford the luxuries that you're used to."

Isabella's slender and elegant hand flutters to her throat, and she lets out a hearty laugh at the accusation.

"Do I look like a bomber to you, Detective? I couldn't even imagine where I would find such a thing. My days are spent shopping for purses and shoes at Neiman Marcus, not purchasing explosives on the black market."

"Did your husband tell you who he hired to take out Sammy Biggs? That's what he had Bartello do, right? Find a hit man to kill the witness?" Navarro goads. "I'm confused why he hired someone to plant the bomb, though, instead of just hiring a sniper to do the job. Seems cleaner that way, unless your husband has no problem taking a lot of innocent lives along with the intended target."

"Detective Navarro, you obviously take me for a fool, which I am not. Not all beautiful women are stupid, isn't that right, Ms. Gooden? I can assure you my husband had nothing to do with the unfortunate attack on the courthouse. It was a tragic coincidence that the bombing occurred during my husband's trial and people involved were hurt. My husband is as much a victim as anyone else. It's a miracle he wasn't hurt in the attack."

"You say Mr. Rossi isn't here. Do you mind if we take a look around for ourselves?" Russell asks.

"Yes, I do mind if you don't have a warrant. Now, if you don't have any other questions for me, I have to return to the hospital. Nick's grandma, Carmella, is in the hospital with pneumonia. She is an old woman, so I hope you will keep her in your prayers," Isabella says, and moves gracefully to the door to escort her visitors out.

"If you think of anything else, please give me a call," Navarro says, and hands Isabella his business card.

"I hope to see you again, Detective."

Isabella reaches into her purse—a soft, butter-colored Prada bag that sits on the entryway table—and pulls out a card that she presses into Navarro's hand.

Navarro, Russell, and Julia exit the penthouse and wait to discuss the encounter until they are out of the populated elevator and back on the street.

"What's going on over there?" Navarro asks as he points

to the front of the Quicken Loans building where the CEO and Mayor Anderson are mugging for the cameras, along with a young man in a wheelchair who is missing the lower part of his left leg.

"Some kind of photo op," Julia answers. "I'm betting Dan Gilbert is starting a fund for the bombing victims."

"He's done a lot for the city," Russell says, and gestures across the street to Gavin Boyles, who now has his hand on the mayor's arm and is hustling him toward a waiting car. "There's your boy, Julia. And he's got a nice ride."

"I prefer American-made vehicles myself," Navarro says.

"And Michigan-made women. I think Isabella Rossi likes you," Russell says as he climbs into his partner's Chevy Tahoe.

"I don't think so. I know that type of woman, but usually it's her pimp, not her husband, trying to use me so I won't make an arrest," Navarro answers.

"You think Rossi uses his wife to help him close business deals?" Julia asks. "Nick Rossi obviously has a huge ego. Do you honestly think he'd let his wife sleep around even if they're separated?"

"Maybe they have an open marriage," Russell says.

"My source told me they believe someone very close to Rossi was the bomber, whether they acted on his direction or not. I think we can rule Isabella out, though. I got the immediate impression Isabella wouldn't want to miss a pedicure appointment, let alone plan an attack on the courthouse," Julia suggests.

"I feel like we're missing something obvious. Russell, did you check Bartello's property records to see if he owns anything else besides that townhome in Wyandotte?" Navarro asks.

"Yeah, and I talked to Bartello's mother, too. She swears she hasn't heard from her son since Christmas," Russell says.

"It looks like he used to own a hunting camp outside of Escanaba in some tiny one-stop-sign town called Perkins in the U.P., but he hasn't paid property taxes on the place in a few years, so it's been foreclosed on. No one has repurchased the property from the bank yet."

"Probably spending his money on drugs instead of paying the mortgage," Navarro says. "Call the local sheriff up there to do a check on the place. If he's got a pair of wire cutters, he can get inside."

"You should hurry," Julia adds. "If you were able to find Jim Bartello's hunting camp through property records, Nick Rossi's thugs will be able to as well."

Jim Bartello combs the sum total of the three aisles in Brandstrom's Convenience Store, Perkins's only business besides the corner bar that has changed hands more times than Bartello can remember, and he loads his basket up with Cheetos, Hot Pockets, and a couple of cans of Dinty Moore Beef Stew. He tops off his purchases with two six-packs of Bud Light. Bartello smiles at the young blond girl who waits on him from behind the counter as he tries his best to look like a regular guy passing through town instead of a fat, sweaty creep with a three-day-old beard who's crashing from a heroin high.

"Just got to town to see an old friend," Bartello explains to the girl. "Who owns the bar across the street now? It used to be Pals when I came up to hunt a couple of years ago."

Bartello's familiarity with the area softens the girl a bit.

"No, the Johnson family hasn't owned the place in a while. Somebody from Marquette bought the bar. They're fixing it up, and it should be open by Memorial Day."

Bartello hands the girl thirty dollars and feels important when he sees her surprised expression as he tells her to keep the $2.40 change. Bartello then loads up and takes the familiar dirt road to his friend Steve Crandall's house. Bartello knows he can trust his childhood buddy to keep his secrets and his whereabouts under wraps, even more so than his own mother. Bartello and Steve grew up down the street from each other in Wyandotte and stayed friends until they drifted apart a few years ago when Bartello started working at the MGM Grand and Steve moved to Michigan's Upper Peninsula after getting laid off.

Steve's maroon Ford F-150 truck is parked in the driveway. Bartello grabs one of the six-packs and a manila envelope he extracts from the glove compartment and heads toward his friend's doublewide trailer.

Bartello can hear Bob Seger and the Silver Bullet Band's "Rock and Roll Never Forgets" playing through the thin walls as he gives a light tap on the door.

Steve opens the door, wearing a plaid shirt and a pair of faded Levi's, his face and hands chafed and red from the elements of a lifetime of working outside in Michigan's unforgiving winters.

"Jesus, Jimmy, what the hell are you doing up here?" Steve asks.

Bartello looks nervously over his shoulder, but the only other life around them is a dozen or so scattered birds pecking hungrily in a field across the street, trying to poke through the still-frozen soil for something to eat.

"Can I come in?" Bartello asks.

"Of course, man."

Bartello follows his friend inside to a place he's been to many times, although it's been a few years. Steve's trailer is neatly kept and smells like freshly cooked eggs and just a hint of marijuana that Bartello figures his friend smoked the previous night.

"You want a beer?" Bartello asks, and cracks one open for himself.

"No, thanks. It's only ten-thirty. I drink this early only when it's hunting season."

"Seven months away, huh?" Bartello asks, and takes a steady chug from the can.

"What brings you up here? I'm glad to see you, Jimmy, but I got to say, it's a surprise, you showing up like this."

"Remember when we were kids, and we'd lie on the railroad tracks behind your house?" Bartello asks.

"Yeah, what a pair of stupid idiots we were, playing chicken with a train. I swear, to this day, every time I hear a Norfolk Southern blasting its horn, I still get a shiver down my spine. You would always wait until the last minute to get off the tracks, but as soon as I could feel the vibration of the train coming, I bolted."

Bartello pulls the envelope out from under his leather jacket and places it on a coffee table between them. "I waited on the tracks too long this time. I got into some trouble downstate."

"What kind of trouble are we talking about? I heard about the heroin bust in the Detroit casinos, but your mom told my aunt you were cleared of all that."

"It's worse than that. All my life, you've been the only person I could trust. I know we drifted apart the last few years, but we're still close, I think."

"Yeah, man. Of course we are. Like brothers," Steve answers. "What did you do exactly?"

"I got involved with the wrong people. When I worked security at Tiger Stadium, I had played around a little, connecting people who wanted to buy coke, so I thought this would be the same type of thing. I got approached by this guy when I started heading up security at the MGM Grand. His name is Enzo Costas and he works for Nick Rossi."

"That big Detroit criminal dude I've been reading about."

"That's him," Bartello answers, and finishes his beer before he continues. "It was easy money. I'd arrange for Rossi's pickups to get the VIP rooms in the MGM Grand."

"What were they picking up in the VIP rooms?" Steve asks.

"Drugs. High-end stuff. Rossi also ran an illegal gambling ring in the VIP suites. These rich dudes would put down tens of thousands of dollars on games. Sometimes even over a hundred thousand. My role, I just made sure Rossi's guys got the rooms they needed. That's all I did. It's not like I was setting up old guys to bang young kids up there or anything. This cop Navarro posed like he was a high roller and started talking to people. Then he put the heat on some assistant for a movie producer in L.A. who was there to buy smack, and this guy spilled his guts and ratted out the whole operation. The Detroit cops did a sting up in one of the rooms, and Rossi got busted. From there, Navarro and his partner swept in and started arresting almost everyone involved."

"You didn't get arrested."

"No, Navarro and this other cop interviewed me and sweated me hard. But they couldn't prove I was involved, and Enzo Costas said he and Rossi would protect me and not tell the cops of my involvement if I continued to work for them. It got worse, though, man. I felt like I was their bitch. Instead of arranging meetings between the gamblers and dealers, they made me run errands. I was blackmailed. Enzo Costas made me hire a hit man to take out the witness at the courthouse the day the bomb went off. I don't know what freaking happened, though, with the bomb going off like it did. That wasn't what was planned."

"You should go to the police," Steve says.

"It's too late for that. I ran away and came up here because I knew Rossi's guys were going to get me. I'm behind on money to them, and they think I botched the courthouse job. With all the pressure they put me under, I started using."

"What, like coke?"

"No. Heroin," Bartello answers.

Steve's face falls in surprise and disappointment as he looks at his old friend.

"I'm still the kid you knew back when we were growing up. I just got a little lost," Bartello says, his words sounding desperate and whiny in the confines of the small trailer. "That's why I need you to take care of something for me."

"I care about you, Jimmy, and we go way back, but I can't do that. I'm not getting involved in some drug deal, no matter how much history is between us."

"That's not what I'm asking. If something happens to me, I want you to go to the police. Don't open this now," Bartello says, and slides the manila envelope across the coffee table to his friend. "I'm going to hide out for a while in my hunting camp. If I'm murdered or it looks like I killed myself—which, believe me, I wouldn't do—you give this envelope to the police and call Detective Ray Navarro at the Detroit Police Department. His card is in the envelope. He gave it to me after I got questioned after the drug bust. There's a flash drive in the envelope and a note that explains everything and will implicate Enzo Costas and Nick Rossi."

"I don't like this. What if those guys come for me?"

"They won't. I'm leaving and I won't come back here until this blows over. Rossi is going to move the majority of his operation to the West Coast, so maybe they'll leave me alone."

"Yeah, maybe," Steve answers, but neither man believes it. "You got enough food up there?"

"I'll be fine for a couple weeks. It's not the food I'm worried about, though. I'm going to have to go cold turkey off the drugs in a couple of days when I run out."

The once childhood friends give each other a quick man-hug, and Bartello wipes away a tear before his buddy can see it.

"Take care, man," Steve calls out from the doorway as Bartello walks across the frozen ground to his car.

Bartello waves, feeling his head start to pound from the heroin crash, the beer obviously not helping. He grabs another Bud Light from the fresh six-pack sitting on the passenger seat and pops the top as he heads down the three-mile stretch of dirt road deep into the woods, where the only other people who ever bother to go there vacated their bluffs last November after the deer season ended.

Bartello reaches the camp and does a slow drive-by first, looking for any fresh tire tracks, but all is clear. He parks his car behind the rear of the structure that he and his uncles built when he was fifteen, and he pulls out his wire cutters from the trunk, swearing at the stupid bank as he cuts the padlock sealing the door.

Inside, the place smells a little musty but like home, where he and his five uncles played cards, drank beer, and talked tits and the Packers while his dad made a pot of deer chili on the makeshift stove.

Bartello relaxes a little, drops his groceries and suitcase on the floor, and reaches inside the hidden compartment for his heroin.

"Just a little bit, got to make it last," Bartello says as he coaxes the balloon out of its hiding place.

"Did you forget something?" a husky male voice asks from the hallway.

Bartello freezes and opens his mouth to speak, when two men emerge from the dark corridor. One carries an ice pick and a blowtorch.

"Wait, this is a mistake, guys. I just came up here for the weekend. I was going to come back with your money, I swear. Please, just give me a few more days."

The smaller man easily tackles Bartello to the floor. He places Bartello in a headlock and forces his forearm against Bartello's windpipe. Bartello starts to lose consciousness, but the smaller man eases his grip from Bartello's neck, enough so Bartello is alert and can feel and experience every minute of his torture session.

His screams go unanswered for the next thirty minutes, heard by no one in the desolate woods, until a final gunshot rings out and nature resumes its peaceful vigil.

CHAPTER 16

Julia gets to the hospital first thing to discover David awake and alert for the first time since the bombing, and although he isn't able to speak yet, his progression to conscious but unresponsive is a step and, for Julia, a cause for celebration. Julia pops the cork to a bottle of sparkling cider and pours five glasses—two for Logan and Will, one for Helen, and two for her and David.

"Daddy can't pick up his glass or drink, but be sure to cheers his plastic cup for luck, guys," Julia says, and brushes her red Solo cup against her husband's on the table next to his bed.

"He looks good, don't you think?" Logan asks.

"Yes, Mr. David looks very good. He has nice color in his cheeks," Helen says. "That is a sign that his circulation is pushing the bad things out of his body. Good circulation, good health."

Julia doesn't bother to question Helen's medical acumen and lifts Will up so David can see him. Will buries his head into Julia's shoulder, uncomfortable in the new situation and more uncomfortable still with his daddy lying motionless in a bed with tubes and wires connected to his body.

"Want to go home," Will pleads.

"We just got here. Say hi to Daddy, sweetheart," Julia answers.

"No. Daddy looks funny," Will says.

"Logan, get the picture Will made for Daddy," Julia suggests.

Logan pulls out a crumpled white paper with blue and red scribbles strewn across it and hands it to Will.

"Give Dad the picture," Logan tells Will, sounding more like a lecturing parent than an eight-year-old.

"No. Go home now," Will says.

"Shhh," Julia whispers in her son's ear. "Will drew you a picture, David. The kids spent most of the afternoon making you their cards."

Julia's phone signals its ring in her purse, and Julia puts Will down next to his brother. "Why don't you two see what else you have in that backpack for your father?"

"Stop saying stupid things in front of Dad," Logan warns Will.

Will begins to sob in earnest now over his brother's rejection and the strange appearance of his father, who now looks like a marred wax mannequin impersonating the man he knew just a few days ago.

Julia looks at the caller. Navarro. She knows she has to take it and nods at Helen to play cleanup with her boys.

Julia scoops Will back up in her arms and wipes away his tears as Navarro's call slips to voice mail.

"No fighting, you two. Will is trying his best, Logan. This is all strange for him," Julia says.

"It's strange for me too," Logan answers.

"I know. I'm sorry. I'll only be a minute on the phone. I promise," Julia says.

Helen swoops in and catches the boys' attention by pulling out Julia's iPad from Logan's backpack. Logan takes it from Helen's confused hands and he expertly navigates to the camera icon. He sits down next to his dad on the hospital bed and begins to show his still-unresponsive father recent family pictures. Will easily sidles up to his brother's side so he can see the action on the screen.

The boys now occupied, Julia goes inside David's private bathroom, shuts the door, and calls Navarro back.

"Navarro, what've you got?" Julia says, her voice slightly above a whisper.

"Do you want to call me back?"

"No. I'm in the only semiprivate place I can find in the hospital where I can use my cell phone."

"Bartello is dead," Navarro says.

"Oh shit. There goes anything he could've told you about Rossi."

"Not exactly. His buddy found his body up in that deer camp Russell mentioned. Apparently, the friend was worried and went to check on him. From what the sheriffs told me, it sounds like he was tortured before he was killed, like it was payback or the killers were trying to get something out of Bartello."

"I'm betting the murderers have to be the same guys we saw outside of Bartello's townhome. Do you have any proof?"

"On the killing, not yet," Navarro continues. "But Bartello had a change of heart at the last minute and gave his buddy an envelope an hour or so before he was killed. There was a letter in there addressed to me. The Escanaba sheriff looked it over already and told me it's a detailed laundry list of Rossi's drug and gambling operations."

"But Tarburton claimed double jeopardy on that, so he probably can't be charged."

"Let me finish. Bartello also says some guy named Enzo Costas . . ."

"Nick Rossi's second-in-command. My source told me," Julia interrupts.

"Anything else you failed to share?"

"Sorry. I didn't know his role in the Detroit operation," Julia says.

"Yeah, so in this letter, Bartello claims Enzo Costas blackmailed him and made him hire a sniper to take out the Butcher on the day he was scheduled to testify."

"Enzo Costas may have been laying down the orders, but Rossi was still calling the shots from prison. There's your attempted murder charge," Julia says.

"Right now, all we've got is a dead guy's word against Costas. But Bartello did give us something we can work with—the name of the sniper. Jason Meter, an ex-army guy who lives in Dearborn. I brought him into the station already for questioning. Meter sold out his employer in under ten minutes. Meter confirmed Bartello hired him and Bartello bragged about how he was the head of Rossi's Detroit operation. The sniper swears up and down that he wasn't involved in the bombing."

"That should be enough for you to at least arrest Rossi. You bring him in on the attempted murder charge and then sweat him about his role in the courthouse bombing attack."

"I would if I could find him. Rossi's in the wind. He's not allowed to leave the country, but a friend of mine in the FBI told me Rossi has a place somewhere in California. I reached out to an L.A. police officer I worked with a few years ago. If Rossi is on the down low there, my cop friend may be able to help me find him. He thinks Rossi has some mountain retreat somewhere near Santa Barbara."

"I know where Rossi's hiding."

Julia can hear Navarro exhale heavily in frustration on the other end of the phone.

"If you're going to California to question Rossi, I want to go," Julia says.

"No, you're not," Navarro answers.

"I'm the one with the address."

"Don't you want to stay with David?"

"He's not out of the woods, but David's condition is improving. I know he'd want me to go after Rossi for what he's done. I'm comfortable leaving for a day trip."

"With the flight back and forth, it's more like a two-day trip minimum."

"Okay. Let me think about it. Will's having a hard time seeing David like this, and I don't want to upset the kids any more than they already are."

"If you're going to come along, you need to let me know pretty quick."

"I will. Sorry to hear about Bartello, but at least he did the right thing in the end by giving everything up in the letter."

"There was something else in the envelope, a flash drive. I told the Escanaba sheriff to look at it before he sent it my way. He said the flash drive has what looks like a surveillance video on it. The recording is pretty grainy. It's a couple having sex in a hotel room."

"If the quality is bad, I doubt it's anyone's porn stash. It sounds more like blackmail to me."

Julia ends her conversation as Helen raps lightly against the bathroom door.

"I'm so sorry. I had to take that. Is Will okay?" Julia answers, and pulls Will out of Helen's arms.

"The boy is fine now. The children and I will take a walk to the gift shop, and that will give you a few minutes alone with your husband," Helen says.

"That would be wonderful. I appreciate everything you've been doing for my family."

Julia waits until Helen leaves with her sons and then closes the door to David's room.

Julia sits on the edge of the bed, gently lays her head against David's chest, and then brushes her lips softly against his cheek.

"You did so great today, babe. I know you're fighting your way back. I'll keep doing my part too. I'm getting closer to Nick Rossi. I met his wife, Isabella. I know she's hiding something. And Navarro arrested a sniper who Rossi hired to kill Sammy Biggs, so all we have to do is find Rossi so he can be arrested in connection to the bombing."

David's body twitches underneath Julia, and she jumps up in surprise. She stares back at her husband, who gives her a laser-sharp stare.

"David, are you okay?"

"Hard to talk," David says in a dry whisper. He fumbles for a paper and pen on his bedside table and scratches something down in an unsteady hand:

Box twenty-two. Three. Two. One. Thirty. Infinity.

"I'm going to call your doctor," Julia says, and pushes the button to the nurse's station. "What do those numbers mean?"

"Money code," David answers. "The bomber . . ."

"Is Rossi the bomber?" Julia asks.

David's eyes burn bright, and he nods his affirmation.

"Rossi knows. You've got to find Rossi in California, or you and the boys will be killed. Rossi already tried once."

"Jesus, David. What do you have on him?"

"Rossi knows about the surveillance video."

"What video? Just start from the beginning."

"The bar video, the footage from the case. Rossi will come after Logan and Will if you don't stop it. Then you'll be next," David warns. "Find the money and the surveillance footage from the bar. Rossi will hide out in California."

"How did you know that?"

"The bomb wasn't meant for Sammy Biggs," David says.

"Who was the target then? You?"

David's eyes roll back in his head, and his body begins to jerk underneath the bedsheet.

"Where the hell is the doctor?"

Julia jumps up from the bed as the door opens and the on-call physician breezes in.

"I think my husband is having a seizure. Do something!"

The doctor moves quickly to David's side and begins to check his vital signs. He then injects a clear substance into David's IV line, which stops the tremors. David closes his eyes and his breathing steadies. The doctor hovers over David for several minutes and then turns around with a calm expression.

"Your husband is fine, except for a slight increase in blood pressure and heart rate, but nothing that I can see as a concern. Your husband is still very weak. I gave him a sedative to calm him down."

"Something is wrong, I know it. Why was he shaking like that?"

"Ms. Gooden, I don't see any cause for alarm right now. David's rise in blood pressure and heart rate is probably related to the excitement at his sudden ability to verbalize for the first time, which set off a temporary physical reaction. From his chart, it looks like his Glasgow Coma Scale score was an eleven, so although nothing is definitive at this point, a good percentage of patients who score in this range are able to make a full recovery. So I wouldn't be too concerned. It's common for coma patients to be alert and awake for only a few minutes at a time at first."

"He was really upset. He was trying to tell me something."

"Another commonality. When patients first come out of a coma, they oftentimes use inappropriate words that don't make sense to anyone else but themselves. Their memories, their thoughts, get jumbled. Imagine everything you've ever experienced in your entire life gets tossed together in a cup and then is thrown out randomly on a table. Whatever your husband said, he may be piecing together disconnected parts of his memory that he thinks fit together."

"David knew exactly what he was saying."

Julia quickly stuffs her overnight bag with the bare essentials she pulls from her closet and dresser. She grabs a tape recorder and her reporter's notebook, and before she puts them in her purse she tears out a single sheet of white paper from the notebook and writes down the phrases and numbers David scribbled down on the hospital pad: *Box twenty-two, three, two, one, thirty*, and then the words *infinity* and *money code* after them.

She pulls out her cell phone and calls Don Brewbaker, who was David's second chair on the Nick Rossi case. He answers on the first ring.

"Julia, great to hear from you. I hope you're calling with good news about David," Brewbaker answers.

"Thank you for asking. David made some major strides today. The doctor isn't promising anything, but we're all hoping he'll make a full recovery soon. Look, the reason I called, and I'm not sure of the legalities of what you can tell me, but I wanted to talk to you about the case David was going to present against Nick Rossi."

"Go ahead and ask, and I'll tell you what I can."

"Great. Were there any issues David was going to bring up about money during the trial?"

"Well, sure. Sammy Biggs was going to testify that Rossi was bringing in a half-million dollars worth of sales a month."

"How about the numbers three, two, one, thirty? Do they have any kind of meaning to you? Or box twenty-two?"

Brewbaker is silent for a moment. "No, not that I can recall. I could check, but David's files were in his briefcase. I'm not sure if those were ever found after the bombing. If they were, the Detroit police or FBI would have them."

"Okay. Sorry to take up your time. One more question, though. How about a money code? Did David ever talk to you about this?"

"Rossi and Biggs used shell companies, mainly the Detroit laundry business that belonged to Rossi's uncle. The laundry company had existing contracts with the MGM Grand and a few other hotels."

"Was the name of one of Rossi's front businesses Infinity?"

"No. That's the first time I heard of it."

"One more question. Did you have surveillance footage of Nick Rossi in a bar that would implicate him?"

"We had plenty of surveillance footage shot throughout the casinos, but the smoking guns were the videos we caught in the hotel rooms of the drugs, bribes, and gambling bets being exchanged for cash. And, of course, there's former mayor Slidell's payoff in the VIP suite of the MGM Grand. But to my knowledge, there wasn't anything significant we captured in the casino bar."

Julia ends the call with Brewbaker, chalking her hunch up to a temporary dead end.

She lays her phone on the dresser next to the box from the hospital holding David's cell phone and his wallet. Julia feels for an instant like the snooping Bianca as she picks up her husband's thick brown wallet and begins to scour through it for any clues. Three credit cards, five twenty-dollar bills, a stack of business cards, and some kind of rectangular stub.

Julia turns the white piece of paper around and instantly recognizes it as an airline-boarding pass. The date is stamped two weeks ago. Julia is about to stuff it back inside the wallet, recalling David's recent trip to Washington, DC, to meet a member of the DEA's office. But her eyes catch the arrival location just as she returns it to the billfold.

LAX. Los Angeles International Airport.

Julia feels her pulse quicken as she realizes that David most likely took the trip to recruit Sammy Biggs and didn't tell her to shield her from the case. Regardless, he lied to her. Just like he had about Brooke Stevens on and her role in the Rossi case. And if David knew that Rossi was going to come after her and their boys, why hadn't he told her before so she could be warned before something happened?

Julia drops the wallet on the desk, feeling a steam of red bruising her cheeks, grabs David's cell phone and scrolls through his recent calls. All are local except for one to the Washington, DC, area code and three calls in the Los Angeles area code. Julia notices fifteen phone calls to the same number over a two-week period, just before she and the boys moved back in with David to their Rochester Hills home. The caller is listed as unknown.

Julia feels like a sleazy voyeur as she begins to go through the entirety of David's text messages, the majority of them banal exchanges with Julia about his schedule and another late night at the office.

Julia's finger continues to scroll down the screen until she hits on messages between David and Brewbaker. One from David reads, "Found the Butcher's location in L.A. Will try and arrange meeting. Easier and safer if I go alone."

Mayor Anderson's name comes up next, and there is an exchange about an upcoming meeting in city hall. Julia is about to ignore texts from an unknown ID, figuring it's spam, but decides to check the messages, just in case. Her eyes freeze on a photo of a woman's naked back, and her round derriere hanging out the sides of a pair of pink lace underwear and the message: "Everything set for California. Get over here now," followed by David's response, "Wrapping up. Be there in fifteen minutes."

"Son of a bitch."

Julia sits down hard on the side of the bed. She grips the phone and stares at the woman's barely clothed backside frozen on the small screen and makes herself keep searching. Six more messages between the woman and David follow, including his praise over similar photos of the woman's perfect body posed from front to back. In every image, the woman has carefully hidden her face from the camera, just like a lawyer, Julia thinks. But not any lawyer. Brooke Stevenson, who obviously joined David on the trip to recruit Sammy Biggs, Julia realizes.

The fuzzy yet still safe line between nagging paranoia and actually knowing about her husband's infidelity now crossed, Julia throws David's phone across the room and begins to weep. The life that she thought she and David could have again, the one she believed as a child she could never attain, slips through her fingers like loose sand. She curses herself for not listening to her internal misgivings about the reconciliation, and for moving back to Rochester to be closer to him, putting their boys at their most vulnerable by believing their parents' reconciliation would be imminent. She suppresses a scream at the realization she ignored the fast and hard rule that cheaters, whether separated from their spouses or not, don't ever redeem themselves.

A dark and vindictive fantasy spools tightly around Julia as she pictures herself tearing to David's bedside where she would raise holy hell and announce to the world that Mr. Ivy League lawyer is nothing more than an adulterous pig, and force him in his weakened state to answer for what he put his family through. Julia holds her face in her hands and knows the fantasy has to stop there. No retribution, at least not now. She stares at her suitcases and realizes that sometimes being the bigger person is all you've got left.

David's warning that Nick Rossi will kill her sons if he isn't apprehended momentarily pushes out her fresh wounds of betrayal. Julia breathes out hard, resolute in her decision to hunt down Rossi, and closes the bag with one fast zip.

"That's the last time, David. No more chances," Julia says.

Logan pops his head inside his mother's room. "Uncle Ray is here."

"Can you please tell him I'll be a minute?" Julia answers. She takes a quick look at herself in the mirror and brushes away a stray tear so Logan won't see.

"I wish you didn't have to go," Logan says.

"I won't be long. I'll be back tomorrow night."

"Why are the police going to be watching our house while you're gone?"

"Just a precaution. An officer will be keeping an eye on all of you for a little while, even after I get back."

"Kind of like a bodyguard? Is someone trying to hurt us?"

"Of course not. The police are just here to make sure everyone is safe."

"What about Dad? Don't you need to stay in case something happens?"

"I promise you, I wouldn't leave if I felt for an instant that your dad was going to get worse. Dr. Whitcomb assured me your father is getting better. Helen is going to take you and Will back to the hospital when you get home from school tomorrow. I'll have my cell phone on the entire time, and you can call me whenever you like."

"Julia, we've got to go to make it to the airport on time," Navarro calls from the hallway.

"Don't worry, Mom. We'll be fine," Logan rallies. "The

police officer will be following us wherever we go. Uncle Ray promised."

Julia makes her final choice, no time to deliberate anymore.

She trails Logan to the living room, where Will sits on top of Navarro's back as her friend pretends to be a wild, bucking horse on all fours.

"You're going to hurt the boy," Helen says.

"I've got a firm hold of his legs," Navarro answers.

"Again!" Will cries out to Navarro, who abruptly stops the game and pulls Will off his back as he picks up a shift in Julia.

"Everything okay?" he asks.

"I've just got a lot on my mind. Logan, can you help Uncle Ray load up the car?"

When the boys are out of earshot, Helen, who stirs a pot of potato and leek soup on the stove with angry strokes, unloads.

"You go to California and get that son of a bitch who hurt your husband," Helen says. "I don't understand why we have the police here, though."

"David has something on Nick Rossi. I don't know what it is, but David said Rossi would come after the kids and me if I didn't find him. David's doctor thought David was just confused when he told me, but I think David meant it. You need to be extremely careful while I'm gone. That means no going anywhere without telling the officer out front. He'll be tailing you and the kids wherever you go. Are you sure you're okay with my leaving? It's not too late for me to cancel the trip."

"Of course. I won't let anything happen to the children. You have my word."

Navarro returns through the front door with the boys and a

young, barrel-chested police officer who looks like he spends all his waking hours in the gym when he's not on duty.

"Helen, this is Officer John Rodriguez," Navarro says. "He'll be on the first shift. If you have to leave the house for any reason with the boys, he'll be right behind you."

"Officer Rodriguez, you call me immediately if anything happens," Julia says. "And I mean anything."

CHAPTER 17

Julia tries to get comfortable on the second leg of the flight from Chicago to LAX and stares out the window as the plane taxis down the runway for takeoff, Julia's most anxious part of the flight. The wheels go up and the engine roars to life in the background, and Julia clutches the sides of her seat as hard as she can. She keeps her eyes closed and tries to ward off images of the plane doing cartwheels across the sky before it takes a suicide nosedive and explodes into a giant fireball on impact with the ground. Her visions of imminent death are suddenly replaced by David's warning and the provocative photographs she found on his phone.

"Gooden, you're okay," Navarro says, trying to downplay his amusement over her obvious phobia. "I forgot you aren't a flyer. Are you all right?"

"I've got some personal issues going on right now."

"Do you want to talk about it?"

"No," she answers, and stares vacantly at the quickly disappearing Chicago skyline below. "Did Russell meet with David yet?"

"Russell tried to interview David this morning, but he was still pretty out of it. He'll swing by the hospital again this afternoon."

"I've been thinking about what David said. If Rossi didn't plant the bomb to take out Sammy Biggs, then who was the intended target?" Julia asks.

"My guess would be David," Navarro answers.

"David uncovered something that got him in trouble, something that Rossi had to stifle at all costs, including killing my family."

"I have twenty-four-hour surveillance on your sons and Helen. Nothing will happen to them while we're gone."

"I wouldn't be here if I thought otherwise. We need to find the money and the video recording David told me about."

The pilot turns off the FASTEN YOUR SEAT BELT sign and Navarro gets up, a big man at six-foot-three and 220 pounds, freeing himself from his relatively small seat, and stretches his muscular frame to get the kinks out from the confines of his seat. A stewardess pushes a drink cart in their direction and gives Navarro an extra-special smile.

"Anything to drink?" she asks, sounding about as friendly as a stewardess can get without openly soliciting a passenger.

"I'll take a Heineken and so will my girlfriend," Navarro answers.

The female flight attendant realizes she has no chance and hands the two cans of beer over without another play. Navarro hands her fifteen dollars and tells her to keep the change.

"Girlfriend?" Julia asks.

"Just trying to call off the dogs, so to speak," Navarro answers. "And considering the fact you almost hyperventilated during the past two takeoffs and the last landing, I think if anyone ever needed an alcoholic beverage right now, that person would be you."

"You started drinking again? I thought you quit for good," Julia says, recalling the times when she had been roused from her sleep by the sound of Navarro vomiting outside the apartment they once shared after another late night of his binge drinking. Navarro had hit the bottle hard after Julia rejected his marriage proposal more than a decade earlier. Julia ultimately left the relationship as painful childhood memories of her mother, a raging alcoholic, cemented her decision. Navarro sobered up in an attempt to win Julia back, but by then Julia had moved on with David.

"Just a beer or two once in a while. I'm not falling back to the sins of my youth, Mom. I promise."

Julia takes a long sip of the beer and feels the warmth of the alcohol spread nicely through her body.

"Something else is bothering you. Something more than the bombing and David being in the hospital. Like that wasn't enough, but I can tell," Navarro says.

"It's nothing."

"None of this was your fault," Navarro says. "I know you. You find a way to blame yourself for everything, like a black cloud is always hanging over you, and you deserve every bad thing that comes your way. But you don't. You can't blame yourself for what happened to David like you did with your brother. You couldn't have saved David in the courthouse. And you were only seven when your brother disappeared. Can I ask you something I've always wondered about?"

"If it's about David, no."

"Well, not exactly. You told me once that you kept your maiden name, Gooden, to be consistent with your byline and professional career instead of taking David's last name of Tanner when you two got married. I always thought, though, that the real reason you kept going by Gooden was in case Ben was still out there looking for you."

"You're the only person who's ever put that together. You know me very well. And by the way, I'm not the only one who blames themselves for things that happened in the past," Julia says.

Julia doesn't take it any further. She knows Navarro's memory of seeing his mother choked to death by his abusive father when he was just eleven still weighs him down like a thorny, lifelong anchor and is ultimately the reason why he became a cop.

"Who's your police friend in L.A.?" Julia asks.

"Felix Espinosa. I trust him. He reached out to me when Rossi began to set up shop on the West Coast."

The pilot's voice announces that they are about to go through a patch of turbulence, and the FASTEN YOUR SEAT BELT sign chimes a reminder.

Julia slams back the rest of her beer for courage and closes her eyes, seeing the words David wrote in the hospital room flash as if they were backlit by exploding camera bulbs before her eyes: *Box twenty-two. Three. Two. One. Thirty. Infinity.* Julia then sees a crystal-clear image of David, fully coherent and dressed in his blue business suit but trapped inside his own broken body as he desperately tries to tell her something. She starts to drift off to sleep, the effects of the alcohol and her lack of rest over the last forty-eight hours finally kicking in, and sees a vision of herself as she slips into the subconscious. In her dream, Julia turns her back on David, still in the blue suit, but this time he's covered in the sticky cocoon of a spider web. Julia runs quickly away from him and to the safety of her brother's voice.

"This way, Julia!"

The hot summer sun beats down on Julia as she chases Ben, running along the town of Sparrow's boardwalk. She can hear the sound of the carousel music from the seaside amusement park up ahead. Julia reaches out to try to touch Ben, but her hand slips through him as if he is nothing but fog and dim yellow light. Julia feels the familiar and profound sense of wanting and loss move through her again as she realizes that what she sees is nothing more than a black-and-white shadow, like a quickly moving image from an old movie projected on a screen.

"Ben, wait!" Julia calls, and tries to run faster. She feels the thump of her heart keep rhythm with her bare feet, which slap against the boardwalk's weathered wood, long distressed from the elements and wear.

Ben, now bathed only in pale silhouette, turns around to face his little sister as the boardwalk disappears. Julia stops running and keeps her eyes focused on her big brother, who now stands far away from her on the edge of a vast, barren field.

"Here's the thing, Julia. You're not looking at the situation clearly, kid," Ben says. "Look at each piece of the puzzle without emotion. Then you'll be able to find your answer. But be smart, little sister. No one is who they seem to be."

A hum of a thousand wings beating as one thumps above Julia's head. She looks up to see a single ebony spot tucked up in the sky's highest peak. The tiny speck quickly descends and grows to a mobile black mass that gets bigger as it approaches.

"I know what you are now," Julia cries.

She feels an odd sense of relief as she watches a massive storm of blackbirds swoop down and circle Ben in a protective cylinder until the sheer force of their wings lifts him up and carries him away.

"Wait, Ben!" Julia calls out for her brother.

But it's too late. He's already gone.

* * *

"Julia, you all right?" Navarro asks.

Julia sits up quickly in her seat and feels a light film of sweat lace across her chest and the back of her neck. She takes a deep breath as the airplane's wheels land on the dark runway of LAX.

"I'm fine. Just a strange dream."

CHAPTER 18

Nick Rossi uses the sharp blade from his folding knife to clean his fingernails while he sits with his feet propped up on a wicker table outside his Santa Barbara mountain hideaway. The warm spring breeze makes him feel lighter and like a human being again after his recent lockup in his hometown of Detroit, and he spits on the ground in disgust over the memory.

Enzo Costas, a short, squat man, walks out to the patio armed with two Coronas.

"You bringing me good news this time?" Rossi asks.

Costas sucks the lime between his teeth before he takes a drink and shoves the spent slice of fruit deep into the bottle's neck.

"Some good, some bad. Bartello was killed just the way you wanted."

"I should have killed his family, too."

"That can still be arranged. My source at the Detroit police station tells me the sniper Bartello hired was brought in for questioning, and he confessed to everything."

Rossi digs the blade of the folding knife deeper into the edge of his thumbnail until it draws blood. "Get Tarburton on the phone for me. I need to be sure he did his job and I won't be retried on the drug, gambling, and bribery charges. This sniper is a whole other issue. Is the dumb-ass incarcerated?"

"Yes, at Wayne County Jail."

"Then make sure he's killed. By tomorrow. Do we still have people inside there?"

Costas's smile is proud and lethal. "Of course. I'll make a call. I've promoted Duncan Broudette to take over Bartello's position. He's done a pretty good job for us in Flint."

"Stupid-ass will probably think a move from Flint to Detroit is like getting transferred to Hawaii. Last couple of years, Detroit's been nothing but bad luck to me. I used to love that city. I thought it was just like me, you know. An underdog. When I was a kid, I'd sit out on the roof of my uncle's house at night after everyone went to sleep and I'd look out at Detroit for hours. I swear, I thought I could see my name written in lights across the skyline. I told myself back then, one day I'd own that city. But I don't want it anymore. Detroit's a good place for Isabella, though, don't you think? She screwed up her job with the lawyer and that almost cost me everything."

"And her punishment was deserved," Costas answers as his tongue darts to either side of his mouth. He pulls a gold necklace out from under his shirt. A medallion of the Virgin Mary hangs in the center of the chain, and Costas brings it to his lips and gives it a respectful and reverent kiss.

"She messes up again, I'll kill her myself. And what about the lawyer?" Rossi asks.

"Soon, boss. I promise. The police at the hospital will thin out in a few days and we'll be able to get to him without any trace coming back to you."

"Soon isn't good enough."

"You have my word he'll be taken care of. There's one more piece of news. My source in the Detroit PD tells me an officer, Ray Navarro, is flying into LAX this afternoon to meet a local cop. I hear Navarro is coming to California to look for you."

"Get some guys down to the airport and have them follow the Detroit cop. I know that guy. He was part of that sting that busted me, and he's obviously still gunning for me now."

"You want me to have him killed?" Costas asks.

"No. Not yet anyway. I don't need any more trouble following me from Detroit, especially with this bomb investigation still going on, so tell them to kill the cop only if he gets too close."

"You got it. One other thing. I checked the airlines. Navarro is being accompanied by another passenger."

"Another cop?" Rossi asks.

"No, Julia Gooden, the lawyer's wife."

Nick Rossi tilts back his head and laughs.

"The prosecutor's wife," Rossi says. "Classic."

CHAPTER 19

Julia and Navarro bypass the baggage claim area since they only brought carry-ons and search for their pickup, Felix Espinosa. Julia spots a young man, probably early twenties, wearing a pair of dark khaki pants and an olive green shirt, staring directly at her. She trained herself long ago not to make eye contact with a passerby in a strange place, but his gaze feels uncomfortable and almost intimidating, and Julia reciprocates with a straight-on stare right back at the man, who looks away and busies himself with a call on his cell phone.

"That guy was looking at me," Julia tells Navarro.

"News flash. Plenty of people look at you. Just stick close, though. I wouldn't be surprised if Nick Rossi heard about our meetup with Felix."

LAX is a huge, always-moving airport, and Julia quickly scans the hundreds of faces in the fast-passing crowd for anyone who resembles a police officer. She rules out an older lady in a wheelchair, a man in an expensive suit who looks like a banker, and a glamorous woman wearing skintight jeans and zebra-print high heels whom Julia is certain she recognizes from an obnoxious reality TV show.

Navarro steers Julia through the crowd, always the protector with his hand on her elbow, until he reaches a short man, probably in his late forties, heavyset with salt-and-pepper hair and a thin, dark mustache. Navarro shakes the man's hand, and the two give each other a knowing nod of their shared history as a greeting.

"Your flight was good?" Felix asks.

"It was fine. Felix, this is my friend Julia Gooden. Her husband is Detroit Assistant District Attorney David Tanner."

Felix studies Julia for a moment, and Julia realizes Navarro probably didn't mention she would be tagging along.

"I've been watching the news and heard your husband was injured in the bombing. I hope he's doing okay. But just so we're all straight with each other, why are you here exactly?"

"I'm a journalist. I was covering the Rossi case, but I'm not here to write a story."

Felix shoots Navarro an annoyed look, clearly unhappy with his colleague's decision to bring a reporter along.

"Julia is the best journalist I know. We go way back, and I trust her."

Julia feels awkward, knowing she is being judged, and trails the two men, settling for an unfamiliar place of subservience, until they reach Felix's car. Navarro offers her the front seat, but she declines.

"I made reservations at a hotel by the Santa Ynez Mountains, where we believe Rossi is holed up. I didn't know there was going to be two of you, so I reserved only one room."

"Don't worry about it. We'll figure it out when we get to the hotel," Navarro answers. "I thought Rossi's West Coast operation was in L.A."

"L.A. and Long Beach. That way he can have direct access to the ports. Rossi's got some compound, like his own personal version of a safe house. But we haven't been able to pinpoint the exact location."

"I know where it is," Julia says.

Felix's eyes burn dark into Julia from the rearview mirror. "I've been working this case for years since Rossi first set up shop out here. I don't even know where Rossi's place is. But you do?"

"I got it from someone who's been there before. Listen, Mr. Espinosa, you obviously don't like the fact that I'm here. But I have valuable information I can share, specifically Rossi's likely location. I'm only here to make sure Rossi is arrested for the bombing back in Detroit."

A few seconds of silence fill the car until Felix speaks up. "My partner and I helped a journalist once. Big mistake. We knew what off the record meant, but the reporter apparently didn't. Serial rapist case. We were about to make an arrest, but the reporter stuck a bunch of facts in the story we told her to hold off on. The rapist got wind of it, figured we were looking at him, and took off. The guy moved up to Oregon. The Portland cops caught up to him six months later, but he'd already raped two women and killed one of them. The woman he killed was a kindergarten teacher."

"Julia would never burn a source. Like she said, she's not here to write a story. She wants Rossi to pay for what he did," Navarro says.

"You've got my word," Julia says.

"In all due respect, I don't know you, so your word doesn't hold any water with me. But if Navarro vouches for you, I'm okay with you being here to give us information. As long as you understand, when it's time to bust Rossi, you're out of sight. I don't want to play babysitter, and I don't want you to get hurt."

"I understand," Julia answers.

Navarro and Felix talk shop as they take 101 North toward Santa Barbara and the city slips away.

"I've been thinking about the sniper and the bomb that killed the Butcher," Felix says. "The two things seem to cancel each other out. Rossi wouldn't order both attacks to kill just one man."

"Meter, the guy who was hired to take out the Butcher, claims he was in position in an abandoned building across from the courthouse when the bomb went off," Navarro says.

"He may be lying, or if he is telling the truth, then who would benefit from the bombing?" Felix asks.

"Rossi," Julia quickly interjects. "I know he did it."

"But he already had the sniper in place to kill his snitch, Sammy Biggs."

"Then maybe it was someone else working independently, trying to protect his boss," Navarro says.

"Possibly, but I'd think the person would know about the sniper. Have you looked at any of Rossi's enemies?" Felix suggests. "They could've been trying to take out Rossi with the bomb."

"That was one of the first theories we kicked around, but Rossi's holding cell was on the other side of the building. The explosive was strong but not strong enough to take out the entire courthouse," Navarro says. "Julia's husband told her Rossi was the bomber. And he indicated that Sammy Biggs may not have been the target."

"Then who was?" Felix asks.

"That's the million-dollar question," Navarro answers.

Felix takes a rural road just north of Santa Barbara, and the lush Santa Ynez Mountains make their pristine appearance on the horizon.

Julia stares through the scenery and turns the pieces of the bombing case over in her head until she sees a black SUV with dark-tinted windows in the rearview mirror, speeding toward their vehicle. She feels the first fingers of trepidation circle around her as Navarro notices the van and pulls out his gun.

"We may have company," Navarro says. "Get down, Julia. On the floor. Now."

Julia spins around in her seat to look at the SUV that is now directly behind them, just inches away from their bumper. Julia tries to peer inside to see the SUV's occupants, but the windows are nearly black.

"Hold on," Felix says, and slams his foot on the gas, but the SUV follows and then begins to pull into the passing lane, where it holds pace with Felix's car for a few seconds until it speeds up and shoots down the road until it's out of sight.

"Rossi's men?" Navarro asks.

"Yeah. Most likely watchdogs for the boss," Felix answers. "They're giving us a warning."

"They must have been blowing a hundred miles plus when they passed us. Did you get a plate?" Navarro asks.

"Those guys didn't want to be tracked. There wasn't one," Felix says.

Felix pulls into the hotel that is nestled along the base of the Santa Ynez Mountains. Although it is early evening, Julia can still see the beauty of the original Indian and later Spanish Mission influences that have been kept intact or restored. Rust-colored cobblestones dot a tidy square in the center of Main Street, and well-kept buildings in shades of pastels and rich browns line the streets like proud elder statesmen.

"It's getting late. You two check in and I'll swing by the sheriff's to see if they got any more leads on Rossi. Good guys up this way, but the biggest crimes they bust around here are speeders. So your info on Rossi's possible locale will be a big plus, Julia."

"I'll go with you," Navarro says.

"Don't waste your time. The local sheriffs aren't convinced Rossi's even up here, and I doubt they've dedicated any manpower to it. They think it's an L.A. problem. We'll head out first thing in the morning to try to confront Rossi. How about we meet up later? I hear they've got a top-notch restaurant in the hotel."

Navarro agrees and grabs the bags out of the trunk. He and Julia then thread through the lobby of the boutique hotel, its dark wood and contrasting bright yellow walls warm and inviting after the confines of the long flight and car ride.

The man behind the desk gives the pair a smile. Navarro pulls out his credit card, and the hotel employee hands him two keycards to the same room.

"Wait a minute. Don't they have another room?" Julia asks.

"I'm sorry," the man answers. "The hotel is completely booked. If something changes, I'll let you know. Breakfast is served in the dining room from 6 a.m. until 10 a.m., and I have a listing of the attractions in the area, if you want to go sightseeing."

"We won't be staying long," Julia says. "The hotel dining room, is it formal?"

"Yes, it's five-star. Authentic Mexican cuisine. Although jackets are not required, they are preferred."

"I don't think I brought anything appropriate to wear," Julia says.

"We have a beautiful women's shop right around the corner," the man says. "It will still be open for the next half hour. I'm sure you'll be able to find something to your liking."

"Thank you. What's the room number, Navarro?"

"Two-thirty-six. I'll take your bag and meet you up there."

"And can you send up a rollaway?" Julia asks. "One bed isn't going to cut it."

"Of course. My name is Luis. Please let me know if there is anything I can do for you during your stay."

Julia turns the corner, passes a green parrot in a cage that whistles at her when she goes by, and reaches the women's boutique. She hurries through the racks, shopping never a sport she enjoyed, and picks out a simple black dress that will fit loosely on her frame.

"That's a nice choice, but probably for someone a bit older," a female salesclerk calls from the checkout counter. The salesclerk is an attractive woman, somewhere in her midfifties, and wears a bright red pantsuit that contrasts beautifully with her silky black hair. "You are what, a size two?"

"Four or six is better."

"Ah, you don't like to show your figure. You're a runner, I bet, from your physique."

"I am, or was at least until the last few days. There's a place I'd like to run to tomorrow. I understand the mountains are very beautiful around here."

"They are very beautiful, but it's always good to go hiking or running with a partner. With the wildlife, you'll never know what you'll find up there. Now, here's the dress I was thinking for you. It will match your eyes."

The salesclerk hands Julia a bright blue dress that Julia can tell is going to be body hugging. "This really isn't my style."

"You obviously work hard on your figure with your running, so why don't you show it off? Try the dress on, and if you like it I'll give you a good deal."

"That's not why I run," Julia answers, but takes the blue dress along with the black one into the changing room.

The salesclerk hands her a pair of black high-heeled sandals from underneath the curtain.

Julia hurriedly puts on the black dress, gives herself a brief assessment in the full-length mirror, and is satisfied with its simplicity.

"Let me see, dear," the salesclerk calls out from the other side, still lurking.

Julia realizes the clerk won't be dismissed easily and walks out from behind the curtain to a bad review. "Hmmm. No. That dress swallows you. Go try on the blue one. You'll see."

"I'm not going to get out of this store without trying it on first, am I?"

"You are most observant," the salesclerk answers.

Julia pulls the blue dress over her head. The dress, while showing off her figure, isn't as body hugging as she thought. She adjusts the neck, which scoops down low in both the front and the back, and tugs at the hem of the skirt, which ends two inches above her knees. On the short side, but not too short.

"It's pretty, but I'm not sure."

"Come on out and let me see."

Julia leaves the dressing room, feeling self-conscious, but is greeted with rave reviews this time.

"You look stunning. If that dress was made for anyone, it was made for you," the salesclerk answers. "Tell you what. I'll sell you the dress and the shoes for a hundred and fifty dollars."

"Oh, no, that's much more than I wanted to spend."

"One hundred, and I'll include the blue topaz earrings I saw you looking at when you came in. I was about to put them on sale tomorrow, so you're lucky."

Julia hesitates but then agrees, feeling slightly foolish over the purchase as she takes the stairs up to her room on the second story.

Navarro lets her in the room, which is spacious with a

queen-sized bed and chaise lounge underneath a white curtain that dances along to the tune of a light breeze wafting through the open window.

"Did you find something?" Navarro asks while toweling his damp, dark hair dry from the shower. Navarro is already dressed for dinner in a fitted, button-down blue-and-white-striped shirt and dark blue dress pants. "Lucky I brought a jacket along, or I don't think they'd let me in the restaurant."

"I picked up a dress in the shop. Any chance I have time to take a run before dinner?"

Navarro sits down on the edge of the bed and fastens the buttons on his shirtsleeves. "Not a chance. Not tomorrow either, even if I'm with you. The last thing I need is for you running around by yourself out here. Rossi's guys are obviously on the lookout for us. We have dinner tonight and you stay put tomorrow. If we can find Rossi and bring him in for questioning, you can be there. That was the deal. But no freelancing on your free time, it's too dangerous."

"I understand," Julia lies.

"Felix called while you were downstairs. I'm going to meet him at the bar to talk strategy for tomorrow. Does it still take you under half an hour to get dressed?"

"I've got two kids now. I can beat that record."

"I swear, Gooden, you're more like a guy than a chick sometimes. Yeah, get dressed and we should still be at the bar. Meet us there and then we'll all go over to the dining room."

Julia takes a fast shower, forcing herself to turn off the nearly scalding hot water that feels soothing on her tired skin, and quickly dries her hair. With no time or rarely an interest in styling her hair, she lets her dark curls hang loose below her shoulders and puts on the newly purchased dress. She stares at her reflection looking back at her and feels suddenly ashamed and guilty, all dressed up for dinner some two thousand miles away when her sons are alone with neither parent there, only the housekeeper. She removes the necklace David gave her, forgetting it was still around her neck after the discovery of his infidelity, and wonders if he cheated because of something she did, something she wasn't that he sought in someone else. She shakes off the insecurities and guilt, knowing David is the one who made the final mistake in their marriage. She slips on the new shoes and the topaz earrings, takes a deep breath, and leaves for the bar.

Julia pauses before she opens the door to the stairwell leading to the lobby, feeling awkward in the outfit and out of her element in her new surroundings, but then she remembers what Margie once told her. "If you find yourself in a situation where you don't feel confident, be the only person in the room who knows that."

Julia pushes through the door and makes her way to the bar, visualizing Nick Rossi's face when he's finally arrested again. She spots Navarro and Felix sitting on two high stools next to a table in the corner. Navarro is deep in discussion with Felix, the two huddled and leaning over the table in what appears to be a high-charged conversation. Navarro sees Julia, his eyes stay on her as she approaches, and his end of the conversation ceases as she makes her way toward him.

Navarro jumps up from his stool to offer Julia his chair.

"Please, let me get you a drink," Felix says, and beckons a waitress over. "We're drinking beer, but I think for the lady, a glass of wine?"

"Perfect," Julia answers. "Something white, on the dry side."

"She'd like a glass of Sauvignon Blanc," Navarro says.

"You have a good memory," Julia says.

"And that's one hell of a dress."

Julia is glad the bar is dark as she blushes over the compliment.

"Please bring our drinks into the dining room," Felix asks the waitress.

The three follow the waitress into the restaurant, lit mostly by candlelight from a vast array of chandeliers strategically placed throughout the restaurant, and take a seat at a table in the back of the room at their request. Felix and Navarro take seats facing the entrance—a force of habit—and Julia sits across from them, not worried about seeming subservient at this point.

The waitress puts the drinks on the table, and Julia lifts her glass to her lips, still feeling the weight of Navarro's stare.

The waitress approaches the table, and Felix takes the lead. "If this works for my colleagues, we'll take the chef's nightly special, which I'm told is always excellent. The chef is originally from Los Angeles, I believe."

The waitress takes pride in Felix's knowledge. "Yes, he was a former sous chef at Spago. Our pastry chef also worked there."

"The special sounds good, right, Julia?" Navarro asks.

"Sure."

Felix settles back in the booth and takes in his surroundings, looking somewhat relaxed.

"I'd like to retire out here. Five more years. It's all open space, and you're not crammed in like L.A. I've been thinking about starting a new career once I pull the pin."

"Security?" Navarro asks.

"No. Too predictable. I've always wanted to teach. I wanted to be an English teacher when I was in high school, but things didn't work out that way. I've been looking at online courses I can take to earn my teaching degree by the time I'm out of the LAPD."

"You like books?" Julia asks.

"Usually more than people," Felix answers, and raises his beer bottle to toast. "This is the calm before the storm. Let's take a minute and enjoy it."

"You've piqued my curiosity as a journalist. You said you wanted to be an English teacher. What made you decide to become a cop instead? " Julia asks.

"I grew up in East L.A. My dad drove a bus, and my mom worked in the cafeteria at the middle school. They worked hard and made sure my little brother and I stayed out of the gang life. The White Fence was everywhere. They owned my neighborhood. When I was a teenager, there was a block party on my street. The local city councilman at the time wanted to strengthen the community, so it was his idea to get people together. It was summer, the Fourth of July, and I remember they had this big mariachi band playing. My little brother, Carlo, was on top of my father's shoulders when both of them were shot. They were in the cross fire of two stupid rival gangbangers, both trying to be harder than the other one."

"I'm so sorry," Julia says.

The pain of the memory reveals itself in Felix's eyes for just an instant and then it's gone. "Julia, you have the address of Nick Rossi's compound?" Felix asks.

"Yes. I gave it to Navarro. There are two roads that lead there on either side of the mountain and a separate path that runs parallel to the main road, which I understand can be accessed with an off-terrain vehicle."

The waitress returns with their food, served in bright yellow bowls. "Pasta al Mojo de Ajo con Camarones, Chipotle y Queso Anejo, the chef's specialty this evening," the waitress says.

"Linguine with seared shrimp, chipotle and queso anejo," Navarro, whose first language was Spanish, based on the roots of his Spanish father and Mexican mother, whispers to Julia.

"Yes, it looks delicious," Julia says, and realizes the last thing she ate was a bag of pretzels on the plane some three hours before.

"Rossi's compound will likely be guarded," Felix says. "Enzo Costas has been running Rossi's West Coast operation while he's been in jail. Costas is dangerous and crazy, which is a deadly combination. The guy's a religious zealot, and he believes everything he does is righteous and ordained by God. There used to be a convent just on the outskirts of the mountains here. One of the sheriffs told me there was a young woman who was circumcised and then brutally raped and murdered while she walked alone along one of the trails there about a year ago. No one was ever arrested, but I'd bet money Costas did it. He's got some heinous crimes on his record dating back to when he was in juvie."

Julia suddenly loses her appetite.

"It's late. We have a big day tomorrow," Felix says as he looks up at the burning candles on the chandelier above them as though hypnotized by their light. " 'All is visible and all elusive, all is near and can't be touched.' "

"That's beautiful. Did you write that?" Julia asks.

The spell broken, Felix looks back at his guests and laughs. "No, not me. I was quoting the poet Octavio Paz. Like I told you, I've always liked words and books. I can admire writing and recite it, but I can't create it. You're the only true writer in our group this evening."

Felix stands up and reaches his hand out for Navarro to shake. "I'll pick you up in the hotel lobby at seven tomorrow morning, Ray."

Julia gives Felix a kiss on the cheek. "Dinner was lovely. Thank you very much. I'm sorry that we got off on the wrong foot earlier today."

"Some of the best friendships start out that way."

Felix heads up to his room, and Julia follows Navarro to the front desk as he checks to see if another room has become available. Then Julia steals out to the patio, the night air feeling warm and luxurious, and she is drawn to a three-tiered, slowly trickling fountain. She pulls out a coin from her purse and tosses it into the water, watching it land against tiny silver and blue tiles that sparkle against the strands of white lights that wind around the base of a palm tree above them. She makes a silent and ardent wish that she will always be able to protect her boys, and right now, especially from Rossi.

"If you were making a wish that the hotel had an extra room tonight, you're out of luck."

"That wasn't my wish, but that's too bad."

"I'll take the rollaway," Navarro says.

"As if there was ever any question."

The two walk in silence, the worries of the next day and the three-hour time difference starting to catch up to them.

Inside the room, Julia moves to the window, still open from earlier. She closes her eyes, the night air feeling exotic and wonderful, and realizes she can't lose her edge. She shuts the window quickly and catches a reflection of Navarro in the room's full-length mirror. He leans against the dresser and stares at Julia in the blue dress, unaware she has caught him checking her out when her back is turned.

She spins around quickly, and Navarro plays it cool.

"As I said, you can take the bed," he says, and begins to unpack his bag.

"I'm uncomfortable with this setup," Julia answers.

"It's not like I planned it," Navarro says.

He unbuttons his shirtsleeves and heads into the bathroom. Julia glances at Navarro through the open door as he removes his shirt. Something deep and primal goes off inside

Julia, and she quickly casts her eyes to the floor, feeling surprised over her unexpected reaction. She realizes how easy it would be to come on to Navarro and convince herself she earned a pass card in light of David's deceit. But deep down, she knows revenge is a fleeting satisfaction and not worth ruining a friendship over.

Navarro emerges from the bathroom wearing a Detroit Police Department T-shirt.

"Come on, Julia. I'm not some kind of beast, you know. What do you think is going to happen? I'm going to try and come on to you? You don't know me at all then, and I figured out of all the people in the world, you still did."

"I'm sorry. Sometimes I think you're looking at me a certain way, and it makes me feel strange. I realize there's a good chance I'm probably wrong and I'm sounding like a complete idiot right now."

Navarro sits down on the edge of the rollaway bed and turns in the opposite direction of Julia, not wanting to face her. "Well, I do look at you that way, probably more than sometimes, and I guess I'm the one who should be sorry. You're a beautiful woman. But it's more than that. You're the one who left me, and I never got over it. But that's my issue, not yours. The day you walked out, I told you if you ever wanted me back you'd have to be the one to tell me you were ready. At first, I hoped to God every day you were going to change your mind, but you didn't. You found someone else, and you created a beautiful life for yourself. So I walked to the sidelines and that was okay, because what I want for you most in the world is for you to be happy, even if it isn't with me. So if you want me to stop feeling, I can't, but don't think I'm going to make a pass at you just because we're alone in a hotel room, because I'm not that guy."

Julia escapes into the bathroom and closes the door, feeling stupid and wishing she and Navarro could continue the dance without her knowing the truth. Julia stares at herself in the mirror, feeling cheap in her blue dress and dirty about the way she felt when she saw Navarro changing his shirt.

Navarro raps on the bathroom door.

"I bet you want these," he says, and hands Julia a pair of her sweatpants and a baggy T-shirt from her bag. "We're okay, right?"

"Yes, of course," Julia lies.

CHAPTER 20

Julia pretends to still be asleep as Navarro gets dressed to meet Felix in the lobby. She lies motionless in bed and watches Navarro out of the corner of her eye as he writes a note and leaves it on the dresser. He stands over her for a few seconds and then grabs his wallet and gun and pulls a light suit coat on over his shoulders. Julia waits until she hears the hotel room door close and then stays in bed an extra minute to be sure he is gone. When she is certain, Julia gets up and peeks from behind the window curtain to watch Navarro walk toward Felix's van parked in the valet area of the hotel.

The van drives away, and Julia quickly dresses in her running shorts and top. The note Navarro left catches Julia's eye, and she turns the paper over.

Dear Julia,
I'm sorry about last night. Please know your friend-ship means the world to me and is more important than anything else. I know you well enough that you aren't going to want to sit around in the hotel all day, but as

your friend and as someone who cares about you, I'm asking you to stay put until we bring Rossi in for questioning. In other words, don't do anything stupid.
    Navarro.

Julia crumples up the paper, tosses it in the wastebasket, and pulls out her cell phone to call Helen.

"Did you catch the man who hurt your David?" Helen answers, cutting to the chase sans the need for a hello.

"Not yet. Are Logan and Will okay?"

"Yes. A policeman stayed up all night in the living room and another was in a car parked outside the house. Logan just got on the school bus."

"Navarro arranged a police tail, and another plainclothes officer will be outside Logan's classroom. I'd still prefer if Logan were at home."

"All this police protection, we're fine."

"Can you put Will on the phone? You can just put it on speaker."

Julia hears thirty seconds of fumbling and Helen probably swearing in Polish until she likely gives up trying to figure out which button to push and hands the phone to Will.

"Hi, Mamma," Will says in his high-pitched, little-boy voice.

Julia feels a painful tug in her heart and wishes she were back home keeping a constant eye on both her children instead of about to embark on a lone mission to try to bring down the man threatening them, but she realizes what she needs to do to keep them safe long term.

"Hello, beautiful boy. I'll be home tomorrow. Just one more night, I promise. Listen to Helen while I'm gone. Mamma loves you."

Julia says good-bye and shifts from Mamma mode to investigative reporter. She reaches inside her suitcase and extracts her reporter's notebook, which has the location of Rossi's compound—not the address, since there isn't one, but a series of coordinates and distances between landmarks that Tyce Jones gave her. Julia looks at the strange chase of directions in front of her and realizes Rossi took great measures to stay hidden.

Julia estimates the distance from the hotel up the mountainside to his location is around twelve miles, not a measure that daunts her. She folds the directions into her waist pack, and puts in a bottle of water followed by her phone and driver's license. She grabs the folding knife from her luggage, fits it in her pack, and then zips it shut.

Julia stretches before she embarks on her journey, thinking herself not foolish but driven. Julia flashes to the little boy, Michael Cole, and his mother, whom she met in the hospital after he died, and the last thing she asked of her:

Make sure you kill that bastard when you find him.

Julia wishes Navarro had left one of his guns behind. She has never physically harmed anyone in her life, but the idea of hurting Rossi for what he did gives her a rush that feels hot and thrilling. The seductive pull of revenge moves through her like an opiate, and she doesn't want it to stop. Before she succumbs to it completely, a decades-old memory takes its place, the one of Ben wiping away a gush of fresh blood from his nose after he got beat up by a pack of older kids who taunted him and Julia about their stringy-haired, alcoholic mother, who had passed out in front of their trailer again.

("Hold your head high and just keep walking. We'll fight the bullies, but not with our fists. I'm going to go tell their parents what they did to me. Then they'll really get it. Use your smarts, Julia, and only punch back when you've got no other choice.")

Julia waits for a moment until she is clear-headed again

and peers out cautiously at the hotel entrance from behind the curtain. Across the street is a dark sedan with a single driver who has been waiting there since Julia first looked out the window some thirty minutes earlier. She connects her pack around her waist and closes the hotel room door behind her. In the hallway, a chambermaid pushes her cart in the opposite direction. Julia follows the woman to a back stairway with a posted sign that reads HOTEL EMPLOYEES ONLY, and ducks in behind her. The woman turns around at the sound of approaching footsteps, and Julia throws up her hands as if indicating she is lost and hurries down the internal corridor until she reaches a loading dock in the rear of the building. She jumps down and starts sprinting in the opposite direction of the busy center of town and away from any roads and Rossi's lookouts.

Julia arrives at the place Tyce told her about. She turns around to find her first marker, the Santa Maria Temple directly to the south, as if she could reach her arm out and touch the silver cross that sits atop its white steeple now far in the distance. She turns in the opposite direction to find the path once used by ranchers and farmers some fifty years ago as they brought their livestock down the mountain to sell. The path is barely visible, long overgrown by low-lying shrub bush, but Julia can find what is left of it and the footpath that will run parallel to the road that leads to Rossi's compound. Julia starts off, the rough brush slapping against her bare legs, and she can hear what sounds like a truck heaving its way up the grade on the road next to her, but she remains protected by a thick shroud of jagged rock and brush that lines the path and keeps her out of view from passing motorists. She feels comfort in knowing that Navarro and Felix will take the back route to the compound along an old road that was closed off years ago on the other side of the mountain.

Julia runs farther along the path into the palm trees, and plants seem to double in size. She looks up to the sun, now in a northeast position, and heads in its direction. She sees a clearing up ahead where her second marker should be and sprints faster up the mountainside. To her left, she spots a fast and fluid movement in the brush. She turns toward the flash of motion, refusing to stop, and spots a mountain lion leaping from a rock covered with an intricate map of clinging green moss and gray mold. The animal lunges with deadly grace in the opposite direction. Julia pounds forward, just catching the mountain lion snatching the neck of a wild hare before it disappears with its breakfast into the trees.

Julia pats the front of her waist pack, feels the hardness of her knife for reassurance, and continues on. She reaches the clearing and the second marker, the former convent, abandoned now for at least twenty years. The probably once magnificent structure now looks like a Roman ruin, left alone to die with no one around to care anymore or witness its tragic collapse. The path in front of Julia forks, one route to the west and one to the east of the rotting building. Julia takes the western trail, which leads her around the back of the convent and into what was most likely a beautiful garden and meditative spot for the nuns. Julia spots the back of a statue of a figure with shoulder-length hair wearing what looks like a robe. The statue is slightly off the trail, but Julia is drawn to it, and against her better sense she runs in its direction. Julia reaches her hand out and lightly grazes the back of the statue's robe, the metal burning hot against her fingers. She runs in a semicircle until she faces the statue, the beautiful and grotesque remains of Christ. The statue's nose and left arm have been decomposed by the elements. The Christ statue reaches out its one good hand toward Julia as if beckoning her closer, as two thick garden snakes slither through his fingers.

Julia takes a surprised step back and begins to run faster away from the disconcerting scene. The rush of air makes her lungs ache, and Julia feels her muscles working harder as the trail laces up the mountain's incline. She keeps going, pushing down her fear of what lurks in the bushes around her, and concentrates on what she will do when she reaches Rossi's compound. Julia takes stock in the fact that she has put herself in danger on more than one occasion as an investigative reporter and always relied on her smarts to get what she needed and out of harm's way in time. Julia feels certain she'll be able to find the bar surveillance footage and the money David told her about more easily than the police, since they have rules and she doesn't.

A twelve-mile run is no stranger to Julia, but the mountainous terrain is. She feels her calf muscles strain as she makes the final push to her third marker, refusing to stop. She knows she hasn't come this far to quit. Julia spots the glint of tired rust just a quarter mile ahead, and she forces herself to run faster, her breath now hard and ragged against the staccato sound of grasshoppers quickly flapping their wings together with a sound like a fast-moving pair of castanets.

At the top, she sees a dilapidated barn. Its roof sags sadly to one side as if it will cave in at any minute, and its front wall is long gone, giving her a bird's-eye view inside. Still hung in the interior of the skeletal structure are black-and-white photos of early settlers who worked this land, proud and virile as they rode horseback, luring their animals back in line with expert hands. Adjacent to the remains of the barn is an old motor home, somehow with all four of its wheels intact.

Julia doesn't allow herself to stop and concentrates on her final marker, the one on top of the mountain, where she will stay hidden until Navarro and Felix arrive.

Julia looks up at the sun still straight in front of her and runs forward in its brilliant path.

She reaches the top of the mountain and falls down underneath the shade of a massive citrus tree, pulling her knees against her chest until her breathing becomes normal.

From the distance and on the other side of Julia's protective canopy, the sound of rap music plays in the background. Julia pulls her knees in even closer to her body and tries to temper her loud breathing until it steadies, lest whoever is playing the music can hear her.

Two men converse on the other side of the trees, and Julia hears the sound of Jay Z rapping with measured veracity about his ninety-nine problems.

"Do you think we're going to get ambushed? I heard talk about a Detroit and L.A. cop sniffing around. But there's no way they'll get inside the compound if they can find it."

"The cops are pussies. They talk tough, but they don't have the courage to confront Rossi. If those officers show up today, we'll take them, easy. Costas called me a few minutes ago and said the police will likely come through the road in back of the compound. Costas has an ambush already in place to kill them. It's hidden along the road, and they won't have a clue."

Julia reaches toward her waist pack and retrieves her cell phone. The signal is weak, but she still has one bar. She tries to move silently away from the two men, holding her breath as she goes into the thickest part of the forest.

She hits the speed dial number and prays.

Julia hears her outgoing call ring shakily in her ear. "Come on, come on!" she whispers.

"Navarro, here."

"You need to abort your attempt to enter Rossi's compound from the backside. Rossi has an ambush waiting for you."

"Julia, what do you think you're doing? I told you not to go there. You're going to get killed."

"It's too late. I'm safe. Turn your crew around."

"Felix is coming up the back route. I'm on the main road."

"You need to call Felix now."

"Get out of there," Navarro yells.

"I can't."

"Stay out of sight then and as far away as you can from the compound," Navarro says. "Now run and hide. Do you understand me?"

Julia is about to answer when she feels the barrel of a gun shove into the middle of her back. A heavyset man with a gold necklace and a Virgin Mary pendant hanging from its chain grabs Julia's phone from her hand and puts it to his ear.

"Ms. Gooden is busy. She has to go now."

Enzo Costas shuts Julia's phone off and sticks it in his pocket. He roughly takes Julia's hands and quickly ties them behind her back. He grabs her arm and forces her through the thick vegetation and into a black Hummer that waits on the side of the main road.

"Hail Mary, full of grace, the Lord is with thee," Costas says as he starts the powerful vehicle.

"Hold on," Julia cries. "You kill cops, you'll have a mark on your head. You think it was bad before, wait until you and your boss face charges as cop killers."

Enzo Costas gives Julia a sadistic laugh. "Blessed art thou amongst women, and blessed is the fruit of thy womb, Jesus."

"Why are you praying?" Julia asks.

"Holy Mary, Mother of God, pray for us sinners, now and at the hour of our death. That is *Hail Mary, Full of Grace*. But don't bother to pray for your safety. Your prayers don't matter," Costas says. "And neither do you."

* * *

Felix's sedan creeps up the back of the mountainside. Felix's body feels charged with adrenaline and ready for the fight. As he approaches Rossi's compound, Felix is surprised to find himself thinking about what it would have been like to be an English teacher instead of a cop. To Felix, poetry and verse sound unique in the tongue they are spoken in, and he would have taught his students to train their ears to pick up the subtle differences of a language's meaning and inflection when it is spoken in English and then in its native tongue. Dostoyevsky works in Russian, Victor Hugo's books in French, and Octavio Paz's poems in Spanish.

Felix stops the van when he sees a young, well-dressed man dart out from the trees and out into the road, waving his hands for him to stop.

Felix's opens his window a crack and warily assesses the teenager.

"Oh, man, thanks for stopping. My mom and I got lost driving up here. Our car ran out of gas. She's just around the corner up there with the car."

"How did you and your mother get up here?" Felix asks.

"The gate to the road was open. We're visiting from Arizona, and we wanted to see the view from on top of the mountain. Listen, I have to get back to my mom. I went into the woods to take a leak and left the gas can back there," the teenager says, and hooks his thumb toward the trees. "Let me just grab it and then we can go pick up my mom."

Felix feels something ring inside him, like a warning buzzer, alerting him that something is wrong.

A black SUV bursts from the underbrush behind him, and Felix hits the gas, but a second vehicle, a black Hummer, roars to life in front of him and comes to a stop sideways across the road so he can't pass. Felix jams his vehicle into reverse as his cell phone rings on the dashboard. Navarro's name flashes across the screen, the call coming in a minute too late.

Felix tries to ram the black SUV that has him pinned in the front. He braces for impact when shots ring out from the SUV and Felix's windshield shatters. Felix feels something burn hot on the right side of his body and realizes he's been hit. He struggles against the air bag that deployed as his door opens wide and two big hands pull him out of the vehicle.

Felix prays that the person is Navarro, who has somehow gotten there in time. Felix's wounded body is tossed to the ground like garbage, and he looks up to see not a savior but a devil, Enzo Costas, smiling sickly over him with his gun drawn and pointed at his face.

Felix spots his new friend, Julia, captured and screaming in the passenger seat of the Hummer. Felix then sees something distant in the shimmer of heat that bakes above the hot pavement, a mirage of what his mind's eye wants to be there, the image of his father carrying his little brother on his shoulders. The two smile happily and call out for Felix to join them.

"Stupid idiot," Costas says.

Felix feels the steel muzzle of the gun as it is pushed into his mouth. He recalls the Octavio Paz line from his poem "Between Going and Coming." Felix closes his eyes and wraps his soul around the words "All is visible and all elusive, all is near and can't be touched."

A warm breeze touches Felix's skin as Costas pulls the trigger, and all that is elusive and mysterious in the world that Felix has known disappears like a puff of smoke carried away on the wind.

CHAPTER 21

The road back to the compound is rough under the Hummer's tires, and Costas laughs when Julia bangs her head against the passenger-side window. Costas reaches across the seat and pinches the skin under Julia's tricep, squeezing until she cries out. She bites the side of her cheek to make herself stop as she realizes Enzo Costas gets off on his victim's pain.

"I saw you murder Felix Espinosa. You'll go to prison for what you did to him," Julia warns.

"You tough-acting women think you're so hard. But you beg for your life the loudest of all."

Costas steers the Hummer through a makeshift path sifting through an especially dense part of the vegetation until they reach a security gate. A mammoth guard, who is about six-foot-five and 300 pounds, doesn't move out of the way of the gate as the Hummer approaches. He finally leaves his post when Costas rolls down his tinted window and pokes his head out so he can be identified. The guard opens the gate, and Costas motors inside.

A quarter mile up, the compound begins to look more like

a resort than a criminal's hideout, with rows of well-tended red dahlias gently sloping the path up to the main house. The Hummer passes an Olympic-size swimming pool, two smaller houses, and what looks to be an industrial-size warehouse. The main house is a brownish orange and looks like a modern-constructed square box, the kind of design Julia has seen on the covers of architectural magazines.

"Come on," Costas says gruffly.

He yanks Julia by the arm across the seat and out the driverside door along with him, as if she needs to be reminded who is boss.

"If you try to get away, you won't make two steps before you're shot."

Costas pushes Julia ahead of him up the stairs and into the main house. Inside Rossi is stretched out on a white couch watching the Detroit Pistons land a three-point shot against the L.A. Lakers on the biggest wide-screen television Julia has ever seen. Rossi wears a tangerine-colored button-down shirt open at the chest and a pair of pressed light tan pants. He glances away from the game and jumps up from the couch when he sees Julia.

"What the hell is she doing here?"

"I caught her near the gate."

"This is a problem. A big problem, Enzo. Was she with the cops?"

"No. The L.A. cop is dead. I'll dump him on the other side of the mountain so his body won't be found. The animals will get to him before night."

"What about the Detroit cop?"

"He's coming up on the other side of the mountain. We've got two guys there who'll take him out."

Rossi strides over to Julia and pulls her away from Costas as if she were a cow being inspected for purchase at a livestock auction.

"How did you get up here?"

"I ran," Julia answers.

"You ran all the way up the mountain?" Rossi asks. "You've got creativity, I'll give you that. I recognize you from the courthouse. You're the one who wrote those stories trying to pin me for the Tyce Jones shooting."

"I wasn't trying to do anything. I was just reporting the facts, just like I did with your uncle."

"So you think I owe you or something because in your mind, you got my uncle off? You shouldn't have come up here. I don't like killing women. I really don't."

"You want me to take care of her now?" Enzo asks.

"In a minute."

Rossi moves to the bar and pours himself a shot of tequila.

"The one thing I can't figure out is why you ordered the courthouse bombing," Julia says. "You already hired a sniper to take out Sammy Biggs. He wasn't the target, though, was he? You were trying to kill my husband."

"You ask a lot of questions for someone in your position," Rossi answers.

"David had something on you that was going to come out in the trial, so you had to be sure the trial didn't go forward. That's why you did it. My husband told me."

"Your husband is a liar. Arrogant prick tried to screw me. He has something of mine that I want back."

Rossi gives Enzo a subtle nod. Enzo reaches into his pants pocket and pulls out a switchblade that he snaps open and presses against Julia's neck.

"Where did he put it?" Rossi asks.

"Put what? I don't know what you're talking about," Julia answers, and tries to keep herself from trembling.

"I think you do."

"The FBI and the Detroit police have what's left of David's

case files. I don't know what was in them. David wouldn't talk about the case with me."

Rossi leans into Julia so his face is inches away from hers and stares at her unblinking for a long minute until he finally pulls away.

"One of the biggest skills a businessman can have is knowing if someone is telling the truth or if they're a lying sack of shit. Tell you what. I think you're being straight with me. Your husband probably kept you in the dark about everything, including what he'd do to make sure people he prosecuted went to jail. Love and loyalty make you stupid. Case in point, you," Rossi says.

"Little kids died in the courthouse attack. They were innocent, just like your daughter was. How could you do that to a child after your own was taken in a violent act?"

Rossi flies around in Julia's direction with the eyes of a madman. His arm jerks up in the air, fist clenched, and Julia closes her own eyes as she braces for impact.

"Don't you ever . . . ever talk about my daughter again," Rossi seethes.

Julia opens her eyes and sees Rossi has dropped his fist to his side and now paces back and forth in front of her, talking in rushed, whispered sentences to himself until he abruptly stops and jerks his thumb in Enzo's direction.

"What do you want me to do with her, boss?" Enzo asks.

"Slit her throat."

Costas's eyes seem to burn bright, and his fingers move up to his Virgin Mary medallion hanging from his neck. He quickly drops the charm as a volley of gunfire rings out in the distance and Rossi shoots him a warning look.

"You told me the Detroit cop was handled," Rossi says. "How many times are you going to screw up today?"

"The Detroit officer is handled. I promise."

"He doesn't sound handled to me. Lock the lawyer's wife

in Isabella's place until you've taken care of the problem. The local sheriffs are a joke and probably won't come up here because they think it's not their coverage area, but I don't want to risk it if one of the yokels at the base of the mountain hears anything. And, Enzo . . ."

"Yes, boss?" Costas answers.

"You screw up again, you'll pay for it."

"Don't worry. I'll take care of everything. None of this will come back to you."

Rossi looks at Costas with disgust and turns his back on his failed employee.

Julia can hear Costas begin to chant the Hail Mary prayer quickly under his breath as he wedges his gun against the small of her back. Costas steers Julia out of Rossi's place and across the compound to another building, which is smaller than the main house but a duplicate in design, another square box.

Before the door shuts behind her, Julia screams as loud as she can, causing Costas to cuff her on the back of the head with the gun.

"Shut up," Costas says as he shoves Julia inside the new building.

Julia does a quick search of the space to see if she can find anything she can use as a weapon.

As if he can read her, Costas grabs Julia's face and constricts his hands around her jaw with such force, Julia is afraid her bones will snap.

"You try to escape, I'll cut your heart out," Costas says, and hurries to the door.

Before he leaves, his wide finger quickly taps a series of numbers on a security system pad.

"You open any doors or windows, the alarm will go off."

Costas closes the door and locks it from the outside.

Julia waits until she hears the Hummer's engine disappear and then begins to comb Isabella's place before Costas returns. Julia does a quick scan of the small bungalow and from the scant décor decides Isabella spends very little time here. The main sitting area is sparsely furnished with just a sofa and a small side table with a framed picture of a very young Isabella, vibrant and happy, running along a beach with another little girl.

Julia runs down a small corridor that dead ends to a single room with just a bed and table. Julia works her way through the room and then into a large closet lined with shoes and rows of designer clothing. In the corner is a shelf of mannequin heads with wigs of various shades and styles. Julia searches through a tall dresser in hopes Isabella would be the type of woman to hide something from her husband, and quite possibly a gun for her own protection against the man she married.

In the last drawer, Julia finds a stack of bank deposit statements and a business card from a Detroit vault and safety deposit company called Infinity Holdings, Inc. Underneath, Julia spots a DVD with the words "Anthony Ruiz in Bar" written across it in a black Sharpie pen and a thick, sealed file. Julia tears the file open and finds a sheet of paper with her home address clipped to the top of the sheaf of papers. Julia quickly flips through the file, which includes a detailed list of the cases David tried as a public defender and prosecutor. At the very bottom of the file is a series of glossy photos. The first image captures David outside the Detroit courthouse stairs. In the second photo, David is dressed casually in khaki shorts and a short-sleeved polo, smiling back at the camera against the backdrop of what looks like the local Santa Maria Temple. The bottom three shots are black-and-white: one of Logan getting off the school bus, a picture of Helen strapping Will into his car seat, and a photo of Julia in the parking garage across from the newsroom.

Julia grabs the disc, and her mind works through the name

written across it until she recalls the Anthony Ruiz case David tried and won when he first started at the D.A.'s office. Ruiz was a day laborer accused of the rape and murder of a wealthy mother and her daughter.

Julia hurries through the bedroom and catches a glimpse of a DVD player next to a slim, wide-screen television and a stereo. She shoves the Anthony Ruiz disc in, realizing her curiosity may waste valuable minutes in finding a potential weapon, but she hits the play button regardless.

The recording starts, but the screen remains dark. Julia waits for twenty seconds and is about to stop the player when a steady buzz of static sounds from the tape. Julia turns the sounds up to full volume when a conversation begins.

"You got the money?"

"Fifteen thousand in the envelope. Where's the surveillance footage?"

Julia feels cool pinpricks move down her arms as she realizes the second voice belongs to David.

"Here it is. I don't want any trouble coming back to me about this."

"No trouble as long as you're being honest with me," David answers. "This is the original and you didn't make any copies? Nick Rossi or the cops or another lawyer approach you about this?"

"No way, man. But Nick Rossi's guy, Enzo Costas, knew about the recording. His local guy told him. Saw your man in here the night it went down. I wish I knew why a guy sitting at a bar doing shots would be worth so much money."

"Just be smart. Keep your mouth shut. That's what the money buys me."

"You got it, man. I'd never go back on my word."

The audio part of the recording goes quiet, and a grainy video appears on the screen. A black-and-white scene of a small, sparsely populated bar plays out. Two men are at the bar drinking; each man sits at either end of the circular counter. There's a time and date stamp at the bottom of the recording, which indicates it was taken roughly seven months ago, and the location—Wayne, Michigan. Julia studies the tape and focuses in on a good-looking, younger patron, most likely Latino, who appears to order another drink from the bartender and smiles his thanks as he raises his glass to the bartender when it arrives. The Latino man downs his shot as the other patron across the bar gets up, walks toward the men's bathroom, and disappears inside. The Latino man rises from his seat a minute later and quickly follows in the same direction. He looks over his shoulder and goes inside the bathroom. Julia stares at the closed men's room door and watches the time elapse at the bottom of the screen. Five minutes go by, and the Latino man reappears. As he walks back to his seat, his gait this time is uneven and sloppy, like a clown trying to walk a straight line in giant shoes. He makes it halfway back to his seat and grabs a passing barstool to steady himself. The Latino man seems to regain his balance and begins to walk in cautious steps when two small, round balloon-looking shapes slip out from his coat and roll across the floor. The young man snatches them up and stuffs them back into his coat. He slaps some money down in front of his spent drink and exits through what looks like the front door of the bar. Less than a minute later, the other man emerges from the bathroom and reclaims his seat. The screen goes black, and Julia pops the disc out of the player to continue her search.

With only one room left to hunt, Julia prays Isabella left behind a razor in the shower, but it is void of any toiletries, and Julia realizes Isabella likely hasn't been to the compound in a long time.

Now out of options, Julia runs back to the entryway to try the door and spies the picture of Isabella as a little girl.

Julia shimmies the glass away from the picture and hits the glass against the desk, trying her best to connect the small pane so it severs right in the center. In her haste, a sharp sliver of glass catches the meaty part of her hand underneath her thumb, and it starts to bleed. She sucks the blood away with her mouth so Costas won't be tipped off and takes the two uneven halves of the now-shattered pane and breaks them into two more pieces. She singles out one that looks like a perfect but dangerously jagged square, its four corners pointy and sharp, and carefully slips it into her running bra. She then whisks the remaining pieces of glass into a single drawer in the entryway table.

The sound of gunfire between Costas and Navarro silences, and Julia knows only one side has won.

The growl of the Hummer's engine approaches, and Julia slides the DVD back in its original place as the beep of an alarm being deactivated sounds from the front room of the cottage and Costas enters.

"Where's Navarro?" Julia asks.

"Dead. Let's go."

"You killed him," Julia cries, and instinctively starts to reach for the broken glass hidden in her bra, but Costas grabs her arm and pushes her outside and toward another small building on the property. Before he goes in, Costas does the sign of the cross and begins to chant the Hail Mary prayer.

"Inside, now," Enzo says after he finishes.

Julia works to adjust her eyes in the dark room and realizes this must be Enzo Costas's place, which is decorated to look like a shrine. Above Costas's bed is a three-foot gold cross and a statue of Christ crucified, drops of crimson blood slipping from his hands. On a table is a Virgin Mary statue. The likeness of the serene holy mother wears a white shroud, a pair of rosary beads hangs from one of her arms, and her hands are clasped together in prayer.

Costas shoves Julia on the bed.

"Take off your shoes," he demands, and turns his back on her so he can kneel down before his Virgin Mary altar. Julia reaches for the broken glass piece still tucked above her chest. She holds it between her right thumb and index finger and hides her hand behind her back.

Costas finishes his prayer and undoes the fly of his pants. He opens up a gold jewelry box on his dresser and removes a razor blade that glints a deadly silver warning against the light.

He begins to recite the Hail Mary prayer again as he forces Julia down on her back. She quickly moves her hand with the glass piece so it dangles on the other side of the mattress away from Costas's view. Costas straddles Julia with his hips, and she can smell the sour mash of cigarettes and tequila from his warm breath as he prepares for his work. Costas lifts Julia's shirt up and prays as he moves the dull side of the razor blade down her stomach. Julia stares at the thick veins in Costas's neck as he concentrates, and she knows what she has to do.

He turns the razor so its sharp side now teases against the inside of Julia's thigh as it makes its way back up. Julia closes her eyes as she hears the lonely cry of a blackbird mourn outside her window, and she realizes she has to make her move.

Costas begins to chant his prayer again, his head bent down near the razor, and Julia's hand comes up, fast and unexpected, as the jagged edge of the glass piece slices through the left side of Costas's neck, cutting directly through one of his bulging veins.

Costas drops the razor and his hand scrambles up to clasp his throat to stop the blood. He staggers forward off the bed, and Julia rushes to her feet, no longer pinned under his weight. She tries to reach the door, but Costas hurtles after her like an enraged bull just pierced by a matador's sword. Julia screams when a gunshot rings out, and Costas drops to the floor. She looks to see Navarro standing in the cottage doorway, his gun still pointed at Costas. Costas makes one last guttural moan as blood leaks from his chest, and then looks up unblinking at the ceiling, as if praying to heaven one final time to save his soul.

"Are you hurt?" Navarro asks.

"I thought you were dead. I'm okay."

"We have to get out of here. Come on," Navarro orders, and grabs Julia's hand. He then reaches inside Costas's pockets and pulls out the keys to the Hummer.

They race outside of the cottage and hurry inside the vehicle, quickly locking the doors. Navarro starts the car and peels out toward the main gate.

"We've got maybe a couple minutes before Rossi goes and checks on Costas."

"I can't believe you're alive," Julia says.

"I figured Rossi was going to have another crew ready to ambush me on the main road after your call, so I was prepared."

"Felix is dead. Rossi's guys ambushed him. Costas pulled him out of his car and shot him in the head."

Navarro's jaw tightens as the news hits about his friend.

"There's a huge guy at the security gate. The guard is armed and made Costas look out the driver's window so he could identify him before he opened the gate," Julia says.

"The windows of the Hummer are tinted, so we should be okay until we get up on the guy. I want you to crawl into the back seat, lie down on the floor, and stay down."

Julia does as she is told and spots the guard from before. She lies flat across the floor as the Hummer approaches the security gate. Navarro slowly opens the passenger-side window, and the guard begins to lean inside the vehicle when

Navarro pops off two shots into the guard's face and he goes down.

Navarro jumps out of the car, the engine still running, and punches a green button to open the gate. It slowly opens, and Navarro hits the gas hard.

"We're never going to escape down the main roads. There's a trail, a path, I took to get here," Julia says. "The Hummer can go off-road, right?"

"That's what it's made for."

"You were ambushed right before you got to an old barn. You couldn't see it from the road, but the path is there."

Navarro takes a sharp turn, and the Hummer dodges a thick nest of trees until they reach a clearing parallel to the main road.

"That's it. The old barn. Right there. There's a path, barely visible, but it's just high brush all the way down the mountain."

"Rossi has his crew scouting both ends of the mountain. I don't know how we're going to get out of here. I called the sheriff's department for backup when I got to the compound. We're in no-man's-land. They're at least forty minutes out."

On the dashboard, a cell phone rings. Navarro looks at the phone. "That's yours."

"Costas took it when I was talking to you."

"Did Rossi and Costas assault you, Julia?"

"No. I was able to get out in time."

"What did you hit Costas with? He was bleeding out from his jugular."

"A piece of glass. I know someone I can call who may be able to help us get out of here."

"Do it," Navarro says, and throws the phone back to Julia.

Julia calls the number she memorized back in Detroit.

Tyce Jones answers.

"Julia Gooden. Girl, where you been? I've been looking for your story online about Rossi hiring a sniper to take out his snitch. That was Grade A prime dope I fed you right there. You going soft or what?"

"I need your help. I'm at Rossi's compound. He's trying to kill me and a Detroit cop."

"You shittin' me? I told you not to go there. Cop or no cop. You need a better army than that."

"Rossi's got the main roads blocked. I'm driving on the trail you told me about."

"Mmm, mmm, mmm. Rossi know your vehicle?"

"We stole it from Enzo Costas. He's dead. He killed an L.A. cop."

"You put me on the hot spot, mama. I got guys in L.A. but not up where you are."

"Come on, Tyce. I'm desperate."

"Let me make a call to one of my high rollers. The badass I'm thinking of has a helicopter in the back of his pad. Let me see what I can do. That map I told you about that Rossi showed me? You followed the trail and saw a convent, right?"

"Yes, I ran past it."

"Ditch the car and hang there until I can secure you a ride. You owe me big-time now, girl," Tyce says, and ends the call.

"Who was that?" Navarro asks.

"It doesn't matter. There's a convent that will be coming up in a couple of miles. Park in the rear of the building, away from the path. My contact is going to call me back, and he told me we should wait there."

"Are you kidding me? If your source is who I think he is, the guy's probably calling his buddy Rossi right now to tip him off."

"I don't think so. Rossi turned on him a couple years ago."

"You think or you know?"

"I know."

Navarro drums his index finger on his thigh next to his gun and pulls behind the convent next to the Jesus statue, the snakes now gone from his fingers.

As promised, Julia's cell phone rings.

"I pulled a mother-f'ing favor for you," Tyce says. "You nail Rossi, we're squared. My guy's got an employee up your way. He'll pick you up at the convent and get your ass to a safe place. From there, you're on your own until you get to Detroit. You dig?"

"I got it. Thank you."

Julia hangs up the phone while Navarro continues to scan for Rossi's men.

"How did you find me?" Julia asks.

"I killed a guard and made it through the gate at the back entrance of the property. I heard you scream."

"I'm sorry. I didn't mean for Felix to die," Julia says. "I feel like it's my fault he got killed."

"You shouldn't have gone to the compound. That was stupid. But you found out about the ambush, and I tried to warn him. He would have died whether you were there or not. And I was on high alert the whole drive up after you tipped me off, which may have saved my life."

A dark blue Cadillac Escalade with heavily tinted windows pulls around the side of the convent and stops, the motor still running.

The driver-side window of the Cadillac SUV cracks open, and a muscular, middle-aged man with a shiny bald head, black aviator glasses, and a prominent space between his front teeth nods for Navarro to open his window. Navarro does, and points his gun at the man who responds with a single slow and heavy blink. The driver of the Cadillac then peers inside the Hummer at Julia.

"I'm looking for a Julia Gooden? That you?" the man asks.

"Yes. I'm Julia."

"My name is Barry. My boss says you need a ride."

Barry does a quick assessment of Navarro. "You're a cop?"

Navarro nods his answer, and the Cadillac driver considers the situation. "You don't ask any questions about me or my boss or tell anyone about this little meetup here, I'll take you where you need to go. Otherwise, I'm gone."

Navarro looks to Julia and concedes. "Okay. Let's get out of here."

Julia and Navarro hurry out of Costas's Hummer and jump into the SUV with their new acquaintance. The Escalade easily dodges through the tall grass and the maze of trees until it lands back on the road.

"Lie down on the seat and don't get up until I tell you it's safe," Barry says.

"You got a gun?" Navarro asks.

"I told you. No questions."

Julia lies curled in a ball, and Navarro covers her head with his hands in a protective gesture.

Julia can hear the hum of cars accelerating past the Escalade at a fast clip down the mountain road.

"Those were Rossi's men. There's a roadblock up ahead. Don't even think about breathing as we go through," Barry says.

Navarro reaches for his gun, ready for a final showdown. Julia can hear the click of a briefcase open as Barry retrieves his own weapon.

The Escalade slows, and Julia can see the shadowy figures of two men in front of the roadblock. Julia can hear the men talking, and she recognizes the voices as those belonging to Rossi's men who were listening to Jay Z right before Costas caught her outside of the compound. The two men study the

Cadillac for a minute and then the larger of the duo cocks his head to the right, indicating the Cadillac is free to pass.

The three drive in silence for the next twenty minutes until Barry stops the car.

"We're here," Barry says.

Julia sits up in the backseat, her back aching and her body now bone-weary. She looks out the window to see that they are back at the hotel.

"Thank you," Julia says, and reaches her hand across the seat to shake Barry's.

"No need to thank me. This never happened."

CHAPTER 22

Julia can begin to make out the skyline of Detroit beckoning her home. She fastens her seat belt and closes her eyes, still uncomfortable with the upcoming landing, even in the plane that so far has carried her and Navarro safely back to Michigan.

"The police are still at my house?" Julia asks.

"Around the clock."

"Rossi's going to come after me now, even harder than before."

"We can move you and your family to a safe house. Just give me the word."

"Let me think about it. I don't want to disrupt Logan and Will's world more than it already is."

"What happened to you back at Rossi's?"

"I found a file in Isabella's cottage. It had photos of the kids and David and me. One of the pictures didn't look like a surveillance shot. It was taken somewhere near Rossi's compound, outside the Santa Maria Temple. David looked comfortable, like he knew the person taking his picture. I figured out he took a secret trip to California to recruit Sammy Biggs, but I think whatever happened in California was more than that. Rossi told me David was a liar and tried to screw him. Rossi claims David took something of his and he wants it back."

"You think David was dirty, that he might be wrapped up in this thing?"

"I'm leaning that way. Rossi said David broke the law to make sure the defendants he prosecuted went to jail. I found a DVD in Isabella's cottage with "Anthony Ruiz in Bar" written across it. I tried to take it with me, but I left it behind when Costas came back."

"I remember Ruiz. The guy was found guilty for raping and killing that mother and daughter over in Troy. David tried the case and won. It sounded like a clean win. There was a DNA match to Ruiz on the semen found inside the daughter."

"I played the disc. The beginning is just audio, and it sounds like David was paying off someone to buy the recording. Then video came on. Just a couple of guys drinking in a bar. And probably a drug deal that happened in a bathroom away from the camera. There was also a time and date stamp."

"When was it?"

"September fifteenth of last year. Eleven twenty-five PM."

"That was the night of the murders. We figured the mother and her daughter were killed around eleven PM."

"Margie had the reporter for Troy cover that story, since I was covering something else. But I remember David talking about it."

"Was one of the men in the video a young guy? Hispanic, good looking?"

"Yes. That sounds right."

"Maybe we're thinking about this from the wrong angle. Maybe David didn't have something on Rossi. Maybe Rossi had something on David," Navarro suggests.

"Do you remember what Ruiz's alibi was the night of the murders?"

Navarro runs his fingers through his hair as he pieces together the memory. "He claimed he was home in bed alone."

"That's a pretty thin alibi."

"Ruiz could have lied about his whereabouts if he was at the bar doing something illegal."

"Like buying drugs," Julia suggests.

"Ruiz had two prior convictions for drug possession and intent to sell."

"I'm pretty sure a drug deal went down. Ruiz, if it was him, looked like he was high when he came out of the bathroom, and something fell out of his coat. Could have been heroin."

"Maybe Ruiz threw the dice. He figured he'd be acquitted of the murder charges, so he made up a fake, safe alibi. If he told his defense attorney he was actually at the bar, the surveillance recording could have been introduced as evidence. That would have been his third strike on a drug conviction and a hefty sentence. The bar surveillance footage was never introduced during the trial."

"But David knew about it. That's a Brady violation," Julia says.

"Right, evidence tampering. Prosecutors are required to turn over any and all exculpatory evidence that could affect a verdict or sentencing. Prosecutors are known to do that all the time."

"But if it was found out that David was withholding evidence, he could've been disbarred. A Texas prosecutor got jail time a couple of years ago for evidence tampering. David's D.A. run would've gone down in flames before it started. Not to mention the fact that he paid someone fifteen thousand dollars for the recording."

"It's got to be connected to Rossi's case. You know your husband. Do you honestly believe he would be wrapped up with Nick Rossi?"

"Despite our issues, I always thought I knew David, but I was wrong. Before we left on the trip, I found out he cheated on me. We were still separated technically, but we were trying to work things out and I assumed he was being faithful."

"With that woman he was seeing from the D.A.'s office when you guys were separated?"

"I'm pretty sure it was her. I found naked pictures on David's phone."

"I'm sorry, Julia."

"For a lot of years, I never felt good enough for David, like I was damaged goods that could never measure up. But I finally realized David did a lot to perpetuate that myth before he walked out the first time. Blaming our first split entirely on my paranoia over the boys' safety and the fact that I couldn't let go of my brother's disappearance, that wasn't fair. He had his share of the blame too with being controlling and when he wasn't telling me what to do, he was absent and always working. My only saving grace is that I wouldn't let him move back in with us until I was sure."

"What are you going to do?"

"About David? Nothing right now. When he gets out of the hospital and back on his feet, the boys and I will move out and back to our lake house in Sparrow."

The airplane taxis down the runway at Detroit Metropolitan Airport. It lands easily, and the attendant opens the door and secures the stairs to the tarmac. Julia hurries off the plane and heads toward the terminal, anxious to get back to her sons.

Julia grabs her cell phone and dials her home number. She listens as her house phone rings twelve times without anyone picking up, thrusting her into panic mode.

"Hello," Helen finally answers.

"Thank God. You scared me. Is Logan home yet?" Julia asks.

"Yes," Helen says, and tries to catch her breath. "That's why I just picked up. Logan just got off the school bus, and then we all rushed inside when I heard the phone ringing. Did you find that man who hurt your David?"

"We'll talk about that later. The officers are still there?"

"Well, they were. The man who stayed with us in the house overnight left in the morning, and there was a single officer in his car out front until a few minutes ago. There was a major accident on I-75, a twenty-five-car pileup with the snow and lots of casualties. The officer promised that another police officer would be here soon, but the person hasn't arrived yet."

"This is important, Helen. I want you to go to the window and be discreet. Look outside. Do you see anyone out there?"

Helen puts the phone down and then returns a few seconds later.

"There was a dark car I saw park across the street when I heard the phone ring. It's still there and someone is sitting inside. The windows are tinted, so I can't see a face, but I know someone is in there. Is this person going to cause trouble?"

"Listen to me very carefully. Is the front door locked?" Julia asks.

"Yes. You always tell me to lock it."

"Get out right now. Don't go anywhere near the front of the house, and stay away from the windows."

"My purse is in the living room on the coffee table by the bay window," Helen says.

"Leave it. Go out the back door and go to the neighbors. The Wilsons should be home. Stay there until the police arrive."

"You scare me, Julia."

"Don't let Logan and Will know you're scared. Now go."

Navarro and Julia hurry through the terminal to his car in the parking garage. Navarro turns on his siren, and they cut through the late-afternoon rush hour traffic leaving the city.

Isabella Rossi watches the boy, Logan, walk toward his house with an old woman and the lawyer's other child, the younger one a miniature version of the assistant district attorney, with their white-blond hair and fair skin. The older boy looks like the lawyer's wife, she thinks.

Isabella's cell phone on the car's inner console begins to ring, and Nick Rossi's number comes across the screen.

Isabella stares at her reflection in the rearview mirror and recalls the first time she laid eyes on Nick. It was at an L.A. club called the Black Sunset. Isabella was waiting with her sister behind the velvet rope with all the other wannabes, hoping to God they'd get in, when Nick pulled up in a black Ferrari, tipped the valet a cool hundred, and then disappeared inside. Isabella wasn't going to let that kind of opportunity pass, so she used what always worked for her. Isabella pressed her body against the bouncer and whispered what she would do to him at the end of the night if he would just let her into the club.

Ten seconds later, Isabella and her sister were in. Isabella slinked her way to the VIP section, where Nick was holding court in the center of the best table in the house.

"You're from Michigan? No shit. What's you name?" Nick asked as he palmed Isabella's ass.

"Isabella Ferrari," she lied, still thinking about the car.

Isabella was a half truth. Sort of. She took the stage name Isabella Thorn after the guy who snapped her headshots suggested it sounded much better than the name she was born with: Kathleen Murphy.

An hour after her new name debuted, Isabella left with Nick in the Ferrari, and one of Nick's guys stayed behind to beat the crap out of the disappointed bouncer who didn't get what he thought was coming to him at the end of the night.

Her first beating came on their honeymoon, when Isabella asked her new husband why he never told her what happened to his mother, a revelation she heard from Uncle Sal's wife during the wedding reception. If Isabella was supposed to know about it, Nick would have told her. That's what he screamed while he continued to kick her even when she had curled up in a ball and tried to seek refuge under a table. The next morning, Nick acted like nothing happened. And no one noticed. Nick was a smart beater who knew not to hit his woman in the face. If no one can actually see the bruises, it's like it never happened.

Isabella taps her manicured fingernails against the steering wheel and rationalizes that she took the beatings because the money was just too good. And when their daughter, Christina, was born, things got better, as if Isabella had finally done something right in her husband's eyes. But when her Christina was murdered by one of Nick's rivals, Isabella felt an icy blackness in her chest, like any small part of her that had ever been good had died. She promised herself then that she would not only leave her husband, she would get even.

Isabella removes a revolver from a briefcase lying on the passenger seat and begins to tuck it inside her coat when a police siren sounds in the near distance. Isabella hurriedly puts the gun back in the briefcase and catches the old woman peeking out from the kitchen curtains.

An image quickly flashes across Isabella's memory: Christina's little hand sliding into her own whenever they took a drive. Isabella would stretch her arm into the backseat of the car until Christina reached out for her mother. Isabella would not let go of her daughter's hand until the ride was over, even when her arm fell asleep. It was always so beautifully worth it.

Isabella shudders and puts the car in gear, knowing the next part of her end game will have to wait.

"Okay, Julia. Calm down. I just ordered another officer to go back to your house," Navarro says. "Logan and Will are at your neighbor's with the housekeeper. Everyone is okay for now, but things are getting complicated. I got a message while we were on the plane. Jason Meter, the sniper, was killed in prison this morning. A fight broke out in the dining hall and Meter was stabbed to death. Meter ratted out Enzo Costas, but Meter didn't say anything about Rossi's involvement. Costas is dead. Meter is dead, and I got a call from the LAPD that Rossi took off and is nowhere to be found. So we don't have anything to directly tie Rossi to the sniper."

"Rossi ordered the hit on Meter," Julia says.

"He's obviously got someone else running the show in Detroit now that Bartello was killed and whoever that is must have made sure Meter was taken out before he pointed the finger at the boss."

"So we're left with what? Nothing?"

"Did Rossi tell you he planted the bomb? I'm not sure we can extradite him back here based on David's confirmation alone, considering the condition David was in when he indicated that Rossi ordered the courthouse attack."

Julia runs through the entirety of her conversation with Rossi in her head. She feels tempted for a moment to lie and implicate Rossi, but ultimately she can't.

"No. Rossi didn't cop to anything."

Navarro pulls into Julia's driveway, the ride seeming to take an eternity.

"I'm going with you," Julia says, and reaches for the door.

"Not a chance. Sit tight."

Julia keeps her eyes trained on Navarro until he disappears inside her house. Julia looks at the dashboard clock and decides to give Navarro three minutes before she goes inside. She watches the minutes slowly creep past until the three-minute mark is reached. Julia grabs the passenger door handle when Navarro surfaces and hooks a finger for her to join him.

"It's all clear, like the other officer said. But come with me for a second," Navarro says, and leads Julia inside and down the hall to David's office. "Does David usually leave his office like this?"

David's meticulously kept files are strewn across his desk, and a filing cabinet is upturned.

"No. I was in David's office before I left. Someone came in here looking for something. I asked another lawyer in the D.A.'s office about the Rossi case file, but he thought it went missing in the blast."

"Then someone came into your house looking for something David had in the file. And whoever did it is an amateur. A professional would've left the place exactly how they found it. That rules out Rossi."

"Miss Julia, are you here?" Helen calls out from the front door as she and Julia's boys are escorted inside by a uniformed police officer.

Logan and Will rush to Julia's side, and she gets down on her knees so she can wrap her arms around both of her sons.

"What happened in this room?" Helen asks. "I dusted Mr. David's office this morning. It was neat and tidy when I left it."

"Something's wrong, isn't it?" Logan asks.

"No. Everything is fine. We're just going to pack a bag and stay somewhere for a few days," Julia answers. "Like a vacation."

"This has something to do with the bombing in the court-house, doesn't it?" Logan asks.

"Stop worrying so much, honey," Julia says, and gives Helen a subtle signal to get Logan and Will out of David's office.

"Come on, boys. We'll go pack a bag now," Helen says, and leads the boys to their rooms.

Navarro sifts through the papers on David's desk, old case files from his work at the district attorney's office and even a few dating back to his work as a public defender.

"Looks like David saved everything," Navarro says, and turns quickly to Julia as something clicks.

"Was David supposed to escort Sammy Biggs into the courthouse?"

"I'm not sure."

"If David was supposed to meet Biggs and bring him up to the courtroom, then David would have been at the exact location where the bomb went off. Like we thought, he must have been the target. Rossi wanted to be sure David was taken out."

Isabella Rossi waits patiently in the stairwell on the twelfth floor of the hospital, having been there enough times to study and learn the patterns of the staff. She knows there is a nar-row window when the nurses change shifts, the prime op-portunity to enter David Tanner's hospital room unnoticed.

Isabella scans the floor for police officers and then slips into David's room. He is sleeping, lying pale on the bed with his shaved light blond hair now starting to grow back into rough stubble, except around a deep red scar on the left side of his scalp from the surgery. David opens his eyes, and Isabella is almost amused at the attorney's frantic recognition as he stares at her now sitting by his bedside.

"Where's the money? Give me the box number and the

combination," Isabella whispers. "You tell me or I'll leak the Ruiz recording from the bar. I got a copy and a confessional of you paying off the bar owner for his silence."

"Go ahead. Leak it. I don't care about it anymore."

"As you like," Isabella says, and strokes her hand down the length of David's thigh above the hospital bedsheet. "You don't care about the recording now, but you care about your family. Tell me where the money is, or I'll kill them."

David struggles to pull himself up from the bed, but Isabella pushes him back down.

"Logan is such a handsome boy. He's a very good basketball player. I watched him play a few days ago."

"You were at Logan's school?"

"I warned you before. No more chances."

"Don't touch my family. If you do, I'll tell your husband what you did. The money is at Infinity Holdings. Box number one hundred two. The combination is thirty-three, ninety-one, forty-seven."

Isabella turns her back to David and removes a long syringe from her purse. She works her hand down David's left arm until she finds a meaty vein and injects the substance, enough, she was told, to make the lawyer's heart explode, and pats David's thigh until the syringe is emptied.

David opens his mouth as if to beg her to stop. But it's too late. Isabella drops the empty syringe back in her bag, slips out of his hospital room, and heads back down the staircase to the street.

Julia sifts through David's files in his office with Navarro and feels the buzz of her cell phone in her pocket. The call is within the local area code but from an unfamiliar number.

Julia is tempted to let the call go to voice mail but picks up at the last second.

"This is Dr. Whitcomb," the caller says. "David went into cardiac arrest. We were able to get his heart going again, but he's in critical condition and back in intensive care."

"Is he going to be all right?" Julia cries.

"His body was in a severely weakened state before this happened, so we'll be monitoring him closely. He had a major heart attack."

"I don't understand how this could happen. He was doing so much better. You were worried about a stroke, not a heart attack."

"No outcome can be predicted exactly. I'd suggest you come to the hospital as soon as you can," Dr. Whitcomb answers.

Julia keeps her eyes steady on the machine that monitors David's heart rate in his hospital room. She is afraid that if she looks away for even a single second, his heart will stop again, as if she could keep it beating at a normal rhythm by her pure will alone.

Julia clasps David's hand, careful not to squeeze too tight. Despite his recent infidelities, Julia can't help but break down as memories of their life together take over her thoughts.

She pictures David, the two of them dancing barefoot in the kitchen, his body pressed tightly against hers as Logan and Will gagged in fake horror over their father giving their mother a warm, wet kiss on the mouth.

(I love you so much, Julia.)

And she sees David poring over his case files late into the night as he prepared for trial the next morning to represent the family of a teenage boy who was killed by a drunken driver as he rode his bike home from the library.

(Go back to bed. I'll be up for a while. This kid deserves everything I can give him in court tomorrow.)

"Julia."

She looks up suddenly, David's voice no longer just in her head.

"David! Let me get your doctor."

"I'm sorry," David whispers. "I tried to stop Rossi. I made a mistake. He was blackmailing me. But I was going to make it right."

"Just relax, okay?"

"I crossed the line on a case I was working. I knew it wasn't right, but I was sure the guy was guilty. And then when things exploded between us, when you were still at the lake house and wouldn't forgive me, I was lost. I was mad at you, and I made a mistake. Find the money before she does and give it to the police," David begs, his green eyes intense and frightened.

The machine monitoring David's heart rate makes a loud warning, and a nurse hurries inside.

A doctor and two other medical technicians rush inside the room, and Julia is forced out into the waiting area. She collapses on a chair and puts her head between her hands, nothing making sense anymore, knowing the life she worked so hard to create with David and the boys has completely unraveled.

An instinctual fear goes off inside her, and Julia jumps up from the chair and hurries back to David's room. Before she can reach the door, the doctor comes out, looking grave and red-faced.

"I need to see my husband," Julia pleads.

"I'm sorry. We did everything we could. Your husband suffered another major heart attack, and we couldn't get his heart working again."

"What are you telling me?" Julia screams.

"Your husband, David. He's dead."

CHAPTER 23

Julia stares at the light gray wall in her bedroom, her body facing away from David's side of the bed. Logan is curled up in his father's former space, and Will sleeps in a nest he made with his blankets at the bottom of the king-sized bed.

The bedroom is cool, but Julia lies on top of the covers after enduring another night when sleep was elusive, and in the rare snatches when it was found, Julia would dream David was still alive. In the first few seconds between dreaming and waking, she would believe he truly was, and he was waiting to finally explain to her what had happened, what dark hole he climbed inside and the reason he slid down it. When Julia was a child, she always carried a tiny spark of hope that if she worked hard enough, she could change her fate. But this time, Julia realizes she is completely powerless and there is nothing she can do to bring David back, death being the one thing that can never be overcome. No matter what David did, in the end, they shared a history, a deep love once, and brought two little boys into the world together.

The sun begins to rise outside Julia's bedroom window.

She knows the security detail is still parked out in front of her house, as he has been all night, which provides a hollow comfort.

Julia looks over at Logan and Will and wishes desperately she could take all their hurt over the loss of their father and suffer it for them instead. Will's questions about where his daddy was had abated in the last few days. Julia recalls the last time Will saw David, his single hospital visit just a few days prior, when Will told her he wanted to leave because his father didn't look the same anymore and the strange beeping machines hooked up to David frightened him. Julia prays if Will carries one memory of his father in his life, it will not be that one. Logan, six years older than Will, is more aware of the permanence of the circumstances. Logan is taking David's death much harder and has quickly learned that the world is not the safe place he thought it once was but is instead randomly merciless and unforgiving.

Julia walks quietly to her bathroom so as not to wake the boys. She looks at her reflection in the mirror and knows she looks beyond haggard but doesn't care.

A light tapping sounds on the door. Julia splashes cold water on her face before she opens it and finds Logan, whose thin shoulders appear to now carry an almost impossibly heavy weight on them.

"I didn't know where you were and I got scared," Logan says. A tear slips down his cheek, and Julia wipes it away.

"I'm right here, and I'm not going anywhere." Julia kneels down and hugs Logan as hard as she can.

"I feel like it's my fault Daddy died," Logan says, his sweet, still-high-pitched voice now a ragged whisper. "Maybe his heart broke because I only went to see him a couple of times in the hospital. If I had visited him more, maybe this wouldn't have happened."

"Of course it's not your fault. You and Will were the light of your dad's life. You brought him so much joy." Julia pauses and waits for Logan to speak, as she takes the cue from the grief counselor at the hospital who gave her some insight on how to help her children cope with the loss of their father.

"Daddy told me when we went to the lake house this summer, he and I would play basketball like we always did."

"He would have loved that."

"I can't do that with him anymore."

"I was thinking we could create a memory book about Daddy with pictures and stories, and we could fill it up with all the things he loved to do with you and Will," Julia says as she struggles for the right thing to say.

"He and I used to get up early on Sunday mornings and make eggs and pancakes for everyone. That was my favorite," Logan says.

"That's a great memory."

"When do I have to go back to school?"

"When you're ready. Don't worry about that right now."

Julia pulls Logan in her lap and the two sit on the bathroom floor, mother and child comforting each other. Logan curls up against Julia's chest. His body feels almost limp against Julia. She strokes Logan's hair and makes promises that sound phony even to herself: that everything will be okay and they will get through it. Logan's breathing becomes slow and steady, and Julia realizes he is asleep. She picks him up, struggling under her once small boy's quickly growing frame, and carries him back to bed.

Julia approaches the kitchen and can already smell coffee brewing. She hesitates for a moment, since it's only six-thirty and she told Helen to take the morning off. Julia grabs a sturdy glass vase from the hallway table and moves stealthily forward.

Helen stands in front of the kitchen island making breakfast. She looks curiously at Julia with the vase in her hand and reaches for a mug in the cabinet.

"You didn't sleep again," Helen comments, and pours Julia an extra large cup of coffee. "There are pills your doctor can give you to help you sleep. If you're too exhausted, you'll be useless to your boys."

Julia takes a long sip of the steaming coffee, savoring its warmth and smell, and sits on one of the tall barstools along the kitchen island.

"I don't like pills. I need to be alert at all times. If something happens in the night, then I'll be useless to Logan and Will," Julia says. "You weren't supposed to come over this morning. You've been with us around the clock for over a week now, and you need to take care of yourself, too. I know your husband misses you being at home with him."

"Alek is retired and is always at home now. Maybe I need a little break from him once in a while."

"You've been so wonderful to me and my children. There aren't enough words to thank you for all you've done for us."

Helen moves to Julia's side and puts her hand on the younger woman's shoulder. "When I was a girl, my parents sent me and my older brother out of Poland to stay with relatives in London, because they were afraid of the Nazi occupation. My brother and I made it there safely, but I never saw my parents again. I can still see their faces as I looked out the window of the train the day I left Poland. My mother pretended to be happy, but deep down she feared that moment would be her last memory of my brother and me. I was eight, the same age as Logan, when she said goodbye to us. It's been over sixty years since that day, but every morning when I wake up, I still see her on the train track, waving at me, bidding me our final farewell. For a child, you see, the loss of a parent never goes away, no matter how many years slip by."

Helen pulls Julia's head to her chest, and Julia lets out a deep sob, feeling like a child being comforted by her mother, an experience Julia never had.

"You're like family to me, and you've suffered a terrible tragedy. I'll stay by your side and your children's sides until I know you're ready for me to go."

Helen keeps holding Julia until Julia pulls away.

"You go on now," Helen tells her. "You must have much preparation to still do for David's service today. I will get the boys ready, so take care of whatever else you need."

Julia heads to David's office to look for any overlooked family photographs to take to the service. She hesitates at the door, unable to go inside at first. This was the room David spent most of his time in as he worked tirelessly and late into the evenings in preparation for his cases the next day. Julia can picture David still sitting in his office chair, dressed in his Harvard Law T-shirt, going through his files and jotting down strategy on one of his constant supplies of yellow legal pads.

She finally enters and sits down on David's chair, wishing desperately the police had been able to find her husband's case file on Rossi that was either lost or destroyed in the attack. Julia absentmindedly runs her hand across an unused legal pad on the desk, and an image of two letters, clear and exact from the day of the bombing, surfaces into Julia's memory.

I.R.

Those initials with a question mark after them were written in David's handwriting on a yellow legal pad that sat on the prosecution's table. Julia spotted the initials on the paper as she searched Judge Palmer's courtroom for David and Logan right after the bomb went off.

Julia turns the letters over in her mind, swiveling David's chair back and forth as she hunts for a meaning. Julia's leg grazes something that feels unnatural underneath the desk, and her fingers search for the object until she reaches a piece of paper. She gets down on her knees and peers under the desk. Taped carefully to its underside is a plain white envelope. Julia tears it free and from the envelope, pulls out a simple business card with the inscription INFINITY HOLDINGS and a Detroit address written across it. Julia feels a trickle of electricity go through her as she starts to connect the pieces and remembers seeing the same business card from the vault and safety deposit company when she was in Isabella Rossi's cottage.

I.R. Isabella Rossi.

Julia grabs her house phone and calls Navarro. When the call goes to voice mail, Julia tries his partner, Russell, instead.

"Hey, Julia. A bunch of us will be at David's service later today. Is there anything you need?" Russell asks.

"No. Listen, I need to meet with you and Navarro this morning. It's urgent."

"Sure, of course, if you have time, come on down to the station. Ray should be back in about half an hour. He went to pick up a flash drive at the University of Detroit Mercy. That Bartello guy who was working for Rossi gave the drive to a buddy of his before he died, and the friend gave it to the local cops, who forwarded it to Ray. The recording on it is pretty grainy, but Ray knows a woman over at the college in the video production department who's helped us out before. Ray just called and said she got it cleaned up a bit, so we're going to take a look to see if we can get anything on it. Probably a long shot, though."

"Okay. I'll be there. This is important. Tell Navarro I found a business card hidden under David's desk from a company called Infinity Holdings. David kept saying the word *Infinity* along with a series of numbers when he came out of the coma. He was trying to tell me something. This Infinity Holdings is connected to the trial somehow and to Rossi.

Right before David died, he told me to find the money before *she* did. It's all connected somehow."

"Infinity Holdings. That's one of those high-end vault places," Russell says.

"I bet Nick Rossi isn't the only one wrapped up in this. I think Isabella Rossi is too."

Julia rushes to the police station, carefully eyeing the clock. It's nine AM, and David's service is at noon.

The receptionist buzzes Julia through the security glass door, and Julia politely thanks the murmuring chorus of "I'm sorry for your loss" as she passes by police officers who know her well from her beat and David from his work as a prosecutor and public defender.

Julia takes the familiar route to Russell and Navarro's office, and the two men are bent over Navarro's computer screen. Russell leaps to his feet and gives Julia a big, protective bear hug.

"How are you doing, sweetheart?" Russell asks.

"We're all just working through it," Julia answers, and then cuts to the chase. "Like I told Navarro, David knew something about Rossi that got him killed. I'm sure of it now. I found this card hidden under his desk at home. Isabella Rossi had the same card in her cottage in California. David kept saying the word *Infinity* back at the hospital, and he had the initials *I.R.* written on a yellow legal pad the day of the bombing. *I.R.*, Isabella Rossi."

"I know you want Rossi to pay, but do me a favor and go home. The service is in a few hours, and I promise you, we'll handle it," Navarro says. "You need to take care of yourself and your kids right now. I promise I'll look into this as soon as we view the video."

"I have some time," Julia answers. "You need to look at Isabella Rossi hard."

Julia pushes the Infinity Holdings business card into Navarro's hand, and he studies it for a second. "Russell and I will go over there to see if Rossi has an account with them. Isabella said she planned on being here in Detroit for an extended period of time, so we'll find her."

"Russell, can you give me and Navarro a minute?" Julia asks.

Russell looks to Navarro and then shrugs his okay as he leaves the office and closes the door behind him.

"Do me a favor and stop telling me to go home," Julia argues. "I need to find out what happened."

"I'm not trying to tell you what to do, but I don't want you weighted down with anything more. You've been through enough. Just go home and I'll call you if we find anything."

"I don't want to go home. Don't block me out of this, and stop trying to take care of me all the time."

Navarro sighs and lets Julia's words sink in. "Okay. If that's what you want, then fine. I'll go get Russell and we'll all look at the video together."

Russell returns, looking between his two friends for any clues of their conversation, and then sits down at his desk.

"I won't take this personally," Russell says.

"It wasn't about you," Julia answers.

"Pop the drive back in your computer," Navarro tells Russell.

"We just saw a couple seconds of it before you got here, Julia," Russell says. "Hopefully it is in better shape since Navarro had his friend over at the college give it a once-over. All you could see before was the outline of some guy banging the shit out of a blond chick."

Navarro shoots his partner a look as Russell puts on a pair of drugstore reading glasses and puts the drive back in his computer.

The recording comes on, and the date and time appear on the bottom of the screen.

"March 1. That's just over a month ago and almost two months after we did the sting at the hotel and arrested Rossi," Navarro says. "Keep going."

The video continues to play. The first few minutes capture only an empty hotel room.

"This recording is in worse shape than the Anthony Ruiz one I found back in Isabella's cottage," Julia says.

"Hold it right there," Navarro says. "Can you zoom in to the desk?"

"I don't know how," Russell answers.

"Let me try," Julia says as she grabs the computer mouse.

"You see that stationery? What's the name on top?" Navarro asks.

"Detroit MGM Grand," Julia answers.

"Okay, we got the location. The MGM Grand was Rossi's home base for his gambling and drug ring," Russell says.

"Go ahead and keep playing the video," Navarro says. "This is the part my friend at the college says was fuzzy, but she tried her best to clean it up."

As predicted, the quality of the recording diminishes, and the video becomes extremely dark and grainy.

"Okay, they're coming in now," Navarro says.

In the right-hand corner of the picture, the hotel room door opens and two people walk inside.

"It's a tall guy in a suit and a blond woman with a kicking figure, kind of like that Tandy Sanchez reporter from the *Detroit News*, but that's all I can get from this," Russell says. "The images look like mud."

The blond woman hands the man a briefcase, which he takes over to a table and opens.

"Again. Zoom in there, Julia," Navarro instructs.

"Those aren't bricks," Russell says. "Those are bundles of cash."

The man takes the money out of the briefcase and looks like he's counting it.

"It's unlikely that's a drug deal or gambling payoff unless Rossi is an idiot and uses the exact same location to sell his stuff where he was just busted," Navarro says.

"Probably a payoff of some kind," Russell says.

"If we could just get a full headshot, that would help," Julia answers.

The blonde hurries across the room to the man in the suit.

"I think the next part of this video won't be suitable for children," Russell says.

"Shut up, will you?" Navarro tells Russell.

The blonde pulls her dress over her head, and the man's hands are all over her body. The blonde unbuttons his shirt and works his belt and zipper until his pants fall away at his feet.

"Looks like the blonde is going south there," Russell says as the woman's face moves down toward the man's crotch.

"Russell, I swear . . ." Navarro starts.

"They're shot from the side. Just turn around so I can see your face," Julia implores the people on the screen.

The man strips off the blonde's underwear in a quick snap and pushes her down on the bed.

"The guy's fair haired," Navarro comments. "Tall, and wiry."

"That fits the description of about two thousand guys in the metro Detroit area," Russell comments. "Oh, wait. I see a hand. She's got a firm grip on his ass, and the waistband of his underwear is going down. And there's takeoff. Wait . . . and now liftoff. My friends, the *Eagle* has landed inside the blonde, and he's giving her the ride of her life."

"Russell, easy on the play-by-play, all right?" Julia asks.

"Sorry about that," Russell concedes.

"There's something on the guy's ass, on his right butt cheek. What is that?" Navarro asks. "Can you zoom in, Julia?"

"It looks like a shit stain to me," Russell answers.

"One more comment and I swear I'm kicking you out of this room," Navarro says.

"I'm zooming," Julia says.

Julia freezes the frame and does a close-up.

The three do a quick assessment, and Julia pushes herself abruptly away from the computer screen.

"If you're uncomfortable looking at this, it's okay," Navarro says.

"What you see on the screen, that's a birthmark," Julia says quietly.

"Yeah, it's unique. Kind of looks like a crescent moon with a shooting star underneath it," Russell says.

"I know who the man in the video is," Julia says. "It's David."

"Is that Brooke Stevenson?" Russell asks.

Navarro inspects the still frame frozen on the screen. "Could be with a wig."

Julia looks back at the brick colonial in Detroit's Boston-Edison District and wonders how many times David frequented the place to visit its owner. She curses herself for not pushing harder with Navarro to let her sit in on the interview with Brooke Stevenson, whom she saw opening the front door of her home twenty minutes earlier.

Julia checks the clock on Navarro's car dashboard again and is about to get out and bang on the door when Navarro and Russell make their way down a tidy flagstone path to the street.

"She looks like she's got the same figure as the broad in the video, but Brooke Stevenson swears that's not her and she didn't know anything about a payoff," Russell says as he works his way into the passenger-side front seat. "She seemed genuinely shocked that David might have been involved in something illegal."

"She's not the only one, but Brooke's lying about the video," Julia answers. "I saw the pictures on David's phone."

"Claims that wasn't her either. Brooke said David dumped her when the two of you got back together," Navarro says, and starts the car. "Did you see her face in the photos on David's phone?"

"No, but I assumed. I guess the woman in the pictures could be someone else."

"We're checking out Brooke's alibi, but it sounds pretty tight. She was second chair on a case down in district court at the exact same time of the recording's date stamp."

"It could have been altered," Julia insists.

"I don't think it's her, Julia," Navarro says. "Some balding guy was getting out of the shower when we walked in. Turns out it's her boyfriend. He's a law professor over at Wayne State University, and the two have been living together for the past couple of months."

"Then who was sending David the pictures?" Julia asks.

"Must be the mystery blonde in the video," Russell answers.

CHAPTER 24

Isabella Rossi hurries across her Detroit penthouse and gathers the last of her things she will take with her. She checks the local headlines online before she packs up her computer, and catches an article about the attorney's funeral scheduled for the afternoon. Isabella fantasizes for a moment about attending. She closes her eyes and steals off to a memory four months prior with her unexpected business partner.

"Hold on, I have to take this. And please be quiet," David says as he puts his index finger to his lips.

David answers the call and looks away toward the sliver of light coming through Isabella's penthouse bedroom window as Rossi's wife moves on top of him.

"Hey, Brewbaker. Yeah, I'm heading to California tomorrow. I'm confident I can get Sammy Biggs to flip."

Isabella tweaks David's nipple, and he shakes his head until she stops.

"No, I don't need anyone else from the D.A.'s office to join

me. I've got it covered. I'll call you after my meeting. . . . No. Don't worry about police protection. I'll be fine."

David turns off his cell phone and throws it on the floor.

Isabella arches her back and tilts her long, slender neck toward the ceiling. David grips her waist with both hands as the two of them finish together.

Isabella pulls off David's body and nestles on the bed next to him.

"What happens after my husband goes to jail?" she asks.

"Just like we agreed. We split the money Rossi gave me to pay off the juror and you get out from under your husband's abusive thumb."

"I should be getting the payoff from Enzo any day now. Once the trial starts, Nick wants me to go back to California."

"I'm working on getting the security box set up for the cash."

"Where?"

"I looked at a vault and safe company called Infinity Holdings this morning," David says. "I've got two more places to check out before I decide. I need to be sure the place is discreet and there's no way anyone can trace the cash back to us."

David gets up from the bed, slips his clothes back on, and hands Isabella the business card from Infinity Holdings.

"How much does it cost to run for district attorney anyway?" Isabella asks.

"I don't care about the money. Your husband has something on me. Or at least he did until this morning. That's why I had to agree to go through with this initially. I withheld evidence in a case that could've helped prove the innocence of a defendant. I was prosecuting a murder trial. Anthony Ruiz. He was accused of raping and killing a mother and her teenage daughter after he broke into their *house over in Troy. The father was away on a business trip at the time. The father killed himself because he thought he could have protected his family if he had been home. I knew that asshole Ruiz did it. Ruiz was a day laborer with a drug problem and picked up a job blacktopping a neighbor's house across the street for a week straight before the murders. A neighbor saw Ruiz talking to the girl a whole lot that week. He was a good-looking kid."*

"So?"

"Ruiz got pinned for a DNA match on the semen that was found inside the girl. That sealed the case for us. But my investigator found something, a security surveillance video from a dive bar down in Wayne that showed Ruiz at the bar around fifteen minutes after we think the women were killed. He was stupid. He made up a fake alibi claiming he was home alone at the time of the killings, because the footage caught him scoring drugs from one of Rossi's guys. Ruiz already had prior drug convictions, and he was probably scared shitless that if he told the truth, he'd wind up serving a good chunk of time on the drug charge."

"And this security video. You didn't turn that in as evidence?"

"No. Troy to Warren is ten miles. Ruiz could have conceivably made it to the bar if he floored it the whole way, but I couldn't risk letting anyone see the footage. It could have put doubt in the jurors' minds. The defense played it that the DNA match between Ruiz and the girl was because the sex was consensual. But I know Ruiz did it, and I couldn't take the chance that he'd walk. He killed those women."

"Ah. Those who follow the law always get screwed. How does Nick tie into this?"

"His guy who sold Ruiz the drugs used the bar as his distribution ground. He saw my investigator there and knew

about the recording and what he was up to and told his boss. Rossi backed me into a corner and threatened me when he found out I'd be leading the prosecution against him. Either I could agree to throw the case and buy off a juror with the money he supplied, or he'd leak what I'd done on the Ruiz case. Rossi blackmailed me. I could be disbarred or go to jail if anyone finds out what I did."

"Where's this recording?"

"I bought it this morning from the bar owner for fifteen thousand. He promised there were no copies and he'd keep quiet. The only other person who knows about it is my former investigator, but he died two months ago in a car crash. So your husband doesn't have anything on me anymore, even though he thinks he does. If he claims I withheld evidence in a case, it's his word against mine. So now I try the case honestly—"

"With Nick completely in the dark about what we're doing," Isabella interrupts.

"Right. And Rossi goes to jail."

"And we split the two million dollars," Isabella answers. "What about the juror?"

"I got as far as pinpointing two I thought would be candidates, but I never approached them. So there are no loose ends."

Isabella turns to the wall so David won't see her smile over his naivete. She knows all too well anything can be purchased for the right price and the right threat, including a copy of bar surveillance footage. She turns back to face David and tries to give him a look that she cares, even though she knows she's already one step ahead of David in ensuring she has something on him if she needs to use it.

"What if Nick finds out what we're going to do?" Isabella asks.

"He won't. I set up the meeting with Sammy Biggs already. We'll have a car waiting for him in the rear parking lot of the Santa Maria Temple. Your husband will never find out."

Isabella smiles and stretches her naked body across the bed like a cat.

"How's your wife? Are you still trying to get her to move back to Rochester so you can be one big, happy family again?"

"Don't talk about Julia," David warns. "She's off limits. This is the last time we do this, understand? It's business from here on out. Things went too far between us."

David stares back at Isabella, realizing he made a horrible mistake crossing the line sexually with her. But once he got sucked in with Rossi, another dark alliance seemed to come naturally.

"Fine. You go back to your little wife, but you better not screw me on my share of the money, or I'll swear I'll come after your family," Isabella says. "I'll start with your oldest son first. Once I'm through, he'll be in so many little pieces, you won't be able to ID the body."

A black cloud of fury moves through David, and he desperately wishes he could go back and act like the man he thought he was before all this mess started, someone who would spurn Rossi's bribe even though it could mean his own professional and most likely personal downfall. David looks on in disgust at Isabella naked in bed, her lithe body now coiled like a snake, and lets in the realization that maybe the true test of a man is not what he does when the chips are down but how far he allows himself to slither deeper into a pit with the devil.

David jumps to Isabella's side, throws her back down on the bed, and wraps his hands around her throat in a chokehold.

*"You touch my family, I'll kill you," he warns. "Do we
have an understanding?"*

*Isabella nods her agreement. David releases her, gets up
from the bed, and stares coolly back at his reflection in the
vanity as he knots his tie at his throat.*

*Isabella sits up in the bed proudly and tries to recover her
position.*

*"You can't take a joke. I lost a child. Do you really think
I'm capable of killing one?"*

"I think you're capable of anything."

"Such tough talk from a pretty boy."

*"I mean it. Leave my family alone. Julia's moving back
home and things are going to work between us this time. We
had a rough patch, but we love each other."*

*"Whatever you say. I'm sure you'll win the husband of the
year award. You going to take that?" she asks as David's
phone rings again.*

*"No. It's the mayor," David answers as he looks down at
his phone. "He's trying to get me to come work for him."*

"How rich."

Isabella thinks wistfully about the expression "the best
laid plans" and curses herself for nearly getting caught. But
she knows she's lucky she got out with her life by lying and
narrowly convincing her husband and Enzo Costas she didn't
know that David planned to double-cross them, until the day
Costas caught her in the room at the MGM Grand.

Isabella grabs her purse, feeling flushed with excitement as
she prepares to head to Infinity Holdings to pick up the
bribe money, more than enough for her to disappear and escape from her life with her husband. Isabella gets as far as the
penthouse door when her phone sounds and her husband's
name appears across the screen. Isabella pauses for a moment
and then picks up.

"I booked you a flight. You're coming back to California first thing in the morning," Rossi instructs. "Things are getting messy. Enzo was killed by the lawyer's wife and a Detroit cop."

"Christ, is that all?"

"The lawyer died."

"Ah, I didn't know that," Isabella lies.

"It saved me some trouble, him dying of natural causes. He screwed me, and I already planned to kill him after the trial. But this way the police won't try to pin me for his death. I called Tarburton. He said the police don't have anything to connect me to the bombing. Enzo worked it out so there was no direct link to me with the sniper, so Enzo will be blamed for the L.A. cop's murder and hiring Meter to take out Sammy Biggs."

Isabella digs her fingernails into her palm until she can feel the skin break. "So you won't face any new charges?"

"Yeah. Good luck is finally turning my way. What did you find out about the two million?"

"Spent. David Tanner was a liar. He never used the money to pay off the juror. The lawyer stole your cash and used it to buy property, and the rest he invested in his upcoming run for political office. Don't worry, though, Nick. You can recoup two million dollars in two minutes."

"That stupid lawyer and his wife."

"Don't worry so much. I'm leaving the penthouse right now so the police won't know where to find me if they want to question me again."

"Just lay low until you hear from me. Tarburton thinks we're okay, but he wants me to take it easy until things quiet down."

"Of course, Nick. Whatever you say."

"You've redeemed yourself," Rossi says. "I'll give you something special when you get back to California, something that will make you feel good all night long."

Isabella rolls her eyes, grabs her Prada bag, and turns off the lights to the penthouse.

CHAPTER 25

The portable heating lamps strategically positioned in Julia's backyard take the bite off the late-afternoon April chill and draw a gathering crowd away from Julia's house and the spread inside that Helen laid out for guests after David's service.

The somberness of the day has temporarily lost its effect on Logan, who plays with Will and some of his friends from school up in the tree house David built three years earlier.

(*Stop worrying, Julia, I took woodshop in high school, and this tree house is as sturdy as our own home. How about we meet up here tonight after the kids are in bed? I'll bring a bottle of champagne.*)

Julia puts her hands over her ears, as if trying to drown out David's voice.

"Julia, we've been looking for you."

Julia looks up to see Gavin Boyles and Mayor Anderson hovering above her. Gavin rubs his finger in nervous circles around the parameter of the port wine stain on his temple, and Anderson offers Julia his hand and a sympathetic smile that looks sincere.

"I've been at a loss when I heard about David," Anderson says, and kneels down next to Julia. He leans in for one of his trademark hugs, but Julia pulls away.

Anderson settles for Julia's hand instead and reaches out to grab it before Julia can object.

"Are you taken care of?" Anderson asks.

"I'm sorry?"

"I mean with money. Did David leave you enough for you to get by? You can't be surviving on what the paper pays you with two young kids. I realize there's nothing I can say or do to help you right now, but I need good talent on my team. Whenever you're ready, I'd like you to come work for me. I guarantee I'll pay better than what you make reporting."

She notices that Boyles has left his boss's side and is now weaving in her direction with a male news anchor and a TV camera crew from the local Fox news station.

"Thank you for the offer, but if you want to do something for me, get your boy out of here with the TV people, or I'll sic the cops on him."

Anderson turns his back and notices Boyles and the rabid media quickly approaching. He holds up his hand to warn Boyles and his entourage to stop.

"Oh Lord. I'm so sorry, Julia. I'll be damned if that boy isn't such a horse's ass sometimes."

Mayor Anderson kisses Julia's hand lightly and then puts an arm each around Boyles and the cameraman as he corrals the group away from their hoped-for shots of the mourning widow.

Julia rolls her eyes at Navarro as he approaches with a Sierra Nevada Pale Ale. Julia grabs the cool green bottle of beer from his hand and downs its remains in a series of rapid swallows.

"I can get you your own," Navarro says. He takes off his suit coat and drapes it around Julia's shoulders.

"No thanks on the beer. I just needed something to take the edge off."

"You need me to ward off the press for you?"

"No. Mayor Anderson took care of it. I'm starting to think he's not such a bad guy. Just the people who work for him are pretty slippery."

"It's cold out here. Why don't we go inside?"

"I want a minute to breathe without everyone hovering over me saying how sorry they are."

"I'm going to Infinity Holdings in a little while. If David took a bribe, Infinity Holdings is probably where he stashed the money. But the question is, who did he take the money from? The thing that doesn't make any sense is, if it was a bribe from Rossi, why did David go to all the trouble of bringing Sammy Biggs in to testify? And the other part that I never understood is why David was in Judge Palmer's chambers all alone at the time the bomb went off without opposing counsel there."

"Maybe David recruited Sammy Biggs before Rossi got to him. And then Rossi paid David to throw the case and David got a freebie thrown in with the blonde who Rossi used as the money currier," Julia says. "David knows Rossi is going to plant the bomb when the Butcher enters the courthouse, so at the last minute David tells the cops and everyone else he can't escort the Butcher because he has to meet with the judge."

"It's possible. But David told you he thought the bomb was meant for someone else."

"The more I think about what he said in the hospital, the more I'm starting to believe David's doctor. David was confused and piecing together memories that didn't connect."

"But what about the bar surveillance footage? Nick Rossi had something on David, so why would he give David money if he already had a hold over him?"

"Maybe to ensure his future services. We need answers. Rossi is in hiding. How about Isabella?" Julia asks.

"Russell just paid a visit to her penthouse. She didn't answer, and the property manager said she terminated her lease this morning. Big surprise, she didn't leave a forwarding address."

"Can we go to Infinity Holdings now?"

"You tell me. You're the host, and if you feel it's okay to leave an hour after your husband's funeral with a guy you used to date while everyone else is still here, I'm game."

Julia shrugs her shoulders, not worried about what anyone thinks of her. She looks back to the tree house and can see Logan's dark hair through the rectangular window David almost lost his thumb trying to cut out and makes her decision.

"All right. We'll stay."

"Russell and I can leave now."

"No way. I'm coming too."

The door to the rear deck opens, and an attractive redhead in a tight black dress carrying a giant floral arrangement cranes her neck as she searches the yard for someone.

"Your girlfriend is here," Julia comments.

Navarro quickly turns toward the house and grimaces when he sees Bianca.

"We broke up. I have no idea why she's here. Let me get rid of her."

"I'm sure she's here to pay her respects, so don't worry about it," Julia says.

Bianca spots the pair and carefully picks her way down the stairs in her stiletto heels.

"Just try to be civil," Julia says, and walks in Bianca's direction. "I'm not up for anything else today."

Bianca leans in and gives Julia a light hug, leaving a strong remnant of her perfume behind.

"I couldn't make the service, with the lunch hour and everything. I'm so sorry about David," Bianca says. "I also wanted to apologize for the way I acted in the restaurant. That wasn't my finest moment."

"Don't worry about it. If you haven't eaten anything, there's a lot of food inside. Navarro, can you show her?" Julia asks, using her friend to get rid of the unwanted company.

Navarro raises an eyebrow at Julia, game to her maneuver. "Yeah, sure," he answers.

Navarro leads Bianca back inside, and Bianca laces her arm through Navarro's as she tries to climb up the six steps to the deck in her ridiculously high shoes.

Julia drops down on the tire swing underneath the maple tree and kicks at the ground with the toe of her black boot. She faces the woods in the rear of her property and fantasizes what it would be like to just take off and run as fast as she can, far off through the trees. She'd never be able to escape her problems, she realizes, but at least she would be alone.

"Hey, Julia," a female voice calls from behind.

So much for being alone, Julia figures, and spins the tire swing around. Tandy Sanchez, the *Detroit News* reporter, stands above Julia, her usual gravity-defying perky cleavage covered up this time in a conservative black wool dress.

"Really?" Julia asks. "Please don't tell me you've come to try to interview me."

Tandy stands firm, prepared to take the expected barbs. She tucks a strand of her platinum blond hair behind her ear and offers Julia a sympathetic smile.

"I'm not here to write a story. This obviously wasn't a good idea."

"You're right. It wasn't. Why did you come here? Are you going to try to corner Logan again for a quote?"

Tandy casts her eyes to the ground. "I'm sorry, Julia. I was just doing my job. You know how it is."

"I don't. I've never stooped that low before," Julia answers.

"Well, then, you're a better person than me if that's what you want me to say. Look, I knew I wouldn't be welcome here, but I wanted to tell you personally that I'm so sorry about David, and I feel terrible for you and your children. I apologize for approaching your son in the hospital. As a journalist, it seems sometimes when we're trying to do our job well, we wind up not being very nice people."

Tandy begins to walk away and retreat toward the house when Julia calls her back.

"The story that you wrote, the one from the first day of the trial."

"About the Butcher, the prosecution's last-minute witness?" Tandy answers, and turns around.

"Right, and the profile you wrote on David. Who was your source?"

"You know I can't tell you that."

"You owe me for the hospital incident. Was it my husband?"

"I'm sorry. I'm not the terrible person you think I am, and I'd like to help you, but I can't burn a source."

"Then how about this. If Charboneau, from Rossi's defense team, told you about the witness, walk back into the house and don't say another word. You won't technically be telling me anything," Julia says.

Tandy chews on her thumbnail, considering the request, and then holds Julia's gaze, ready to play the game.

"You're still here, I see," Julia says, and continues. "If David was your leak on the Butcher, go back into the house and leave the screen door open."

"I don't want to do this anymore."

"That's fine. But you're not burning a source if you rule out my husband as your leak. We both know how this works."

"All right. It wasn't David. I tried to get it out of him, but he wouldn't budge. It was someone else. I won't give you a name, but the person is in your house."

Julia looks out the window of Navarro's car and watches the abandoned shells of buildings slip by as she, Navarro, and Russell approach the city's core and Infinity Holdings.

"Are you all right back there?" Navarro asks Julia.

"I'm fine," she answers.

"That was quite a surprise seeing Bianca show up like that," Russell goads. "Are you two back together?"

Navarro keeps his eyes on Julia in the backseat for a beat and then returns them to the buckled road, left in infinite ill-repair until the city of Detroit can find a way to pay to fix it, a priority buried way down deep on the already daunting list of its more dire needs.

"No way," Navarro responds. "She was nice and conciliatory as hell until she asked me to come to her house, and I told her that was never going to happen. Then she got ugly. I had to escort Bianca to her car before she caused a scene."

"I guess you just never know some people, just like David, right, Julia?" Russell says. "There are usually clues about someone's real intentions, you know that, and you've always been really good at figuring out the true story behind the lies people tell. You and David were married for what, ten years? Did David give you any indicators that he was the type of guy who would take a bribe, possibly throw a case, and screw around on his wife?"

Russell's dead-on summary of her husband makes Julia visibly cringe.

"Russell, shut it," Navarro orders.

"No, it's okay. Maybe it's never really possible to ever truly know another person," Julia says.

"Everyone has a face they want to hide," Navarro tells Julia. "For you and me, we hide what happened to us when we were kids. For others, they hide their duplicitous acts."

"That's some heavy philosophy there, Ray," Russell comments, and turns around in his seat toward Julia. "You and David got married pretty quick after you got together. Maybe you didn't know him as well as you thought."

"I was pregnant with Logan."

Navarro gives Julia a hard stare from the rearview mirror as if something has finally been explained and pulls into an open parking space a street away from Infinity Holdings.

"You think they'll let us take a look around without a warrant?" Russell asks. "The judge didn't sign it yet."

"Go in first, identify yourself as a cop, and see what you can find out. Chances are, they won't give you much without a warrant, but press the issue that this place probably doesn't ask for much identification when people set up their accounts, and Infinity Holdings could be abetting a crime as a result. Make whoever you talk to think they could get arrested if they are storing anything illegal in the place."

"What about you?" Russell asks.

"Julia and I will wait here for you. If you're successful, then call me and I'll come in. If you're not, Julia and I are going to pose as a couple interested in getting a security box, and we'll dig around and see what we can find."

"Do me a favor and move up to the front seat. I feel like a taxi driver up here," Navarro says as Russell disappears around the corner.

Julia takes Russell's place and, not wanting to talk, slips one of Navarro's CDs into the car stereo. Stevie Ray Vaughan belts out with passionate, raw soul, "The Sky Is Crying." They've listened to the first half of the blues artist's posthumous album when Russell appears on the street in front of them and makes his way back to the car.

"They're slick," Russell answers as he gets in the backseat. "Polite little bean counters gave me a tour of the place and they were professional enough, but they 'hold their clients' confidentiality in the highest regard.' "

"You didn't threaten them with an arrest?" Navarro answers.

"Of course I did. That got their knickers in a big old twist. The head guy, Greg Spanier, comes out from his office, all apologetic, saying he just got back from lunch and the broad helping me out front is new. This Spanier guy looks through his files and says no one by the name of Rossi has ever had an account there. But David Tanner does, and he gives up his security deposit box as number twenty-two."

"David told me 'box twenty-two' when he was in the hospital, so that has to be where he hid the cash," Julia says.

"I explained to Spanier that David died because of the injuries he sustained in the bombing, and we have reason to believe he was involved in criminal activities regarding Rossi, which gets Spanier all sweaty and nervous," Russell continues. "That's when things go bad. Spanier tells me a woman came into the place just a few hours ago and claimed she was a secretary from the district attorney's office and was picking up something for her boss in one of the boxes. Turns out she had the wrong safety deposit box number and security code and asks if he can give her the correct information. Spanier tells her to call her boss with the account and heads to his office, thinking she'll follow, but before he can take two steps, she's out the door. Then Spanier stops talking to me all of a sudden after he realizes maybe what I'm asking him about and the mystery woman are connected and he realizes he could be in trouble, so he tells me he won't be able to assist

me any further without a warrant or consulting with his attorney."

"Someone is a step ahead of us," Julia answers.

"Probably Isabella on behalf of her husband. All right.
We've got this," Navarro says. "Give me fifteen minutes. If
we don't come out by then, go back inside Infinity Holdings
and demand you have to see Spanier again."

"About what?" Russell asks.

"Make something up," Navarro answers.

Navarro and Julia exit the vehicle and turn the corner to
the vault and safety deposit box company.

Infinity Holdings, the alternative for people who want to
put their valuables in a safe place other than a bank, looks
exactly like one, institutional and secure, complete with a
fake circular copper vault door on the inside back wall for
show.

Navarro, who could pass for a legitimate businessman,
still in his suit coat from the funeral instead of his usual
leather jacket that makes him look like a hood or a cop, puts
his hand on the small of Julia's back and leads her inside.

A mousy, tense-looking woman in a conservative navy
blue dress and a name tag that reads JUNE pinned to her lapel
gives the couple an anxious smile as they enter.

"Good afternoon. Are you here to deposit something?"
June asks.

"No, my fiancée and I are getting married next month, and
we're looking for a place to keep our valuables. With the
economy the way it's been, there have been a couple of break-
ins in my neighborhood, and I want to be sure our belongings are safe."

"Of course," June answers. She pulls out a glossy brochure
of the place and hands it to them across the counter. "Let me
just call my boss."

Julia and Navarro pretend to pore over the brochure with

interest as the manager, Greg Spanier, emerges from a back office. He strides over to Julia and Navarro and pumps Navarro's hand up and down in a firm grip.

Navarro gives him the same spiel as the receptionist, and Spanier's eyes shine with fake enthusiasm. "So when's the big day?" he asks.

Navarro looks blank for a minute, and Julia speaks up. "We're getting married next month."

"You're a lucky man," Spanier tells Navarro. "And smart. We've had a spike in the amount of vaults and security deposit boxes we've rented out due to the rampant crime epidemic here in Detroit. And as a business owner, let me just say the police have done little to stop it."

Navarro presses his hand against Julia's waist over the irony of the comment, and Julia forces herself to suppress a smile.

"You don't have to worry about your valuables here. We have twenty-four-hour surveillance and twenty-four-hour accessibility. All we need is your thumbprint. Now, how about a tour?" Spanier asks.

"I was ready to go home, Mr. Spanier. It's almost five," the receptionist says.

"It's only four forty-five," Spanier says, and taps his index finger against his Rolex. "We'll be through the tour in just a few minutes."

Spanier walks past the fake vault door and brings Navarro and Julia to a back room.

"Sorry, June is a new hire. Although she works bankers' hours, as I said, all our clients have round-the-clock access to the facility."

Spanier presses his thumb into a keypad mounted on the wall, and an exterior door opens. Inside the climate-controlled cool room is the real vault door, a mammoth circle with gold-colored bars running vertically through it. Spanier opens the heavy door with a key and takes Navarro and Julia inside the space that is filled from floor to ceiling with rectangular silver security deposit boxes on one side and larger vaults on the other.

Spanier knocks off the list of all the features of Infinity Holdings, until June's voice interrupts them from the other side of the vault door.

"Mr. Spanier, that police officer is back," she says.

Spanier is the one who looks nervous this time, the makings of a bead of sweat appearing on his brow.

"I'm very sorry," Spanier says. "Tell you what. Why don't you take a look around for a minute, and when you're done, just press that red button on the wall and June will let you out."

"That will be perfect," Navarro says.

"If you're interested in a larger space, our six-foot vaults are right around the corner," Spanier says as he leaves.

Julia and Navarro wait to hear the exterior door close, and then they hurry down the narrow corridor of polished metal boxes infused into the walls.

"Russell said David's security deposit box is number twenty-two," Navarro says.

The numbers start at the rear of the vault, so David's space is tucked far back from the entrance. Navarro gets down on his knees and inspects the rectangular box that has the number twenty-two etched across it.

"We need a key or a code, and we have neither," Navarro says.

"When David was in the hospital, he told me the numbers three, two, one, thirty, and then the word *infinity*. We've obviously hit on the 'infinity' part of what he was trying to tell me. Maybe the numbers are the code."

Navarro's finger quickly taps the numbers in sequence, and the door of the box pops open.

"Bingo," Navarro says. He reaches inside and pulls out a

worn leather briefcase. "Let's hope there's no code or key involved this time."

Navarro snaps the briefcase easily open and lifts the lid. Inside, the briefcase is piled with thick stacks of carefully bundled hundred-dollar bills.

Navarro quickly runs his hand down the side of one stack to count the money.

"There's got to be over a million dollars in here. David was dirty," Navarro says.

"I realize that, but why did he want me to find the money?" Julia asks.

"He knew Rossi would come after you and your kids if he couldn't find the cash."

The sound of shoes clicking a fast path across the fake marble floor in their direction puts Navarro and Julia on instant alert. Navarro swiftly puts everything back into the briefcase. He snaps the briefcase's locks back in place and thrusts it into the security deposit box.

"Sorry about the delay," Spanier says, letting himself back into the vault with a key. "Now, how was the tour?"

"I think we found everything we hoped for and more," Navarro answers.

Navarro drops Russell back off at the station to secure the warrant for Infinity Holdings and then pulls in front of Julia's house. A few red-and-orange Chinese lanterns that Helen placed for the reception still hang on the porch to welcome those who came just a few hours prior to pay their respects to David.

The police officer parked in front of Julia's house flashes his beams at Navarro's car.

"I'll be right back," Navarro says. "Stay here and I'll walk you inside when I'm done."

Navarro huddles over the security detail's open front door

window for a few minutes and then heads back in Julia's direction, the streetlight casting a dim yellow spotlight as he approaches.

"My guy says there's been no suspicious activity going on all day, even with all the people coming and going during the reception. I wish you'd take the gun I offered you, though. It would make me feel better."

"Thanks, but not with kids in the house," Julia says. "Even with a safe, they scare me. Do you want to come in for a few minutes? You can have a beer since I drank most of yours this afternoon."

"Sure, if you want me to," Navarro answers.

Navarro and Julia head inside the house and find Helen packing up the last of the reception food into clear Tupperware containers.

"You're late," Helen says. "The boys were exhausted, and they fell asleep about forty minutes ago."

"I wanted to say good night to them. How are they doing?"

"A day like this? As well as could be expected. Logan wanted to stay up until you got home, but I made him go to bed. He and Will are asleep in your room again. Go give them a kiss," Helen tells Julia, and then turns to Navarro. "And you, you are staying?"

Navarro searches Julia for an answer.

"Yes, I asked my friend to visit with me for a bit," Julia says.

Helen puts her hands on her hips and shoves the remaining Tupperware containers into the already-packed refrigerator, obviously not happy with Julia's response.

"Feel free to get yourself a beer. I'll be right back," Julia tells Navarro.

Julia walks quietly to her bedroom and gives each of her boys a soft kiss. She pulls off her black skirt and top, tired of looking like she is in mourning for a man who she realizes she never really knew. She changes into a light blue tank top and jeans and turns down the thermostat in the nearly unbearably warm house, caused by Helen's usual nightly routine of turning the heat up to nearly eighty to ensure Julia's room in the back of the house is warm when the boys go to sleep.

Julia returns to the kitchen, which is now empty. Julia decides Navarro changed his mind and went home. She reaches into the refrigerator to search for a beer. The back screen door opens, and Julia's hands scramble across the counter for her cell phone to call the officer out front.

"Hey, sorry, I didn't mean to scare you there," Navarro says as he heads down the back hallway toward the kitchen. "I walked Helen home, although she clearly didn't want me to. I get a very strong feeling she doesn't like me very much."

Julia pulls out another bottle of Sierra Nevada Pale Ale from her refrigerator and hands it to Navarro.

"You changed," he says, his eyes doing a quick and discreet sweep of Julia's body.

"Helen turns this place into the Sahara Desert at night. I needed to put on something cooler. And yes, she's overprotective and might be worried you have bad intentions. Don't take it personally. She's just playing mamma bear with the boys and me right now."

Navarro takes a long pull of his beer, and Julia motions him into the living room.

"How are you doing with all this?" Navarro asks.

Julia moves to the large window that overlooks the backyard and flicks on the porch light, taking in all the things that were once so wonderfully familiar.

Navarro comes up from behind and puts his hand on Julia's shoulder. His touch feels warm and strong, and Julia flashes back to the recording of David having rough sex with the blonde. She realizes how good it would feel to do the same right now. She pictures herself and Navarro starring in the video instead and, for a second, savors how good it would feel to be desired by someone who wouldn't hurt her or continue to lie and betray her trust.

She picks up her beer instead and finishes half the bottle easily in a matter of seconds.

"I forgot you could drink a beer faster than most guys I know."

"Why do you think David did it?"

"You want my dime store psychology? If David wasn't being blackmailed, then it was all about sex and money. Those are potent drugs. I assume you guys were pretty well off financially?"

"Not on my salary, but David made a good income in the D.A.'s office."

"So unless David has some gambling or drug problem, which I don't think he had, the money is all about power, and so is the sex."

"You're good. Maybe you should switch professions."

"No, thanks. I wouldn't want to sit around and listen to people's problems all day," Navarro answers. "Do you want some company tonight? I can come back here after I meet Russell at Infinity Holdings to pick up the briefcase. Mr. Spanier is about to get a late-night call he wasn't expecting. And I can sleep on your couch. I don't want to leave you alone if you need someone to talk to."

"No, it's been a long day. You look tired. Go home and get some sleep when you're done with Spanier."

"If you're sure then, okay. I can swing by and pick you up in the morning if you like. I'm going to the hospital to see if Judge Palmer has come around yet. It's worth a shot. I'd like to talk to him about what David was doing in his chambers at the time the bomb went off."

"Yes, definitely count me in," Julia answers. "I'm going to take the boys to Eastern Market in the morning. I know I can't make everything better overnight, but at least I can get them out of the house for a while. There are too many memories here for them."

Navarro picks up his coat and heads to the front door.

"Hey, you," Julia calls after him.

Navarro turns around and flashes Julia his perfect smile.

"Thanks for everything you've done for me," Julia says. "I owe you after this is over."

"No, you don't. I'll see you in the morning. Are you sure you're okay?"

"I've survived things as hard as this."

"And come out stronger. I'm here for you."

"That's one of the few things I'm sure of."

CHAPTER 26

Henry Ford Hospital is the one place, besides Rossi's compound, Julia never wanted to return to, and she feels out of her body as she, Navarro, and Russell make their way down the fifth-floor corridor to see Judge Palmer. Russell, the one who always lightens the mood with his off-color comments, is unusually quiet, and Julia understands that the hospital is the last place on earth he would rather be.

"It was pretty ballsy of you to go right back to work after you got hurt in the bombing," Julia says to Russell, speaking his language.

"Balls of steel," he answers, a slight smile forming at his lips as he gets his mojo back.

"Are your injuries all healed?" Julia asks.

"Pretty much everything except for the groin. I pee more than I used to, but that could be age," Russell answers. "You know I just turned forty."

"Add on another ten years, my friend," Navarro says.

Russell grabs his chest, pretending to be hurt.

"Hey, forty is just three years away for you, and don't

think I won't keep reminding you about it. Viagra and Rogaine, baby," Russell jabs at Navarro.

"I've got to talk to Judge Palmer's doctor first," Navarro says, bringing the conversation back in line. "The judge has been in and out of surgeries, so I just have to get the green light that he's stable enough for me to interview him. I've gotten nothing but no's so far."

"Maybe today will be your lucky day," Russell says.

Russell and Navarro sidle up to the nurses' station, and Navarro easily wins the attention of a pretty young brunette RN who drops what she's doing to help him. Julia pulls out her reporter's notebook and succumbs to her usual habit when she tries to figure out a missing piece of a story. She writes down the one thread she hasn't been able to solve:

If David took a payoff, why did he recruit the Butcher to testify against Rossi?

Julia searches the space for Navarro but instead spots David's physician, Dr. Whitcomb, walking through a door that reads ADMINISTRATION ONLY. Julia tries to turn around, not wanting to see David's doctor again and relive the last few days, but her move is too late. Dr. Whitcomb notices Julia and beats a path toward her.

"Julia, I'm surprised to see you here."

"I'm at the hospital on business related to the bombing," she answers.

"I was just on my way to call you. You ordered an autopsy of your husband's body, and I just got the preliminary results a few minutes ago."

"Right. I wanted to know his exact cause of death."

"Was your husband a drug user?"

"No," Julia quickly answers. "At least I don't think so."

"The toxicology report shows David had cocaine in his system."

"Cocaine? That's not possible. One thing I'm sure of, David never took drugs, and there's no way he would ever touch cocaine. He was a high-functioning attorney, and I would have known if he'd fallen into something like that. Even if he was using before he got to the hospital, the drug would have been out of his system by the time you did the toxicology report, I would think."

"The level of cocaine in his system was extremely high," Dr. Whitcomb answers.

"Something happened then. You and I both know there is no way David could have been doing lines in the hospital. He wasn't strong or steady enough to even pick up a cup to take a drink of water."

"Well, it got into his system somehow."

"Did the cocaine cause the heart attack?"

"We won't have the full results of the autopsy for several weeks, but that amount of cocaine could certainly cause major cardiac distress and overdose, if not death."

"Somebody tried to kill him," Julia answers.

"It's certainly a suspicious finding, and enough to alert the authorities. I've asked the nursing supervisor who was on shift the day your husband died to check if her staff can re-member any visitors David had that afternoon. I'll have my secretary make you a copy of the preliminary report that will also be sent to the police."

Dr. Whitcomb leaves Julia with the bombshell revelation, now her second unanswered question. Julia closes her eyes and envisions David right before he died, looking up at her with a mix of fear and grave regret. David's last words to Julia, his apology and confession of his colossal mistake, ring in her head like a desperate mourner's wail. David's death from natural causes, despite his betrayal, is something Julia isn't sure she will ever get over. But the possibility that David was murdered is a game changer.

Navarro and Russell emerge from the hallway leading to Judge Palmer's room, and Navarro waves his fingers for Julia to follow. As Julia approaches, she makes a silent promise that she will find out the truth, no matter the potential cost.

"Judge Palmer is still pretty beat up, but his doctor says he wants to talk," Navarro says. "He suffered some major internal injuries and he's still weak, so most likely we won't have a lot of time with him."

"I just saw David's doctor. I don't think David died because of his injuries from the bombing. I think someone tried to kill him because of what he knew about Rossi. David had high levels of cocaine in his system when he died."

"Sounds like someone came into the hospital to finish him off. And we know who could supply a lethal supply of blow in a hurry," Russell answers.

"I would have known if David was a junkie. You can hide an affair, but not drug use. My mother was an alcoholic, and I could never forget the signs of an addict," Julia says. "I don't know exactly what David was doing in the end, but I think he got himself into something he couldn't handle anymore."

"I'll look into the cocaine angle. Let's see if Judge Palmer has any other answers," Navarro says.

The three enter the hospital room, and the once personally imposing Judge Palmer looks like a child in the bed. His left leg is swallowed by a thick white cast and juts out from the hospital bedsheet.

"Water," he asks, and jerks his thin face toward the pink plastic pitcher on the bed stand.

Julia pours the judge a glass of water and tips the straw to his lips for him to take a drink. The judge gives Julia an attempt at a smile and indicates for her to sit.

Julia pulls up a chair next to the bed, and the judge reaches out his hand to take hers.

"I heard about David. I'm sorry," he says, his once-rich baritone now reduced to a light treble.

"Judge Palmer, thank you for agreeing to meet with us. David Tanner was in your chambers at the time of the explosion. What were you two talking about?" Navarro asks.

The judge moves his head back and forth slowly as if shaking away cobwebs from his memory. "I got a call from my clerk, telling me David wanted to see me and it was urgent. So I finished up my lunch early and met him in my chambers."

"How come Defense Attorney Tarburton wasn't in your chambers too?" Navarro asks.

"David didn't want him there. He told my clerk he had to meet with me alone. When I got back to the courtroom, David was sitting by himself at the prosecution table and he was upset, really agitated. We went into my chambers, and David told me he had just received a tip that there was going to be an assassination attempt on his new witness. I pressed him on his source, but he refused to tell me. Then he got a call on his cell phone from the police officers who were waiting to escort Sammy Biggs into the courthouse, and I could tell from the conversation that they were asking where David was. David insisted that the officers had to wait in the car and not come inside the building. Then David started telling me Rossi hired a sniper to take out his witness on the courthouse stairs at exactly twelve-thirty. I remember looking up at the clock, and it was twelve twenty-nine. David was really worked up at this point and said the sniper was across the street positioned in an abandoned office building. He told me he did something very wrong and needed to come clean. The next thing I can remember, there was a massive explosion and the ceiling above us caved in, and something that felt like an elephant fell on top of me. Before I lost consciousness, David asked if I was okay. He said he was trapped and couldn't help me."

"That's really helpful information. Was there anything else David said to you?" Navarro asks.

"David told me if something happened to him and he couldn't get out, to tell you, Julia, he was sorry for everything he did. Then I must have lost consciousness, because that's all I can remember."

"Did David say anything about taking a bribe to throw the case?" Navarro asks.

"No, nothing like that. He was genuine and tried very hard to persuade me to add Biggs as a last-minute witness the morning of the trial. I've worked in the legal profession for more than thirty years, so I'm pretty good at reading people," Judge Palmer says, and musters a weak smile.

"If you can think of anything else, here's my card," Navarro says. "And get better."

"When I get out of here, I'm going to play a game of golf, drink an ungodly expensive single-malt scotch, and eat a thick steak with enough cholesterol to stop my heart."

"Call me up and I'll join you," Russell says.

The three leave the hospital and walk silently until they reach Navarro's car.

"Sounds like David had a last-minute change of heart," Julia says.

"David told Judge Palmer about the sniper, but nothing about the bomb," Navarro comments.

"Which means he probably didn't know about it," Russell says.

"Right. If David was being paid off by Rossi to throw the case, even if he gets a conscience at the eleventh hour, he'd know about the bomb, which means Rossi wasn't the person behind the courthouse attack," Navarro says. "But David told Julia that Rossi planted the bomb. Which leaves us with what?"

"My source told me he believed the bomber was someone close to Rossi who was trying to protect him," Julia says.

"My bet goes to Enzo Costas or Salvatore Gallo," Navarro answers.

CHAPTER 27

Isabella Rossi tries to take care of her other unfinished piece of business following the Infinity Holdings fiasco and banks on the fact her husband hasn't called his uncle, the one exhausted moral compass in his life. She keeps her pace far enough back from the older man as he finally gives up on his daily afternoon regimented exercise, a brisk stroll along Detroit's RiverWalk, that he took up and stuck to after his heart attacks.

Salvatore Gallo drops down on a bench that faces the Detroit River. Isabella watches the older man try to catch his breath as she moves in for the kill.

As she approaches Gallo, Isabella realizes that her husband is the luckiest man in the world. If none of the cops, prosecutors, or reporters could get any charges to stick against her husband that would put him away for good, Isabella knows she has to be the one to ensure that Nick Rossi's luck finally runs out.

"Sal!" Isabella calls.

Gallo rises with his right hand stuffed inside his silver

tracksuit and scowls as he turns his head in the direction of the stranger's voice.

"Oh, it's you," Gallo says, and sits back down on the bench. "Hold on. I've got to check my heart rate."

Gallo reaches two fingers up to his neck and holds them there for a minute.

"What are you doing here?" he asks.

"I need to talk to you. But it has to stay between us. You tell Nick, he'll kill me."

"If this is about my nephew, that's between the two of you."

"Nick ordered the bomb at the courthouse. He told me."

"Nicky told you this?"

"You need to go to the police and tell them Nick was the bomber. I hate to be the one to tell you this, but Nick said he was going to testify that you managed most of the illegal ends of his business if his case had gone forward."

Gallo stays poker-faced, but Isabella thinks she can detect a slight tic in the corner of Salvatore's right eye.

"Why should I believe you?" he asks.

"You've been covering Nick for years. But the courthouse situation is different. Innocent people were killed, including children. You know you couldn't live with that if you try to protect your nephew this time."

"I need to talk to Nicky to verify that what you're telling me is the truth."

"You talk to him about this, he'll kill me. What happened at the courthouse was wrong. How long are you going to keep covering for him?"

Gallo gazes out at the shards of broken ice that skim the top of the Detroit River as he answers the question.

"You tell lies every day, they aren't lies anymore. They become part of the narrative and get mixed into the fabric of your day-to-day life until you convince yourself that's what really happened. But there's always something nagging just out of sight, because deep down, you know."

"You've been carrying around all this guilt for years because you're a good man and you knew lying for Nick was wrong. When was the last time you were happy?"

"Happy? Do you know anybody who's really happy? Any magic starts to die the moment you're born. When something bad happens like the murder of Nicky's mother, any joy, any hope that's left, it just sputters out like a balloon losing air as it flies out of your fingers."

"Nick witnessed what happened to his mother. It turned him into a psychopath. He's got problems," Isabella goads.

"That's family business. End of story."

"Nick went too far this time," Isabella says, and reaches for Gallo's hand but he jerks it away.

"You know what he's done to me?" Isabella asks.

"Like I said, that's between you and Nicky."

"He got our daughter killed."

"I'm sorry for that. I truly am. No harm should ever come to a child. But that's your grudge to bear."

Gallo gets up from the bench and begins to walk back toward Rivard Plaza and the idle Cullen Family Carousel, closed for the season.

"Salvatore!" Isabella cries before he reaches the merry-go-round.

Gallo keeps on walking and answers without looking back.

"I'll think about it," he says.

CHAPTER 28

Isabella Rossi leaves Gallo at the Riverfront and waits impatiently one block away from the hospital in her leased dark blue Lexus, having switched cars the day prior in case her other luxury vehicle had been spotted when she killed the lawyer.

Isabella adjusts the rearview mirror so she can get a better view of her near-perfect reflection. She plays with the knot of her Hermes scarf, tied loosely around her neck, and feels the ache of the anticipation of when she will force Julia to give up the real safety deposit box number and code and she'll finally get the money. Isabella pulls out a travel brochure for Spain from her Prada bag and calculates that she can live comfortably there with the two million dollars, in addition to the other one million she stole from Nick, and be far enough away that he'll never find her.

Isabella scans for her target at the entrance of the hospital again, and tugs at her hair she dyed back to blond in an attempt to evade being recognized, and carefully drapes a long strand along her jawline to cover her one mar—her missing earlobe, the one Enzo Costas cut off at the MGM Grand when he caught her with the lawyer.

From her rearview mirror, Isabella sees Julia and the two policemen leave the hospital and feels a stab of hatred torch through her. The poor little lawyer's wife always has someone around to take care of her and soothe her grief.

Isabella feels her anger burn brighter as she is sure Nick is already planning a hit on her for not being able to manage the lawyer, and she knows she would already be dead if Nick knew of her true involvement with David and their failed plan. Isabella looks over at her Prada bag and the gun inside and wishes her husband were in the passenger seat so she could tip the barrel against his ear and watch his brains spray across the window.

Isabella cuts her dark fantasy short as she spots Navarro pulling away down the street in front of her. But she doesn't follow. She knows Navarro is too smart and shrewd and would recognize that he is being followed.

Instead, she weaves through the three miles of city traffic until she gets to Greektown. She parks outside of Plaka's Restaurant, where she searches the front of the building for the person she solicited to help her with Julia.

Isabella spies the young man walking around the corner of the restaurant. He is in his early twenties, tall and thickly muscled with broad shoulders and a sloping waist, resembling a younger version of her husband. Isabella slowly opens the Lexus driver-side window and calls him over.

"Franco, the job I told you about, it's happening earlier than we discussed. I need your help right now," Isabella says, and reaches out her pinky finger to stroke the back of the young man's hand.

"Now? That's not possible, I'm sorry."

She looks up and down the empty street, takes his hand, and cups it over her breast.

"Oh, I think you can and you will," Isabella says.

Franco swallows hard, his Adam's apple bobbing up and down in his throat.

"Okay. How much will you pay me?" he asks.

"Five hundred dollars and a night with me in my hotel room," Isabella answers, knowing she would go up to a thousand dollars if need be, but Franco looks like he'd jump in the car and do it to her right in front of the Greek restaurant during the lunch rush if he could.

"That sounds good. Real good," Franco answers.

"I'll call you when I'm ready. You'll drive me first to a residence in Rochester Hills. Have you ever killed anyone before?"

Franco's beautiful olive complexion pales to two shades lighter.

"Don't worry, little boy. I'll handle it. Do you know where the Packard Plant is?" she asks.

"Of course. Everyone in Detroit does."

"Very good. Go there now and set up a room on a high floor. And stop by a hardware store on your way. I'll need a chair, some chains, duct tape, and bleach," Isabella says. "Find a location in the Packard Plant that is secure. Clear out any vagrants or drug addicts you find in there. I don't want any witnesses."

Franco looks back at Isabella like a scared child, and he quickly retracts his hand from Isabella's breast.

"Are you in or not?" Isabella asks, her voice now a razor-sharp stiletto.

Franco looks back at the gorgeous woman inside the car, his decision made.

"I'm in."

Isabella watches the tight curves of Franco's hips as he walks away and knows now all she has to do is find a moment when the lawyer's wife is alone.

CHAPTER 29

Eastern Market on any given Saturday draws a crowd. But throw in the first nice day when the temperature spikes to fifty degrees after another brutal Michigan winter, and Detroiters come out from the woodwork en masse. Julia curses the good weather for luring the larger-than-usual crowd to her destination with her boys and leaving her without a parking space.

"Can I take off my coat?" Logan asks.

"No. I don't know where I'm going to be able to find a place to park, so we may have to walk a ways and I don't want you to get cold," Julia answers.

"Take my coat off, too," Will chimes in, echoing his brother.

"Stop tag teaming your mother, you two," Helen says from the passenger seat. "This is a nice family afternoon she planned for everyone."

"Thanks for that," Julia tells Helen. "I don't care what other people are wearing or not wearing. Everyone in this car keeps a coat on, at least for now."

"Helen, too?" Logan asks.

"I'm going to ignore that," Julia answers.

She gives up trying to find a space on the street and pulls into a paid parking garage instead.

"I'm going to take Logan and Will to get coneys at Zeff's, but is there any specific place you'd like to go, Helen?" Julia asks. "We've got all afternoon."

"I must stop at the pierogi booth for Alek. It is his way of taunting me, making me buy someone else's food for him when he knows mine is better," Helen answers with a dramatic sulk.

Julia finds a parking spot on the highest floor of the garage. She extracts Will from his car seat and Helen takes Logan's hand as they make their way to the elevator. Julia lets Will push the down button, and she notices a dark blue Lexus circling their floor for the third time since they left their car. The Lexus disappears down the exit ramp, but a nagging worry still hums in Julia's chest.

"Let's take the stairs instead," Julia says.

"We're on the ninth floor," Helen says. "Is something wrong?"

"No," Julia answers, not wanting to scare the boys.

Julia eyes the stairs but changes her mind when the elevator arrives. Julia lets Helen and the boys enter first and stands guard by the door until it is ready to close, and she slips inside at the last second.

The parking garage elevator levels with the street, and they get off and blend in with the crush of other people moving in the direction of Eastern Market.

"Can I go listen to that guy?" Logan asks, and points across the street to an older black man singing a silky Motown rendition of The Temptations' "Ain't Too Proud to Beg," accompanied by his acoustic guitar.

"No. We stay together," Julia answers, and steers the group toward Shed 3, the largest of the open air stalls in the public marketplace, and Logan and Will take their place side by side in front of the two women.

"I'm surprised your police friend isn't here," Helen comments.

"He's working. What do you have against Navarro anyway?"

"He's lying in wait to make his dirty-boy move on you. Just you wait and see," Helen whispers to Julia in a conspiratorial tone. "Your husband is gone and he is now plotting to replace that good man."

"I've known Navarro for a long time, and he's not that person. He's one of the good guys."

"Sometimes it doesn't matter how long you know someone, because the sly ones can hide their true faces," Helen says.

"Yeah, I know."

Helen pauses to peruse a stall filled with spring's first blooms of brilliantly shaded tulips, daffodils, and pansies while Julia scans the scene, second-guessing her decision to bring her children to such a busy location, with Rossi and his wife still on the loose.

"I have to go to the bathroom. Can you take me over there?" Logan asks Julia, and points to the public restrooms on the other side of the shed.

"Go to the bathroom too," Will repeats.

"Okay, that's fine. Let's go over to the Russell Street Deli after this and then go home," Julia answers.

"Something is the matter," Helen says quietly to Julia. "I thought you said we would be here all afternoon."

"No, nothing's wrong. I guess everything is just catching up to me and I'm suddenly not feeling well," Julia lies as her cell phone sounds from inside her purse.

She pulls out the phone and sees Navarro's name as the incoming caller. Julia lifts her finger to tell the boys and Helen to hold on as she starts to answer.

"I really have to go," Logan says while dancing in place.

"I can take the boys," Helen says.

"I have to use the girl's room?" Logan asks.

"You will live. I will not let you go into a public bathroom in the middle of the city all by yourself," Helen responds, and walks the boys toward the women's restroom sign.

Julia searches for a quiet corner to take the call and answers.

"Can you hear me?" Navarro asks. "It sounds like you're in the middle of Comerica Park. What's all the noise?"

"I'm at Eastern Market with the kids and Helen," Julia answers, and moves to the side exit and out into the alley where she can hear Navarro better. "I'm starting to wish we didn't come here. There are so many people, and I swear I thought I saw a car following us in the parking lot earlier."

"Just stay alert to your surroundings like I'm sure you're doing," Navarro says. "I got a tip from one of my informants a little while ago. The guy is a big doper and shoots up over at the Packard Plant. He tells me one day a few weeks ago, he's huddled up against a side of the building and sees these two young guys walking out of the plant, and one guy is carrying a suitcase. He says the window of a Mercedes parked across from him opens, and the two guys get popped by the driver. From the informant's description, the suitcase sounds like a fit for the one the courthouse bomb was in. My guy hid when the driver got out of the Mercedes so he couldn't give me an ID, but he got a partial on the plate."

"How accurate can a partial plate from a drugged-up informant be?" Julia asks.

"Let's just say he was scared sober from what he saw. I'm running the plate now to see if anything connects."

"I bet money it belongs to Nick Rossi."

"I'm heading over to the station to see what I can find out about the two dead guys and then over to the Packard Plant to interview the junkie."

"Let me know if anything comes out of it," Julia answers.

"I will. Be careful out there," Navarro answers.

Julia starts to end the call when she is interrupted by a woman's voice coming from behind her.

"Mrs. Tanner." The name sounds peculiar in Julia's ears since no one calls her by David's last name, the one she never legally took as her own.

Julia shoves her phone in her pocket and slowly turns toward the voice.

Standing a foot behind her is a woman clad in a black, long-sleeved silk shirt, tight black jeans, knee-high black boots, and a turquoise necklace with a long, silver chain.

"You're a very difficult person to find alone," Isabella says. "How nice it is for you to have so many sad little male faces following you along with their limp dicks tucked behind them as they trail you like puppies, just hoping they'll do something right so you'll open your legs for them."

Julia studies the woman with platinum blond hair that carefully frames her nearly perfect face. The stunning beauty suffers from a single imperfection—her mangled left ear, the lobe missing, the flesh where it was once connected now a blobbed matrix of twisted red scars. Julia instantly gets beyond the new blond hair color and recognizes the woman as Isabella Rossi.

"Don't act as if you don't know me. We've met before in my penthouse when you and the officers questioned me. You don't have any idea how difficult it was for me to keep from telling you how hard your husband screwed me."

"I know who you are. You're Isabella Rossi. You're the blonde in the video," Julia says.

"My starring role, but your husband and I had many encounters that weren't recorded. I'd be happy to share every detail with you, if you like. I can assure you, he was very, very good. But you know that already. Now, do you see the Lexus parked across the alley?" Isabella asks, and waves at the vehicle.

The darkened driver-side window of the car opens, exposing Franco, who waits obediently with a gun pointed directly at Julia.

"My friend in the car has been instructed to shoot you if you try to run or cause a scene," Isabella says.

A man wearing a white chef's coat and carrying a crate of mushrooms hurries down the alley toward the Eastern Market loading entrance, and Isabella slips her arm around Julia's waist, as if they are two sisters or best friends having a pleasant little chat.

"Don't even try it," Isabella hisses in Julia's ear.

Isabella looks in the other direction as the man passes into the rear market entrance and then pushes Julia toward the waiting Lexus.

Isabella scans the now-empty alley, then throws Julia roughly against the side of the vehicle and knocks on the passenger-side window for Franco to open.

"Is everything arranged?" Isabella asks.

"Yes, I got the supplies you wanted and set up a room in the Packard Plant up on the seventh floor," Franco answers.

"Good," Isabella says, and then tosses Franco the keys to her Lexus. "You'll drive."

Isabella pulls the back of Julia's hair in one quick snap and slams Julia's face against the side of the car. Julia's jaw makes a popping sound, and she tastes something metallic as her mouth begins to fill up with blood.

"You move, and I'll kill you," Isabella says.

Isabella frisks Julia and stops when she feels the cell phone still in Julia's pocket. Isabella pulls the phone out, smashes it under the heel of her boot, and kicks the broken phone into an opening of a sewer grate along the sidewalk.

"There's no policeman for you to call for help this time," Isabella says. She shoves Julia into the backseat of the Lexus and slides in beside her. "David told me he thought you were seeing the policeman behind his back."

"David was the only person cheating in our marriage," Julia answers.

Isabella lifts up her hand and smacks Julia across the face.

Franco watches the backseat, nervously looking from woman to woman.

"Don't you get scared on me, little boy," Isabella says. "Now drive."

Isabella pulls a gun out from her Prada bag and holds it on her lap, the barrel pointing at Julia's chest.

Franco turns the car on Wilkins Street, and Julia feels awash in desperation as she watches Eastern Market, where Helen and the boys still are, disappearing in the rear window.

"If you're going to kill me, I at least want to know the truth. How did David get involved with your husband?"

Isabella studies the quickly passing downtown core as if she can see the memory in its backdrop.

"As you wish. Nick got word to Enzo Costas from prison that he wanted me to meet David."

"You were the currier who gave him the money," Julia says.

"Two million dollars for David to pay off a juror. Nick had dirt on David, a video that proved your husband hid evidence in a case he was prosecuting. If it got out, David would have lost everything."

"The Anthony Ruiz trial. I found the DVD in your cottage in California. Rossi blackmailed David."

Isabella shrugs, obviously not caring about the consequences to her former business partner.

"For me, David was just another one of Nick's jobs at first, but then I realized we could work together for the good of our individual interests."

"You used David," Julia says.

"Everyone uses everyone, and if they don't, they're just stupid," Isabella answers. "I used your husband, and he used me. David figured a way out. He bought the Ruiz video from the bar owner and thought he was off the hook with Nick, so he planned to try the case honestly and we'd split the two million. And when Nick went to prison, I'd be free from that asshole. I needed the money because Nick's assets would be frozen when he went to jail. I lied to Enzo that David bribed a juror, and I told David about Sammy Biggs."

"The Butcher," Julia answers.

"I went to California with David when he went to recruit Biggs to testify against my husband. I knew Biggs's testimony would be my ticket out of my life with Nick. I told David where to go, and I stayed in the hotel for most of the trip so I wouldn't be seen."

"Except when you were outside of Santa Maria Temple, where you took the photo of David."

Isabella gives Julia a gloating smile as the Lexus crosses city traffic and makes a turn on Mt. Elliott Street.

"I was sure Nick didn't know about the trip," Isabella says. "I got instructions from Enzo to bring the two million dollars to David at the MGM Grand, and David agreed to meet me there. Nick had Enzo plant the camera in the room before we got there. One of his people saw David in California, and Nick got suspicious he was going to screw him at the trial. We got to the hotel . . ."

"I saw the video," Julia answers.

"So you know how good I look when your husband is doing me," Isabella says. "Enzo showed up to confront David and me, but David had already left. The only good thing you did was kill that monster Enzo. Look what that bastard did."

Isabella lifts up her blond hair to expose her scarred ear.

"Your husband saw you and David having sex on the tape. I have a hard time believing Rossi didn't have any problem with that."

"Nick didn't care who I screwed as long as I got the job done for him."

"So Rossi knew David double-crossed him. Why didn't he kill him?"

"He still needed David to throw the case, so he had Enzo instill the fear of God into David. One night, Enzo waited for your husband in the parking garage across from the D.A.'s office. He held a knife to David's throat and warned him that if he didn't go ahead with his original agreement, your children would be killed. And you too."

"David never told Rossi about your involvement?"

"No. But he was going to screw me over, so he's no good guy. The morning of the trial, I called him. David said he was going to come clean. He was going to tell the judge and your cop friend about everything, including the Ruiz tape and the money. He said he didn't care if he went to jail. He would have hung me out to dry with the cops if Nick didn't get me first."

Franco turns the Lexus onto Holburn Avenue, and Julia can see the Packard Plant in the distance.

"Rossi planted the bomb to take out David," Julia says. "David told me in the hospital that Rossi was the bomber."

"He got the wrong Rossi. Poor brain-addled David meant me, not Nick. I told your husband I would come after you and your children, starting with your oldest boy first, if David refused to give me my share of the money. Logan was to arrive at the courthouse the time the bomb went off, right? Very logical reasoning for a lawyer. I'm impressed."

"You set the bomb to try to kill Logan as a warning to David about the money."

Isabella looks away from Julia and stares out at the quickly passing city blocks outside her window.

"I know too well the pain of losing a child," Isabella answers, and then turns back toward Julia with a stone-cold expression. "Your husband lied to me in the hospital about the security deposit box number and code. You're going to give it to me now, and then we'll take a drive down to Infinity Holdings where you'll take out the money and give it to me."

"The police have the money and they're onto you."

"You're a bad liar. You could have made this easy, but I'll make you tell me the truth."

Franco parks the Lexus in the rear of the Packard Plant. He jumps out and then pulls Julia from the car. He grabs both her wrists and wraps them tightly in front of her with duct tape.

"You go first," Isabella commands Franco.

Franco takes the lead as they approach the building, and Isabella pushes Julia to follow as she walks behind Julia with her gun pressed against her back.

Franco enters through what remains of a rusted metal door at the far side of the building, and Julia looks up at the once-mighty Detroit landmark, the Packard Plant's now helpless ruins bearing silent witness to what is about to happen to one of its own.

* * *

Three miles away, Helen rushes through Shed 3 at Eastern Market, a cold pit of dread growing in her stomach. She pulls each boy along with her until she gets to the one area she hasn't checked. Helen darts out to the alleyway and quickly moves the boys behind her so they won't see Julia's purse spilled across the sidewalk.

Helen fumbles for her phone in her coat and finds the sheet of paper Julia gave to her with the number Julia said she must call if there was ever an emergency.

Helen's hands shake as she dials the number.

"Mr. Raymond," Helen says, her voice cracking as Navarro answers. "Something has happened to our Julia."

CHAPTER 30

Franco bounds up the maze of crumbled concrete steps of the Packard Plant, and Isabella cuffs Julia in the back of the head with the butt of the gun to make her keep up. Julia knows she could easily outrun Franco, but she slows her pace as she searches for an exit route.

At the center of the seventh-floor stairwell, Franco stops abruptly in his tracks.

"What's going on?" Isabella calls from a story below.

"There's a guy up here," he calls back.

"I told you to search the place to be sure something like this didn't happen," Isabella yells.

"I did. I swear, this guy wasn't here before."

Isabella shoves Julia forward until the two reach the seventh-floor landing. Sitting huddled on a flat cardboard box is a scrawny man in a yellowed T-shirt with greasy, long hair and a stringy brown beard pocked with thick white patches. A hypodermic needle almost drained of heroin sticks out of his right arm. The man, well on his way to being high, looks up at Isabella.

"Who are you, man?" the junkie asks. He scoots like a crab across the cardboard box as he tries to get away from his unexpected company.

"Shoot him," Isabella commands.

"You didn't tell me I'd have to kill someone," Franco answers, a heavy film of sweat now covering his face.

Isabella jams the barrel of her gun next to the junkie's temple and pulls the trigger.

"Jesus! His shit got all over me!" Franco screams as he tries to wipe off the remnants of the junky from his own face. "I'm going to throw up."

"Get up. If you can't do what I paid you for, then stay here and make sure no one else comes up."

Franco gives Isabella a quick nod and succumbs to an undulating series of retching and dry heaves.

Isabella turns her back on her employee and pushes Julia inside the seventh-floor entryway. The massive space of dirty gray concrete is littered with beer cans, garbage, and disintegrating car parts that even the most desperate pickers didn't want.

Isabella shoves Julia toward the back corner of the long room and into a chair. She takes the butt of the gun and gives Julia a hard punch with it against the side of her temple.

Julia scrambles to get up but is snapped back as Isabella wraps a heavy chain around both of Julia's ankles and the rear legs of the chair. Isabella then secures the rest of the chain to a narrow strip of frame connecting the passenger door to the caved-in roof of a green truck, an old metal carcass of a vehicle but still sturdy and Detroit made.

Isabella busies herself looking at the contents of two large brown bags. She extracts a switchblade, and her knee-high black boots tattoo a path through the rubble in Julia's direction. Isabella opens the blade, its silver point glinting menacingly in the muddied light of the Packard Plant. Isabella gathers Julia's hair in one hand and jerks her head back so her neck is exposed.

"I like the way you carved up Enzo," Isabella says, and eases the blade down Julia's neck. "Now, where's the money?"

Isabella works the knife until Julia can feel it begin to pierce her skin.

"Is it still at Infinity Holdings? You'll tell me the security deposit box number and the security code, or I'll start cutting."

"The police have the money. I told you," Julia cries.

"Hey, someone is coming," Franco yells from the stairwell.

Isabella drops the knife and hurries to the stairwell for a better look, then she finds a position where she can lie in wait, hidden behind the door.

"You say one word and I'll shoot you in the head," Isabella warns.

"I'm in here!" Julia screams.

Isabella, as promised, fires off a shot, and Julia recoils as a bullet ricochets off the concrete a few inches above her head.

Three shots echo from the stairwell as Franco exchanges gunfire with the person below. The steady thud of a body tumbling down the steps reverberates into the space as Russell cautiously enters the room with his gun drawn.

"No, Russell!" Julia screams. "She's behind the door."

Russell tries to retreat, but Isabella is too fast. Her bullet connects, and Russell flies back against a concrete wall. The downed officer collapses to the floor.

Isabella stands over Russell and places the toe of her black boot on his chest where the bullet went in, pressing hard until the detective lets out a low and animal-like moan.

"If Russell is here, then the police are on their way."

"There's no policeman to save you this time. Oh shit," Isabella says, correcting herself as another set of fast footfalls echoes up the stairwell.

Isabella launches herself back to the seventh-floor landing, panning for the incoming target.

"Russell, are you all right?" Julia calls out.

"I'm hurt bad."

"Can you move?"

"No, I don't think so. I'm sorry. I shouldn't have let Isabella get the shot."

"It's okay. We'll find a way out. How did you know I was here?"

"I didn't. Ray wanted to talk to his informant again," Russell says.

The ricochet of gunfire rings out as Isabella rushes back into the room and crouches behind a thick cement column for cover.

"Drop your weapon!" Navarro calls out as he takes a quick scan of the room, using the door as a blocker.

"She's hiding behind the third column in front of you," Julia shouts.

Navarro ducks back into the hallway just as Isabella takes a shot. Isabella then sprints to the other side of the story and presses her gun against Julia's temple.

"Throw down your gun or I'll shoot her," Isabella warns.

"Don't do it. Take the shot, Ray," Russell begs.

"I'll give you to the count of three. Walk slowly into the room with your hands where I can see them," Isabella says.

"Take the damn shot, Ray," Russell pleads.

Navarro appears in the doorway with his weapon down at his side before Isabella can begin her count.

"Good. Now put the safety on and kick the gun to me," Isabella says.

"Take it easy. No one needs to get hurt," Navarro says as

he secures his weapon and then slides it across the floor in Isabella's direction.

"Jesus Christ, Ray," Russell cries. "You should've shot her."

"Give it up, Isabella," Navarro says, his voice echoing through the vast space. "I called backup when I saw the dead junkie."

"I would have heard you. You should have listened to your partner and taken a shot when you had the chance."

Isabella removes the gun from Julia's temple and advances toward Navarro to finish off her most dangerous adversary in the room.

Julia jumps up from her seat and pulls forward, the chains constricting more tightly around her ankles as she tries to get free. Julia strains against the chains with her strong legs, runner's legs, that made it easily up the twelve-mile steep incline in the mountains to Rossi's compound. Julia pulls forward as hard as she can, pushing through the pain as the muscles in her legs feel like they are on fire. Julia stretches her body forward, like a horse trying to pull an impossibly heavy cart behind it, until she hears the groan of the truck's rotting metal beginning to bend.

"Stupid cop, giving in to a woman," Isabella says as she draws her gun.

Julia pulls forward in the chair again, the chains attached to the thin metal frame of the old truck stretching taut this time until they have no give.

Julia closes her eyes and concentrates. She hears a loud pop behind her as the rusted old bolt that held the truck frame in place cracks loose just as Isabella fires at Navarro, the sound distracting her just enough so that the bullet veers a few inches away from her intended target and clips Navarro in his shoulder.

Navarro staggers backward and drops to his knees as Isabella moves toward him to deliver a fatal shot.

Julia jams her body forward, her muscles feeling like they will explode, until the tired metal strip of the truck the chain is looped around snaps. The chain springs free from the vehicle, and Julia, still trapped in the chair, charges toward Isabella. Julia slams into the side of Isabella like a linebacker, knocking Isabella off her feet. The unexpected ambush causes Isabella's gun to fall from her hand, and it skitters across the room in Russell's direction. Isabella stretches her body across the floor toward the gun until her long fingers graze the barrel.

In a flash of a second, Navarro reaches behind his back, pulls out a gun hidden at his ankle, and shoots Isabella.

Isabella drops to the ground, looking small and pale as she curls her body into a fetal position. Blood leaks from her torso and stains the dirty floor underneath her. Something seems to pass over Isabella's face, and her eyes lose focus.

"Julia, are you all right?" Navarro asks.

"I'm okay," Julia answers. "How's Russell?"

Navarro squats down next to his partner and tries to stop him from bleeding out as police sirens wail their approach.

CHAPTER 31

Julia sits on a hospital emergency room plastic chair, concentrating on the wall clock she checks every ten seconds while she waits to get updated on Navarro and Russell's conditions.

Navarro's phone buzzes in his black leather jacket, which Julia took from the Packard Plant when the police and EMT crews arrived. She instinctively reaches in and pulls out the cell.

"Julia Gooden."

"Uh, yeah. Julia? This is Officer Gary Smith. Is Ray out of surgery yet?"

"No. He should be out soon, I hope. His surgeon thinks he'll be okay. He got a pretty clean shot through his shoulder. It's Russell I'm worried about."

"Geez, poor Leroy. Keep us posted, all right?"

"I will. Do you want me to leave a message for Navarro?"

"Yeah, tell him I got a hit on that plate he wanted me to look up. Granted, Ray gave me only four numbers, but it looks like the car matches a 2014 black Mercedes E-Class sedan that was leased from Deluxe Automotive."

"Let me guess. It's registered to Nick Rossi," Julia says.

"No. The name on the lease agreement is Lester Anderson."

"The acting mayor?"

"That's right. I'm not sure what Ray wanted it for. But those politicians always seem to get themselves in trouble. Be sure to let us know when Leroy and Ray get out of surgery," Smith says, and ends the call.

Julia stares down at Navarro's phone, realizing she should wait until she talks to Navarro, but she can't help herself. She reaches for her own phone and dials Gavin Boyles. The mayor's chief of staff picks up on the first ring.

"Julia, my God, I heard about what happened to you down at the Packard Plant. I left you a voice message. I'm so glad you called me back. Are you okay?"

"Fine. Listen, is the mayor around?"

"No. He's at a fund-raiser for a family who lost two kids in the bombing. Did you change your mind about the ad campaign? It's not too late. The mayor would be thrilled if you were part of it."

"What kind of car does Anderson drive?"

"His car? If you're trying to write something about Anderson using taxpayers' money for personal use, you're totally off base here, Julia. That incident with the missing campaign funds the *Free Press* wrote about, it's been handled. The campaign finance director was fired, and I assure you, Mayor Anderson had nothing to do with it. What are you trying to do here? Bradley Dole announced he was running for mayor this morning on the Republican ticket. Did he put you up to this?"

"No. This is important, Boyles. Did Anderson lease a black Mercedes recently?"

Boyles pauses for a moment, and Julia can hear a door close in the background.

"Yes. Why are you asking?"

"I'm not exactly sure what's going on, but I think Anderson may somehow be involved in the courthouse bombing."

"There's no way. I assumed with what happened at the Packard Plant with Isabella Rossi, she was the bomber. What's this about the car?"

"Well, nothing is confirmed. A police informant who was at the Packard Plant the day the bomb was purchased gave a police detective a partial on the plate he saw. I answered the detective's phone a few minutes ago and just found out."

"Does anyone else know about this?"

"No."

"Now listen, Julia, I know we've had our issues in the past, but I need you to keep a lid on this until I confront the mayor. This has to be a mistake."

"The police need to question the mayor, not you. I agree, it doesn't make sense, but Anderson's car was there. There's a witness."

"Who saw the mayor or the car?"

"Just the car."

"Okay, then. You're jumping to conclusions on a delusion of a drugged-up junkie."

"How did you know it was a junkie?"

"Who else is going to be hanging around the Packard Plant and would be giving tips to the cops? Listen, I've known Anderson for fifteen years, and there's no way he's a part of this. We get the police involved, the mayor gets crucified in the press for no reason, and even if the issue is resolved, the voters won't trust him anymore. I'm already doing damage control with the campaign finance director fiasco. We need to meet."

"I'm at the hospital. I can't."

"I'm in Rochester Hills picking up a campaign check. You still live there, right? I'll meet you at your house in an hour," Boyles says.

"I've got to go."

"Gooden, hold on. . . ." Boyles says, but Julia hangs up as she sees a doctor walking out of the surgery suite and feels as if she is forever stuck in a life-or-death déjà vu moment at Henry Ford Hospital.

She tries to read the surgeon's face as he approaches, and he picks up on it, offering a small nod of reassurance.

"Leroy's out of surgery. We've moved him to the ICU, but he's still in critical condition. The bullet we removed was just a centimeter away from a major artery. If it had been nicked, he wouldn't have made it out of the Packard Plant alive."

"Jesus. Is he going to be okay?"

"We'll be keeping an eye on him, but the surgery went well."

"I need to see Navarro."

"Your other friend is in good condition, and if all goes well, he'll be released tomorrow. But he's still heavily sedated. Why don't you go home and come back later this evening? You look like you could use some rest."

Salvatore Gallo stands motionless in front of his living room fireplace mantel in his Sherwood Forest Detroit neighborhood home, staring at the framed photographs of what was his life.

Gallo Family Cleaners opening day, April 17, 1962, with Sal and his father, Joe, standing out front, proud and smiling, both wearing identical starched white uniforms with the family name stitched in red on their lapels.

A snapshot of Sal and his late wife, Joanie, a pretty little Irish girl from Livonia, as they waved on the deck of the Grand Princess cruise ship en route to the Bahamas on their first day as man and wife.

And two photos of Nicky, Sal's surrogate son since Joanie couldn't have any children, boxing the other pictures in. Little Nicky during his first communion, looking almost angelic in a baby-blue suit, and Nicky and Sal in front of the cleaning business right after Nick returned from California to take over after Sal's heart attack. As if things were really that easy.

Sal looks at the rotary phone on the entryway table and laughs, knowing there's no way he'd call the cops. If Nicky really ordered the courthouse bombing, Sal knows deep down he'll have to take care of it himself. That's what real men do.

Sal lets his potential act settle in but is smart enough to know he needs some help checking the facts. Although the situation isn't entirely without bias this time on her end, Sal calls one person he thinks he can trust to get him the answers he needs.

When his call to Julia Gooden goes to voice mail, Sal grabs his long, black wool coat from the hook on the front door. Time to take care of business.

Julia veers off the I-75 ramp into Rochester Hills, torn between the guilt of leaving her friends at the hospital and seeing her sons for only a few minutes as she was being treated at Henry Ford for superficial wounds from her brush with Isabella Rossi. The agreed-upon plan was for Helen to keep the boys at her house until Julia left the hospital.

Julia pulls into her driveway, thinking how luxurious a shower would feel before she picks up Logan and Will. She feels surreal as she walks in the front door and into her quiet home, knowing just eight hours earlier she, Helen, and the boys were embarking on what they hoped would be a worry-free day at Eastern Market.

Julia pulls off her coat and peels away her sweater and jeans, then heads to her bathroom. *Quick shower, in and out, and then get the boys*, she tells herself.

"Nice view."

Julia shudders, recalling David's same words the day of the bombing when he saw her leaning over the computer in his office.

Julia pivots toward the familiar voice and covers her body up with her sweater.

"How did you get in here?" Julia asks.

"I told you I'd meet you at your house in an hour," Gavin Boyles says, and leans against Julia's living room wall with his hands stuffed inside his pants pockets. "Now, please. Come over here and sit down. We need to talk. Redress at your discretion."

"Turn around," she commands and bends down to pick up her jeans, her sweater still acting as a protective shield across her chest.

Julia quickly pulls her clothes back on and studies the mayor's chief of staff, who continues to stare straight back at Julia with one finger now delicately rubbing the port wine stain on his temple.

"You saw me that day, didn't you? The day you and the cops went to visit Isabella Rossi," Boyles says.

"Right. It looked like you were there for a press conference at the Quicken Loans headquarters."

"I saw you and those two cops on the street while I was getting into a Mercedes," Boyles says.

"Anderson's car. How did you get in my house?"

"Back door. It will need some repairs."

"You broke into my house? I want you to leave, Gavin."

"You don't get to be the one in control anymore."

"Get out of my house, or I'm calling the cops."

Boyles reaches inside his suit coat, pulls out a handgun, and trains it on Julia.

"You're a smart girl. I figured you'd have put me with the Mercedes right away when you got the hit on the plate, but eventually I think you'd have connected the dots. And that would've been a big problem for me."

"The car was leased to Anderson."

"I leased the car for myself in the mayor's name."

"I don't understand."

"I have your attention now, don't I? Destruction, violence, dead kids, that's the only thing you and the press care about. I couldn't get your attention before. No matter how hard I tried to get you and the rest of the media to cover the good things our office was doing, you wouldn't. You kept on dragging the mayor through the sludge of the Rossi case because of the previous mayor's involvement. Guilt by association. Mayor Anderson's popularity numbers were tanking, and I had to do something, otherwise he wouldn't have a chance in hell of winning the election in November and I'd be out of a job."

"What did you do, Gavin?"

"I staged an event, a big damn event, the kind I knew the media would eat up. A horrible tragedy that rocked Detroit and brought everyone together. I got the mayor out in front of the story, and I made sure he looked like the strong, heroic leader he needed to be, just like New York mayor Rudy Giuliani after September 11. I bet you didn't know I'm a scholar of current events. After the courthouse bombing, Mayor Anderson started getting the good press he deserved, and his poll numbers went through the roof. He went from a slapped-in replacement to a bona fide star because of what I did."

"You planted the bomb?" Julia asks. She stares through Boyles and instead sees the melee at the courthouse, the mangled bodies of the dead and the living, and Michael Cole, the little boy who was killed, lying on the pavement, shivering against the cold with half his leg blown off. Julia instinctively moves toward Boyles, wanting to make him pay for all the lives he snuffed out and shattered, but she stops her pursuit as Boyles lunges in her direction, closing the distance for the shot.

"Stay where you are, Gooden, and get that disgusted look off your face. I did what I had to do. Mayor Anderson is going to pull the city of Detroit out of the hell it's in. Most of this city looks like the apocalypse hit. The mayor is going to get people back to work. Detroit isn't going to be a burned-out, overgrown, abandoned ghetto anymore. Sometimes people have to get hurt to ensure the bigger good is realized. That's politics. I also leaked the story about the Butcher to Tandy Sanchez. David told the mayor about Sammy Biggs the morning they met. I wanted to plant the seed early with the article, so when the bomb went off, people would automatically think Rossi was responsible for killing the star witness who was set to testify against him."

"You killed little kids."

"And the two guys who helped me buy the bomb. I couldn't risk that they'd identify me."

"I read about the missing campaign money in the mayor's account. Was that you?"

"I didn't think anyone would notice that the money was gone. It was such a small amount in comparison to what Anderson had raised. I blamed the campaign finance director, and Anderson fell for it. And with your bulldog belief that Nick Rossi was the bomber, you did a superb job of keeping the police off my trail."

Julia stares at the fireplace poker just three steps away from her and tries to figure out how she can distract Boyles so she can grab it.

"What are you going to do to me? Make it look like I committed suicide?"

"No. The police will think one of Rossi's men killed you for taking out his wife. You never made it easy for me, did you? Having to whore myself every day for you to bite on one of my pitches. You wouldn't even help me with the mayor's advertising campaign when your own husband was a victim. You're no better than me, and you never were."

Boyles levels his gun at Julia, ready to pull the trigger. Outside the front door, a board creaks on the porch, and Julia makes her move as Boyles turns his head toward the distraction.

"Who the hell are you?" an older man's voice warns in a calm but threatening bass as the front door opens.

Julia makes it as far as the hallway and turns to see Salvatore Gallo now standing in her living room.

"He's the bomber!" Julia says.

"You sure?" Gallo asks. He stands immobile with his hands still stuffed in his coat pocket, and his eyes burn dark as they stare at Boyles.

Boyles jerks his gun away from Julia and points it at Gallo.

"She's correct. Wrong place, wrong time, old man," Boyles says.

Before Boyles's smile is complete, Salvatore Gallo draws a small revolver from his coat pocket, and in one lightning-quick motion he fires, capping Gavin in the knee.

Boyles screams and drops to the floor, his own gun falling out of his hand. Boyles stretches his splayed body and crabs across the floor as he tries to reach his gun, which now rests underneath Julia's dining room table. Boyles claws for the weapon as Gallo lowers his revolver so it's pointed at the head of the mayor's chief of staff.

"This is my city. You're nothing more than a spineless pussy for what you did," Gallo says.

"Cover him while I call the police!" Julia cries.

Julia grabs for her cell phone when a second shot rings out.

Julia drops the phone and sees Gallo still standing over Gavin Boyles, the once political rising star, who has a fresh trickle of blood flowing from a hole just above the port wine stain on his temple.

"Sorry. I don't follow orders very well," Gallo says.

CHAPTER 32

Julia looks at the FOR SALE sign in front of her house and exhales as she presses her forehead to the front door window, the glass feeling cool and comforting against her skin. During the past two days since the incident with Isabella at the Packard Plant and Gavin Boyles's death, Julia tried to quiet the chaos for a moment to focus on the future. She realized that too many bittersweet memories were experienced in the house she shared with David for eight years. Sometimes, Julia feels as if David's ghost is waiting for her just around the corner, still inhabiting the space, wanting to make amends or at least explain what he had done and why he did it.

The smell of fresh pierogis wafts from the kitchen, and Julia follows the aroma. Helen is at her usual place over the stove, her faded blue apron wrapped around her thin waist.

"I swear, you should patent that smell," Julia says.

"Another reason why you shouldn't move," Helen says. "This is your family home and your boys' center. I'm just up the street if you ever need me."

"I've thought a lot about this and talked it over with Logan and Will. I think we're all ready for a fresh start."

"I read the stories about David, what he did. That was not the man I thought I knew."

"Me neither. I think he tried to make it right in the end, though."

"Would that have been enough for you if he were still alive?"

"No way. I could have forgiven David eventually, but I would never go back to him."

"Where will you go after the house is sold?" Helen asks.

"I was thinking maybe closer to the city. There's been a lot of revitalization efforts in the downtown core, and I'd like to be part of Detroit's second coming."

"The city is too dangerous," Helen lectures.

"Everywhere is dangerous. But I think I can handle it," Julia responds.

"You're a tough broad like me. That Isabella Rossi woman, if I was there at the Packard Plant with you, I swear . . ."

"I know. She wouldn't have stood a chance," Julia answers. "I have a few errands I need to run this afternoon. I was thinking we all could go out to dinner tonight when I get back—you, Alek, the boys, and I. And another guest."

"The policeman," Helen says.

"Do you have a problem with that?"

Helen studies Julia for a long moment and then shrugs her shoulders.

"You like this man?"

"I've known Navarro for a long time, and he's one of the few people, besides you, who's never let me down."

"Fine. Bring Mr. Ray along then. But if he insists on paying the bill, please tell him Alek will order the most expensive item on the menu."

The front doorbell rings, and Julia peers through the curtain before she opens up, her paranoia still fresh after her encounters with Isabella Rossi and Gavin Boyles.

Julia unlocks the deadbolt and lets Salvatore Gallo inside.

"I hope you don't mind me dropping by like this," Gallo says.

"No. It's fine," Julia says.

Julia leads her unexpected visitor into her living room and motions for Gallo to sit down across from her on the couch. Helen pokes her head into the doorway from the kitchen, looking at Gallo suspiciously as if she were about to shoot him with a poison dart.

"Helen, we're fine. He's a friend."

Helen offers up one last "don't even try it" look at Gallo and disappears back into the kitchen.

"I wasn't expecting to see you so soon," Julia says.

"I just got out about an hour ago. The police decided not to file charges against me. They agreed I acted in self-defense. It's a whole different story if the grand jury decides to take a closer look."

"Even if the case goes to trial, I think any jury would have a hard time finding the guy who killed the Detroit bomber guilty."

"Nothing is guaranteed. One promise I'll give you, if charges are filed against me at a later date, I won't ask you to testify on my behalf. You owe me nothing for taking out Boyles. I heard you told the cops I acted in self-defense, that I was trying to protect you and then that kid from the mayor's office tried to shoot me."

"That's what happened."

"You didn't tell them about the second shot I took at Boyles, that he was already down when I did it."

"As I recall, Gavin was reaching for his gun after it fell on the floor. Honestly, that's what I remember."

Gallo gives Julia a slight nod of respect.

"Why did you come here the day Boyles tried to kill me?" Julia asks.

"I had a question I needed your help with."

"What's the question?" Julia asks.

"It's been answered."

"I'm sure you talked to your nephew since you've been out."

"I got kicked loose about an hour ago, so no."

Julia tries to suppress a surprised look, but she's sure Gallo can read her regardless.

"I've got updates on Rossi if you want to hear them."

"Go ahead," Gallo says.

"Your nephew is going to face trial for trying to bribe my husband and attempted murder. The cops tell me his attorney, Tarburton, is pointing the finger at Enzo Costas and Jim Bartello for orchestrating the whole thing."

"Blaming two dead men who can't answer for themselves. That's a coward's way out."

"Can I ask you something personal?"

"Shoot," Gallo answers.

"Are you going to cover for your nephew if he asks you to again?"

Sal takes out a folded white handkerchief from his pocket and dabs his forehead.

"You can take off your coat," Julia says.

"I won't be staying. And, no. I won't be providing Nicky an alibi, if that's what you're asking."

"Why did you come here this time?" Julia asks.

"That thing you said to me back in the restaurant when you were trying to get information from me that would tie Nicky to the bombing. You said just because someone is family, it doesn't buy loyalty. When I was a kid, my dad, my uncles, my grandfather, they all said family was everything. You protected it to the death."

"Sounds like you had a much better foundation than I did."

"Your sister really tried to hustle you?" Sal asks.

"Yes. She learned her tricks from my father. He was the best."

"What did you do when your sister turned on you like that?"

"I kicked her out of my house, and the cops paid her a visit to make sure she wouldn't bother me again."

"You feel guilty about it?"

"Not at all. If people do wrong and refuse to change or if they hurt you purposely with no remorse, cut them out of your life. You're allowed. You can't try to perpetuate a relationship with a bad person because of blood or shared children or family ties. They'll play on your kindness and try to make you believe they care about you, but if they really did, they wouldn't keep doing things that cause you pain. If I'd known what David was doing, I would have told the police."

"There are no beautiful surfaces without a terrible depth," Gallo says, and stands up from his chair. "Sorry about your husband."

"He fooled me. At least with your nephew, I imagine he never pretended to be someone he wasn't."

Gallo takes Julia's hand and gives it a light kiss. He makes his way to the door, and Julia watches the older man cut a straight and certain path toward the street. Gallo pauses before he reaches the gate and turns back one more time to face Julia.

"Family's a bitch," he says.

Julia feels like a regular now at Henry Ford Hospital and confirms her status when the gift shop clerk refers to Julia by her first name. She selects a bouquet of flowers, the only somewhat manly ones in the bunch that aren't pink and laden with lacy baby's breath, and then grabs two magazines, *Esquire* and *Maxim*, she knows her friend will like. The matronly gift shop clerk studies the barely clad woman on the cover of *Maxim*, and Julia offers up a shrug.

"It's for a friend," Julia explains as the clerk quickly stuffs the magazines into a plastic bag.

Julia slips inside her friend's hospital room. Russell sits upright in his bed wearing his pair of drugstore reading glasses and is engrossed in a slew of paperwork that sits on his lap.

Russell starts to get up when he sees Julia but winces in pain from his injuries as his body shifts in the bed.

"Don't you dare get up for me. Stay where you are, you," Julia commands. She moves to Russell's side and kisses him on the cheek.

"Nice posies," Russell says, and nods his head at the bouquet of flowers.

"I know you have a softer side buried way down deep in there," Julia answers, and dumps the men's magazines out of the gift store bag and onto the side of the bed next to Russell.

"Now, that's what I'm talking about," Russell says, eyeing the covers. "I'm knee-deep in paperwork, so this is a very welcome distraction. My rep stopped by a little while ago. I'm going to take some medical leave this time."

"As you should. Give your body some time to heal before you come out swinging again, and I know you will. How's your chest?"

"If the bullet went one whisper to the left, I'd be a dead man. Ray got there right in time."

"He didn't take the shot you wanted him to take."

"He took the shot that mattered. I know he was trying to protect you, and I would have probably done the same thing. But he's lucky he had another gun, because I would have killed him myself otherwise. Are you doing okay with everything, Julia?"

"I'm getting through it. So are the boys. I'm heading to Navarro's after our visit to see how he's doing."

"I'm not going to tell you how to live your life or what you should do. But Ray is a good man, one of the best I've ever known, and he never stopped caring about you. Whether you're ready to get involved in a relationship yet or not, keep him in mind, because if you don't, you're making a huge mistake. But don't wait too long to decide, because I'm tired of watching you two dancing around while you're in the wrong relationships with other people. Deep down, I know you care about Ray too."

Julia smiles at her friend and catches a whiff of expensive perfume as another visitor arrives and stands in the doorway of Russell's room.

"I was hoping you'd be coming back today," Russell tells the visitor.

Julia turns around to see Bianca, Navarro's former flame, dressed in a clingy canary yellow dress. Bianca carries in her black-gloved hand a white to-go bag with her restaurant insignia *Chanel's* written across it. Bianca leans in to Russell and gives him a lingering kiss on the lips.

"Julia, you know my friend Bianca, I believe," Russell says.

"Yes, I do. Nice to see you again."

"What are those?" Bianca asks as she eyes the men's magazines now on Russell's lap.

"You know, Bianca, I had a feeling you and I were exactly alike," Russell says. "My police rep came for a visit a little while ago and left these for me as a get-well present. I never look at these things. Never have. They objectify women in the worst possible way."

Bianca pats Russell's hand as she stuffs the magazines back

inside the hospital gift store bag. Once the offending publications are safely out of sight, Bianca leans in and hugs Russell. He looks back at Julia as she turns to leave and gives her a big wink.

Julia pulls into a parking space across from Navarro's Rivertown Detroit neighborhood complex, grabs three full shopping bags from her trunk, and hurries across the street to Navarro's high-rise. A bird caws overhead, and Julia looks up to see a blackbird perched on the awning of Navarro's entryway.

"Hey, buddy," she tells the blackbird, which seems to stare at her with locked interest until it soars out of sight.

Julia takes the elevator to the seventh floor and can hear the light hum of music coming from Navarro's apartment. The familiar string of Stevie Ray Vaughan's song "Pride and Joy" welcomes her as she raps on the door.

"Hey, come in," Navarro says, looking genuinely surprised. He moves to his living room, where he turns down the stereo. "I would've cleaned up if I knew you were coming over."

"You earn a pass card, a bachelor recovering from a gunshot wound to the shoulder. I come bearing gifts."

"It's not my birthday."

"I told you once the Rossi case was over, I'd owe you," Julia says.

"You owe me nothing, you know that."

Julia digs inside one of her shopping bags and pulls out a white box.

"For starters, here's something for your health."

"You didn't have to buy me anything. I'm not keeping a scorecard, you know."

"Just open it."

Navarro lifts the top of the cardboard lid and pulls out a pair of high-end running shoes.

"With your shoulder still needing some time to heal, you won't be able to hit the gym on your regular schedule. I can personally attest that running is the best exercise to keep you healthy. I was thinking maybe, until your shoulder gets better, we could start running together."

"Thank you, I'll take you up on that. These are really nice," Navarro answers as he inspects his new pair of size 13 Asics GEL-Kinseis.

"But wait, there's more," Julia answers. She pulls out a six-pack of Sierra Nevada Pale Ale and a bottle of Pinot Grigio from the second bag. "Pick your poison. Beer or wine."

"I'll take a beer."

Julia tosses the green beer bottle to Navarro, who raises it up to Julia as if giving a toast.

"I still have visions of you ramming Isabella Rossi from behind in that chair at the Packard Plant."

"Sometimes you just have to work with what you've got," Julia answers.

"Anthony Ruiz's attorney is petitioning for a new trial based on the video from the bar."

"Good. He'll probably get a new trial, and it's deserved. David took the law into his own hands by deciding Ruiz was guilty and withholding evidence that could've exonerated him."

"There's been a lot of media coverage about David and what he did. That's got to be tough on you and your boys."

"I'm trying to shield them from it. I thought I'd always be a journalist. But after all this, I'm not so sure."

"When do you go back to the paper?"

"Maybe never. Mayor Anderson called me this morning and offered me a job with his office. This is the second time he's tried to recruit me. Anderson told me he's not going to pull the plug on his election campaign for mayor, despite what Gavin Boyles did. Anderson believes he's the only person who can pull the city out of the hole it's in. I almost believe him."

"If Anderson offered you a job, he's obviously smart. What would you be doing?"

"Chief of staff."

"Are you going to take it?"

"I turned it down, but then Anderson offered me a new position as public safety policy advisor. Politics isn't really my thing. But the newspaper industry is barely hanging on by a thread, and I feel pretty jaded at this point. So I'm considering Anderson's offer, although the longevity of a job with an elected official always hangs on the voters."

"You'd be good in that role. But don't discount the chief of staff position yet. You have a knack for ordering people around and keeping them in line."

"Thanks for the ringing endorsement. Did you find anything more out about Gavin Boyles?"

"We were able to piece together some details based on what we found on his home computer. Gavin took money from his boss's campaign fund to purchase the bomb, and then he hired a couple of local thugs to buy it at the Packard Plant. He killed the guys because he couldn't risk any residual witnesses coming back to bite him. Gavin knew Sammy Biggs would be escorted into the courthouse at twelve-thirty, so he left a press conference at City Hall early and planted the bomb on the courthouse stairs before Biggs arrived. He wanted everyone to think Rossi was responsible. Gavin was either naive or really lucky. I'm surprised no one recognized him when he left the bomb there. What a twisted bastard, blowing up a building and killing a bunch of innocent people to get his boss positive media coverage and votes. I owe Salvatore Gallo for showing up when he did."

"So Russell and Bianca are an item now? When did that happen?"

A wide grin spreads across Navarro's face.

"I warned Russell. But I think they actually may be a good fit," Navarro says.

"Better him than you, huh?"

"She was never really my type. How are you holding up with everything?"

"I'm expecting a settlement from David's life insurance policy. I'd rather be broke than take the money, though. I'm going to put it in a savings account for Logan and Will to pay for their college and then put the rest in a trust fund when they're ready. And I put my house on the market. I'm thinking about moving closer to the city. Too many memories in that house."

"Lots of changes for you," Navarro answers, and reaches his hand up to his still injured shoulder.

"How's the gunshot wound?"

"It itches like hell. My doctor said that's a normal side effect until it heals completely."

"Can I take a look? I promise I won't faint."

Navarro unbuttons the top of his long-sleeved white shirt and pulls the fabric away from his injured shoulder, which is covered by a thick protection of gauze and tape.

"I've been thinking about your brother's case. When you're ready to look into it again, I can help you," Navarro says.

"I'm ready to do that. I'm almost embarrassed to admit it, but I've been getting some counseling about Ben's abduction, and I think it's actually helped. I'm pretty sure I can go back in and investigate what happened to my brother without it eating me alive."

"I wouldn't let that happen."

Julia strokes her index finger around the exposed skin outside of Navarro's injury, tracing in a circular motion.

"You've been the one person who's always been there for me and never let me down. I ran away from you when we were together because you were too kind, and deep down I didn't think I deserved you."

"You did. You're a good person, and you always have been. I always wondered the real reason why you left, so at least now I know I didn't do anything wrong."

Everything that is usually easy and free-flowing between Julia and Navarro seems to slip away, and she suddenly feels like a teenage girl about to ask a boy if he really, really likes her. She moves away from Navarro and busies herself putting the beer and wine into his refrigerator and stalls until she quells her nerves enough to make a move.

"So, if you're not doing anything later, do you want to go to dinner tonight? It's casual. Helen and her husband and the boys will be there."

Navarro looks back at Julia and flashes her his perfect smile.

"I'd love to. Is Helen okay with me being there?"

"Deep down, I know she likes you. She was just being protective before," Julia says, and then faces Navarro, jumping in while she still has the courage.

"When we were in California, you said if I ever wanted you back, I'd have to be the one to tell you."

"I remember."

"So I'm telling you. I'm ready."

"Are you sure? If this is a rebound situation because of what David did, as much as I want to be with you again, I can't do it that way."

Julia presses against Navarro, and she feels his mouth on hers, wet and open and hungry, and the years of space between them closes as Stevie Ray Vaughan pays testament in the background.

Navarro's hands move across Julia's body, and he begins to steer her toward his bedroom, but Julia pulls away before they venture inside.

"I'm sorry, but I need to take this slowly. The kids have been through a lot, losing their dad. I hope you understand."

Navarro breathes out hard and looks away from Julia. She feels a tug of worry go off inside her until Navarro takes both her hands between his and brushes his lips against her fingertips.

"Slow isn't the pace I want, but I understand. I've waited this long for you, and I'm not leaving. I love you, Julia."

Julia rests her head against Navarro's chest and closes her eyes, feeling as if she's moving toward the place she should be and possibly back to the place she should have never left. Julia stays wrapped in the safe cocoon of Navarro's arms until her cell phone, still lying on the kitchen counter, buzzes.

"It's Helen," Julia says as she sees the incoming caller's name on the screen. "She's probably wondering where we are."

"She's going to be like one of those overprotective fathers sitting on the front porch with a shotgun, waiting for his teenage daughter to come home from a date, isn't she?"

"There's still time to run."

"Come here," Navarro says. He grabs Julia and kisses her until he pulls away first this time.

"I'm trying to abide by the rules. I swear, on my honor, I'll do my best." He raises his three fingers of his right hand in the air with his thumb and pinkie finger tucked together in an "O" like he's doing an earnest Boy Scout pledge. "But if I had my way, we wouldn't be leaving this apartment anytime soon. I better get my coat before I change my mind."

"You were a Boy Scout?" Julia asks.

"What do you think?"

Julia moves to the apartment's living room window and takes in the Detroit city skyline, shining bright and hopeful, the city her kindred spirit, a place that has been beaten down and abandoned, but Julia knows there is still something beautiful at the city's core, something unique and vibrant that can't be taken away or destroyed, no matter what happens to it. Too many people still believe in Detroit to let it crumble.

Julia doesn't fixate on the pain and loss that she has endured, but instead thinks of the beauty in her life, Navarro and her children, the best parts of her day. She takes one more look at the dim lights of the city and smiles as she listens to Navarro humming "Pride and Joy" from the other room and hopes as hard as she can that maybe better days really are ahead.